MAD JACK

MAD JACK

Catherine Coulter

DOUBLEDAY DIRECT LARGE PRINT EDITION

JOVE BOOKS, NEW YORK

This Large Print Edition, prepared especially for Doubleday Direct, Inc., contains the complete unabridged text of the original Publisher's Edition.

MAD JACK

A Jove Book / published by arrangement with
the author

The Penguin Putnam Inc. World Wide Web site address
is http://www.penguinputnam.com

ISBN: 0-7394-0232-3

A JOVE BOOK®
Jove Books are published by The Berkley Publishing
Group, a member of Penguin Putnam Inc.,
375 Hudson Street, New York, New York 10014.
JOVE and the "J" design
are trademarks belonging to Jove Publications, Inc.

PRINTED IN THE UNITED STATES OF AMERICA

**This Large Print Book carries the
Seal of Approval of N.A.V.H.**

To Lesley Delone,
An excellent chef and flower designer,
And best of all, a splendid friend.
I hope we'll be singing Y&R together for a
Very long time to come.

1

St. Cyre Town House
London, 1811
March 25th

Grayson Albemarle St. Cyre, Baron Cliffe, read the single page one more time, then slowly crumpled it in his hand. *Some letter,* he thought, as he threw the ball of paper into the fireplace. Not many words on the page, but most of the few there were vicious and malevolent. He watched the paper slowly crinkle around the edges, then burst into bright flame.

He walked out of the drawing room and down the long corridor toward the back of his home. He opened the door to the library—his room—all somber and warm and filled with books and little else. The heavy, dark gold velvet draperies were drawn tightly against the night, the fire low and sluggish because none of the servants had known he would be coming into this room at this time.

They all thought he'd left five minutes before to visit his mistress.

He thought of the damned letter and cursed, but not as fluently as his father had when he was so drunk he could scarcely walk. He sat down at his desk and took a piece of foolscap from the top drawer, dipped the quill into the ink pot, and wrote: *If I receive another threat from you, I will treat you as you deserve. I will beat you senseless and leave you in a ditch to die.*

He signed his initials, GSC, slowly folded the paper, and slid it into an envelope. He walked to the elegant Spanish table that sat against the wall in the entrance hall and placed the envelope onto the ancient silver salver that his butler, Quincy, cleaned every other day, at one o'clock in the afternoon, without fail.

He wondered as he walked in the cold, clear, early spring night to the apartment of his sweet Jenny what would happen now.

Probably nothing. Men of Clyde Barrister's stamp were cowards.

Carlisle Manor
Near Folkstone
March 29th

There was nothing more to say, damn her. He was panting with rage at her, the ungrateful little bitch. He couldn't help himself. He raised his hand to strike her, then got hold of himself. "If I hit you, Carlton will know it and perhaps not want you."

She whimpered, her head down, her hair straggling long and tangled and sweaty down the sides of her face.

"Silent at last, are you? I never thought I'd see you mute as a tree. It's refreshing for once not having to listen to your complaints and see those looks of yours. Silence and submissiveness are very charming in women, in you especially, though I'm just now seeing them for the first time. Well, perhaps it's over, eh? Yes, you've finally given up. You won't go against me anymore."

She said not a word. When he grabbed her chin in his hand and forced her head up, there were tears in her eyes. But still he frowned. He stared down at her hard, still breathing hoarsely from his pacing and yelling. But his face was no longer as flushed as it had been a minute before, and his voice no longer trembled with rage when he spoke. "You will marry Sir Carlton Avery. He will return tomorrow morning. You will smile shyly at him and tell him that it is your honor to become his wife. I have given him my blessing. The marriage settlements are agreed upon. Everything is done. You will not disobey me, or when I next see you, I will make you very sorry."

He grabbed her chin again, saw the tear streaking down her cheeks, and smiled. "Good," he said. "Tonight you will bathe and wash your hair. You look like a slut from Drury Lane." He swiftly left her bedchamber, humming with his victory. Still, because he didn't want her to forget that he was serious, he slammed the door behind him. She heard his key grate in the lock. She heard his heavy-booted footsteps receding down the long corridor. She drew in a deep breath, looked upward, and said, "Thank you, God. Thank you, God."

He'd forgotten to retie her hands.

She lifted her hands, looked at the ugly, raw bruises on her wrists, and began to rub feeling back into them. She bent over to untie her ankles, then rose slowly from the chair where she'd been trussed up like a criminal for three days. She relieved herself and quickly downed two glasses of water from the carafe that sat on her bedside table. Her breathing calmed. She was very hungry. He hadn't allowed her any food since the previous evening.

But he'd forgotten and left her hands untied. Perhaps he hadn't forgotten. Perhaps he believed he'd finally broken her and tying her hands didn't matter. Well, she'd tried to make him believe that. To hold her tongue had cost her dearly. To squeeze tears out of her eyes hadn't proved so difficult.

Would he come back? That got her into action more quickly than having Farmer Mason's bull Prixil racing toward her across the south field would have. She had to leave in the next three minutes, perhaps sooner.

She'd thought of this so often during the long hours of the past three days, had meticulously planned it, modified her plans, pictured everything she would be able to carry in the small, light valise.

The next two minutes she spent tying the ends of her two sheets together, slinging them out of the second-floor window, and praying that she would fit through the tall, narrow opening. No doubt she was thinner now than she had been three days ago. She'd stared at that window off and on during the past three days, knowing it was her only way out. She would have to squeeze through it. She had no choice at all.

She managed, barely. When she was dangling six feet above the ground, she looked briefly back up at her bedchamber window, then smiled. She let go and rolled when she landed on the soft, sloping ground. When she stopped, shook herself, and found that she'd gained only a few bruises from her jump, she looked back at her home once more, its lines soft and mellow beneath the brilliant light of the half-moon. A lovely property, Carlisle Manor, one that had belonged to her father, Thomas Levering Bascombe, not this bastard, not this man who'd married her mother after her father had died. And now Carlisle Manor was his, all his, and there was nothing anyone could do about it.

With luck she wouldn't be missed until the

morning. Unless he remembered and came back to tie her hands. Then things would be a bit more difficult.

At least Georgie was far away from here, all the way up at York, and thus would be safe from their stepfather's rage when he discovered that his pigeon had escaped the cage.

His pigeon also knew where to go.

2

St. Cyre Town House
London
April 2nd

"My lord."

"Keep your voice down, Quincy," Gray said, not opening his eyes. "Eleanor's asleep."

Quincy eyed the sleek Eleanor and lowered his voice to a whisper that he soon realized wasn't all that much of a whisper, since Eleanor opened her eyes and frowned at him. "It's important that you come to the drawing room, my lord. You have visitors."

The baron lightly stroked his fingers over Eleanor's soft back one more time, patted her head, trailed his fingers along her jaw, which made her stretch out beneath his hand, then stood. Eleanor raised her head, blinked at him once, twice, then flattened herself again. She didn't move.

"She's still sleeping," Gray said. "She does that sometimes, have you noticed? She'll look you straight in the eye, then just blink out again. I don't think she wakes up at all. Now, it's very early for visitors. What visitors?"

"Your two great-aunts, my lord." Quincy eyed the silent Eleanor. He would have sworn that Eleanor had been very much awake when she heard him.

"What two great-aunts?"

"From what Miss Maude said, they are your mother's aunts."

He was frankly surprised. He remembered them, but it had been so many years, too many years. He'd been a young boy, perhaps seven, when they'd last visited.

He stared at the soft, pale brown leather chair his mother had loved. He could still see her lightly rubbing her palm over the seat. It was odd that he would remember such a thing, since they'd stayed in London seldom over the years. "Those old ladies. I haven't heard from them in more years than I can count. I wonder what's going on." His mother had been an only child—more's the pity, Gray had thought many times. If she hadn't been, perhaps there would have been a brother to protect her; her father had died in the colonial war in a place called Trenton and there'd been no man at all to take her part. There'd only been her son, a very little boy, who'd been helpless to save her until he was twelve.

He shook his head. Long-past memories, dead memories that should stay buried since there was nothing to be done about them at this late date.

Gray had eaten his breakfast some two hours earlier and had been working a bit in his library, his only companion his prideful Eleanor. He stretched as he walked toward the front of the house. The St. Cyre town house stood in the middle of the block at Portman Square. Its drawing room gave onto the park across the street, just now coming into its spring plumage.

It was a wretched morning, gray and drizzling, the air damp and cold. It was the second of April and there wasn't a hint of sun— not that the sun was ever really expected in London.

When he walked through the drawing

room double doors, hearing Quincy say in his gravelly voice, "Lord Cliffe," he nearly stopped dead in his tracks.

Two old ladies were standing there in the middle of the large room, all muffled up in scarves, bonnets, cloaks, and gloves, staring at him like he was the devil himself.

"You are my great-aunts?" Gray asked as he walked toward them, smiling easily because he was a gentleman. Today, which had promised to be rather boring until he took himself off to Jenny's apartments to make love to her until he was scarcely breathing, had now changed course.

One old lady stepped forward, taller than most females he knew, thin as a post, her face long and narrow, her skin dry and slightly yellowed, like aged parchment. She looked at least old enough to be long dead, but her walk was spry, the look on her face determined.

"We need your assistance," she said, her voice low and quite beautiful. She had a very long neck and a lovely mouth that still held nearly a full complement of teeth, from what he could see. He bowed, waiting, but the old lady just looked at him, then stepped back, like a soldier returning to formation.

The other old lady, this one short and very slight, looked briefly at her sister, then took three steps toward him, dainty little fairy steps. "I'm Maude Coddington, my lord. What Mathilda would have said if she'd felt like it, which she rarely does, is that we're your great-aunts. We were your grandmother's younger sisters. Unfortunately your dear grandmother, Mary, died birthing your mama, our little niece. Our other sister, Martha, died of an inflammation of the lung three years ago, and that leaves only Mathilda and me."

Maude looked fluffy, what with all the ribbons and bows that adorned what he could see of her gown. There were even several swags of fruit on her bonnet, grapes and apples. She probably came only to the top button on his waistcoat; Mathilda came to his forehead. These two were sisters? He wondered what his great-aunt Martha had looked like. He'd once seen a portrait of his grandmother, painted when she was eighteen.

"It was the vicar's fault," Aunt Mathilda said.

"I beg your pardon?" Gray said. "What was the vicar's fault?"

"Martha," Aunt Mathilda said.

"What Mathilda would mean, were she to feel like telling you of the incident, is that our sister, Martha, was walking with the vicar and it began to rain and he did bring her home but it was too late. She became ill and died."

"Oh. I'm very sorry." He smiled at them because he was exquisitely polite and because he was frankly curious. They'd also made him smile. He said, "Thank you for explaining things more fully. Now, please, won't you be seated? Yes, that's right. Ah, you're here, Quincy. Do bring us some tea and some of Mrs. Post's lemon rind cakes." He waited until the two old dears had arranged themselves on the settee opposite him. Then he sat down. "Aunt Mathilda said you need my assistance. What may I do for you?"

"Not money," said Mathilda.

"Exactly," said Maude. "How very distasteful that would be, two old ladies coming to you with their mittens out. No, we have no need to beg financial assistance from you, my lord. We live near Folkstone. We are comfortably situated. Our father left us very well off indeed."

"Rich husbands," Aunt Mathilda said.

"Yes, well, our husbands left us well situated as well. They were good men, as men go, and thank the good Lord that they always go, eventually." Aunt Maude drew a deep breath and added in a very dramatic voice, "No, my lord, we beg your assistance as head of the St. Cyre family."

"Very young," said Mathilda.

Gray said slowly, "I suppose I am rather young to be the head of the family, not that there's all that much family to head. I just turned twenty-six. I have some cousins that I never see, who probably don't care if I'm above the ground or under it, but no one else until now. I'm very pleased to have you as my aunts. I will naturally offer you any assistance I can. Ah, here's Quincy with Mrs. Post's cakes and the tea."

Gray watched as Quincy, who'd been very thin as a young man and now, in his middle years, had become as plump as one of Mrs. Post's buttocks of beef, laid out all the food, poured the tea, and then assisted the two old ladies out of their myriad layers of clothing. Mathilda was dressed entirely in black, from the old-fashioned bonnet on her head to the slippers on her long, narrow feet. All black. Even the cameo at her throat was black. He'd never in his life seen a black cameo.

Maude was dressed in purple. No, that wasn't exactly right. There was some brown and pink mixed in there, diluting the purple, which was a visual relief. There was a word for that color. Oh, yes, it was puce, a very ugly word, he'd always thought—sounded like the color of day-old remains. Her bonnet was puce, the slippers on her very small feet were also puce. Puce, he thought, looked rather nice on Maude.

When the two ladies were seated again, cups of tea held gracefully in their veined hands, Gray said, "Pray tell me what you would like me to do."

Mathilda took a sip of her very hot tea and said, a wealth of information in her eyes, "Flood."

Maude bit into one of the lemon rind cakes, sighed, showing teeth as nice-looking as her sister's, then swallowed and said, "We recently had a fire at our lovely home just north of Folkstone. It's called Feathergate Close, has been for three hundred years. We're not certain why, but it is a charming, rather romantic name, don't you think? Not, of course, that it matters much, after all this time. Actually, after Mathilda and I die, Feathergate will come to you." Maude paused, beamed at him, then continued quickly after a quick nudge from Mathilda—more of a sharp poke, actually.

"Yes, dear, I'm getting to the point. One doesn't want to rush things. The boy must be softened up properly."

She gave him a beautiful smile. He supposed that meant he was properly soft. "Now, in any case, after this dreadful fire, there were many repairs to be done. We would like to remain here with you for a while, until our house is habitable again."

"What about the flood?"

"Oh," said Maude, delicately wiping her fingers on the soft white napkin after she put another lemon rind cake into her mouth. "The flood came after the fire. Our dear mother's Chippendale dining room chairs nearly floated out of the manor. Unfortunately the flood didn't come in time to put out the fire, but rather a full three days later. Then it rained and rained. It was more depressing than having the vicar propose yet again to Mathilda, which he did just last Sunday morning, after services, right there, in the nave of our church."

"What did Mathilda do?" He was sitting forward, fascinated.

"What? Oh, she told him yet again that she'd had her taste of the marital flesh and she believed, given the evidence of him standing right there in front of her, that he would provide her nothing that would enhance either her experience or her current well-being."

"Aunt Mathilda, you said all that?"

"It's what she would have said if she'd wanted to," said Aunt Maude. "Your great-aunt Mathilda is a moving speaker, an orator of great breadth, when she wishes to be. I believe with the vicar, however, Mathilda merely had to look down her nose at him and let it quiver just a bit. It told him quite enough. She does not believe him to be worthy of any of her excellent oration."

Aunt Mathilda nodded complacently. "That's right. Mortimer killed Martha, after all."

Maude cleared her throat again. "He probably didn't do it on purpose, but he did take Martha for a walk, as we already told you, it rained, and she died. He was very sorry. But now he wants Mathilda." She stopped, gave a deep sigh, and continued. "It's a pity that he couldn't have prayed to prevent the fire and the flood. But he didn't. There is quite a bit of damage from both the fire and the flood, and so there was no choice but for us to come to you and throw ourselves upon your mercy. Will you let us remain with you for a bit of time, dear boy?"

This was quite the strangest thing that had happened to him in some time. Gray looked from Mathilda, the orator if only she felt like orating, to the slight, more informative Maude, pictured their mother's Chippendale dining room chairs floating out of a house onto a front lawn, grinned at them, and nodded. "It would be my pleasure, ladies. May I also offer my assistance in the repairs being made to your home? I can send my man down to Feathergate Close to ensure that everything is going the way you wish it."

"No," said Mathilda.

"Actually, my lord . . ." said Maude, leaning forward. Then she just stopped. Gray blinked as he saw his mother's lovely pale green eyes in Maude's face, pale green eyes that were also his. Maude looked briefly at Mathilda, then cleared her throat. "We have men we trust entirely doing the work. We feel that everything is being done as swiftly as possible. We are content."

"I see," said Gray. He took a drink of his own tea, now tepid. "Naturally you are welcome in my home."

"Alice," said Mathilda.

"My mother Alice?" Gray asked, an eyebrow up in question.

"Ah, yes, your dear mother," said Maude. "She was such a lovely little girl. We missed her sorely when she was wedded to your father, although that was so long ago we're not really certain if that is precisely what we miss. But you know, your father took her away immediately. We saw her only twice between her marriage to your father and your birth. Why, I believe the last time we saw you, you were a very little boy. Ah, yes, whenever we thought of dear little Alice, we missed her."

"Bloody rotter," Mathilda said and stared hard at Gray.

"What Mathilda means, if she felt like explaining things more fully, is that we weren't at all certain at the time if your father was truly an excellent enough gentleman for our little niece. Your mother was so very gentle, so loving, so—well, weak, to spit out the truth of it. I imagine that had your father been a saint, Mathilda would still feel he wasn't good enough for your mother."

"He was a vicious rotter," Mathilda said again, more forcefully this time. She was staring hard at him.

Gray looked from one old lady to the other, then slowly nodded. "Yes, you're quite right. My father was a rotter of the first order. Ah, I see. You wonder if I'm like my father. There's no reason for you to believe me, but you should. I'm not at all like my father." They obviously didn't know what had happened those many years ago. He wondered why not. Surely anyone who'd wanted to know could have easily found out everything.

"Now, ladies, allow Quincy to bring Mrs. Piller to you. She is my housekeeper, was my mother's housekeeper before I was even born. She will know exactly which bedchambers would please you the most."

"There's Jack," said Mathilda. "Jack needs a room as well. Close."

More than one word, Gray thought. This

must be incredibly important to her. Perhaps she was readying herself to orate.

"Jack?"

Maude patted Mathilda's knee and nodded, making the fruit on her bonnet tilt to the side. "Yes. We brought our young, er, valet with us. His name is Mad Jack. Since he assists both Mathilda and me, we would appreciate it if he could be placed near us. Perhaps he could sleep in a dressing room off one of the bedchambers?"

"Mad Jack is your valet? A boy whose name sounds like a highwayman's sobriquet?"

"Well," Aunt Maude said, after a very brief eye flicker toward Mathilda, "it's really just Jack, but our boy, Jack, is also a bit on the energetic side, not wild, mind you, but he does many things, some of them stimulating enough to turn an old lady's hair quite white."

"Hmmm," was all Gray could think of to say. He did blink, but if either of the great-aunts noticed it, they paid it no heed. They really had a valet named Jack whom they called Mad Jack? It wasn't at all expected, but on the other hand, who cared? Gray said, "Perhaps you'd care to give me just a hint of some of the stimulating things that Mad Jack might do here at my house?"

Mathilda said, "Not a blessed thing. Forget 'mad.' "

"Yes, that's right," said Maude. "Our little Jack is all that is calm and serene when he's in a stranger's house, particularly one as grand as this."

Fascinating, Gray thought, and said, "All you have to do is consult with Mrs. Piller. Where is this Jack?"

"He's probably sitting quietly in the entrance hall," said Maude, "guarding our luggage. He's a very good boy, very well mannered, very quiet, at least most of the time, at least in strange houses. You'll never know he's here. We've had him with us forever, very nearly. Yes, Jack's a very sober lad, loyal as a tick, and he prefers to keep to himself when he's not keeping us. He won't cause any harm, no ruckus at all, he's a studious, quite inoffensive boy. Do just as Mathilda said. Forget the 'mad' part of his name. It is simply a fancy, a silly name that an old lady simply plucked out of the air of her burned and flooded house."

"Jack is also welcome, with or without his highwayman's sobriquet. Now, since we're all related, and perhaps you ladies do care that I'm above the ground and not under it, I should like it very much if you would call me Gray."

"Grayson," said Mathilda. "That's your name."

"Well, actually, that's a bit much, I've always thought. My friends as well as my enemies call me St. Cyre or Cliffe, but usually just Gray."

"That will be just fine, my boy," said Maude as she rose and shook out her puce silk skirts.

Mathilda rose as well, turned toward the drawing room doors, and shouted, "Jack!"

3

The baron didn't get a good look at Jack the valet, mad or otherwise, as he was wearing a wool cap pulled to his ears and had his head turned away, seemingly staring hard down at the aunts' two valises. He did see, however, a boy about fifteen years old, skinny as a toothpick, clad in baggy breeches, scuffed boots, and a bilious jacket the color of pea soup left too long in the pot. He didn't look in the least like a boy who would deserve such a dashing handle. Skinny, ill-garbed little nit. He supposed that to two old ladies, any youthful behavior at all could easily be deemed mad. What had he done? Hurled a teacup to the floor and stomped on it?

He saw the valet pick up the aunts' valises, grunt, and promptly drop them. He stared down at them, then seemed to gird his loins and began to drag them. What did he plan to do with the valises once he reached the stairs? Gray wondered. And was he totally untrained? A valet wouldn't haul valises up the main staircase, even a mad one.

Gray nearly burst out laughing when Jack the valet began to nudge the valises forward with the toe of his boot, first one valise, then the other, each gaining perhaps three inches per boot poke. Quincy observed this for a very brief couple of seconds, then called for Remie the footman to assist, which he did. Remie, big and blond and Irish, clapped Jack on the back, nearly knocking him over, grabbed both valises in one huge hand, and walked toward the back of the town house to the servants' stairs. He called out for Jack to follow him.

Mrs. Piller, the St. Cyre housekeeper—very pink in the cheeks, for what reason Gray couldn't imagine—came forward to curtsy to the two aunts. Within moments, the aunts were on their way upstairs to bed-chambers that were connected by a large dressing room where Jack the valet would reside.

"I'm leaving," Gray said. "See to their comfort, Quincy. The aunts will be with us for a while. A fire and a flood—both—hit their home near Folkstone. They will remain here until their house is repaired. A fire and a flood," he repeated, frowning toward the picture of the third Baroness Cliffe, a pro-claimed witch, who had died in her bed of natural causes at the age of eighty-two. "It sounds rather odd, don't you think?"

Quincy, who privately thought the two great-aunts and that unripe and untrained valet to be impecunious interlopers, looked severe and said, "Their carriage was hired, my lord. Their luggage is easily from the last century."

"Well, I suppose that makes sense since they're going to be remaining here for a while. We have no room for an additional carriage in the stables. As for their luggage, why shouldn't it be old? They're ancient themselves. Now, I'm off."

"Your lordship will enjoy yourself."

Gray grinned as Quincy, who was nearly

as short as Aunt Maude, helped him into his cloak. "Was that a bit of impertinent wit, Quincy?"

Quincy, an artist at his craft, affected the stolid, unaffected butler look and said nothing at all, but Gray always saw the impudent wickedness in his eyes, no matter how hard he tried to hide it.

"Gray, do please taste the apple tarts. I made them once before, but the butcher, a big hairy ape who claimed I was much too pretty to cook, thought the crust was too dry. I put a bit more butter in the pastry this time, just in case he was telling the truth. The apples were very fresh. The boy who sold them to me was a crude little fellow who wanted to give me a kiss, so I clouted his ear. Now, do try a tart. I made them especially for you."

Gray was lying flat on his back, naked, happy, sated, and just beginning to breathe normally again. And here was Jenny, wrapped up in a peach confection that, to his mind, looked more edible than the apple tarts she was sticking in his face. Her glorious black hair was tangled about her head, tumbling all the way down to her very nice bottom, her lips still red from all their kisses. He wanted her again—well, perhaps in another five minutes. Now he just wanted to rest a bit, so he could once again replenish his manly vigor. But he saw the excitement in her eyes, knew his duty, and took an apple tart. At least she was always ready to feed him after she'd exhausted him.

"You've never before made apple tarts for me," he said as he examined the small square of pastry with hot apple sauce dripping off the sides.

"You said that the roast duckling with sweet Madeira and apricot sauce was a bit heavy after lovemaking, so I thought to give you just a bit of dessert today."

He took a bite and lay back against the pillow. He closed his eyes and clasped his hands over his chest, careful not to smash the tart. He chewed slowly, knowing she was already hopping from her right foot to her left, waiting for him to pronounce her apple tart the best in the land. He kept his eyes closed, took another bite, chewed it slower than he had the first bite, then—finally—popped the last bite into his mouth. He looked at Jenny from beneath his eyelids. She was very nearly ready to shriek at him.

He opened his eyes and said, "It isn't enough. I'm not certain that the taste is exactly what one would applaud. Give me another one."

She nearly crammed it into his mouth herself.

He ate the second tart, still silent and thoughtful, still chewing each bite until he knew if he didn't say something very quickly, she would throw the plate at his head.

He smiled up at her, scratched his belly, and said, "Jenny, just a dollop of Devonshire cream for the apple tart, and it's perfect. The pastry with the addition of more butter makes it nearly as smooth and creamy as the flesh on your belly."

"I have some Devonshire cream," she shouted and ran out of the very feminine bedchamber, hung with soft peaches, light yellows, and pale blues. The naked man lying atop her unmade bed sighed, stretched, and fell asleep.

Before he left two hours later, once more sated and more content than a vicar who'd found three gold coins in the collection plate, he ate another apple tart, this one dripping with Devonshire cream. It was beyond delicious, and she licked the cream off his mouth, laughing. "Give me the recipe for Mrs. Piller," he said. "My guests will not want to leave the table." He then saw himself telling the ancient and ever-so-proper Mrs. Grainger-Jones, wife of an equally ancient old general from the colonial wars, that the recipe was from his mistress.

Jenny kissed his mouth, then helped him to dress. When he left, she was humming, doubtless dreaming up a new recipe. She would probably be cooking in her kitchen in the next five minutes, never heeding that she was wearing a peach silk confection that would make a randy man want to eat his elbow. He'd spent more money having her kitchen remodeled just as she wished it than he ever had for clothes or jewels or trips to Vauxhall Gardens or the opera.

St. Cyre Town House
April 7th

Gray wondered how the aunts were doing. He'd seen them only on two occasions since their arrival, both at the table for dinner. And on both evenings, Mathilda had worn a black gown, circa 1785, few flounces and severely corseted; her very beautiful, thick hair was piled high on her head and was so white it could have been powdered.

As for Maude, her gown was the latest style, high-waisted, with fluttery puce silk swathing her meager bosom.

He heard more details about the infamous fire and flood that had ravaged Feathergate Close and kept the two old ladies in an elevated state of misery. He heard more stories of how Mortimer the Vicar had tried to steal a kiss from Mathilda behind the vestry and had even patted her posterior when the sexton was ringing the church bells. On both evenings when dinner was finished, he found he didn't want to sit in isolated splendor in his dining room sipping a glass of port.

That first night he'd followed the aunts into the drawing room. Before they could be seated, Mathilda said, "Piano."

And so it was that Gray was treated to some flawless Haydn by the very talented Maude.

That had been two nights ago. He wished, as he stroked Eleanor now, sprawled out along the length of his right leg, that he'd had his great-aunts in his life throughout the years. He quite liked them.

He smoothed Eleanor out over both his legs, picked up his quill, dipped it into the exquisite onyx ink pot that the lovely widow, Constance Duran, had presented him after he'd removed a noxious problem from her life, namely her husband, and wrote a letter to Ryder Sherbrooke, a man with not too many more years on his plate than Gray, a man Gray admired more than he'd ever admired any other man in his life.

He had just finished the letter when Quincy entered the library, his rheumy dark eyes narrowed.

"What's wrong, Quincy?"

"It's a gentleman, my lord—actually, a gentleman I've never seen before. He gave me his card." Quincy handed Gray a small, very white visiting card with the name Sir Henry Wallace-Stanford written on it. He didn't know this man. He looked up at Quincy again. "I heard it in your voice. What's wrong with him?"

Quincy said slowly, "It's something about his eyes. It's what he's after. I believe that greed, pure and simple greed, is what he's all about. Actually, perhaps that is over-

flowing in melodrama. We will see. However, I don't think Sir Henry is a very good
man." Quincy shook himself. "Nevertheless,
he asked very politely to see you. He claims
it's important."

"This should prove interesting," Gray said
and rose. "Bring in our Sir Henry."

"Lord Cliffe?" Gray nodded at the extraor-
dinarily handsome man who walked confi-
dently into the library, his hand out. He was
tall, straight, and of middle years, with thick
dark brown hair flecked with gray. He shook
the man's hand automatically, then bowed
slightly. "Yes, I'm Cliffe. I'm afraid I don't
know you, sir."

"I'm Wallace-Stanford. I'm a friend of the
Feathergate Close sisters, Mathilda and
Maude. I happened to be in London and decided to see if they were enjoying their stay
with you. I'm very fond of the old ladies."

Now this was a revelation. The man had
jumped right in, not a single nicety, no prelude at all. He was also anxious. Gray could
see the sheen of sweat on his brow. "I see,"
Gray said, not really seeing a thing. He invited Sir Henry to be seated, which he did.

"Would you care for a brandy?" Once the
brandy was pressed into Sir Henry's elegant

hand, Gray said, "So, you are acquainted with my great-aunts. Are you calling to see them or just to inquire about them?"

"No, actually, I'm here to inquire if the dear old ladies have a young guest with them."

"A young guest?"

"Yes."

He looked at Sir Henry Wallace-Stanford's eyes, so very dark, thought of Quincy's words, and said, "No, the aunts brought no guest with them."

"Ah, I see," said Sir Henry. He slowly rose. "I'm sorry to have disturbed you, my lord. You are certain they brought no person with them?"

Now this was mightily interesting. Gray just shook his head. "No guest in sight," he said. "Are you certain you don't wish to speak to them? At the moment I believe they are at Hookham's bookstore or perhaps at Gunther's, enjoying an ice. Perhaps you'd care to wait for them?"

"Oh, no, it's not all that important, really." He gave Gray a long look, then slowly nodded.

Once Sir Henry was out of his house, Gray stood in the entrance hall beside

Quincy, staring at the recently closed front door. "This is very strange," Gray said.

"Shifty man," Quincy said. "Very shifty. If you would like to tell me what he wanted, my lord, I would be pleased to cogitate on its implications."

"If I'm not mistaken, I think he was after Jack."

"Jack the valet?" Quincy said, tapping his fingertips lightly on the silver card tray he was holding. "I can't imagine why. A most unprepossessing lad. Not much of a valet, I heard Horace say. Needs training. Your Horace said he'd be happy to see to it, but the lad avoids all the servants, stays to him- self in the great-aunts' bedchambers. The boy also needs proper clothes. I wonder why your two great-aunts haven't provided for him? And why would Sir Henry want Jack the valet?"

"Good question."

Mad Jack, who wasn't Jack or mad at all, was scared. It had been four days since she'd escaped from her bedchamber down the knotted sheets and flown to the aunts' house. And now they were here in London and she was supposed to be a boy because the aunts said that her stepfather would surely track them here and there simply couldn't be a young lady with them, else it would give all away immediately, and that would lead to trouble, and their great-nephew didn't deserve any extra trouble. He'd been nothing but amiable, they told her every evening, always solicitous, not a rotter at all. Still early days, though, Mathilda had said.

She had to remain a valet so they could protect their great-nephew from any possible violence offered by her stepfather. They'd paused, cycled looks back and forth, then said that the baron was also the son of a very dishonorable man and they didn't want to take the chance of the baron being like his father, in other words, taking one look at her, slavering, and trying to seduce her. Jack couldn't imagine any gentleman slavering over her, but no matter. It was what the aunts were concerned about, and they should certainly know more about slavering than she did, being that they were triple her age, at least, so she'd kept quiet.

Mad Jack. She grinned now, just for a moment, thinking of it, laughing a bit as she remembered when Jack had been created.

Aunt Mathilda had looked at her, up and down, finally nodding her long, narrow face. Jack remembered Mathilda's deep, musical voice saying only, "Breeches."

Aunt Maude, her small hands fluttering, had said, "Yes, that's a good idea. She will be a boy, with a cap pulled down over her eyebrows, a boy with breeches bagging down to her knees. Ah, the church rummage barrel. It will have all that we need. Our great-nephew, poor dear boy, won't be tempted by her exquisite self if it turns out he carries his father's bad blood."

She'd rolled her eyes. "I'm as exquisite as a turnip, Aunt Maude."

"Jack," Aunt Mathilda had said, ignoring her.

Aunt Maude had nodded. "Yes, Jack's a very good name. Solid, unromantic, a name to trust, not question. But wasn't there a highwayman some years ago with that name? Wasn't he Mad Jack or something equally silly?"

"Black Jack," said Aunt Mathilda. "But 'Mad' is better. That's our boy."

"Yes, a very romantic bad man, that one," Aunt Maude had said. "Now, the baron, if he thinks anything at all out of the ordinary when he sees her, will think 'Jack' and then go about his business."

She'd been Jack for four days, and Mad Jack only in the company of the aunts. How long would it take her stepfather to find her?

She'd seen the baron only on that first morning when they'd arrived, and just for a moment before she'd quickly turned her head away. In all honesty, she realized that just about every woman she knew would say the poor dear boy was too handsome for his own good in a blond, blue-eyed Viking sort of way; every woman would probably dance right up to him, sigh in his face, bat her eyelashes, and fall metaphorically at his feet. She felt her flesh ripple with distaste and fear.

She'd had just a brief glimpse of him. Was the young man like his father? Bad to the bone? Was he like her stepfather? Rotten to his heels?

Yes, his great-aunts had said that the baron's own father had bad blood, something common in the St. Cyre males, they'd said, their voices matter-of-fact. She believed the great-aunts implicitly. If he was a womanizer—like her stepfather, like his own father—then she would remain Jack, and she would loathe him to the toes of the great-aunts' stableboy Jem's old boots and avoid him at all cost.

Just for that brief moment when he'd looked over at her, her hands overflowing with the aunts' valises, she'd seen his eyes, seen that weary sort of arrogance that bespoke the kind of knowledge that a man as young as the baron shouldn't have. It was a pity, but it was likely that he was a rotter, a debaucher to his boots.

She drew her knees more tightly to her chest.

She saw her stepfather's face in her mind, his devil's handsome face that her mother had seen once and loved until she'd died. She heard his deep, brilliant voice raging.

Now they'd found out yesterday in a message sent by the great-aunts' housekeeper, that Georgie was back at Carlisle Manor.

Dear God, what should she do?

4

Gray was tired. He was also still furious, calmly and coldly furious now, back in control, but he knew that if Lily's husband hadn't been lying sprawled in a drunken stupor in the corner of the bedchamber those first minutes after he'd arrived, he would have pounded him into the floor, with deadly enthusiasm. At least Lily was now safe, because Charles Lumley had regained his wits enough to understand that Gray would kill him without warning, without hesitation, if he ever touched his wife again. Lumley, still on the drunk side but no fool, had agreed. Gray didn't trust him, but he'd wait and see.

He drew another deep breath. Only an hour had passed. And he was still so angry he could spit.

Charles Lumley was a weak sod who was a bully and vicious only when his victim was half his size, as was his wife, Lily. Well, no more would he strike her. No more, or Gray would bring him down.

He had the hackney stop at the corner of Portman Square, paid the driver, and walked to his town house. He didn't want to awaken anyone, particularly his great-aunts, and their bedchambers faced the front of the house. He had his latchkey in his hand, raised to fit into the lock of the front door, when from the corner of his eye he saw a light flash. *No,* he thought, *it was nothing,* but still, even as he dismissed the flash of light as nothing important, he turned. There it was again—a flash of light coming from the stables. So his head stable lad Byron was up with one of the horses. What if it was serious? What if Brewster, his bay stallion, was colicky? What if Durban had hurt his hock? He turned quickly and walked toward the stables, set just back from the house and extending nearly to the street.

The light went out. The stables were completely dark now. This was very odd indeed. His heartbeat picked up. The door to the stable was cracked open. It wasn't Byron, then.

It was a thief.

Jesus, that a thief would break into a gentleman's stables at Portman Square. It made no sense. He knew the stables well. Once he had eased inside, he immediately flattened himself against the wall directly to his right. His three riding horses were in separate stalls some dozen feet away. He stood quietly, listening. He heard a voice then, speaking to one of his horses. He could make out an open stall door, heard that low, soothing voice again, and knew he was covered with shadows and the thief wouldn't see him. Then he saw his gray gelding, Durban, his head jerking up and down, snorting low. The thief was leading him out. The thief bridled the gray, then, with the ease of long practice, swung up on his back. Slowly Durban was coming right toward him.

He felt himself smile. He'd not been able to pound that drunken animal, Lumley, but now he had his very own thief, and there was no doubt at all about his guilt. He'd caught the bugger in the act. He felt viciousness flood him. He felt good. He said very softly, "You bloody little sod. You'll not escape me." And then he grabbed the thief's leg and jerked him off the gray's back. The thief went flying to the ground.

Gray raised his leg and brought his foot down into the man's ribs. He heard a satisfying thud. At least he'd bruised a rib. Damn, but ribs were sturdy.

"You rotten scum, I'm going to kick your ribs through your back."

"You already did."

The thief didn't sound like a very old thief. Pain laced that faint voice. It was a boy— he saw that now—a slight boy who had tried to steal his horse and would have gotten away with it if Gray hadn't come home at just the right time.

"I should beat you to hell and gone, you puking little bandit. You don't steal one of my horses, you bloody beggar." He reached down, grabbed the boy by his arm, and jerked him up. He shook him. He drew back his arm. He wanted to smash the thief's jaw. He was smiling.

The thief kicked Gray in the leg. Pain laced through him and he saw red. He picked up the boy by his neck and hurled him against William the Conqueror's stall.

The Chief, as he was called by the stable lads, neighed loudly. Brewster whinnied back.

"Go back to sleep, Chief, Brewster. I'm just beating the sin out of a boy who was stealing Durban, and because Durban hasn't an ounce of sense, he would have let the thief take him without a sound." Durban was standing placidly, munching straw now. Gray saw that the thief was lying there in the straw, shaking his head, and he laughed.

"I rattled your brains a bit, did I, you little blockhead? Come here and let me have a go at those skinny ribs of yours again." But the thief didn't move, just lay there. Gray walked to him, leaned down, and dragged him upright. "You kick me again, and I'll beat you from here to the Thames."

He shook the boy.

"Don't you dare groan on me." Then he sent his fist into his jaw. The thief crumpled to the floor.

"That was just a light tap. Damn you, get up." The thief didn't move. Well, hell.

The cowardly little bugger had the gall to faint. From a stupid kick in the ribs? From a little tap on his jaw? He hadn't even gotten started yet, and the little sod had collapsed on him? He picked the thief up, shook him, and slapped his face several times, but the thief didn't stir. Gray was holding him up. He was a dead weight, nearly pulling Gray to the floor. Gray let him go. The thief fell onto his side.

"Well, damnation," Gray said and knelt down beside the fellow. He lit the stable lantern and brought it close.

Before he got it in the thief's face, the fellow lurched up, slammed his fist into Gray's jaw, then frantically crawled away, finally coming up on his knees some six feet away.

"You're a damned boy," Gray said, lightly rubbing his jaw. "I thought so. You're little and you're skinny. You don't even have a whisker on that chin of yours, do you? You're not even old enough to shave. I think I'll still beat you from here to the street. Perhaps then you'll think again before you sneak into a man's stable and try to steal one of his horses."

He kept rubbing his jaw even as he lunged toward the boy. The boy tried to twist out of the way, but he wasn't fast enough. Gray slammed down on him hard. He drew up, straddling him, his right hand fisted just above the boy's jaw. "You have the gall to strike me?" he said, then brought his fist down. The boy jerked away, but Gray's fist got the side of his face and his left ear. He growled deep in his throat even as Gray closed his hands around his neck and began to squeeze. The boy grabbed his hands and tried to pull them free. It was at the exact moment when the boy's hands dropped away that the haze of anger fell away. Gray shook himself. Dear God, he'd nearly killed a boy for trying to take his bloody horse. He lurched off him and came up on his knees. The boy just lay there, saying nothing, his eyes closed.

"Say something, damn you. I didn't kill you, I can see you breathing. You'd best get yourself together before I deliver you myself to Newgate."

The boy still didn't say anything. He raised his hands and began to rub his throat. Then he opened his eyes and said, "I think you broke something."

"You deserve it, but I didn't break any of your bloody ribs. I just gave one a little tap. Don't whine. Get yourself together. You try to steal a man's horse, the very least you deserve is to have a rib cracked, which I didn't even do. Consider it just a beginning punishment for this evening's work."

Then Gray fell silent. Dead silent. *Oh, no,* he thought. *Oh, no.* He reached for the lantern and knew he didn't want to bring it close. But he did. He stared down at the boy.

The boy tried to jerk away, but Gray simply clamped his hand around his upper arm and said slowly, "Well, hell. You're Jack, aren't you? Mad Jack? You're the valet to the great-aunts? Why were you stealing my horse? Come on, you little sod, answer me." He raised his hand, now a fist. He saw that his knuckles were bruised. He'd hurt his knuckles on the little bastard. It wasn't fair.

"Yes, I'm Jack." Then the boy turned over and vomited into the straw. "I'm not at all mad. I wish the aunts hadn't told you that."

"Well, they did and now I begin to understand why. They said you were energetic. They didn't indicate at all that you were also a thief." Gray sat back on his heels. He pulled a handkerchief out of his waistcoat pocket and poked it into the boy's hand. "There, clean yourself up. I don't want you stinking when I haul you to Newgate. If this is an example of what the aunts meant, you're mad enough. And stupid to believe you could get away with stealing one of my horses."

The boy wiped his mouth with the handkerchief. Slowly Jack rose, forcing himself to straighten. Then, with no warning at all, he kicked the lamp away from Gray, plunging the stable into darkness. Gray was up in an instant. In the very next instant, he heard movement, but he didn't scramble away in time. The lantern hit him hard on the back of his head and he went down and out.

He didn't know how long he'd been unconscious, hopefully just a minute or two. Yes, that had to be all. He lurched to his feet, groaned when he realized his head felt like it would fly off his neck, and ran out of the stable. He saw the thief riding Durban hell-bent for leather down the street.

He cursed, got a bridle on Brewster, and swung up onto his back. By the time they reached the street, he couldn't see Durban. He nudged his heels into Brewster's broad stomach and sent him galloping in the direction he'd seen Durban running.

Gray was dizzy, his head was beginning to throb, and he wanted to kill that little bugger Jack. And he *would* kill him the minute he got his hands around his skinny neck. Thoughts of murder made him begin to feel better.

Who the hell was Jack? Why did he steal Durban? Who was Sir Henry Wallace-Stanford? Why was the boy with the aunts? Well, they could all have their Mad Jack back after Gray finished with him.

The night was cold, the clouds hanging low and dark. Only a few scattered stars shone down. The moon, currently just a quarter of itself beaming down, was veiled by the sluggish black clouds.

There, finally, he saw Durban, the boy lying nearly flat against his long neck. Where the hell was the boy heading?

This was certainly an unexpected ending to an already distressing evening. He thought of Charles Lumley, lying there dead drunk on the floor of his bedchamber, saw him as he'd left him, bending over a chamber pot puking up his guts, his vow hanging in the air that he would never again strike his wife. He thought of Jack and what he would do to the little puke when he caught up with him. All his anger at Lumley was easily transferring itself to Durban's thief.

Traffic was light. No one stopped to stare

at the one horseman chasing after the other. No one cared, and why should they?

The boy didn't turn in the right direction. Gray had assumed he'd go to the Folkstone road heading south, but he didn't. He was riding due west out of London. But that made no sense at all. Hyde Park disappeared into the distance, fog-laden, all the trees huddled together in the heavy darkness.

For a few minutes, Gray lost sight of Durban in the thick fog. Ah, there he was. Gray saw him as they rounded a turn. Durban was flying, his hooves eating up the ground. He was as fast as Brewster and he had a good lead.

Well, damn. Sooner or later the boy would slow, he'd have to. Brewster couldn't maintain such a pace for very long—no horse could, not even his. He was aware of the boy looking back every few minutes. Gray didn't think Jack had seen him yet. Good. He would probably pull Durban up soon, slow him to save his strength. They were out of town, on the Reading road, stretching long and flat into the distance. Gray knew that if the boy left the road he would probably lose him. The night was simply too black to see much of anything, despite that bit of moon. He had to catch him and he had to catch him soon, or else he just might lose him, and then what would he do? Inform the aunts, saying, "Well, Aunt Mathilda, Aunt Maude, your valet stole one of my horses, but I lost him on the Reading road. Do either of you know why he did this? What's on the Reading road? Perhaps he left because of something to do with that hard-eyed Sir Henry Wallace-Stanford who was looking for him?"

Why the hell was the boy riding to Reading? Then possibly onward to Bath? Wasn't Jack the valet from Folkstone, just as his two aunts were?

He said now to his horse, "Brewster, my boy, our Durban is in the hands of the valet Jack, who's up to no good, and I have no clue as to what the no good is. Is the little bastard indeed mad? Just what I need, a bloody real-life mad valet who's completely untrained, according to my valet, Horace. Mad Jack. Now that has a ring to it, doesn't it? Or was he there at my house to steal my silver? We've got to catch him so Durban can come home. Can you give me the speed, boy?"

Brewster was a thoroughbred, with a racer's heart. He stretched out his neck, bunched his muscles, and flew forward, surprising even Gray, who'd trained Brewster himself some four years before.

He would lose sight of Durban, curse loudly into the dark night, then catch sight of him again. He didn't believe Jack knew where he was going. But if he was lost, why didn't he just stop and return to London?

Because he thinks I'll be there waiting to kill him and then take his body to the magistrate. Not a bad idea, all things considered. The boy isn't stupid, at least about saving his hide.

It started to rain about two o'clock in the morning. The temperature plummeted. It needed but this, Gray thought and hunched down against Brewster's neck. Brewster, unhappy about the weather, snorted and stretched his neck out even longer.

There was no traffic at all. Not a carriage or another rider. Nothing, just the heavy rain and fat, bloated clouds and air that was growing colder by the minute.

Gray cursed, unable to think of anything else to do. And always he was thinking: *Who the hell is Jack?*

Brewster came around a bend. Gray was expecting to see Durban in the distance, but he didn't see anything at all. He rode farther. He didn't see Durban, not a whiff of him. He'd just vanished. No, that was impossible. He rode another mile. When he was certain that Jack must have left the main road, maybe finally realized that he was going in the wrong direction, Gray pulled Brewster to a stop and sat there in the rain, freezing and thinking. Then he turned back toward London. He saw a small country road that forked off the main road. Jack had to have come this way. Gray nudged Brewster onto the rutted, muddy country road.

Gray was exhausted, soaked to the marrow, and so worried about Jack that his anger at the boy had cooled below the boiling point. Brewster was tiring. He had to do something.

Brewster slowed to a walk, both he and his master nearly cross-eyed with fatigue. Suddenly Gray heard a familiar whinny.

Durban.

He pulled Brewster to a halt and said, "That's our Durban. What do you think, Brewster? Do you know where he is?"

Brewster raised his great head and whinnied loudly. He was quickly answered. Durban was close, just off to the left. It was then that Gray saw a very old relic of a barn set back from the country road at the far end of a barley field. There was no farmhouse in sight, just the dilapidated old barn, probably deserted a good half century before.

The rain was coming down even harder, though Gray would have thought that impossible. It was difficult to see three feet in front of him. Without any instruction from his rider, Brewster left the road and gingerly made his way through the muddy field which had sharp rocks sticking up here and there to catch the unwary. At a patchwork wooden fence Brewster had to jump, which he did, clearing it easily.

At least Jack was inside that barn, out of the rain, nursing his bruised rib—the worthless little bastard. He obviously didn't have any notion of direction.

Durban whinnied again, and Gray's eyes narrowed.

He slid off Brewster's back, nearly falling because his legs wouldn't hold him up after the five-hour ride. He steadied himself and led Brewster into the barn. At least it provided some shelter, though rain came hard through a good half dozen holes in the roof. Then suddenly the rain stopped—simply stopped. Well, that was something.

He called out, "Jack? Where are you, you damned idiot?"

No answer.

He removed Brewster's bridle and led him to Durban, who was tied by a badly frayed rope in one corner of the barn where the rain probably hadn't reached. Durban was chewing on old straw. Gray left the two horses together, Brewster nuzzling Durban's neck, and walked to the only other protected corner of the barn.

"Jack?"

No answer. He cursed. When he saw the boy finally, he saw only his head, covered with what looked to be thick dark blond hair. He was covered with straw up to his nose, an attempt to keep warm. He seemed to be asleep. *Sleeping sound as a babe in the straw while I was riding like a bat out of its cave trying to find him.*

Gray came down on his knees beside the boy. It was near to dawn and growing lighter. He pushed the straw off and shook the boy's shoulder. Then a shaft of early-morning sunlight knifed through two board slats.

Gray sat back on his heels and stared down at the boy. He was shaking his head even though he knew he wasn't mistaken. "Oh, God," he said, "I don't believe this. Jesus, you're no more a Jack than I am." Gray leaned forward and swatted the straw from her face and stared down at the girl he'd badly wanted to smash into the stable floor. "You're a damned female. I could have killed you. Not that it should make any difference, but of course it does. You were stealing my horse. Why? Who the devil are you?"

She moaned.

5

"What's wrong with you? Wake up."

He lightly slapped her cheeks. "Come on,
open your eyes." She moaned again, turning her face away from him. She was wet.
This wasn't good. He couldn't be of much
help since he was wet to the bone himself,
and his only clothes covered those bones.

He pressed his palm to her forehead, her
cheeks. She didn't have the fever. He said
again, this time right in her ear, "Wake up.
I don't like this. I came after you because
you stole Durban and here you have the absolute nerve to act ill. You have even more
gall to be a female. Damn you, wake up."

She opened her eyes. It hurt, but she did it. The man's voice sounded very irritated. At first she'd believed it to be her stepfather's voice, but then she knew it wasn't. It was his voice, the baron's voice. Her vision cleared and she saw him not an inch from her nose. He looked worried. Why?

Then her stomach clenched and she lurched up. She felt his hands on her arms, pulling her back down. "I'm going to be sick," she said and felt him pull her up fast and hold her steady. She drew deep breaths, shuddered, breathed through her mouth. No, she wouldn't vomit; she refused to. She swallowed, took several more shallow breaths, and said, "The great-aunts don't know about this. Please don't tell them."

"Why the hell not? They've got a thief disguised as a valet, and you're also a girl. Is this why they call you Mad Jack? You pull ridiculous stunts like this? Dress like a boy and parade about? Damnation, what is going on here? Who are you, damn you?"

"Stop cursing." She felt pain pounding in her jaw and head; her ribs ached, drew, and pulled, and she wanted simply to close her eyes and fall back into the straw. She was cold, yes, that was the worst of it—not her ribs, not her cramping belly. She was cold and she didn't know what to do about it.

She looked up at him and said, "I'm cold. Please, do you have a blanket or something?"

"I'm as wet and cold as you are. Just where do you think I'd find a blanket? Do you even have any idea where you are?"

"In an old barn. Durban brought me here. We can't be too far from Folkstone."

"Here, let me cover you with straw again." He paused a moment as the shaft of bright sun hit him in the face. "No more rain. All right. I have no idea where we are, but we're nowhere close to Folkstone. We're somewhere west of London."

"No, no, we're south of London."

"If you were a man, you'd know in your bones what direction you were going. It's an automatic thing, this knowing where you are, bred deep in a man's bones. But you're not a boy, you're a damned girl and you were riding poor Durban as hard as you could, due west. On the Reading road, toward Bath."

She groaned and closed her eyes. "Oh, dear." She opened her eyes and blinked.

"Do you really know the direction automatically because you're a man?"

"Naturally. Without men, women wouldn't find their way home. It's a sorry thing, but there it is. Now, take off as many clothes as you can and I'll hang them out in the sun to dry. There's nothing else we can do, so get on with it. Oh, your ribs. Do you need help?"

"No, go away."

"Fine," he said, rising. "I'll strip myself."

He heard her breath whoosh out from behind him. He spun on his heel and saw her weaving where she stood, but he wasn't in time to catch her before she fell back down onto the straw. He let loose with a string of curses that had Brewster neighing loudly at him, and then she whispered, "You're cursing again."

"I'm cursing because it's simply the only thing to do. It's what a man does when he doesn't understand what the devil is happening or why it even dared to happen to him since he is completely innocent, and thus his spleen demands venting. You were stealing my horse, I chased you down, and now you have the gall to be a girl and a mad valet to my great-aunts. On top of everything, you're sick, damn you." He smacked his hand to his forehead. "It's a new day and I had a bloody awful evening and night."

"What happened last evening?" She didn't move, just lay there on her side, trying to control the god-awful pain in her one rib that he'd kicked into her back and the sick throbbing in her head. She felt less cold now, which didn't make a lot of sense but was true nonetheless. And here she was talking. Who cared about his blasted evening? "Did your mistress tell you she'd found a better protector?"

"Ah, so there's still a bit of hornet left in you, is there? What would you know about mistresses and the men who keep them?"

"Every man has mistresses if he has the money. Everyone knows that. It's the way things are." Slowly, she tried to pull herself upright. She managed it, breathing hard, still feeling a bit sick to her stomach, and hating the dampness of her clothes sticking to her. "But it isn't right. It really isn't. Men might automatically know directions, but if they aren't faithful to their promises, then they shouldn't be admired."

"Maybe it's only other faithless men who admire them. Now, are you going to fall down again? You're a female, so I suppose

I should expect it." He paused a moment and frowned. "You got the best of me twice last night. I don't understand that."

"Men have direction and women have brains—well, and a bit of luck too. Now, I'm going to get up and I'm going to get these wretched clothes off. Yes, I'm going to do it right now. Turn around. Thank you."

"When you get your clothes off, I'll look at your ribs."

"No you won't, my lord. If you try it I'll smash you to the ground again."

Gray laughed, he couldn't help it. "We're somewhere in the wilds of nowhere—well west of London—but at least it's not raining, so I won't complain. Look, Jack, or whatever your name is, the thing is—" He'd turned as he spoke and there she was, standing in a chemise that came to her knees, and one riding boot on the other lying in the straw beside her. Dark blond hair spilled over her shoulders and breasts. She looked utterly, amazingly female. He hadn't a clue as to what he had been about to say. He quickly gave her his back again. "Toss your clothes over near me and then get under as much straw as you can."

He stripped down to his breeches, had his

hand on their buttons, then sighed and shook his head. No, Jack wasn't a Jack. He couldn't strip all the way. He picked up her clothes and his shirt, waistcoat, and great-coat and left her.

She lay there, shivering like a loon, wondering what would happen now and knowing it wouldn't be good. She closed her eyes, felt nausea stir in her belly, and began breathing lightly and quickly.

He said from above her, "Now, think about your ribs. Did I get one or two?"

"One."

Without saying anything else, he knelt down beside her, wearing only his breeches. She'd never seen a half-naked man before, and the surprise of it made a little noise in her throat, which brought his face to hers. "What's wrong?"

"You don't have a shirt on. I've never seen a man's chest before."

He sat back on his heels, frowning down at her. "Don't be a twit. You dress like Jack the valet, hide in a barn older than my grandfather, and then make silly little noises just because I don't have cloth over my up-per parts? Close your eyes, then." He un-fastened her chemise and pulled back the soft white batiste just a bit. It wasn't enough. He pulled the material wide, baring her breasts. She was so surprised her eyes popped open. She just lay there staring up at him, not knowing what to do. Then she raised her hand in a protective gesture. He gently shoved her hand back down. She just sighed, closed her eyes, and said, "I'm not a twit."

"Good." He lightly touched his fingers to a lower rib that was yellow and blue, edged with fingers of green and black. She tried to pull away, but it hurt so badly she just groaned instead. "That's right. Make noise, but hold still. Now, let's see what we've got here." He pulled the material fully apart. Though he didn't want to, he saw that her nipples were puckered from the cold. Dear God, it was amazing how a woman's breasts could do a man in very quickly; on the other hand, her breasts were lovely. No, he was looking at the rib he'd smashed with his foot, not at two very nice female breasts. She lay there, stiff and shivering with cold as he ran his fingers over her ribs, up and down her arms, felt her belly, asking over and over, "Here? Does that hurt? No? Good."

It was a relief, she thought, looking at him because she simply couldn't keep her eyes closed. He didn't appear to notice her womanly parts at all. She could have been Jack for all he cared. No, he was looking again at her ribs and now he was lightly stroking his fingertips over that particular rib that hurt so badly she had to bite her lip to keep quiet. Then he pressed harder and she cried out.

He looked up at her briefly. "Sorry. Just hold still. I had to see how bad it was. No, it isn't broken, thank God, but you're not going to feel like performing the cotillion for the next week or two." He sat back on his haunches. "Well, you deserve the pain. Stealing my Durban, a solid old boy I've had since I was fourteen years old. The chances are he would have brought you low, you know. Whenever Durban sees any dandelions—it doesn't matter where—even on the side of a road that's filled with carriages and other horses, he has to have them. Dandelions are ambrosia to Durban. It doesn't matter what you do. Indeed, the only thing you can do is simply let him eat all the bloody dandelions he wants. Only then will he move another hoof in the direction you want, even if it's the wrong direction.

"Now, I'm not going to feel sorry for you. I'm not going to apologize. No matter what you are, you were still stealing my horse. I'll bet the aunts had no idea what you were going to do, did they?"

"They know me very well. If they'd put their brains to it, I'm sure they would have realized that I'd do what I did. I left them a letter."

He could only stare at her. "Bloody hell. Actually, that's just perfect. What should I have expected? You're a damned female, after all. Now, tell me your name and tell me right now."

He was staring at just her face, not her womanly breast parts, which were still very bare.

She was white and silent.

"Is it Jacqueline and you shortened it to Jack?"

She shook her head.

"What else is there that goes with Jack? Jennifer? Jasmine?"

"My name is Winifrede Levering and I'm very cold."

"Winifrede? What's a Levering?"

"Winifrede was my grandmother's name and Levering was her family name. My grandmother on my father's side. My father loved his mother very much and I got stuck with the results."

He grunted, closed the chemise over her breasts, and covered her with handfuls of straw.

"Your family name?"

She shook her head. Her jaw hurt, the side of her face hurt. She held herself perfectly still and said, "I don't want to tell you that. If I do, it will be all over."

"What will be all over?" He tossed more straw over her.

"I didn't mean to say that, precisely. My family name is McGregor."

"You're not any better at lying than you are at stealing. I'll accept the Winifrede Levering—it's too dreadful not to be true. It's a name that really doesn't suit you at all—it even nearly hurts to say that name aloud, so, yes, there's no doubt in my mind that you're telling the truth about that. But *McGregor*? The truth, please, now."

She sighed. Why couldn't she think of a name that he would accept? She wasn't about to tell him who she was. She had no idea what he would do. Probably he'd return her directly to her stepfather.

"I must leave," she said, and he heard the desperation in her voice. There was also pain. What was he supposed to do now?

"Very well," he said, his voice as cold as the month of February had been last winter. "Once our clothes are dry, I'll take you back to London and turn you over to the aunts. I'm certain they'll tell me everything I want to know. They can also deal with you. Of course, they didn't do a very good job of dealing with you before, but what choice do I have? Poor old birds, stuck with you. They do indeed have my sympathy."

"They did an excellent job of dealing with me. It was just that I had no choice. I had to go back to Folkstone. The aunts are wonderful. They're trying to protect me. They won't tell you a thing."

"I'm cold as well," he said, as he lay down beside her and pulled straw over himself. "I came home last night expecting to pour a nice bit of brandy down my gullet and then stretch out on my back and dream sweet dreams, perhaps about my mistress, who doesn't want another protector. But no, it wasn't to be." He gave her a look of loathing. Then he blinked. "Damn. I thought I'd covered you well enough but I didn't. That straw on your skin will tear you apart."

He was over her in an instant, brushing off straw, then pulling her chemise completely together and fastening the small buttons, his fingers lightly brushing over her left breast. She nearly heaved she was so frightened. "For heaven's sake, hold still. I'm not a bloody rapist."

"Stop cursing."

"You'd curse too if you had a half-naked girl whose name is Winifrede Levering alone with you in a wreck of a barn and you were freezing your—well, never mind that. Just hold still. There, now you're covered again. Oh, yes, you look like someone smacked you in the head."

"You did. I tried to jerk away, but you still got me."

He frowned at that, lightly touched his fingertips to her temple, then frowned again. "I don't like to see bruises on a woman. Actually, I've always hated it. What's worse is I've never been one to do it." He threw some more straw over her, then lay down beside her.

"How many mistresses have you had?"

His eyes came open. "Why? You want the job?"

"No, I don't even want you near me, but you fastened my chemise like you've done it many, many times. You even had your eyes closed."

"I have done many little services. I remember the first chemise I fastened. It was swiftly and very well done. I'm not a clod. I was never a clod. I closed my eyes because looking at your breasts wouldn't be the right thing to do. Actually, I'd already looked my fill at your breasts. Thus, doing the right thing this time wasn't that difficult. What am I supposed to do with you now?"

He sounded like a reasonable man, but she couldn't be certain. She hadn't really known many men in her life, other than her father and the two she'd known better than just simple acquaintances hadn't been reasonable. "Perhaps," she said, feeling her way since she well realized that she was mired in a very big problem, "you could simply help me back to London. I will just lie low until I am well again. I'll convince the aunts that I'm all right. You could perhaps just forget all of this?"

"And when you could, you'd try to steal one of my horses again?"

He had a point there.

"No, don't even try to lie. You're no good at it. Now, I think it's in your best interest to tell me the truth and let me decide what's best to be done."

Total silence.

"Very well. Tell me about Sir Henry Wallace-Stanford."

He thought she'd fainted, but when he came up on his elbow to look at her, he saw that she'd squeezed her eyes tightly shut.

"Who is he?"

"Not a good man."

"I know that. Even Quincy knew that. Quincy has something of a second sight about people, inherited all the way down from a great-great-grandmother. Yes, Sir Henry came looking for you."

"Oh, God. What did you say?"

"He told me he was in London on business and just wanted to see if the aunts were doing all right. Then he asked if the aunts had brought a guest with them."

"What did you say?"

"Jack the valet wasn't a guest. I said no. I'm not certain if he believed me, but he had no choice but to leave." He saw that her hair was nearly dry. He himself was finally warm again. Her skin had lost that waxy gray color. She must be warmer as well. He came up on his elbow and began picking the straw out of her hair.

"Since you said you'd never seen a man's chest before, then I assume that Sir Henry isn't your husband."

She groaned.

"No. Well, then, your father?"

"No. My papa's dead. Mathilda and Maude will be frantic. We must get back to London."

He was untangling hair from around a crooked piece of straw. "Since we're both covered with straw, I think I'll take my breeches off." He rose, stripped, laid out his pants, then returned to lie next to her, straw poking him in places he hadn't thought vulnerable since the time when he'd been fifteen and made love with sweet Florence Dobbins in the shade of a sand dune on the beach at Torquay. "If the sun holds steady, our clothes should be dry in a couple of hours. Now, how do you feel?"

"Fine," she said. He heard some strange noises, turned to face her, and saw that she'd stuffed her fist into her mouth and tears were slowly trickling down her face.

6

He didn't think, just acted, pulling away the straw and bringing her close. Her body was incredibly warm against him, which was a surprise, since she'd been shivering just a minute before.

She stiffened tighter than a virgin in a brothel, which, he supposed, wasn't all that much of a surprise. He just pulled her closer and pressed her cheek down against his shoulder. Her arms were as bare as her legs, which were against his, all smooth and delightful. He turned his face into her hair and said, "It's all right. Don't cry unless you're hurting, and not just feeling miserable about this impossible situation that you, I might add, are responsible for getting us into."

"You didn't have to come after me. You could have let me have Durban for a while. I would have returned him."

He started to burn her ears, but he felt her tears on his neck and cursed instead, then stopped cold. "No, I won't curse again, at least until it's impossible not to. I have this feeling that with you near at hand, cursing will become a regular habit with me."

"My mother hated cursing. Once I said 'damn' when I was just a little girl and she made me eat a bowl of turnips. She wouldn't let me add any salt or butter, nothing. I came to hate turnips very quickly. I can't look at a turnip now without thinking about that one small 'damn,' which felt very good saying at the time."

"Turnips, huh? A better punishment than having a mouth full of soap, which I understand is the time-honored curse punishment. Now, you're warming up and so am I. Let's just rest here a couple more hours until our clothes are dry."

"Then what?"

"We'll go back to London."

His skin felt itchy from her tears and he shifted just a bit, bringing up his hand to scratch himself. When she realized what he was going to do, she did it for him, lightly digging her fingernails into his shoulder and neck.

"Thank you," he said. "You hair smells good."

She sighed. "You shouldn't say that. I'm nineteen years old. I don't know you except for what the aunts said, and they aren't sure if you're nice or very wicked. You're naked. I can feel your legs and they're hairy. My rib hurts and so does my head."

"All right. Take a nap. Oh, yes—I'm not wicked. I'm staid, even proper. This one small incident with us lying here bundled together isn't the norm. Trust me."

"I don't know about trusting you just yet. Yes, the aunts wondered if you were like your father. They didn't like your father."

"I didn't either. Go to sleep." He was the one, however, who was lightly snoring five minutes later.

She'd never before lain half-naked against a fully naked man. It was at once strange and just a bit exhilarating. What to do now? She lightly scratched his shoulder again.

When she woke up, she was quite alone, packed in straw like a fish on the dock. She opened her eyes and stared around her, not moving until she remembered, and then she sat up quickly. She was so dizzy that she nearly fell over. She sat very still, waiting. Finally her head cleared. She saw him some six feet away, shrugging into his waistcoat.

"Are the clothes dry?"

He turned around and gave her a smile. She'd never seen him smile before. It was quite nice. In fact, it was a smile that would have knocked her flat—would have knocked any female flat, she imagined—if she weren't sitting here with only her chemise on, with straw sticking out of her hair. If she hadn't believed him to be a womanizer, and possibly just like her stepfather, she would have thought his smile quite the nicest smile that had ever been bestowed upon her. On the other hand, he'd assured her that he wasn't wicked. In her meager experience, however, men weren't to be believed.

"Yes, they're dry. How do you feel?"

She was no longer dizzy, thank God. She silently queried her body, from her rib to her head. It wasn't too bad, just light throbbing in both places. She did feel a bit heavy, perhaps on the dull side, and that was odd, but it wasn't bad enough to say anything about. "I'm fine, but I don't want to go back to London, unless it's just to leave you there with Brewster and make certain I'm on the road to Folkstone."

"Not likely," he said, giving more attention to the wrinkles in his coat than to her very serious statement.

She didn't think it was very likely either, but still, he could have perhaps explained, apologized, even smiled at her again. She watched him walk to her and drop her clothes onto the straw.

"Get dressed. I'll see to Durban and Brewster. They're probably thirsty."

She was fastening her breeches when he came back into the barn. "The sun's brighter than a woman's smile when her lover gives her a diamond necklace."

"I've never heard it put quite that way."

"I'm sometimes a poet," he said. He narrowed his eyes and looked at her closely from toe to head. "You look like a wreck."

"So do you."

"Yes, I suppose neither of us would be

welcome in a London drawing room. On the other hand, my face isn't a mess of blue and green and yellow bruises like yours is. Let's go get something to eat. There must be a town nearby with an inn."

The Corpulent Goose was the premier inn in the market town of Grindle-Abbott. Set in a small yard surrounded by oak trees and a little stable, it faced the town square on High Street. The Corpulent Goose was at least three centuries old and looked every decade of it, but still somehow managed to retain a touch of bygone elegance, what with its slate roof that sloped sharply and dozens of small diamond-paned windows that were sparkling clean.

The taproom was very small, holding only four square wooden tables with benches so old they looked worm-eaten.

A man with a huge belly that was covered with a stained apron came to their table and bellowed, "Wot be fer ye lads?"

"Something to eat, please," Gray said, "for my brother and me."

"A lot of something, please," she said, her voice as deep as she could make it.

"Yer a purty little pullet, ain't ye?" the innkeeper said, as he rubbed his belly with a huge hand. "Even with yer face all bruised up."

"I'm not a little pullet. I'm just a little rooster."

The innkeeper eyed them both and said, "Ye both look like ye slept in yer clothes. Wot did ye do to yer face, little un? Yer brother here belt ye a good un?"

"My brother fell afoul of a door," Gray said. "Actually we did sleep in our clothes. Food, please. A lot of it. My brother's a growing boy."

"Aye, don't flap yer feet." He looked at her again, frowning. "Ye'd best pray Mrs. Harbottle's good food will 'elp yer little brother grow up straight, but I don't think so. Aye, I know. I'll bring one of me Millie's roasted pork knivers, that'll help the lad if anything will."

"Thank you, sir," she said.

Gray saw that she was staring after the innkeeper. "What is it?"

"I've just never before seen a man quite like that one. He was very familiar. What did he mean that the pork knivers would make me grow straight? I have excellent posture."

"I don't believe we should visit that subject. The aunts wouldn't approve. Actually I don't know if the aunts would themselves understand, so just forget the straight business.

"Now, do you want me to tell the innkeeper that I'm a baron and that he should bow, slinging that huge belly low, to show me proper respect, and then charge me twice as much?"

She laughed. "Oh, no, I'm sure he couldn't keep his balance. Oh, goodness, do we have enough money to pay for the food?"

"If you don't eat too much, we should be fine."

"That's good—you look too dirty and wrinkled to be a baron." She giggled behind her hand, a very white hand with long slender fingers. Gray saw another man who was drinking a glass of ale in the corner look up, his nose twitching, sniffing out that sound.

"Be quiet," he said, leaning toward her. "Boys don't giggle. They particularly don't giggle behind their hands with their eyes all wicked. Keep your head down and your mouth shut."

Actually, he thought, just one look at that

face of hers and no man worth his salt would for an instant think she was male.

The innkeeper brought a platter of baked chicken, a single pork kniver for the purty little rooster, an entire loaf of bread, still hot from the oven, and two large glasses of ale. She fell on the chicken before the ostler had taken two steps away from their table.

"Oh, goodness, it's the best chicken I've ever tasted in my life," she said after she'd dropped a breast bone on her plate. "Indeed, I never had a clue that chicken could be so delicious. Is that thick leathery-looking thing a pork kniver? I've never seen one before." She gently hefted the slab of pork off her plate and onto his. "If I have to eat this to grow straight, I think I prefer taking my chances."

He laughed, picked up his fork, and dispatched the pork kniver in half a dozen bites. "I just realized that I was ready to take a bite out of that table leg," he said. He followed the kniver with half the chicken. When he saw her take a long drink of ale, then swipe her hand across her mouth, he laughed. He couldn't help it.

"If you weren't so damned pretty, I would

believe you a boy. The mouth swipe was well done."

"I watched Remie do that once after he'd kissed an upstairs maid and heard Quincy coming. Remie's very manly, you know. I decided that mouth swiping after drinking was just the thing to make me more believable in my rooster role."

"Well, just don't drink too much of that ale. It's got fists. You've already drunk most of that glass. Do I see crossed eyes?"

"Naturally not." She was feeling just the slightest bit dizzy, perhaps a bit light-headed, perhaps almost like she was going to fall in a wrinkled lump onto the taproom floor. She got her strength back when she saw there was still a single heel of bread left. She snatched it up before he could draw a bead on it himself.

Gray sat back in his chair, his hands folded over his belly. "That was quite excellent. Now, are you full yet? It's time we got back to London. Perhaps on the way you'll be so kind as to tell me who you are and why you're the aunts' valet, Jack—their valet, Mad Jack, to be exact. If you've still got a taste for talk, you can tell me why you felt you needed to steal Durban and why you were planning to return to Folkstone."

She sat as still as the man three tables away who was still staring at her, his head cocked to the side.

"If you don't tell me, why, then, I'll just let the aunts know that the game's up. Then I'll have Quincy find Sir Henry Wallace-Stanford."

"Oh, no," she said. "Oh, please, no, Gray. You wouldn't do that." Then she blinked at him, tilted her head to one side, opened her mouth, and closed it. She fell forward, her nose hitting a thigh bone in the middle of her dinner plate.

Gray looked up at the dark-timbered eaves of the taproom. "Why me?" he asked no one in particular.

She wasn't drunk. She was ill, and he was scared to death—and furious. He'd done his best by her, even fed her until her breeches' buttons probably were ready to pop, and she'd had the gall to get ill. She was roasting with fever, limp as her breeches, which were now folded neatly over the back of a chair that looked to be older than the aunts.

Gray watched the little man straighten.

His name was Dr. Hyde, and he was Jack's size and completely bald. He was also clean, which was a good sign. Gray had been relieved no end when Harbottle, the innkeeper, had brought him up. "My lord," said Dr. Hyde, who recognized a lord when he saw one, since he himself was the second son of a baronet, "the girl—yes, I know this is a girl despite the ridiculous clothing— she's indeed ill, as anyone can see." He raised a small, narrow, very clean hand when Gray opened his mouth. "No, I don't need to know anything about either of you. She's got the fever. It's evident she was in the elements. It was a heavy rainstorm last night."

"We were on our way to London."

"If you want her to remain alive, you won't go anywhere," Dr. Hyde said. He placed his palm on her forehead again, then slipped his hand beneath the blankets to lay it over her breast. He closed his eyes and was quiet for a good minute. Finally, he looked up and said, "She should survive this if you keep her very warm and pour water down her throat, else she'll just shrivel up and she'll die, my lord. Now, here's a tonic for her. It's good for many things, a fever among them.

I'll return this evening. If she suddenly worsens, have Harbottle send for me." Dr. Hyde cleared his throat. It took Gray a moment to realize that he wanted money. He pulled out a wad of notes from his waistcoat pocket. It wasn't all that big a wad. He paid the doctor, not moving until the little man had let himself out of the bedchamber—the best bedchamber in his inn, Mr. Harbottle had told Gray when he'd followed him upstairs, carrying an unconscious Jack over his shoulder, since she was a little rooster and thus couldn't be carried in his arms.

Gray cursed and nearly ran from the bedchamber, calling out when he saw Dr. Hyde at the end of the hall, "Dr. Hyde, the boy is my younger brother, Jack. I ask that you not forget that. It's very important."

Dr. Hyde frowned down his very thin nose, then slowly nodded.

Gray was cursing again an hour later when Jack shot up in bed, looked straight at him, and said, "If I don't get Georgie, he'll realize that he can use her against me, and I don't know what he'll do."

Then she simply collapsed back onto the bed, her eyes closed, the fever hard on her now.

She was shivering violently. He took off his wrinkled clothes and climbed in beside her. Her chemise was damp. He managed to get it off her without ripping it, then pulled her tightly against him. He rubbed his hands up and down her back, over her hips, as far down the back of her legs as he could reach.

He said quietly, hoping that at some level she could hear him, "Come on now, Jack, you're ill and that's all right, but for just a little while. I'm getting you all warmed up, and soon you'll be sweating like a mistress I once enjoyed who hated the summer heat because she sweated and she thought it would revolt me. Can you begin to imagine anything more silly than that? No one could, at least no man could. Come now, breathe more slowly, stay close to me. Yes, that's it."

He thought he'd die of heat prostration when, suddenly, without warning, she lurched up again and yelled, "I can say 'damn,' I can. It's not a really bad word. Mrs. Gilroy says it under her breath when Mr. Gilroy eats garlic and then tries to kiss her. It's a better word than 'turnips.' No, don't make me eat those horrible turnips. Oh, goodness, it's hot in here." And she flung off the covers, pushed herself away from him, and jumped up from the bed.

He stared at the naked girl just standing there, staring down at him, her expression blank as a slate, her dark blond hair tangled wildly around her face. She was very nicely knit together, and had breasts made for a man's mouth and his hands, although which part of himself a man would select first would be hard to decide. Damnation, he couldn't think like this. She ran to the long, narrow window and flung it open. She leaned out, breathing in the fresh, crisp air. He looked at a white backside and a stretch of long legs that nearly made him swallow his tongue. A man's mouth or a man's hands—tough decision.

"No, Jack. Good God, you're buck naked and leaning out the window. No, don't wave." He pulled her away from that open window, relieved that no one on the ground below had yet noticed her, and towed her back to the bed. "Come on now, you're ill, Jack. You've got to keep warm."

"I am warm, you fool," she said, even her breath hot against his bare flesh. "I'm burning up. Flames are near my skin. Oh, goodness. Where are some scissors? I want to cut off this dreadful hair."

She started pulling on her hair. Then she groaned and collapsed forward, her face against his belly. He gently eased her onto her back, then straightened over her.

"All right, I'll try to cool you down." He was stymied for a moment, then eyed the basin of cool water beside the bed. He wet her chemise, since he didn't have anything else, and began to wipe her down. He would swear that when that cool, damp chemise stroked over her, she stretched and purred just like Eleanor.

He kept rubbing her with the damp cloth until finally she opened her eyes, smiled up at him, and said, "That's very nice." Her head fell to the side.

"Oh, no," he said, bringing her head up into the crook of his elbow. "You've got to drink some water." He got nearly a full glass down her before she fell completely slack against him.

He felt utter panic, then saw that this time she was asleep, not unconscious. He eased her back onto the bed and brought the covers to her chin, spreading her hair out in a halo around her head. Then he rose and dressed in his ravaged clothes. He felt her forehead again. She was cool to the touch. Thank God. She was asleep.

He quickly left the bedchamber.

7

The rain slammed against the narrow windows in the bedchamber. The windows rattled when lightning followed by a crash of thunder shook the table beside the bed. It was a god-awful day, dreary, cold, and gray. And there was nothing for him to do except wait. He wasn't all that patient. It was a chore for him not to pace a hole through the very old rag rug that covered the oak floor.

At some deep level she was aware of the drumming rain. Hours later, it was the absence of that rhythmic rain that woke her. She lay there, aware finally that things had changed, but she didn't know what exactly had happened. She thought she was back in the barn again when she saw the sun shining hard through the panes of the window, right in her face.

She was with some fat bird. A fat bird? Where? No, that wasn't right. She was at the Corpulent Goose inn. She sighed deeply, pleased to have gotten that cobweb cleared out of her brain.

She was here with the baron, with Gray. That was a nice name. He'd never told her his name. She'd heard the aunts speak of him. But she remembered that smile of his, all white-toothed and wicked, that smile that could flatten a female, and she smiled now herself, thinking of it.

He wasn't here. Oh, goodness, had he left her? Had he dusted his hands of her, taken Durban and Brewster and gone back to London?

It hurt now to smile and, she discovered, to swallow. She was thirsty. She was more than thirsty, she was close to dying of thirst. She saw a pitcher of water on a small table beside the bed. She had to have that water—she had to. Then she'd worry about Gray deserting her.

Gray opened the bedchamber door to see

her flailing wildly in an effort not to fall out of bed. She didn't make it. He didn't either. She crashed to the floor, blankets and sheets twisted around her.

He cursed as he came down to his knees over her.

"Turnips," she said, sounding like the creaky gate in Maude's rose garden. "My mother will make you eat turnips."

He grinned at her. "Good, you didn't break your neck." He scooped her and all the covers up and put her back on the bed. Everything was a mess.

"I was trying to reach the water."

"Hold still." Soon she was attacking a glass of water the way he'd attacked that delicious pork kniver. She drank a full glass, then fell back, just a bit of water dribbling down her chin. He flicked the water away with his finger.

She eyed him, then eyed him some more. "You're not wrinkled. You look very much a baron today."

"No more wrinkles. Squire Leon took pity on me." He stopped then. "You're awake and you're making sense. I've become used to a moaning, sweaty girl who occasionally squeaks or sings nasty ditties or tells me about a frog she once had named Fred or how her older cousin used to throw her in a pond on the first day of May every year."

"Poor Fred. A Frenchman got him, I know it. He was visiting in the neighborhood—the Frenchman, not Fred. Fred lived in the neighborhood. I knew the Frenchman was a guest at Gorkin Manor. He must have seen Fred, and it was all over. Fred was gone." She coughed. "My voice feels all rusty. It doesn't hurt that much right now, but it's still strange. May I have some more water?"

After drinking another glass, she said, "I really told you about Fred?"

"Yes. Where's your cousin?" He lightly stroked his fingertips over her cheek, a healthy color now, which relieved him enormously.

"Bernard died in the Peninsula three years ago."

"I'm sorry. Now, do you remember when we came to the inn?"

"This morning. We came late morning and we were starving. I remember the pork kniver that you ate without offering me a single bite."

"As I recall, you tried to eat all the chicken and disdained the kniver. At least you passed out after you'd eaten and not before. Now, you're not quite right about the time. Actually, that happened four days ago. I was very worried about you, Jack. Even the local vicar was here, praying over you. Dr. Hyde told Squire Leon about the two of us, told him I was a peer, for God's sake, and Squire Leon came to visit, took one look at the abysmal state I was in, and offered me clothes. His wife left clothes for you. Yes, everyone appears to know that you're a female, including Mr. Harbottle. I suppose it was just too meaty a tale for Dr. Hyde not to pass on to his neighbors. It's not really that important.

"Now, you've drunk two glasses of water. You're looking desperate. Let me get you the chamber pot."

He left her to herself for a good three minutes before fear that she would fall on her face again drove him back into the bedchamber. She was sitting on the edge of the bed, holding the blankets over her, staring hard at her toes. They were nice toes. An appallingly clear image of himself nibbling those toes flashed through his mind. He cleared his throat.

"The squire's wife, Betty, left you a nightgown. I'll put it on you right after you've had a bath. What do you think?"

"A bath?" she scratched her leg, then touched the thick, oily braid. She nearly shouted, she was so excited. But once he had her sitting in the deep tub, the water just covering her breasts, she didn't have the strength to balance herself. She slid directly down and nearly drowned herself.

"You're weak," he said matter-of-factly, his hands under her arms, pulling her up. "That's perfectly natural. You just keep yourself sitting up, yes, that's it, hang on to the sides, and I'll wash your hair for you."

She was trembling, her lips nearly blue, when finally she was clean, from her toes to her head, and he had wrapped her in towels. She sat bundled in the single chair, watching Susie, the maid, change the bed. When Susie was finished, she curtsied and said, "Shall I comb out your hair, my lady?"

Her hair was nearly dry before she realized what Susie had called her. *Oh, dear*, she thought, but it was a halfhearted *oh, dear* because she was simply too tired to care. She was only vaguely aware of Gray putting her into a nightgown and lifting her into bed. He smoothed the nightgown over her legs and tucked her between those delicious, sweet-smelling fresh linens. She felt his warm hand lightly stroking her wrist as she sank into a pleasant stupor.

"Come on, Jack, open your eyes. You can do it. Can you smell the chicken soup Mrs. Harbottle made just for you? Yes, that's right. Breathe in deeply. Now open your mouth. Good. Just a little bite at first."

He kept spooning in the soup until she simply couldn't hold another bite. He set the bowl aside and leaned back in the chair, crossing his arms over his chest.

She stretched beneath the covers. "I'm alive and I feel clean. It's wonderful."

"Yes." He remembered each and every inch of her, since he'd been diligent, not missing a single patch of her with that washing cloth. He closed his eyes for a moment, trying to wipe that picture out of his mind and not succeeding to any great extent, and said easily, "You've got a lot of hair. I don't recall ever having washed a girl's hair before. It's still not quite dry. Try not to move your head."

"Can I have some water?"

After she'd drunk her fill, he laid her back down and sat in his chair again, leaning forward, his hands clasped between his knees. "A lot has happened in the past four days," he said, watching her carefully. "I sent a messenger to London with a letter to Mathilda and Maude. He waited for them to write me a response."

She closed her eyes against the enormity of life. "Do they ever want to see me again?"

"Oh, yes, you're still their little lambkin. As you can imagine, they as well as my entire household were frantic when I unexpectedly disappeared, evidently taking both Durban and Brewster with me. Naturally the aunts had to spill to Quincy that Jack the valet wasn't Jack at all. Unfortunately, by the time they worked themselves up to the sticking point, Quincy had already notified all of my friends, not just one or two. No, he'd notified at least a dozen, inquiring if they knew where I'd gone to.

"Then Sir Henry Wallace-Stanford came back, nearly ran over Quincy, and was met by the manly Remie, who properly set him back out on the street. While Remie was manhandling Sir Henry, a good friend of mine, Ryder Sherbrooke, came along and was quickly told by Quincy that I was missing and that this man was trying to steal into the house for some nefarious purpose." Gray paused a moment, smiling as he pictured the scene, and said, "Ryder then proceeded to pound him into the ground.

"Ryder was there when my letter to Quincy arrived." Gray looked down at his fingernails. They were clean and well buffed. "Ryder will be coming here to escort us back. I expect him anytime now. There was nothing I could do to prevent it. But we don't have to worry about Ryder. He'll not say a word to hurt me. Since you're with me, you'll not be hurt either."

She was giving him a bitter look that made him angry. He hadn't done a damn thing, and here she was looking all wounded. Now that expressive face of hers was drifting toward desperation. "All because I stole Durban," she said, looking at the ceiling. "What will I do now?"

He sat forward, groped beneath the pile of blankets to find her hand, and pulled it out. He held her fingers, feeling how dry her skin was, and frowned. "We need some cream. Illness does strange things to our bodies. Your skin feels like a dry leaf. This isn't good. I'll take care of it."

He didn't say another word, just got up and left the bedchamber immediately. She lay there because she didn't have the strength to lift her own dry hand. Where had he gone? What was he going to take care of? Everything was a mess. There was indeed life waiting outside this bedchamber, and she didn't like it.

Where had he gone, damn him? She didn't say the curse aloud, just thought it. It surprised her that when she'd even thought the 'damn,' she'd tasted turnips. Her mother had a lot to answer for.

When Gray came back, he was carrying a small jar. "Hold still," he said and began smoothing cream into her hand. He shoved up the arm of her nightgown and rubbed the cream into her forearm, then up to her shoulder. "That feels better," he said, then moved to her other arm. He rubbed slowly; he was thorough. "Now your face."

When he'd finished to his satisfaction, he set the jar beside the water carafe, sat down, and leaned forward, his hands clasped. He said, "Who's Georgie?"

She said, "You're not a bad man, are you? The aunts were wrong to even consider for a moment that you weren't honorable. You're not at all like your father. Was he really bad?"

"Yes, I already told you. He was a nightmare. He's dead. I'm not at all like him. Enough of your attempts to distract me. If you don't think you can trust me now, then you're a blockhead. Tell me, Winifrede, who's Georgie?"

"My little sister."

"You were riding toward Folkstone to visit your little sister?"

"I was going to take her away from my stepfather. I must protect her."

"Because he'll finally think of her and use her as leverage against you?"

"How did you know that?"

"You were delirious. You said that."

She fell silent. She wouldn't look at him. He was so irritated, he nearly threw the pitcher against the wall. He rose and began to pace. The clothing Squire Leon had given him fit him well enough. Actually, she thought, looking toward him, the trousers were black and tight. He looked quite fit, no fat on him that she could see, and he was a good deal taller than she was. It was difficult to tell how tall he was, since she was lying flat on her back. Squire Leon's waistcoat was also black, not terribly stylish, but she thought that with the full-sleeved white shirt he looked quite dashing. His black boots were his own, she assumed, and his attempts to clean them hadn't been terribly successful. Yes, Gray was a man of many nice aspects.

What else had she spewed out when she'd been out of her head? Had she told him about little Tommy Lathbridge putting his hand on her leg when she was six years old and he was seven? Then she'd put her hand on Tommy's leg, and he was so mortified he hadn't spoken to her for a month.

She sighed. Life was here in the room with her, and he was trying to shove it down her throat. There was no hope for it. She either trusted him or she didn't. He'd saved her life. On the other hand, if he hadn't stopped her, she would have—would have what? Ridden to Bath before she'd realized she was going the wrong direction?

She cleared her throat and spit it out. "You saved my life. Thank you. I'll be ready to leave in another day, surely not longer. I'm young and usually very well—not even colds bring me down. Will you loan me some money? Will you loan me Durban? Will you just forget all this happened? Please?"

"Is Sir Henry Wallace-Stanford your father?"

She'd given it her best. It had been worth a try. "No," she said.

He walked to the bed, leaned down with a hand on either side of her head, and said not an inch from her mouth, "You will stop this lunacy. You have already compromised me beyond redemption. You are such a provincial twit that you don't realize what you've done, not just to yourself but also to me. On top of all of that, you won't even trust me to help you. Damn your eyes, Jack, I did save your bloody life. Trust me, tell me all of it, or I'll throw you out that bloody window."

"The window's too narrow. I'd never fit."

"You would now. You're as skinny as that bedpost." He stood up. "Ryder Sherbrooke's older brother Douglas is the earl of Northcliffe. He and his family are also in London. While Ryder comes flying to my assistance, Douglas will see to it that all my friends know that I'm still alive and stop looking for me. He will protect the aunts and my home."

Why had he spit all that out? None of it

made any difference. There was a knock on the bedchamber door. "It's either Mr. Harbottle, wanting to increase the cost of this room, or Susie, come to straighten the room, or Ryder, come to save me, not realizing that it won't matter, that it's already too late."

It wasn't Ryder Sherbrooke. It was Ryder's younger sister, Sinjun, who was married to Colin Kinross, the Scottish earl of Ashburnham.

He'd known Sinjun since she was fifteen and he an ancient nineteen and a friend of the other Sherbrooke brother, Tysen, now a vicar and so righteous and pompous that his brothers continually regaled him with their most wicked tales. To test his character, Ryder said. To determine if he was really so nauseatingly upright, Douglas said. As for Sinjun, Gray remembered that she would just shake her head at Tysen and laugh.

Sinjun at fifteen had been tall and lanky with straggly hair and the most beautiful smile he'd ever seen. That girl was long gone. She was now twenty-two, still tall, but now quite beautiful. Those Sherbrooke blue eyes of hers shone brilliantly in the dim corridor light as she threw her arms around

Gray and said, "What have you gotten your-self into now, sir? Tell me whom I'm to shoot, or what dragon I'm to slay for you.

"Ryder just found a little girl who'd been tossed into the streets by her father who was trying to find a man who wanted a child. It's difficult to believe there are such wicked people, but Ryder says it's all too common. He took her back to Brandon House, to Jane."

Gray said to Jack, "Ryder Sherbrooke rescues children from appalling situations and takes them to Brandon House, a beau-tiful brand-new house that sits very close to his own in the Cotswolds. He takes care of them, sees to their futures. He usually has about fifteen children there at any one time."

Sinjun interrupted him. "Who's this? Goodness, Gray, is this the young lady who isn't really the valet Jack? She looks all green about the gills. What have you done to her? Move aside and I'll see to her."

Gray moved aside. Sinjun was only four years his junior and a major force of nature.

"Where is Colin?" Gray asked, trailing Sinjun into the bedchamber and closing the door.

"He was being a perfect pain in the—well,

never mind that. He's more nervous than the chickens get when I'm practicing with my bow and arrow in the apple orchard. It's absurd, Gray. I'm just pregnant—a very common thing, particularly among women—and you'd think I was afflicted with some strange and nasty disease. I left him in London to drive himself mad for a change."

Gray closed his eyes. "You mean you simply walked out on Colin? You didn't say anything at all to him?"

"I left him a very sweet letter," she said. "Now, enough of that. Let me see to Jack."

"You're pregnant? That's wonderful, Sinjun! Congratulations." Gray hugged her, then lightly tapped his fingertips on her chin. "You didn't ride like a bedlamite to get here, did you?"

"Not at all. I brought a carriage." She just smiled up at him, then moved to the bed. She stared down at Jack the valet for a long moment, then sat on the edge of the bed.

She leaned forward and peered very closely into Jack's eyes.

"I'm really all right."

"You're less green now than you were a minute ago. Yes, you're going to be fine, thank God. Did Gray nurse you? Of course he did, there's no one else. I've known Gray forever. He's never nursed me, but I would imagine he's quite capable."

"It's his fault that I got sick. He wouldn't let me take Durban."

"What a selfish lout. Shame on him. Who's Durban?"

"I'm not a lout," Gray said. "Durban's my horse, not hers."

"Believe me," Sinjun said to Jack, ignoring him. "Gray's not at all selfish. He must have had an excellent reason not to lend Durban to you. He is wonderful, you know. You can believe me about this." She lightly laid her palm on Jack's forehead. "You feel nice and cool. When did you last drink some water? It doesn't matter. Here, drink some more. You're also clean. Did Gray bathe you? He never bathed me either, but again I'll wager he's quite good at it. Gray is thorough. He's conscientious."

"Don't forget to repeat how wonderful I am," Gray said, torn between amusement and irritation and, yes, a dollop of embarrassment as well.

"Your skin also feels healthy and soft. Hmmm, that's lucky for you."

"Gray rubbed cream all over me."

"He noticed your skin was dry? He rubbed you with cream? What a thoughtful thing for him to do."

He saw that Jack didn't stand a chance. No one did with Sinjun. Jack drank the entire glass of water that Sinjun held for her. Gray wanted to laugh. While Ryder would have coddled Jack and let her complain and whine, Sinjun simply rolled over her. Was he really wonderful? And thoughtful?

"Sinjun," he said to a bewildered, silent Jack, "is but one of the Sherbrooke siblings. Just wait until you meet Ryder and Douglas. Incidentally, Sinjun, how is Vicar Tysen?"

"He and that appallingly proper Melinda Beatrice—that's his wife"—she added to Jack—"are working on their third child. Three! They've only been married just three years. Can you believe that? Douglas and Ryder torment him, tell him that God surely can't approve of all the carnal appetite he's displaying." Sinjun Kinross paused a moment, her brow furrowed, her Sherbrooke blue eyes gone dark with intensity.

"As I told you, I brought a carriage, Gray. Actually, it's your town carriage. When Jack is strong enough, we'll go back to London."

"I'm strong enough right now. This very

minute. I've never been called Jack before a week and a half ago."

"What's your name?" Sinjun asked.

"Winifrede."

"You don't look like a Winifrede," Gray said. "Thank God."

"No, you don't," Sinjun said. "Gray's right. I like 'Jack.' It has grit. My mother wouldn't like it; she'd claim it would wither a female's charms and shrivel a man's interest, but I disagree. Yes, 'Jack' has fortitude."

Gray laughed at the look of complete bafflement on her face. "All right. Let me wrap you up and Sinjun here will take us back to London."

8

They made it to the front yard of the inn.
Gray was carrying Jack, with Sinjun giving
him instructions he didn't need, when a
man's furious shout made them stop in their
tracks.

"Oh, dear," Sinjun said, "I believe I'm
about to be brought low."

Gray, who alternately looked up at the
heavy dark clouds overhead and down at
Jack's pale face, said, "I thought you left
Colin a very sweet letter."

"It was. It was mawkish it was so sweet.
It wasn't a thing like me. Perhaps he didn't
have a chance to read it. Or perhaps he saw

I was gone, read the letter, and decided to strangle me anyway. But you know, Gray, Colin is a lot like Ryder and Douglas. One minute he's yelling his head off and the next he's laughing and—"

"I know when a man is gathering himself up to yell his head off," Gray said, "and your husband is on the very brink."

The man striding quickly toward them was waving his fist and yelling, "Damn you, Sinjun, don't you move. Don't you even think about taking another single step away from me. Just stand right there and be calm and don't fidget. And don't breathe too deeply, it might shake something loose."

Jack, all wrapped up like a package and held in a man's arms, against a man's chest—something that had never happened to her in her life—looked up to see a tall black-haired man nearly running across the inn yard toward them. She forgot how weak and light-headed she felt and asked, "Why can't you breathe too deeply, Sinjun? Shake what loose?"

"Because she's pregnant, dammit." Colin Kinross, the earl of Ashburnham, came to a halt in front of his wife, very gently clasped her upper arms in his big hands, and yelled, "Are you all right?"

"Yes, Colin, I'm healthy as a stoat."

"You look flushed, dammit."

"If I am flushed, it's because my husband chased me down in an inn yard and is shouting loudly enough for the entire town of Grindle-Abbott to hear. Look, there is Mr. Harbottle coming out of the inn wielding an empty tankard over his head."

Colin jerked his head up and stopped Mr. Harbottle with a look. His eyes were back on his wife's face in the next moment. "You left me, Sinjun. After I told you to remain very prettily arranged on your bed, reading those ghost stories I bought you myself, you had the gall to leave me. You managed to slip out past the servants, who know you well enough to be forewarned, but you still managed it. They are upset, but not as upset as I am."

"I was needed, Colin. Ryder saved a child and he had to take the little girl back to Brandon House, to Jane."

Colin's mouth was forming around very satisfying full-bodied curses when Gray said, "Hello, Colin. I'd shake your hand, but as you can see, I can't at the moment. I'm holding Jack. Oh, yes, Sinjun said she left you a very sweet letter. Didn't you read it?"

"Hello, Gray, Jack," Colin said with no great enthusiasm, without looking away from his wife. He said right in her face, his voice now a bit more controlled, just a bit lower, "You're a twit. We've been married nearly four years, and the good Lord knows I've patiently tried to guide you, to gently instruct you, to ease you into the pursuit of logic, the exercise of reason. But you remain a twit, at least on occasion, like this occasion here in this inn yard, now with that fat innkeeper standing over there holding that empty ale tankard." He ran his fingers over his wife's face, then leaned down and kissed her lightly. "When I get you alone, I'm going to beat you."

Sinjun laughed up at him. "Enough of that, Colin. I have excellent explanations, all of which I wrote you in my letter. And I already told you, I was needed. Just look at poor Jack, all bundled up in blankets, whiter than your beautiful hard belly in the dead of winter."

"Now isn't the time to distract me with talk of my manly parts. Damn you, I read your explanations. They are pitiful. They hold no weight at all, particularly since I specifically told you to remain in bed, to rest, to nap, to read your novels, and yet you hared off the moment I was out of the house. And just who is this Jack person who doesn't look at all like a 'Jack' to me?"

Gray said, "Colin, Jack here is getting heavy. I know she looks frail and pallid as a netted gailey fish, but even small rocks weigh heavy after a while if there are enough of them in one sack. I'm a manly man, just like my footman, Remie, but nonetheless, I've been holding her for the past ten minutes, all during your touching reunion with Sinjun and even for five minutes before that. Perhaps you can continue to pin Sinjun's ears back after I've loaded Jack into the carriage?"

Colin Kinross turned to Gray St. Cyre, a man he'd met before he met Sinjun Sherbrooke in London back in 1807 when he'd had to find himself an heiress or have his people starve and his lands go to hell. He said, "St. Cyre, you're holding a girl in your arms and her hair's all tangled and blowing in her face. She looks like one of Madame Tussaud's figures, all white and waxy. I'm not blind. She isn't a boy. How can her name be Jack?"

Gray smiled. "I think she looks quite like a proper Jack. If I'd braided her hair you surely would have been fooled. It's good to see you, Colin. Congratulations on the future arrival of your son or daughter."

The earl turned white, which was surely odd, then he seemed to shake himself, and said, "Thank you." He grabbed his wife's hand when she merely took a step toward the carriage. "You're not moving until I tell you to." He said over his shoulder, "Are you telling me that this is Jack the valet?"

"One and the same," Gray said. "Do you ride, Colin, or will all of us pile into the carriage?"

"No, Colin," Sinjun said, "you must restrict verbal assaults if we're all in the carriage together. You're going to have to wait until we're alone. You can't take a strip off me in front of Gray and Jack."

"Why? Your brothers would take a dozen strips off you before they even got to the door of the carriage."

"True, but they're English. You're a Scot. You're more civilized than they are. You have better manners."

Colin Kinross, the earl of Ashburnham, raised his eyes heavenward. "Nearly four years," he said aloud. "I will not survive until I'm thirty."

Sinjun patted his arm, saying to Gray and Jack, "He will turn thirty this year. I believe I will give him another tome of poetry for his birthday. He loves poetry. It soothes him, at least in the normal course of events. Now, Gray, do put Jack into the carriage before you drop her."

Gray closed his eyes. His life had been delightfully tranquil, predictable, quite tolerable, all in all. He'd saved Lily and hopefully threatened her husband sufficiently. His mistress, Jenny, had a new recipe for quail soup that was ambrosia to the tongue. Yes, one day had followed another with ease and comfort—until the great-aunts had descended on him. Until Jack the valet had stolen Durban. Until Jack the valet had become a damned girl and gotten ill. He sighed, stepped up into the carriage, slipped on one of Sinjun's black gloves, and fell forward on his face, hitting his head on the opposite door. He managed to toss Jack onto the seat an instant before he would have smashed her against the carriage floor.

Jack flailed, Gray cursed, and Lynch, the coachman, froze in appalled silence.

"This is a propitious start," Colin said to the dangerously overcast sky, helped Gray dust himself off and straighten Jack into a sitting position, then assisted his wife into the carriage, holding his breath, it seemed to Jack, until she was safely seated and the black glove was removed from the floor of the carriage and gently placed between her palms.

"I'm riding for a while," he said, looking at his wife, Jack thought, with an odd mixture of rage and desperation. "Gray, I wish you luck." He gave him a salute and turned away to a stable lad who was holding a magnificent black barb with a white blaze on its forehead. Once he was in the saddle, he called out, "I've tied your horses to the back of the carriage. All right, Lynch, let's go. It's at least five hours back to London."

Gray was sitting next to Jack, holding her up, just shaking his head. Sinjun was biting her lip, staring at the toes of her black slippers. Immediately Gray took her hand. "What's wrong, Sinjun?" he asked as he leaned a bit more to the left to balance Jack, who was listing.

"Poor Colin," Sinjun said. "I'm such a trial to him, Gray."

"Nonsense. He's the luckiest bastard alive and he knows it, but there's something wrong, Sinjun, particularly with Colin."

Sinjun nearly laughed, but didn't quite make it. "No, I won't complain and whine to you. Ever since we discovered that I'm going to have a child, he's been different, unwilling to let me out of his sight, always fussing over me. He's been very un-Colinlike. It was so good to hear him yell, to have him breathing fire right in my face, to have him turn red. It's the first time he's managed it since I told him about our child.

"Oh, enough of that. Now tell me, why did Jack steal Durban and leave London?"

Jack shuddered and ducked her face in Gray's chest.

"Jack," Gray said slowly, aware that she was wearing only Squire Leon's wife's nightgown, with three blankets on top of it, "will answer all my questions once we're back in London. Won't you, Jack?"

Jack burrowed herself into Gray's armpit. When she emerged some four minutes later, she looked at Sinjun and said, "Gray told me about your brothers, Douglas and Ryder.

But I don't know them. Perhaps I will meet them in London."

Sinjun laughed. "Bless your heart. Certainly you will meet them. It's quite provoking to hear people talk about brothers and other assorted relatives that you've never heard of. Gray probably told you that Douglas is the oldest Sherbrooke sibling. He's the earl of Northcliffe and the very best of brothers. He's all big and dark like Colin, and his smile is so sweet it warms the coldest day. Alex, his wife, thinks he should smile more, but I like to see him look stern and forbidding. Then when he finally succumbs to a smile, it's such a treat. Douglas is smart and loyal, and he takes his responsibilities very much to heart. His family seat is near Eastbourne, Northcliffe Hall, on the southern coast of England.

"Ryder is my second brother, a wicked, utterly charming man, so filled with life and laughter that you can't help but glow whenever you're around him. Unlike Douglas, Ryder always has a smile playing about his mouth. For years now, he has been rescuing little children and taking them to a house we call Brandon House, to Jane, a dear woman who's stronger than ten oxen and as determined as Ryder is to save hurt children.

"Then there's me. I married a Scot because I saw him at the Drury Lane Theatre one night and fell in love with him on the spot. He needed an heiress, and fortunately I was one. It all worked out marvelously well once Douglas and Ryder got used to the idea of their little sister actually knowing a man in carnal ways. Colin's first wife had died, and I have two wonderful, quite notorious stepchildren—Philip, who's ten years old now, and Dahling, who's eight. Is that enough information for her, Gray? She looks ready to topple over the edge of exhaustion."

"Oh, no," Jack said. "Tell me more, Sinjun."

"Well, Douglas is married to Alexandra, who is half his size and at least as strong-willed. Douglas wants to be the absolute ruler, and Alex allows it half the time, which all of us, except Douglas, agree is fair. They have two sons—twins—who are the very image of Alex's older sister, Melissande, who's so beautiful one can only stare at her. Douglas is incensed that his little boys are the most handsome lads in all of England

and will doubtless grow up to be insufferably conceited.

"Ryder is married to Sophie. He met her in Jamaica, of all places, and helped solve a perfectly dreadful situation there. She has a little brother, Jeremy, who's at Eaton. Sophie's a pillar, all serious and proper, until she looks at Ryder. Then she's smiling and laughing and touching him and kissing him, no matter who's close by. They have one son, Grayson, who is the most precious little boy in the world. He has his father's charm and his utter love of life. Ah, but he has Sophie's thoughtful expression, particularly when he wants something."

"Grayson is my namesake," Gray said to Jack. "Now, Sinjun, my godson will be the most precious child in the world until you have your own son. At least that's what I hear happens."

"Perhaps. We'll see. Do you think he'll look like Colin?"

"That would be fine just so long as he has your Sherbrooke blue eyes," Gray said.

Sinjun smiled at that, then said to Jack, "Now, I won't tell you about our mother, not until you have all your strength back. You're nearly drooling, you're so tired. Go to sleep,

Jack. If you have more questions about the Sherbrookes, they're planning to remain in London for a while. Will you be remaining in London as well, Jack?"

Jack mumbled low, indistinct sounds and retreated once again into Gray's armpit.

Gray let her hide, saying only, "She'll have to face up to things soon enough." He pulled a blanket more closely around her.

9

Mathilda looked at Gray who was carrying the still-blanketed Jack in his arms, and said, "Lordy."

Maude smiled, patted the soft curls beside her ears, and said, "I never doubted for a moment that you would see to our Jack, my boy. Who is this tall young lady who's following you and Jack?"

"This is Lady Ashburnham, Aunt Maude."

"Ill-tempered husband," Mathilda said. "But handsome, very handsome."

Maude said, "Yes, Mathilda believes his lordship even more handsome than the vicar Mortimer, who kissed her in the vestry. Naturally, his lordship is just a mite too young for Mathilda—more's the pity for him, poor boy."

"Yes, he is handsome, ma'am," Sinjun said and blinked. She gave Mathilda a beautiful smile. "Isn't he amazing? He can yell at me and then kiss me, all without wasting a single breath. My stepson, Philip, remarks upon that. He wants to be just like his father. He practices on his little sister, Dahling. He doesn't kiss her because he still thinks girls are the very devil, but he does enjoy practicing his father's yelling skills."

Sinjun shook out her skirts, straightened the smart little straw bonnet on her head, and said, "Now, Quincy just whispered to me that my husband is currently in the drawing room with Douglas. I don't know why Douglas didn't come out when we arrived, but I'm sure to be told shortly. Hopefully I won't have to be told anything too shortly, though, since I don't intend to walk into the tiger's mouth. Jack, will you be all right?"

Jack, flattened by rotten bad luck and illness, said, "I'm fine, Sinjun. Thank you."

"You'll tell me everything once Gray has pried everything out of you, all right?"

"We'll see," Gray said, eyeing Jack, who

looked ready to expire. "Maude, where do you want me to gently unload our valet?"

When Gray went down the wide staircase some ten minutes later, Douglas Sherbrooke, the eldest of the Sherbrooke siblings, stood at the bottom of the stairs in the black-and-white Italianate marble entrance hall, his hands on his hips. He wasn't smiling. When Douglas Sherbrooke didn't smile, he looked ferocious indeed, Gray thought, remembering how he'd been fool enough once to go into the ring with Douglas Sherbrooke at Gentleman Jackson's Boxing Saloon. He was lucky he hadn't gotten his jaw broken or his teeth loosened.

"Good day, Douglas. How is your family?"

"Everyone is just fine. Look, Gray, you're probably wondering why I'm here in your house, standing here in your entrance hall, looking up at you like you're an unwanted guest."

"No, not really. I'm so bloody tired I don't really care who's here."

"Where's Sinjun?"

"I believe she went to one of the bedchambers to, er, repose herself, at least that's what she told me."

"Sinjun's never reposed herself in her life.

The girl's incapable of reposing. You'll not believe this, Gray, but Colin just told me she's pregnant. My little sister—pregnant. By God, I can remember holding her right after she was born. I remember her wetting on my brand-new breeches, my shirt, my hands. She also puked on other breeches, other shirts, my same hands. She was beautiful, Gray, and so precious. Damn, but it's difficult to accept that she's now going to have a babe. I think of her as so young and naive and innocent. Then she saw Colin and couldn't wait to learn all sorts of wicked things, which, naturally, he was more than ready to teach her, curse the bounder.

"Now, you know well enough that she gave you that reposing excuse because she knows that I now know and she doesn't want me telling her she's an idiot for scurrying off to God-knows-where to rescue you." He struck the heel of his palm to his forehead. "Reposing herself, hah. Sinjun's never been a coward, but that's what she is now. Ah, it curdles the belly. My little sister has become a coward, and it's all Colin's fault. Dragging her to Scotland, forcing her to live in a bloody castle, throwing local ghosts in her face—when everyone with even a tiny brain knows there's no such thing as ghosts.

"Yes, it's all turned her into a coward. She's avoiding me. *Me.* He's only had her for four years, and she's become a coward. It revolts my innards."

"That isn't true, Douglas," Colin said, striding out of the drawing room toward them, his voice nearing a roar. "Damn you, your precious *little* sister controls everything and everyone in a ten-mile radius of Vere Castle. She controls everything and everyone inside the castle as well. She even has that blackguard neighbor of ours, Bobbie MacPherson, cooing over her white hands, although she wanted to kill him not above four years ago. She'd probably take over the running of bloody Edinburgh Castle if she took a notion to. I don't believe in ghosts any more than you do, Douglas, but she deals quite well with Pearlin' Jane.

"Don't you blame me because she's hiding upstairs in Gray's house and he didn't even have the chance to invite us to stay, which he would have done because he likes us. Yes, Sinjun knows I'm so furious with her I'm just likely to take away all her clothes to keep her in bed for the next week."

"Who's Pearlin' Jane?" Gray asked.

"My family ghost," Colin said, clearly distracted. "But she doesn't really exist. Hellfire, Douglas, Sinjun's pregnant, damn her beautiful eyes, and Jesus, I can't stand this. I just can't."

It was as if the dam had burst. Colin's voice became deep and harsh. He yelled to the chandelier overhead, "Dammit, I don't want her to die. I couldn't bear it if she died."

Gray said quietly, quite aware that every servant in his house was positioned just so to hear every word each of them said, "I think we should go to my study. Quincy, bring us some food."

"Yes, my lord."

Gray shut the study door, turned, and said, "Now, what's all this about Sinjun dying?"

"Nothing." Colin ran his fingers through his hair, standing it on end. "Nothing. I just lost control of my mouth. I've got it back now. I've just been so bloody worried. All right, I've been scared to my feet." He smashed his fist against the leather arm of a wing chair.

"Sinjun won't die," Douglas said, and Gray saw that he was perfectly white. "She won't. I won't allow that. For God's sake, my mother didn't die and she birthed four children. Look at me, I'm not a lisping little fellow, and she came through it all just fine. Your first wife didn't die birthing Philip or Dahling. What the hell is wrong with you? Oh, God, is Sinjun ill?"

"No," Colin said, his voice that of a desperate man.

"Then why do you think Sinjun's life is in any danger?" Gray asked, an eyebrow raised. "Has a doctor told you that she's in danger?"

Colin, who had been standing in the middle of the study, his head lowered, said, "Neither of you understands. Don't you see? It's been nearly four years and she's never gotten pregnant before. I'd just about come to believe that we were simply not supposed to have children, but because I'm a randy bastard, I've forced her time and time again to take my seed, and she does enjoy it so, indeed, she's always leaping on me in our bedchamber or jerking me behind the stairs or bringing me down on the tower steps to my special room, and just look what happened."

"Oh, God," Douglas said. "You sodding

randy bastard. I might have known. I did know, the minute I laid eyes on you kissing Sinjun in the entrance hall of my very own house four years ago—and you barely even knew her name—yet you had your damned hands on her bottom and you had your tongue halfway down her throat. By God, you miserable Scot sod, you've forced her?"

Douglas leaped a good six feet to land on Colin, his big hands going around Colin's neck. Soon the two men were rolling on the floor, tangling in the beautiful Aubusson carpet, threatening to overturn one of Gray's prized Chinese vases that had just arrived from Macao six months before.

The door burst open. Sinjun came running into the study, yelling, "Stop it, both of you. Stop it, now, do you hear me?"

All she got for her effort was grunts and a few ripe curses.

Sinjun grabbed Gray's Chinese vase and brought it down on both Douglas's back and her husband's arm.

Gray's Chinese vase from Macao was shattered. He stared at the shards that were scattered over half the study floor. He watched Douglas and Colin roll away from each other and slowly rise, panting like men who had run all the way from Bath to London.

"Damn you both," Sinjun yelled at them. "Listen to me. I'm not going to die. Can your small brains understand that? I have no intention of dying. Listen to me, Colin: *I will not die.*"

Gray called out to Quincy, who was plastered against the wall beside the door, "Quincy, bring more brandy. I see I've only got half a bottle here." He turned back to Sinjun. "Now, while Quincy drags himself slowly out of hearing distance, tell me, Sinjun, where are Philip and Dahling?"

"They're at Douglas's town house. Oh, I see." Sinjun waited until Quincy had closed the door after himself. Quick as a snake, she turned on her brother and her husband, who were looking at each other with a combination of embarrassment and wariness. She said over her shoulder, "Gray, don't listen to this since it isn't your problem. That's right. Drink your brandy—you need it, particularly with the gentlemen here enacting such a fine melodrama for you. Now, Douglas, Colin, I have no plans to die birthing our son or daughter. I'm healthier than I've ever been in my life."

Colin opened his mouth, but Sinjun just raised her hand. "No, no more out of you. Very well, I'll tell you the truth. I haven't gotten pregnant simply because I wasn't ready to, Colin. But three months ago I decided that both Philip and Dahling needed a little brother or sister. They both came to me and requested that I consider it. I did. Thus, when I was ready, I became pregnant. There's nothing more to it than that."

"A woman doesn't determine when she does or when she doesn't get pregnant," Douglas shouted at her. "Are you an idiot?"

"Leave her alone, Douglas. She's my wife. I'll deal with her. What the hell was that fine bit of nonsense? *You* decided?"

Sinjun walked to her husband, laid her palm lightly against his cheek, and smiled up at him. "I'm going to give you a beautiful son or daughter. I fully intend to be the mother. And then I'll become a grandmother. You and I will become eccentric old curmudgeons together. We will lose our teeth together. We'll help each other totter up the stairs every night. Nothing will happen to either of us, Colin. All right?"

He couldn't answer. He just stared down at her.

"I'm not lying, Colin. I'm not."

Colin just nodded, then very slowly, very carefully, drew her against him. He buried his face in her hair.

Douglas looked on, then said to no one in particular, "I can't imagine any sister of mine not having her teeth."

"You know," Gray said now, "I have an excellent physician friend who lives just two hours from London, near Bury St. Edmunds. His name is Paul Branyon and he recently married the late earl of Strafford's widow, Lady Ann. He's an excellent man and an excellent doctor. I will write him and he and Ann will come to London. He'll examine Sinjun. He'll tell both of you the truth. Sinjun is very likely going to be just fine. Paul will reassure all of you and then you, Douglas, and you, Colin, won't have to try to break each other's heads anymore in my study, and your wife won't have to break any more of my belongings to split you two apart."

Sinjun twisted about in her husband's arms. "Oh, Gray, the vase? I'm so sorry—I didn't think."

"If you will let Paul Branyon examine you, then I will forgive you for breaking the vase."

"Oh, all right," Sinjun said.

"Good," Douglas said. "I'll feel better once I've got some of your excellent brandy down my gullet."

Calm restored, brandy served, Sinjun patted and forced to sit down on Gray's big comfortable wing chair, Colin standing over her to press her back down if she chanced to move, Douglas said, "Now, why don't you tell us, Gray, why this girl named Jack stole one of your horses and was riding toward Bath when you caught her? And stayed with her for four days? Alone?"

"Actually, the great-aunts call her Mad Jack, a small jest, I suppose, amongst the three of them. Well, what she did—stealing Durban, riding not south like she intended but rather due west, then getting ill—well, it is rather mad, so I suppose she deserves the nickname. Now, the answers to many of the other questions still elude me, Douglas."

"Not for long they can't," Douglas said, grim around the mouth. "Jesus, Gray, you've done it this time. There's no hope for you now."

"I know," Gray said, and sighed as he poured more of his fine smuggled French brandy into the men's glasses. He raised an eyebrow toward Sinjun, who shook her head. He gave them a grin and hoisted his glass, saying, "Douglas, you made it sound like a fatal illness. Very well. To my demise. Douglas is right," he continued to Colin and Sinjun. "I'm not long for my shackleless life. Yes, it's all over and I don't even know who the chit is. She does, however, have excellent taste in horseflesh. She went right to Durban, who's got the best blood of all of my horses."

"I didn't know Sinjun, either," Colin said. "Douglas certainly didn't know Alexandra. But that's not the point. There's no reason for you to throw yourself into the well. No one else knows about her except us. We won't tell anybody."

"Not a single soul," Sinjun said.

Gray sighed. "Thank you. But all my friends know that I was missing. For at least four days."

Douglas said, "But they don't know why. None of them knows a thing about Jack. Jack could simply disappear. There's no problem." But he was frowning, obviously arguing with himself.

"She did tell me her name is Winifrede," Gray said. "That curls the toes, doesn't it?"

Douglas said, "Possibly, but that's not to

the point. All women's names are the same in the dark."

Sinjun nearly went *en pointe* once she'd leapt out of the chair. "Douglas! Alex would make you sleep in the stable if she heard such twaddle from you. I should probably do something to punish you, but for the moment I just can't think what."

Douglas gave his sister a harassed look. "It was a mild attempt at humor, Sinjun. Sit down before Colin flings you down."

Sinjun sat.

Douglas said, "Now, I'm sorry, Gray. I have to take it all back. I was wrong. I know London. I know how the gossip mills grind. They'll have you debauching young virgin damsels from here to Bath within twenty-four hours. They'll demand that you produce the most debauched of the young damsels and make a big show of marrying her. Then you'll be forgiven and readmitted to the fold."

Sinjun said, "I don't know London at all, but I know human nature. Douglas is right. Gray is compromised to his boots. For example, it's impossible to guarantee even the silence of all the servants here, and that's only the beginning of the possibilities."

"My lord," Quincy said from the doorway. "I have waited until all the more unrestrained displays of emotion were more contained than not. The fellow who tried to run me down and was foiled by Mr. Ryder Sherbrooke is here again, asking to see you specifically, my lord. I don't believe he wants to get attacked again."

"This man," Gray said, "is the key to Jack the valet. Show him in, Quincy."

10

Gray rubbed his hands together. "Sir Henry Wallace-Stanford isn't her father, I got that much out of her. Nonetheless, she's scared spitless of him. He holds power over her and her little sister, Georgie. That's all I know."

"This should be interesting," Colin said and tossed down the rest of his brandy. He took his wife's white hand in his and kissed her fingers.

Sir Henry wasn't happy to see a roomful of people. He'd hoped to find Baron Cliffe, that cocky young bastard who'd lied to him through his teeth, alone. But there was a young lady present, along with the three men. He looked closely, but none of the men was the wretch who had bashed him to the ground. That one he would kill. All he needed was the man's name.

"Lord Cliffe," Sir Henry said, not moving a foot from the doorway into the room.

"Sir Henry. My butler informs me that you wish to see me."

"I would prefer to see Maude and Mathilda. Or, if you would fetch Jack the valet down here, I would very much like to speak to him."

"Jack the valet? How very odd that sounds," said Gray. He gently set his brandy snifter on the edge of his desk, straightened a couple of papers, and said, "Who are you, Sir Henry?"

"I am Sir Henry Wallace-Stanford of Carlisle Manor, near Folkstone, and I want my property back, my lord."

At midnight, Gray was seated beside Jack's bed in a comfortable high-backed chair blessed with thick cushions for both the back and the behind. He'd lit a single candle against the gloom. He'd been watching her for the past half hour.

Upon their return this afternoon, Mrs.

Piller had had him tenderly carry Jack to the Ellen Chamber, and he had watched while she was tucked into the raised, canopied bed dating back to the third Baron Cliffe. Ellen St. Cyre, that baron's only daughter, had been struck with a strange paralysis very young in life and had spent all her twenty-three years within these four walls. It was a lovely room, and any memories scored into the walls or the furniture were pleasant and warm. He sat back in his chair, his chin propped up on his tented fingertips. He breathed out long and slow. The candlelight flickered a bit.

Jack was riding bareback, pressed against the mare's neck. If she didn't escape, she knew he'd catch her and he'd hurt her this time, hurt her until she screamed. He wouldn't care if he marked her, not now. She yelled when she was jerked off the mare's back and thrown through the air to land on her side at the edge of a cliff. She rolled over, trying desperately to grab at a lone bush to stop herself, but it broke off in her hand and she heard him laughing, and then she was falling, falling, screaming—

"Wake up, Jack! Come on, wake up!"

He was shaking her, but she was still falling. She didn't want him to save her, she didn't want to owe him anything. She didn't hear him laughing anymore.

"Jack, dammit, open your eyes! Here I'm going to have to marry you and I don't even remember what color your eyes are. This is ridiculous. I've seen your breasts and your belly and your buttocks, yes, all of that, and I remember them quite well, and they are very nice memories. I know I saw your eyes any number of times, but I don't remember the color. Does that make me a lecher? Probably. Wake up!"

She bit his hand, hard.

He yelped, grabbed his hand, and began rubbing it. "Why did you do that?"

"Gray? Is that you?"

"Naturally. I hope you don't make it a habit to bite the hand that wakes you."

"No, I thought you were—" Her voice died in her throat. She couldn't see beyond his face, the single candle barely piercing the immediate darkness. She turned her own face away. He'd flung her off the cliff. Oh, God.

"I'm not your damned stepfather, Jack."

Moments of perfect clarity were rare, Maude had told her once, a brief flash when you simply comprehended something fully, knew what it meant all the way to its very core. For the first time she understood what Maude had meant. This man who had awakened her from the nightmare, who had chased her down and nursed her back to health—this man she didn't begin to know, but still, she knew now that keeping anything from him was ridiculous.

She smiled at him, saying clearly, "I told you about my little sister, Georgie. She's really my half-sister, but that doesn't matter. She's mine. I have been her mother for four of her five years. My stepfather has always ignored her, didn't even want to hear about her. She wasn't the son he wanted, you see, and thus she had no value to him.

"After my mother died four years ago, he gave up any pretense at all of affection for her.

"Three months ago, I realized that if he found out how much I loved Georgie he would use her against me in an instant to force me to marry Lord Rye. I made it a point to speak of her in his presence with complete indifference, even occasional contempt. One night she had a nightmare and her screaming woke him. He was so angry that he sent her to his younger sister in York.

"I couldn't say anything, else he'd know how much I loved her. The last thing I wanted was for her to be punished because of what I refused to do. When I escaped from Carlisle Manor, I went immediately to Featherstone, to Maude and Mathilda. They made plans. That's when I became Mad Jack.

"Mathilda told me just after we came to you here in London that my stepfather's younger sister had brought Georgie back to Carlisle Manor. Their housekeeper had sent a message by one of the stable lads. I couldn't bear it. My stepfather isn't stupid. It's just a matter of time before he realizes he's got a gold mine. I waited four days, then I had to go get her away from him."

His fingers steepled again. "I see. You were going to steal Durban, ride to Carlisle Manor, sneak away with a five-year-old little girl, and then do what? She would be a valet-in-training? I assure you, Jack, I would have remarked upon a child in my house. Come, tell me, what did you plan to do with her if you did manage to get her away from your stepfather?"

All of it, she thought. He deserved to know everything, otherwise her actions could endanger him. "I have money. When my grandfather died—my mother's father—he left all his money to me, not to my mother because he detested my stepfather. Nor is my stepfather my guardian. Lord Burleigh is. My grandfather's been dead for nearly ten years now, and Lord Burleigh has managed to keep my stepfather from touching a single sou of that money. I would have brought Georgie to London, seen Lord Burleigh, and he would have given me my inheritance, or at least an income. I wasn't planning on starving in a ditch, Gray. My plan still stands. As soon as I can get Georgie, I'm going to Lord Burleigh. He'll protect Georgie and me from Sir Henry. Don't doubt that."

"Normally females aren't privy to financial affairs," Gray said slowly. "This is particularly true, strangely enough, when the one most directly involved is the female in question. So, how do you know all of this?"

"I eavesdropped on my stepfather speaking to Lord Rye. He told Lord Rye how my grandfather, the devious old bastard, had my money so tied up that he, Sir Henry, wasn't able to use it. Sir Henry said the only way the inheritance would come to me is when I turned twenty-five or if I married.

"Sir Henry roundly cursed Lord Burleigh, my legal guardian. He also told Lord Rye that if I died, the money wouldn't go to Georgie, it would go to the Royal Naturalist Society.

"Naturally, when I married, my husband would take control. Lord Rye knew my stepfather was leading up to this, and so they quickly struck a deal. If I married Lord Rye, then my stepfather would gain twenty thousand pounds and Lord Rye would keep the other forty thousand. I watched them shake hands through the keyhole."

Gray, who had heard quite enough about Lord Rye, said easily, "I gather then that this gentleman doesn't appeal to you as husband material?"

"He's a dissolute lecher who very probably beat his first wife to death in a drunken rage—at least that's the local gossip, whispered behind cupped hands. His other two wives both died in childbirth. He has six children from the three different wives. He's rich—don't get me wrong—but he has a son who's following in his footsteps. He's the type of man who pilfers two coins from the collection plate after he puts one in.

"That is doubtless why my stepfather approached him. He can sniff out baseness in others quite easily."

Gray had heard quite a lot more about Cadmon Kelburn, Viscount Rye, none of it remotely pleasant. It was a pity that three of his children were sons. They didn't stand a chance of becoming honorable men. The thought of Lord Rye having control over Jack, actually having her in his power, repelled Gray to the core.

He sat forward in his chair, his hands clasped between his knees. He studied her face, then said, "What's your name, Jack? Your full name?"

"Winifrede Levering Bascombe. My father was Thomas Levering Bascombe, Baron Yorke."

"My God, you're Bascombe's daughter?" Gray collapsed in his chair, utterly taken aback.

"You knew my father?"

Gray shook his head. Then he began to laugh. He laughed and laughed.

"Come, my lord, what is this? What is it about my father?"

"Ah, Jack—"

"My father called me Levering."

"If you don't mind, I will stay with Jack for the moment."

"Georgie calls me Freddie."

He leaned over and lightly placed his palm over her mouth. He said very close to her face, looking clearly into her very lovely blue eyes, "Your guardian, Lord Burleigh, is also my godfather."

"Oh, goodness. Surely, that can't be right. Oh, dear—" She stared at him a moment, then said, "Life is really strange, isn't it?"

"Yes. It appears there are a lot of ties bringing us together that neither of us knew anything about. Also I believe that my father hated your father, for what reason I don't know. You and I have a history, Jack, even though the two of us have just begun to appear in it."

"I never heard my father speak of yours. I wonder why your father would hate mine. Do Maude and Mathilda know any of this?"

"We can ask them."

"Is it very late, Gray?"

He liked the sound of his name when she spoke it. This, he thought, had to be the oddest courtship ever conducted outside a gothic novel. He nodded. "Nearly one o'clock in the morning. How do you feel?"

"I'm fine. Maude told me that Sir Henry came again today. Please, tell me what happened."

"Yes, Sir Henry was here. Douglas, Colin, and Sinjun were also the recipients of his venom. Actually, he was loath to come right out with it, but he finally had to. He pattered around the point for a while, then realized he was being mocked by all of us. He finally said you were his daughter and that we had to turn you over to him."

"Tell me," she said, and he did.

Gray saw Sir Henry's flushed face, heard his own incredulous voice as he'd asked, deliberately goading the man, "But, sir, why ever would you want Mathilda and Maude's valet?"

"The valet belongs to me, my lord. He was merely on loan to them. They treated him too well. He is mine. You will have him sent for this minute."

"Actually," Douglas Sherbrooke had said, studying his thumbnail, "Lord Cliffe has already offered the valet's services to me while I'm in London, since my own fellow is sick and had to remain at Northcliffe Hall."

"No!"

"Now, Douglas," Sinjun had said, lightly touching her fingers to her brother's sleeve, "you know how Maude and Mathilda adore having Jack arrange their hair, polish their slippers, and file their fingernails. Surely we can find you someone else. How very odd that a valet should be so very much in demand."

Sir Henry was grinding his teeth so loudly he was sure that Baron Cliffe—the bastard—could hear them. "I want Jack and I want him now. I tell you, he's mine."

It was at that moment that Gray had simply stepped up to Sir Henry Wallace-Stanford and said right in his face, "You will leave my house. You will take Jack nowhere. He will remain here where he's safe."

"All right, damn you. Jack is a girl. She's my daughter and she ran away from home. You have no right to her, none at all."

Gray had said, "Why did she run away from you?"

"That is none of your business."

He'd smiled then. "Very well, Sir Henry. I will speak to Jack and find out the truth of the matter. I will also speak to Maude and

Mathilda. You may return on the morrow and I will tell you what will happen."

"You arrogant young puppy, you believe yourself so powerful, but I can break you, I can send you to oblivion, I can—"

It was so subtly done that it took Gray a moment to realize that both Douglas and Colin had moved to stand directly behind Sir Henry. Douglas Sherbrooke lightly laid his hand on Sir Henry's shoulder. "I should take care what I said if I were you," he said very quietly. "My brother-in-law and I are both larger than you, Sir Henry. We also hold Gray a very good friend."

Sir Henry jerked away from him. "Damn you all, I will come back here, and I'm going to bring men with me to remove that bitch from here." And Sir Henry was gone.

Jack, Gray saw, after he'd told her of the interview, was perfectly white. "No," he said, "I wanted you to know exactly what your stepfather said, what he threatened, because it's your right to know. But don't be afraid."

"He's a vicious man."

"It won't matter," Gray said. He stared off toward the shadowed corner of the Ellen Chamber. "Tell me, Jack, must we invite him to our wedding?"

11

Jack jerked up, flung back the blankets, and swung her legs over the side of the bed. She stepped off the bed, tripped, and fell to her hands and knees on the carpet because the bed was raised a good three feet off the floor.

"No," she shouted at him as she scrambled to her feet. He was already halfway out of his chair to help her.

"No! Don't you move." And then she was standing over him, pushing his shoulders back down, staring at his upturned face, her nightgown billowing about her ankles, now shaking her fist under his nose.

Her very nice eyes were dilated. The woman, Gray realized, was seriously perturbed. She leaned close, as if she thought that if she spoke any distance at all from him, he wouldn't understand her. "No, don't you move or say anything more. No, don't you even consider towering over me and believing you'll automatically get your way.

"Now, what you just said, why that's preposterous. I think you're cruel and not a whit amusing. No, don't say a word. I don't want to hear anything you have to say. Nothing, do you hear me? Just be quiet. What the devil did you mean, anyway?"

"As Aunt Mathilda the orator would say: Marriage. Me."

"It's ridiculous."

"Ridiculous, is it? Well, perhaps you're right. It wasn't all that romantic a marriage proposal, was it? Lie down, Jack. I don't want you making yourself ill again. I spent four days leaning over you, wiping your brow and many other parts of you as well. My back hurt. You wore me out. I don't want a relapse."

She sat on the side of the bed, her narrow white feet dangling. He smiled at her. All in all, this marriage business was easier than he'd thought it would be, although it still felt quite strange to ask a girl to marry him whose last name he'd discovered only ten minutes before. She was silent, staring down at her hands, folded in her lap. He waited, but she remained silent.

"All right," he said at last. "If you won't marry me, then I have absolutely no recourse but to give you over to your stepfather. How old are you?"

"Nearly nineteen."

"Eighteen, in other words. You are under his control, Jack. I'm sorry to tell you this, but Lord Burleigh wouldn't have been able to protect you. He's your guardian, in charge of your money, but Sir Henry is your stepfather. At the very least it would be a mess, possibly a scandal."

She was shaking her head frantically, but what came out of her mouth was a whisper. "Life couldn't be so unfair, could it?"

"Life is frequently the very devil. Now, it's time for you to face up to things."

"No."

She was getting perturbed again, perhaps even more seriously this time. He didn't imagine that any more pathetic whispers would be coming out of that mouth. She hadn't braided her hair and it was tangled around her face. He liked the way one long, curling runner trailed down the side of her face and made an interesting twist just above her left breast.

He wasn't at all surprised when she said, her brow furrowed, her eyes mean, "You told me you weren't a womanizer. Stop looking at me as if I were a horse on the block."

"You saw me staring at you, did you? Well, why shouldn't I? I've seen you as naked as the day you came from your mother's womb. I've taken complete care of you, Jack. I've bathed you, washed your hair, wiped you down with cool cloths, pulled you away from the window all white and naked so the men below wouldn't see you. I held you tightly against me when you were freezing from the fever.

"However, if you wish a more subtle, sensitive approach, then let me say it this way: Jack, you're a very nice stretch of land that I've thoroughly mapped."

"I don't know if that's more sensitive or not. It's embarrassing, is what it is. As a metaphor it makes me want to laugh. Goodness, I don't even remember why I ran to the window. It's all very odd. I don't under-

154   *Catherine Coulter*

stand this." She shivered, frowned at herself, and got back under the covers. "Now you'll marry me in order to save me from being forced to marry this Lord Rye? You're truly willing to sacrifice yourself?"

"No, that's not it at all. My fate was already well sealed before I heard about Lord Rye, who is a complete rotter, and, to be honest here, it makes my stomach turn to think of him touching you, having the right to do whatever he wishes to do to you."

She turned as pale as the white satin counterpane, swallowed convulsively, and said in a voice so thin it was nearly transparent, "I never thought of that. That would be dreadful. You mean he would—no, never mind that. My imagination doesn't want to go in that direction. I'd rather think about being a stretch of land."

"It would be his right to do with you as he wished. I daresay nothing he would do to your fair person would send you to heights of delirium.

"Now, the truth of the matter is that once you were with me for four days, alone, my fate was sealed. If you don't marry me, I'll be cast out of my very pleasant life here in London. No one will speak to me. No one will ride with me in the park. It's possible that my friends will spit in my direction rather than acknowledge my presence. It's an unpleasant future I'll have, Jack."

"That makes no sense. No one even knows about me. Even if they did, it wouldn't matter. I'm a nobody."

"Not true. You're quite a somebody. You're Thomas Bascombe's daughter and Lord Burleigh is your guardian. Ah, yes, in case you've still got questions about this, let me tell you just the way our world works. Ladies must be protected since they're helpless to protect themselves from men who are twice their size and have twice their strength. Men don't want other men to ravish ladies they perceive as heir-producing material because it would severely undermine their confidence in succession."

"What does that mean?"

"It means that a man couldn't trust the male child born of his woman to be of his seed. It could be that another man had taken her. Do you understand? Thus a lady has to be protected."

"That's nonsense."

"Tell that to men who've been killed in duels, all for a lady's honor."

She actually shuddered. She began swinging her feet. "Very well. Because of this seed business, you've got to marry me?"

"Yes. Because of this seed business, when a gentleman dishonors a lady, or when he's perceived to have dishonored a lady, he's made to pay. Since neither of us is married, I won't have to fight a male relative. I'll just have to give myself to you for life."

"A long time, life."

"Yes, hopefully. Now, Jack, you're still uncertain. Think of it this way: you'll be saving yourself from Lord Rye, and I'll be saving myself from being ostracized for debauching you, a young lady."

"Does holding me naked mean that you debauched me?"

"Well, no, but no one would ever believe that I had a naked young lady next to me for four whole days and didn't take complete and ruthless advantage of her, since I am a man and thus weak of flesh."

"But I was sick. Who would want to debauch a sick naked young lady?"

"If you were conscious and looked as nice as you do at this moment, most any man who was still breathing would want to debauch you."

"Then why didn't you debauch me?"

"Well, I can't say that I didn't consider what it would be like—debauching you—but I didn't carry through with it because you were really very sick. You weren't all that conscious. You weren't arguing or laughing. Your hair wasn't tousled all over your head, all soft-looking. No man would have wanted to debauch you in the eye of your illness, just perhaps on the periphery."

They stared at each other. She licked her lower lip. He stared at that lower lip as she said, "You didn't debauch me on the periphery either. Why?"

"This isn't a bone. Stop chewing. Let it go."

"What if I were older than you, what then?"

"It would depend, I suppose, on how much older than me you were. Ten years? No, I'd probably still have to hie myself and you to the altar. By the way, I like older women," he said and smiled. "I also like the way your mind works, like a wheel that backs up when one doesn't expect it to."

Then he laughed. "It's late at night, you're

sitting here in your nightgown, we're quite alone, which simply isn't allowed, you know, yet I didn't even think twice about coming into your bedchamber, and we're talking about all the particulars of debauchery.

"No hope for it, Jack, we've got to marry, and soon. Since your stepfather isn't your legal guardian, which is a very good thing, and since I also know Lord Burleigh very well indeed, I don't believe I'll have much difficulty obtaining his permission to be your husband. Oh, incidentally, your father might be dead, but Lord Burleigh isn't, and he's a very powerful man. Were he to find out—and he would—that I was alone for four days with his ward, he'd be on my doorstep with the ink on the marriage agreements scarcely dry."

"I have sixty thousand pounds. That's a lot of money."

"I believe Sinjun was a greater heiress, but you're right, it's nothing to raise one's brows at."

"So, you spend four days alone with me and you earn sixty thousand pounds."

A dark blond eyebrow shot up. "Is that how you translate this mess? Into groats for my coffers? Let me tell you, Jack, I don't want to marry you any more than you want to marry me. My life was pleasant, blessedly predictable, until Mathilda and Maude came trooping in, claiming disasters so they could stay."

"What disasters?"

"As Aunt Mathilda would say: Featherstone—fire and flood."

She laughed. She couldn't help it. "I heard them arguing over the excuse they'd give you, but they never told me what it was. That's very inventive."

"Yes, it was well done of them. Quincy didn't buy it for more than a minute, but I really didn't care enough to question them closely. I knew I'd enjoy having them here. I really have no other close family, you know. Actually, I would have welcomed them without a whimper if they'd just asked to visit me for a while. On the other hand, I can see their need to protect your innocence. They couldn't have known I was a saint among gentlemen."

It was quite fascinating, really, just watching the myriad expressions on her face ranging from absolute terror to rage to even a brief smile that showed the dimple in her left cheek. He sat forward and said, "No,

Jack, I'm marrying you because as a man of honor I have no choice. Your money doesn't matter in the least, at least it doesn't matter in terms of being the catalyst to matrimony. No, your ill-planned thievery of poor Durban is what precipitated this whole thing."

"It wasn't ill-planned."

"You would have ended up in Bath, if some malcontent hadn't robbed you, then tossed you into a ditch. I call that ill-planned, at the very least. If I were more honest and less sensitive to your female feelings, I should possibly refer to your debacle as the end result of brain fever, a supposed common ailment amongst females."

To his surprise, she laughed, actually laughed in the face of his amusing insult and her unamusing situation. She said, shaking her head, "It wounds me to have to say this, but you do rather seem to have the right of it. Oh, dear. It was ill-planned."

She rolled off the other side of the bed and shrugged into one of Mathilda's dressing gowns, a particularly odd affair because it was completely black, the neck a swatch of black feathers. It dragged the floor. She tied the sash, then turned to face him. "Actually," she said, a good fifteen feet between them, "if I want to keep you at a distance from me, I need to light more candles. You're all shadowy over there by the bed."

"True enough," he said. He watched her light the eight candles on a very old gold candle branch and set it on a circular table in the center of the room. The corners were still hidden in deep shadows, but they could see each other clearly enough. "So you want to see me? My face?"

She was twisting a hank of hair around her fingers. "Yes, I want to see you, particularly your face. I'm coming to know what your various expressions mean. Listen to me, Gray. I have quite ruined your life, and the truth of it is that I don't know what I would have done even if I had managed to sneak into Carlisle Manor, grab Georgie, and escape undetected. I'm an idiot. I thought I'd rescue Georgie, then sneak over to Featherstone, cozy the servants there into hiding us until my stepfather gave up on finding me, then sneak both Georgie and me to London, to Lord Burleigh. I don't know him. I can't begin to imagine the look on his face were I to arrive at his front door with my little sister. I wouldn't have come back here. Your good nature never would have extended that far.

"It supposes that everyone else remotely involved would have to be idiots too, even if I'd succeeded." She paused, then, under his horrified gaze, she began to cry.

"Jack, for God's sake, don't do that." He was out of his chair in a flash, across that fifteen feet, and gathering her up against him, black peignoir and black feathers and all. He rubbed his hands up and down her back as he said over and over, "No, don't cry. I can't bear it. Please stop."

"I'm an idiot," she said, tears making her choke. "An idiot. And now you've got to pay because men are afraid that an unacceptable flower could spring up from the female's soil."

He began untangling her hair with his fingers. "All right, maybe you didn't think your plan through. But you're not an idiot. I wager you would have thought of something. Even if you'd ended up first in Bath and then had to change course, you would have managed it. Of course, I would have caught you by then, but I know—I'm positive—that you would have given me an excellent chase.

Actually, you did. It was just your ill luck that I saw your light blink in the stable that night."

"Rotten luck," she said against his neck.

"Perhaps not so rotten. You'll be gaining my manly self as a husband. How is your rib?"

She pulled back, sniffed, wiped her nose with the back of her hand, and said, "It aches and pulls, but it's nothing, really. But your manly self doesn't want to wed me."

He tilted her head back and looked down at her. "The bruise on your face isn't as bad as I'd thought it would be. I think whatever flowers you and I grow together will be quite acceptable. I am becoming rapidly accustomed to the idea of marrying you."

"You like ladies in black feathers who cry all over your collar, do you?"

They both became still as stones at the sudden light tap on the bedchamber door, followed by Maude's face peering into the room. "I heard voices and was worried. Goodness, my boy, why are you in here with Jack? Holding her while she's wearing one of Mathilda's peignoirs?"

"She's going to marry me, Aunt Maude. She was so happy that she began to cry.

I'm a gentleman and thus I'm comforting her in her joy."

Mathilda appeared next, wearing an identical black peignoir. She towered over Maude, like a hovering witch over a fairy who was gowned in dazzling puce. She eyed the two of them. "Mortimer," she said.

"Ah, yes," Maude said. "What Mathilda would have said if she'd wished to elaborate is that the vicar once grabbed her and managed to hold on to her until one of the silly Gifford sisters came by and twittered."

"I didn't know about that," Jack said. "I wish I could have seen that."

"When?" asked Mathilda.

Gray slowly released Jack. He took a step back from her. "Just as soon as I can get us a special license. It is fortunate that Lord Burleigh is Jack's guardian. There will be no problem at all gaining his permission to marry her. You see, he's my godfather. Now, I will see him tomorrow. I'm thinking we should marry on Friday. That's a full four days from now. Is that all right with you ladies?"

Mathilda was staring hard at him. Maude patted her sister's hand. "It's all right, dear,"

Maude said. "Our boy here isn't a thing like his father. Are you, my boy?"

"Do call me Gray, Aunt Maude. Compared to my departed sire, I'm an undisputed saint. By the way, what do you call her? Freddie? Do you call her by that dreadful Winifrede name?"

"Graciella," Aunt Mathilda said.

"What Mathilda means is that Jack's father wanted her named Graciella, but her mother refused, and thus she became Winifrede. Her father called her Graciella upon occasion. As I recall, he called her Graciella in moments of affection. Otherwise, it was Levering, surely a painful name for a girl, but he wasn't to be dissuaded from it. Actually since both Mathilda and I are very fond of her, we also call her Graciella. It has a nice sound to it, doesn't it? It rolls on the tongue."

He tried out the word on his tongue. It didn't sit right. It was a lovely name, but no, he didn't see it fitting her. He looked at her and smiled. "May I continue with Jack?"

"I rather like it myself," she said. She was looking at him strangely, and he wanted to know, just about more than anything at that moment, what she was thinking, exactly.

"Next Friday, Jack?"

"Yes, Gray. Next Friday." He watched her gather up the slithery skirt of her black peignoir, walk back to the raised bed, and climb in. He smiled when she burrowed beneath the bedclothes, covering her head with the soft down pillow.

He couldn't say that he blamed her. He thought of doing some burrowing in his own bed.

He bid Mathilda and Maude good night and went to his bedchamber to do just that.

12

"It is impossible, my lord," said Snell, Lord Burleigh's formidable butler for more years than Gray had been on this earth. He'd terrified Gray as a child with his very precise hauteur, which bordered on the glacial. Now that Gray was a man, Snell still made him want to apologize for interrupting the household.

"It is urgent, Snell. Terribly urgent. I must see Lord Burleigh."

"I'm sorry, my lord, but you don't understand. Lord Burleigh is very ill. He is upstairs in his bed with Lady Burleigh seated on one side of him, one of her hands covering his.

Dr. Bainbridge is seated on the other side of him, staring at the whites of his eyes, which, Dr. Bainbridge says, tell him exactly whether a patient is ready to journey to the hereafter or remain here, hovering but alive."

"But what is wrong with him, Snell? His heart?"

"Yes. It was rather sudden. Just last Sunday he simply collapsed at Lady Curley's card party. I might add that Lord Burleigh didn't wish to go to the card party, but her ladyship very prettily begged him until she carted him away with her."

There was simply no one like Snell, Gray thought, stroking his long fingers over his jaw, to see that things were properly explained and commented upon, leaving no doubt as to his opinion of everything in the world. Lord Burleigh had had difficulties with his heart for years now. He prayed his godfather would survive this. Dr. Bainbridge was a good physician. Well, hell. After this unexpected blow, what the devil should he do now?

"Good morning, Snell. How is his lordship this morning? Any improvement?"

Gray turned to see Mr. Harpole Genner, a lifelong friend of Lord Burleigh's. A man of quiet manner and unassailable honor, he'd known Gray all of Gray's life and had even put him up for membership at White's some seven years before.

"There is no change this morning, sir," Snell said.

"Is that you, St. Cyre? It is. It's been a very long time, my boy. Ah, you've heard about poor Charles. It's a siren's call to us all, this collapse of his. When I awoke this morning, I felt my bones aching."

Gray looked at Mr. Harpole Genner and saw a path to rescue. "Snell," Gray said, "may Mr. Genner and I come in and perhaps use Lord Burleigh's library for a moment? It's very important, as I told you. I believe Mr. Genner may be able to help me, if he wishes to."

"Naturally, Gray, naturally," said Mr. Genner, focusing now on the young baron. "There is something wrong, Gray? Something I can assist you with? Ah, some distraction from this trying time is welcome. Come, Gray. Bring us tea, Snell."

". . . So you see, sir, since it involves such a vast sum of money, I cannot, as a gentleman, simply marry her without Lord Burleigh's blessing. It simply wouldn't sit right with me. He is her guardian and I must have his approval to wed her."

Mr. Harpole Genner slammed his fists down on his bony knees. He was smiling. "By damn, boy, you've given me a splendid tale. My wife will burst her seams when she hears this. The demmed girl was riding west instead of south? No natural sense of direction like we men possess? Ah, and you were her savior?" Mr. Genner rubbed his veiny hands together. "Now the little pigeon's all yours."

"Actually, I believe she sees herself as a flower, or perhaps a gardener of future flowers. No, there's no way around it, sir. But I must wed her quickly, before her stepfather can step in and make this situation even more awkward than it already is."

"Yes, Sir Henry Wallace-Stanford. A wobbly wheel with crooked spokes. A man with no finesse, and a black heart. Aye, a bloody rotter, that one. He's trying to force her to wed Lord Rye, an equally dissolute character. His son's following in his father's tracks, so I hear. Sir Henry wants this, of course, so he can take part of her dowry as his fee. Hmmm. Charles would never have allowed that. Never. I suppose Sir Henry was going to force the girl to wed Lord Rye and then come to Charles and announce it?"

"That, or perhaps Lord Rye would simply have raped her. Once that was done, Lord Burleigh would have had no choice but to give her over to him, and her money as well."

Mr. Genner began to pace about Lord Burleigh's library, a large, square room that admitted little light even on the sunniest of days. It was whispered behind gloved hands that Lord Burleigh preferred the night, the blacker the better, and why was that, pray tell?

"I must speak to Lord Bricker. You know him, do you not?"

"Yes, but not as well as you or Lord Burleigh. I have heard him speak in the House of Lords. He is a very eloquent man."

"A pity he has to be a blasted Whig, but what can one do? I will get back to you this evening, my boy, no later. Theo—Lord Bricker—and I will work this out. I realize this is a matter that must be dealt with quickly, and with a good deal of discretion. Yes, Lord Bricker is just the man to resolve everything properly.

"Oh, dear, if only Charles would wake up and quit this nonsense! I say leave this sort of illness to younger men who would deal with it more quickly. Aye, it's a young man like you who could have his heart beat like a faint drum one moment and then have it pounding hard again the next, all without scaring the wickedness out of his friends." He sighed.

"I'm sure Lord Burleigh would agree with you, sir."

"I must tell Snell to close the draperies in his bedchamber. Charles hates the sunlight and it's fair to bursting in on us today. Yes, he must have the comforting darkness. I'll inform Snell that he is to see to it right now. I will speak to you later, my boy, after Lord Bricker and I discuss the best way to proceed."

Gray and Mr. Harpole Genner shook hands. Mr. Genner patted Gray's arm. "Don't worry about this, we'll see it done. I know how very fond Charles is of you. It will delight him to know that his ward and his godson are to be married. Yes, it will please him very much."

Gray left the Burleigh town house. He hoped that Lord Burleigh would recover. He very much liked his godfather. Odd how one took one's very close friends for granted. He would never do so again.

Now there was nothing to do but wait. He didn't know Lord Bricker well. But surely the man would approve of him—surely.

Douglas Sherbrooke looked at his brother, Ryder, over the top of the *London Gazette*. "I'm glad you're back. How is the little girl?"

Ryder Sherbrooke, full of life and vigor and charm, spread strawberry jam thick on his toast, took a big bite, and said, "Her name is Adrienne. She's only five years old, Douglas, but as brave a little child as you can imagine. As I told you, her father had sold her to men who preferred children. Evidently one man become furious with her because she was so thin and silent. He threw her in the gutter, where I found her. She's safe now at Brandon House with Jane and all the other children, thank God. When I left I heard three of the children around her, all of them interrupting and stumbling over each other to tell her of their own dreadful experiences and how they were the very worst and the other children's experiences weren't even close. The last sound out of

Adrienne's mouth was a laugh, a little one, but it was still a laugh."

"How many children are at Brandon House now, Ryder?"

"Only thirteen. Jane is fretting. She told me her quiver wasn't even close to being full. I just looked at her, for surely that was an odd way of putting it. Your boys are just fine, wreaking mayhem, just as one would expect. Now, our wives will be coming to London a good three days before your auspicious birthday."

"It isn't auspicious. It's depressing and re-grettable," said Douglas.

"You're only thirty-five, Douglas, not yet a doddering grandfather. Although I did hear Alex talking about pulling a gray hair out of your head. I also heard her telling my Sophie that she supposed it was inevitable that you would lose interest."

"What the hell does that mean? Lose what interest?"

Ryder made a big show of examining his fingernails. "Your wife, Douglas, told my wife that you were tiring of her, obviously, since you only made love to her once a day now. She had nearly given up, she told So-phie, all teary-eyed. She'd tried to rekindle your interest in her fair person by singing you an Italian love song in the gardens beneath one of the naked statues; she'd tried to stimulate your passion by hand-feeding you strawberries from Lord Tomlin's hothouse. She'd even gone so far as to write you a sonnet quite in the classic style. However, she said, you laughed so hard you didn't even make it to the fourteenth line, which, she told my wife, was indeed a moving tribute to marital love in all its varied forms. Yes, she said, she'd failed with you and was at her wit's end."

Douglas was laughing so hard he sputtered on his hot coffee. "Those two women are a danger to us, Ryder, a very real danger. Good God, you'd not have believed that sonnet."

"Maybe so, but Douglas, I'm thinking that Alex is right. I've noticed that you've been acting differently lately. You're distracted, you seem disturbed, perhaps even worried about something. And you came to London, dragging all of us with you, ostensibly for your birthday. What's going on with you, Douglas?"

"That's nonsense," Douglas said. "There's nothing at all going on with me. I happen to like London. If I must become a year older, London is the place to do it. Alex is dreaming up difficulties where none exist. I beg you not to do the same thing. Now, as I said, Alex's sonnet nearly curled my toes."

Ryder had his mouth open when Gray said from behind him, "Alex wrote you a sonnet? Can I look forward to Jack penning me verses as well?"

Both men turned to see Gray St. Cyre standing in the dining room doorway. Douglas said, "Well, we've been married nearly eight years. I thought I'd know everything there was to know about Alex by this time, but not a chance of it. That sonnet—she titled it 'Ode to a Flagging Spouse.' I will read it to the two of you sometime. The looks on your respective faces will be worth all your verbal jabs.

"Now, Gray, you're looking a bit flaccid about the mouth. Come in and have some breakfast." Douglas waved away Thurlow, his butler, and rose, motioning Gray to the chair beside Ryder.

Ryder said, "You're right about wives—they're a mystery. Also they're aggravating and adorable, and I count myself the happiest of men to have Sophie's warm self beside me every night and to wake up with that same warm self beside me every morning." Ryder struck a pose, then added, "And perhaps three cats, tucked in behind my knees, stretched out on my chest, or wrapped around my head. The cats love Sophie. Sometimes she wakes up wheezing because one of the cats has his tail wrapped around her nose."

"Eleanor likes to sleep on me," Gray said. "I wake up to feel her kneading the hair on my chest. She only uses her claws if I happen to be sleeping later than she would like."

Ryder said, "I like your Eleanor—she's got long legs and a strong will. Are there any kittens in the future? We could give one to the Harker brothers and let them train it to become a racing cat."

As the two brothers spoke of the cat-racing season in the south of England, at the McCaultry Racetrack from April to October every year, Gray just listened, occasionally shaking his head. A racing cat. He knew about the cat races but he'd never seen an actual racing cat. He'd have to see what Jack thought of that.

There couldn't be two more different men,

Gray thought, looking at the two brothers. Douglas, the earl, was a very big man, all hard muscle, stern-faced as a vicar presiding over a roomful of sinners, a changeling by Sherbrooke standards, what with his sin-black hair and eyes even blacker than sin. Some believed him hard, unyielding, and indeed he could be when the need arose, but his family knew that he would give his life for any of them. His smile, his wife, Alex, was heard to have said, would smite even the newly titled prince regent, which wasn't a bad thing, all in all.

As for Ryder, the second Sherbrooke son, he brought the sunlight into a room with him. His smile could charm the coins out of a miser's pockets. He was carefree, at his ease with a chimney sweep or a duke, and one would assume he was an indulged younger son unless and until they found out about his children, his Beloved Ones.

And then they wouldn't know what to think.

Ryder was a young man granted all he could possibly want, and yet he became an avenging angel when he found a child abused and hurt. After his own marriage some seven years before, Ryder Sherbrooke had built Brandon House not a hundred yards from his own house, Chadwyck House, and there he brought those children that no one cared about, those children hurt, starving, abandoned, and beyond hope. And that, Gray thought, was what he and Ryder had in common. It was a bond that would hold them together for a lifetime.

Gray looked at Ryder, who was chewing on a piece of bacon, his Sherbrooke blue eyes bright and filled with mischief, and just plain joy at no more pressing a matter than chewing on that bacon.

Douglas said, "When you walked in, Gray, you said something about it not boding well for you. What did you mean?"

"I'm getting married on Friday," Gray said. "To Jack the valet. I went to see Lord Burleigh this morning. It turns out he's Jack's guardian and he's my godfather. Odd, isn't it? One just never knows what's around the next bend in the road. In any case, Jack's an heiress, so it's not just a matter of marrying her and damn the consequences."

"Obviously Lord Burleigh wouldn't turn you away from her," Ryder said.

"Lord Burleigh couldn't do anything. He's unconscious in his bed." He told them of

Lord Burleigh's illness, of Mr. Genner and Lord Bricker, and what would probably happen.

"No reason not to let you marry the girl," Ryder said, "but you're awfully young, Gray. What? Twenty-six? Weren't you just twenty-five last week?"

"The same age, I believe as you were, Ryder, when you married Sophie."

Ryder sighed. "Has it only been seven years? Nearly eight? Not thirty years? The woman exhausts me. She teases me, she flays me with that fluent tongue of hers."

"Don't whine, Ryder," Douglas said, tossing his napkin onto his empty plate. "You're a lucky sod and you know it. Now, Gray, you will let us know if you need any assistance?"

"Of a certainty I shall. I'm here to ask Ryder to stand up with me. To support me. To coach me in the ways of artful premarital conduct."

Douglas shouted with laughter. "Now that is something I don't want to miss. What will you teach him first, Ryder?"

Ryder said slowly, thoughtfully, "You know, I doubt there is much of value that Gray still needs for this particular endeavor.

I do, however, have several close-held observations that might serve you well. I will tell you later, when your day of reckoning is at your front door. Congratulations, Gray."

13

Gray was hunched over his desk, writing the betrothal announcement for the *London Gazette*. When he was writing in the bride's name, he wrote "Jack." He grinned and marked it out. Winifrede. Perfectly dreadful, but it didn't matter. Winifrede Levering. Ah, well, he didn't like Graciella any better.

It was nearly midnight. Mr. Harpole Genner and Lord Bricker had visited him earlier in the evening and told him to proceed with his marriage to the young lady whose virtue he hadn't abused at all, but since that didn't matter in society's eyes, she would doubtless make him an excellent wife.

They'd all shared a brandy.

He finished the announcement and looked up at the light tap on the library door. "Come."

It was Jack, looking all sorts of pale and scared and ridiculous in Mathilda's black peignoir, which trailed after her like a witch's train. All she needed was a familiar.

"Just a moment," Gray said. He rose and walked over to where his Eleanor was curled up in front of a sluggishly burning fire. He lifted her into his arms, let her stretch and dig her claws into his shoulder, then said, "Eleanor, this is Jack. She's moving in with me. Come and get to know her since she'll be sleeping with us after Friday."

Sleeping with him? Jack said as she took a limp Eleanor and began to stroke her automatically as she draped over her shoulder, "I didn't think about that, Gray. All of us will sleep in the same bed?"

"That's the way of things, Jack. It's not depraved or debauched or anything very interesting like that. No, the three of us will all be stretched out side by side, snoring and dreaming and perhaps kneading each other to gain attention."

Jack said, still stroking a sprawled-out,

perfectly boneless Eleanor, "This has been the strangest two weeks of my life. My mother used to tell me that I had the imagination of a good half dozen children. But I know that I would have never imagined this happening."

"A wife named Jack trooping into my life hasn't happened to me before either. Actually, I begin to believe that I was too set in my comfortable ways. Perhaps it was time I reimmersed myself in reality. You're not a bad reality, Jack, all things considered. It appears that Eleanor approves of you. Of course, she's exhausted, since she took three hours to chase down a mouse today. Maybe that's it. She'd accept anyone who had gentle hands."

He suddenly saw his own hands on her. His hands had been on her a good deal, but not recently; within the past three days his hands hadn't been anywhere near enough to her. His fingers itched. Her hair was in a braid that was barely braided, all slept in and tangled. He very much liked the tendrils of hair that fell and curled and lazed about her face. A nice face, he thought. Yes, she had a very nice face, full of character and good humor.

She would be his wife.

On Friday. Good God.

"Gray?"

He blinked away the glaze over his eyes, the same glaze that was over his brain. "Yes, Jack? Eleanor is too heavy? Is she weighing down your shoulder? You're still tired?"

"No. I was wondering where my stepfather was. He said he'd come back today, didn't he?"

"He did." He took Eleanor from her and led her to a settee in front of the fire. "Sit down, Jack, before you crumple to my carpet. You're looking a bit white about the mouth. Yes, you can hold Eleanor on your lap."

"Tell me," she said, settling the both of them. "What will he do?"

Gray smiled at the two of them, Eleanor curling, then recurling until she was comfortable on Jack's thighs. One of the black peignoir feathers wreathed her head.

"He said, without any polite preamble, that he had come to fetch you home, that he wouldn't leave until I'd handed you over, and he was fully prepared to bring in a magistrate along with sufficient men to drag you out of here. At that point I offered him a brandy, clicked my glass to his, and fondly called him papa-in-law."

"Oh, dear. What did he do?"

"He spit my very expensive brandy all over the carpet and his waistcoat. Once he regained his breath, he carried on about that not being possible, at which point I calmly told him that I had been to see Lord Burleigh, who just happened to be my godfather as well as your guardian, and everything was in order. I gently inquired if he was at all concerned that it was your guardian approving your marriage."

"Did he choke and spit again?"

"No, he drew a stiletto from his coat pocket and brandished it in my face. He said that wasn't possible, that he was your stepfather, and it would be he who determined who your husband would be, not that damned Lord Burleigh."

Gray leaned over and patted her face, his grin becoming wider as he said, "Your stepfather was utterly sincere when he said that you already had a gentleman who wished to wed with you. He said he feared that you—a wild and undisciplined chit—had already taken him for your lover. It was Lord Rye, he told me, a gentleman of great good nature and healthy enough appetites to suit a young girl."

"That is perfectly appalling," Jack said, tugging on one of Eleanor's ears, to which Eleanor reached up a paw and swatted her hand. "Come, tell me the rest of it."

Gray grinned at her and sat back in his chair. "It's not very edifying."

"At least he didn't stab you. He's always fiddling with that stiletto."

Gray set his brandy glass down and began stroking his long fingers over his chin as he said, "I told him I had heard of Lord Rye. Oh, yes, I told him, I was acquainted with his charming heir, a young man about my own age, by the name of Arthur, if I wasn't mistaken."

Gray pictured Sir Henry's red face, remembered him saying quite clearly, "Cadmon Kilburn, Lord Rye, is a mature gentleman, not a flighty young man who would break her heart with his careless ways."

"Mature?" Gray had said, an eyebrow lifted. "You wish to share fathering duties with Lord Rye? You would wish her to be the stepmama of Arthur, who is older than she is?"

"Enough of this, my lord. Bring me my stepdaughter. She is already betrothed to Lord Rye. You won't get her."

"You mean I won't get all her groats?" Gray had walked to his desk, opened the top drawer, and withdrawn a sheaf of papers. He presented them to Sir Henry. "If you'll read the marriage agreement, Sir Henry, you'll see that I've already got her. Lord Rye may find himself a rich widow to see to him, his debauched heir, and his half dozen other children. Now, either we can be civilized about this or I can beat you to a pulp and toss you out my drawing room window. Or, if you truly distress me, I can take that stiletto of yours and prick your brain with it."

Gray gave her a white-toothed grin. He rubbed his hands together. "At which point," he said, "your stepfather jumped at me, his stiletto at the ready."

Jack was staring at him, utterly frozen. Eleanor leapt up, snarled in Jack's face, and jumped off her lap and onto a wing chair.

"She's sensitive," Gray said.

Jack jumped to her feet. Gray had the presence of mind to jump to his feet before she ran him down. Her hands were all over his face, down his arms, then flattened against his chest. He grabbed them and held her still.

"What's wrong, Jack?"

"Did he stick you with the stiletto? Oh, God, did he hurt you?"

He was pleased. She was concerned that he'd been hurt. She cared, and it more than pleased him. He laughed to hide it. He brought her hands to his mouth and kissed each of her fingers. She became very, very quiet. Then he spit one of Eleanor's hairs out of his mouth and grinned down at her.

"Your dear stepfather didn't stick me with the stiletto. I relieved him of his nasty toy and tossed it onto the grate. Actually, I thought he would cry then. Finally he drew himself up and announced that he would see me in hell before he would see me as your husband." Gray paused a moment, his fingers still lightly stroking her hands. "I find it odd that he looks so very, well, heroic, I suppose. Yes, that's the proper word. He's tall and imposing, seemingly a man who's a leader, a man of apparently fine parts, at least fine physical parts, a man one could trust and admire."

"Oh, no, he's not at all like you, Gray."

He believed in that instant that if his chest expanded any further, he'd explode. She believed him imposing? A leader? She trusted and admired him? By God, he was heroic?

"No," he said, staring down at her, fascinated, feeling so wonderful he was still in danger of bursting. "He's not a bit like me."

"It is such a mystery to me. My mother adored him until she died. If she ever saw through him, realized at last who and what he really was, it just didn't matter to her. Don't misunderstand me. Sir Henry isn't stupid. I imagine that he was properly adoring until they were married and he had her money. Then there would have been no more need for him to be anything other than what he really was."

"A rotter."

"Yes. Only my mother never cared. She worshiped him. When she birthed Georgie, rather than a precious heir for him, I believed she would kill herself. To make her suffer more, he acted as though it were all her fault, that she'd birthed a daughter to torment him. I had disliked him before. After that, I hated him for his cruelty. I still do."

"Perhaps your stepfather and my father

were somehow related in the distant past. I believe I will have to make a study of Sir Henry so as to see how close their similarities.

"Now, Jack, stop this. He didn't hurt me. Why, I even invited him to our wedding. I assured him that if he could present himself as a doting stepfather you wouldn't mind at all. I did tell him that he couldn't stand up with you because Mr. Harpole Genner had that honor."

She didn't know about this Harpole Genner. She frowned. He patted her shoulders. "Don't worry. You'll like Mr. Genner. He's a longtime friend of Lord Burleigh's. He's the one who has seen to everything being right and proper. I could tell that Sir Henry knew about Mr. Harpole Genner, knew he was a man to respect, perhaps a man to fear. Sir Henry won't try to muck up our wedding ceremony, Jack."

She just nodded. She was frowning down at her black slippers, on loan from Aunt Mathilda. "I'm worried about Georgie. She's in his power, Gray. What can I do?"

"I've been thinking about that, Jack. I want you to stop worrying. I swear to you that I'll make sure Georgie is safe and sound. Will you trust me?"

He saw that she trusted him. She just didn't believe he could get his hands on her little sister.

He let it go. "Now, would you like to read your marriage settlement?"

"Yes. I should like to read all your manly stipulations."

"Jack, let the papers sit on my desk a few minutes longer. Come here and let me kiss you. It's the first time."

Actually, he thought, his mouth lightly touching her, it was probably the first time that she'd ever kissed any man. "Pucker your lips," he said against her mouth. "Yes, that's right. No, don't seam your lips together. Open them just a bit—that's right."

She was warm, her mouth soft, and she tasted sweet. His hands went unerringly toward her bottom, only to halt half an inch away. It was too soon. She wasn't Jenny. She had no experience at all. He imagined she didn't cook at all either.

It was daunting, her youth and innocence. He had to go very easily.

He'd never even been close to a virgin before. He was a blockhead, with a short memory. How could he forget even for a moment that he'd seen her naked, cared for her, held her tightly against him. What the devil was wrong with him?

She was conscious and full-witted now, that was what was wrong. "Smooth out your mouth," he said as he nipped at that dimple in her left cheek.

"What does that mean?"

"It means your mouth looks like an ill-sewn seam."

She drew back in his arms and laughed. "Oh, Gray, show me what to do."

It wasn't a good idea. She was so giving and soft and pliant. He could haul her over to the sofa and take her down, right this very minute. She was just an envelope of black silk away.

He set her away from him. "I'll show you everything you want to know on Friday. *No, after our wedding*—not Friday morning over kippers."

"I'll be too scared to eat kippers on Friday morning."

"I'll probably be too scared as well. Go to bed, Jack, alone. I won't come to tuck you in. I wish to spare myself any more suffering."

He saw that she didn't understand. Well, she would come to understand as soon as he had the bishop's blessing on his head to indulge himself in marital bliss until he was exhausted or couldn't stand upright, whichever came first. He took a step back.

His good sense was cracking like an old mirror that had seen too much. He picked up Eleanor, who gave him a lazy look, stretched her head forward, and lightly bit his neck. He looked over at Jack, who was still standing there, undecided. "On Friday night, I want you to bite my neck, just like Eleanor did. All right?"

She nodded slowly. She took a step forward. "Actually, I could bite your neck right now, Gray. Surely no one could consider that debauchery."

His eyes nearly crossed. "Yes, they could. If you did bite my neck and anyone saw you do it then we'd have to get married right now, tomorrow at the latest. Trust me on this. Go to bed, Jack."

"Don't you think it appropriate that you give me just a bit of preparation for my new job?"

A dark blond eyebrow went upward. "New job?"

"I'm going to be a wife. I know nothing about it. At least I know nothing at all about the fleshly side of it. My mother did train me how to deal with servants, from a flirtatious laundry maid to a tearful tweeny to a puff-chested butler. I know how to mend a sheet. I can do beautiful embroidery. I can even cook a bit. But, Gray, I don't know a thing about my duties in the bedchamber."

"Jack, I swear to you that you will learn very quickly, since I am an excellent instructor and you will have as many lessons as I can manage before I fall over in a heap. You don't need to know anything. It's best for your peace of mind that you come into this ignorant as a ball of clay." Ball of clay? He was losing what little he had left of his brain. "Well, hell, all right. Come here."

But it was he who walked quickly to her, grabbed her against him, and trailed his fingertip over her eyebrows, her nose, her jaw. He dipped his head down to kiss where his fingers had touched her.

Then he yowled.

Eleanor swatted him again.

"I forgot," he said and peeled Eleanor off his shoulder. "Sorry," he said, to both Jack and Eleanor, watching her as she strolled away from them, her tail twitching high in the air. Then he turned back to Jack, who just stood there, looking at his mouth. She looked interested, very interested. She also looked just a bit on the scared side. Well, this whole business wasn't for the faint-hearted.

He lightly stroked his knuckles over her jaw. "You and I will deal well together, Jack. Now, don't close your eyes. Look at me straight on." Very slowly he cupped her breasts in his hands. She jerked.

"No, just hold still. Look at me. Tell me how that makes you feel."

She swallowed. Then, very slowly, she let her head fall back. He watched her eyes drift shut, her eyelashes sweep down. He looked at that white neck of hers.

He wanted that white neck, but he had to begin somewhere and he'd already begun with her breasts. He stroked her easily, ever so easily. He felt only soft black feathers and a single layer of silk between his hands and her breasts. He'd washed her breasts, drawn the damp cloth over her breasts when she'd been roasting with the fever. He'd stared at those breasts of hers and nearly swallowed his tongue. He cleared his throat, trying to tell his brain that speech was the best thing for him in this situation. Still his fingers didn't move from her breasts. He cleared his throat again. "Jack, what do you feel when I caress your breasts?"

"I can't see."

"That's because your eyes are closed. Bring your head back up and look at me."

She did, her eyes shining and excited. Even though he was harder than the pink-veined Carrara marble mantelpiece, he kept his hands steady.

He leaned down and kissed the pulse in her throat.

He pulled the peignoir open.

"You're looking at me."

"Yes, your northerly female parts are really quite exquisite."

"Will I find your male parts equally exquisite?"

"Of course," he said, praying desperately that she would. He kissed the tops of her breasts. Then he pulled the black silk back together.

"You will now go to bed, alone. Tomorrow is Thursday, Jack. Think of me kissing your breasts until Friday. Will you try?"

"I'll try, Gray."

When she was gone, he turned to Eleanor, who was staring at him from unblinking green eyes.

"So, what's the matter with you?"

She slowly sat up and began washing herself. He looked at her more closely. "Your belly isn't at all lean, Eleanor. Are you pregnant? Do you have future racing cats inside you?"

Eleanor kept licking.

Gray laughed. He wondered as he walked up the dark stairs toward his bedchamber just how all this had come about. Surely it wasn't an expected thing that a man's wife suddenly appear as a valet who would steal his horse.

He had to visit Jenny tomorrow. He realized that all he would truly miss was her delicious apple tarts, with Devonshire cream.

14

A valet? This girl devised a plot to trap you into marriage by actually playing a valet and stealing Durban when she knew you'd be coming home and knowing you'd see her?"

Gray tried not to laugh, but it was impossible. "Oh, Jenny, she had no notion she would end up being married to me when she stole Durban. No, she had no plans for me to see her. Actually, I strangled her, knocked her in the ribs, hit her jaw, and slammed her to the straw.

"Come now, I just tried to give you an idea of how this has all came about. Jack is a good sort. She will suit me very well, you'll see."

"Have you slept with her?"

An impertinent question, but he let it go. "No, Jenny, nor will I until we're married."

He watched his mistress pace up and down, up and down the full length of her drawing room. She was wearing a quite lovely green muslin gown that would have shown the lovely curve of her breasts if she hadn't had an apron tied around her neck. There were gravy stains on that apron. It was nearly time for luncheon. He sniffed. Roast lamb was only two rooms away, he was certain of it.

"Very well," Jenny said at last, and then she sniffed, as well, nodded, her mind obviously in her kitchen. "You will marry her. I knew you would have to marry to have an heir. It is expected. However, I believe that two weeks should be quite enough. Then you'll be bored with her and come back to me. I shall go to Bath for two weeks and recuperate in the healing Roman waters. Now, I will feed you, my lord. Roast lamb with my special mint sauce."

As he ate Jenny's delicious roast lamb with her special mint sauce, he realized he hadn't even thought about keeping a mistress and a wife at the same time. Most men did, but now, when he was facing the decision, he knew he wouldn't do it. It wasn't right. A man gave his word and kept it. It was that simple. His father, not surprisingly, had enjoyed a score of mistresses during his time with Gray's mother, and it had been no secret, not to his wife, not to his son.

He was still thinking about the business of wives and mistresses as he walked from Jenny's charming apartments on Candlewick Street back home to Portman Square, a full mile to the east. The sky was overcast, but it wasn't raining, not like it had the night before, when Eleanor had burrowed so close to him he'd nearly crushed her when he executed a roll onto his back.

He thought of his mother and felt the familiar pain block his throat. He saw her face suddenly in his mind's eye, her face as it had been when he'd not been more than eight years old and he saw her staring down into the entrance hall at her husband kissing a woman and rubbing her breasts, all in front of whoever wanted to watch, which had probably been the entire household. He saw the tears streaming down her cheeks, the deadening pain in her beautiful eyes. He shook his head. He hated those memories because there was simply no way to control them. They popped up, spread instant devastation, then simply disappeared again back into the past, hovering there until the next time.

No, he would never do that to Jack. Once he was married, he would keep to his vows. However, it was surely odd that he hadn't felt even a flicker of desire when he'd been with Jenny. He'd lusted after the roasted lamb, though.

Gray remembered seeing an advertisement for a new stove, supposedly so modern that it did everything except actually baste the meat. He would buy that stove for Jenny. He would also look for another protector for her, if she wished it, a gentleman who would enjoy her cooking as much as Gray did.

He was whistling, swinging his cane, when he walked up the steps to his town house. The door flew open and Quincy, with both aunts hovering behind him, shouted, "My lord, Miss Jack is gone!"

* * *

Jack couldn't breathe. There was some sort of foul-smelling sack over her head. When she tried to raise her hand to rip it off, she realized her arms were tied behind her back. She couldn't breathe and she couldn't save herself. She choked and struggled.

"Shut up," someone said. "Just shut up."

She continued to struggle, wheezing, knowing she was going to die.

She heard the man curse. The sack was jerked from her head. She sucked in air, concentrating on the fresh, pure air coming into her body. She fell back and lay there, just breathing. Finally, she opened her eyes. She saw a burlap sack on the carriage seat beside her.

She was indeed in a carriage and it was moving fast, rocking hard from side to side. Odd that she hadn't realized that before.

"Well, dear Winifrede, you're back again. I forgot that you couldn't stand closed-in places. No, don't move or I'll hurt you. I might even put that burlap sack over your head again and listen to you choke."

She stared at Arthur Kelburn, Lord Rye's eldest son. She hadn't seen him for a good three months. She wished she didn't have to see him for another thirty years.

"Why?" she said, nothing more, staring at his very fine white cravat and buff riding jacket.

He gave her his special brooding, dark-eyed scowl that sent most of the local girls into swoons of delight. His hair was as black as Eleanor's stomach, long and curling slightly over his neck, a thick lock hanging romantically over his forehead. He was the same age as Gray. There was no further likeness between the two men. Arthur was the antithesis of his noble name. He would very likely prove to be a greater wastrel than his father in the years to come, if he lived that long.

"Why?"

He was sitting on the opposite carriage seat, facing her. His hands were clasped between his knees. His dark, brooding look intensified. He probably practiced that look in a mirror.

"When I was young," he said finally, "I thought you the skinniest, ugliest little girl I'd ever seen. My father would just smile and say, 'Wait, my boy, just wait.' I waited, Winifrede. Now you're eighteen—nearly nineteen, my father told me—a woman grown, and I must say that my father was right. You've turned out quite charmingly.

"I'm a man grown, and I'm ready to marry. My father and I had determined that it would be he who married you. It was all settled. We knew that those witless old ladies had taken you to London. We even knew where you were. Sir Henry would fetch you back. I told my father that you would prefer me to him and that once you knew I would be your groom, you would cease your complaints. It is, naturally, quite true, and so my father agreed to it.

"Then Sir Henry came rushing down to Folkstone to tell us that you were going to marry a bloody baron tomorrow morning."

He sat forward, his knees touching hers, and his brooding look became turbulent, more laced with violence.

"You're not going to marry any bloody baron, Winifrede. You're going to marry me. We're on our way to the border. It will take us at least five days to get there and get married. By that time, it's more than likely that you'll be pregnant with my child."

"Did your father truly believe I would prefer you to him?"

"Ah, yes, ladies do enjoy having many

men fighting over them. It pleases their vanity. Well, my father decided that having you in his bed just wasn't worth all the aggravation, so he gave you over to me. He told me you were willful and obstinate and had too much guile for a woman. He said you weren't to be trusted. He assured me that wooing you would be a waste of time. He reminded me what had happened when your stepfather left you alone in your bedchamber, assuming that you were broken, assuming that he'd won and you would do what he told you to do. He told me to master you, it was the only way.

"My father's an old man—not that he'd appreciate hearing me say that, but it's true. He's forgotten what it's like to take a young innocent like you and teach her what she's supposed to be, what she's supposed to do."

"My betrothed will kill you."

Arthur laughed. "He might wish to, but he won't attempt it. He's a useless dandy, that one. I would shoot him down very easily. He knows it. I have a reputation for my shooting and fencing skills.

"No, your baron will bleat and gnash his teeth because he's lost your sixty thousand pounds, but he's not stupid. He won't do anything, Winifrede, he simply won't. He has no spine and he realizes it."

She was silent, working the knotted rope at her wrists. Her fingers were getting numb. It wasn't a good sign.

Arthur looked out the window when she remained silent. He was pleased that she was holding her tongue. He stared at the passing green hills and the interminable yew bushes that lined the road as far as the eye could see. He saw an occasional herd of cows, an occasional flock of sheep. The carriage was well sprung. His father liked his luxuries. He didn't want his son to be uncomfortable in this venture.

He turned to look at her again. He stretched out his legs, one on either side of her, clasping her legs between his. "That scares you, doesn't it, Winifrede? Well, after tonight, you'll like having me all over you. I trust you're still a virgin?"

She continued silent. If she'd had her way last night, just maybe she wouldn't be a virgin this morning. But Gray was a man of honor, curse him. She kept working the knot.

"Yes, I suppose you are. Since you were

the aunts' valet, they would have protected you." He pressed his legs more tightly inward, trapping hers. She didn't move, didn't breathe, just kept twisting and pulling on the knot.

"You know, I began to believe you pretty after your sixteenth birthday. You've turned out well. You're not as pretty as your mother was—at least that's what my father says—but I shan't repine. Your hair is thick and quite lovely, many interesting shades of blond." He leaned forward and removed the clasp that held her hair at the nape of her neck. He fanned his fingers through her hair, arranging it about her shoulders, bringing over some of it to cover her breasts.

He sat back again, crossing his arms over his chest.

To his surprise, she smiled at him. "I would like you to return me to London now, Arthur. Gray won't kill you if you turn the carriage around right now and go back."

"I already told you that he won't try to kill me, no matter what I do to you. Are you stupid?"

"Very well. Then I will tell you this: I refuse to marry you. You can't force me to."

"I will simply take you until you have no

other choice. I will keep you with me until you're with child. I'm a potent man. I have three bastards at least to prove it."

"I don't care if you rape me. I still won't marry you."

His brooding look now bordered on the petulant; he looked for all the world like a small boy who'd been thwarted and hadn't expected it. "That's ridiculous. You're a girl. You know nothing about anything. You won't have a choice. I'm a man. I'm handsome and charming. I will please you in bed as I've pleased more girls than I can count. You will admire me. You will be pleased that I'm your husband. You will obey me, but I will never trust you."

She continued to smile at him even as she turned her face against the squabs and closed her eyes.

"Damn you." He was on her then, jerking her chin back, his hands wrapping themselves around her hair. He was kissing her, thrusting his tongue into her mouth. He pulled her over on top of him, holding her legs still between his.

Gray said to his horse, "She stole you. You never even had a chance to bite her for what she did. If you find her for me, I'll let you nibble on her to your heart's content."

Durban snorted, flicked his tail, and lengthened his stride. They passed a farmer in a cart piled high with hay.

Gray was on the North road. She'd been gone for only an hour. She was probably in a carriage. If the bastard who took her was thinking about a quick wedding, then he'd be dragging her to Scotland.

Five days to Scotland.

He didn't think he'd want to try to hold Jack prisoner for five days. Not when she didn't want it. It would be five very long days. Who had taken her? Her stepfather? In that case, Gray was wrong to his boot heels, for Sir Henry would be hauling her back to Folkstone. Then Douglas would get him. Perhaps it was Lord Rye, the lecherous old fool. Would he try to take her to Scotland? Or perhaps to Bath, where he'd hide her in one of the many houses for rent in the area? If so, then Ryder would find them.

No, it wasn't either of them, and that's why Gray was riding hell-bent for Scotland. He'd immediately believed Aunt Mathilda when she'd said, "Young and determined."

And then Aunt Maude had said thoughtfully, "Any man who took her would have to be not only strong and determined. He would have to be desperate."

Aunt Mathilda had nodded slowly and added in her deep, beautiful voice, "Arthur."

Mathilda and Maude knew all the possible bounders who could have snatched Jack. They believed it was Arthur, Lord Rye's heir. Yes, the aunts had assured him. Arthur was strong, not as strong as his namesake, but he wasn't a weakling like many young men who wenched and drank and played cards until dawn.

They were just an hour ahead of Gray and Durban, not much more. He pressed his cheek to Durban's smooth neck and urged him on faster.

He was groaning, his breath hot on her cheek, his hands furiously kneading her breasts. Her hands slipped loose of the knot. She reared back suddenly and slammed her fists into his neck.

He gave her a look of disbelieving horror, then gurgled. He was holding his throat, turning blue. She didn't wait. She opened the carriage door, grabbed his arm, and flung him to the floor. He slid down onto his hands and knees. She managed to squeeze behind him, plant her feet in the center of his back and kick with all her strength. He went flying out the open door. Unfortunately, the coachman saw his master crash onto the road and roll to the side.

She would have given anything for a gun, for a stick of wood to use as a weapon.

The horses came to a sliding halt. The coachman jumped off the seat and rushed to look into the carriage at the girl his master had kidnapped.

"What happened to Mr. Arthur? What did ye do to him? Poor lad, he didn't do nuthin' except steal ye out of Portman Square. Ah, there he be, poor lad, lying on 'is face in the dirt, all still. Ye kilt him, ye did. Fer shame, and ye a lady an' acting like a floozy with no sensibility."

The coachman ran as fast as he could toward the fallen Arthur. Without hesitation, Jack jumped onto the box, grabbed the reins, and flicked them over the horses. She yelled at them, jerking on the heavy reins, slapping them against the horses' necks.

She heard the coachman shout, "Stop! No!"

She took a quick look over her shoulder

to see Arthur lying in the middle of the road, still. Too still. Oh dear, was he dead?

She saw herself deported to that place nearly a world away called Botany Bay. She urged the horses forward even as she considered going back to see to Arthur. She looked back one more time. He was sitting up, holding his head. No, he was rubbing his villain's neck. Good.

The road was wide, the ruts deep and dry. She pulled back a bit on the reins, for there was a curve coming up. She thought she heard a horse coming. The horses didn't pull up at all. They didn't even pause.

The lead horse, a huge bay, jerked his head up and snorted, then stretched out and lunged forward, bringing the inside horse with him.

Jack had never driven a pair before. It wasn't at all the same as riding. She tried to pull them back. It didn't work. They flew around the curve directly into the path of an oncoming horseman, galloping hard right at them.

She heard the man's yell, saw his horse rear back onto its hind legs. She saw that it was Durban and his eyes were wild. Gray's eyes were wild too.

She saw that he'd kept his seat on Durban's back, but not for long. As the horses galloped away, Durban went crashing off the road into a thick stand of yew bushes. Gray was thrown off Durban's back and slammed into an oak tree.

She closed her eyes for an instant, every action she'd taken in the past ten minutes careening through her brain. Oh God, Gray would have caught them if only she hadn't thrown Arthur out of the carriage.

Jack gritted her teeth, sawed on the reins, got no results, then finally, having no idea how to stop the beasts, she just looped the reins loosely around her hands and sat there, feeling the wind tear through her hair, shivering because the air was cold at this colossal speed, closing her eyes because they were tearing and burning from the harsh wind. And she prayed.

To her relief and surprise, the horses began to slow. It seemed forever, but surely it didn't take them too much longer to pull up, winded.

They simply stopped in the middle of the road.

She jumped down from the box, went to their heads, and stroked both faces, thanking them, promising them oats, promising them her steadfast devotion for a lifetime.

"Now," she said, fastening her hand tightly about the lead horse's reins, close to his mouth, "we've got to go back and see to Gray. We're going to walk back."

It took only five minutes to cover the road at a nice slow walk, the same road that they'd flown over but minutes before.

"Gray."

There was no answer.

Durban was standing in the shade of an elm tree just up the road. He raised his head when he heard her voice.

"Durban, don't move, boy. Just stay there. We've got to find Gray."

She did find him, in an unconscious heap at the foot of the oak tree.

15

The cold air grew suddenly colder. The sky, until just five minutes before, had held nothing but rippling white clouds. Now those same clouds were fast becoming bloated and dirty gray.

Jack carefully tied the horses' reins to a yew bush, then ran to Gray, lying beneath that oak tree. She knelt beside him, her fingers finding the heartbeat in his neck. Slow and steady, thank God. There was a thin line of blood from his forehead down his left temple, where he'd struck the tree as he fell.

She sat back on her heels. What now?

It began to rain.

Durban neighed.

How to get a full-sized man back to the carriage and into it? Gray wasn't a giant of a man, but he was still nearly twice her size. There was no hope for it. She could but try.

She clutched him beneath his arms and began to drag him back toward the road. It was uphill, and strewn with rocks. She wasn't going to be able to do it.

She stared at Durban.

She tied his reins around Gray's chest, then urged Durban to back up. She was in-utterably relieved and frankly dumbfounded when Durban began taking tentative steps backward—a plan of hers and it was actually working! Durban dragged Gray beside the open carriage door. She kissed Durban's nose, told him he was magnificent. Then she stared down at her betrothed, once again flummoxed.

How to get him into the carriage?

The rain was coming down harder. She shoved her wet hair out of her face. Somehow she had to get him to stand up. Then she could tip him onto the carriage floor. She knelt down and slapped his face. "Gray, please, wake up. I've got to get you warm.

Please, Gray." She slapped him several more times, but he didn't respond at all.

She propped him against the side of the carriage as best she could. His back was against the step-down. She was winded when she stood.

"Now, Durban, you've got to back up again, only this time go very slowly. You're going to pull your master toward you and upright, I hope." Durban took a step backward. The reins tightened and Gray came a foot off the ground. She crouched down behind him, pushing him more upright as Durban took another step back. Then another.

He was nearly standing. She guessed it was as high as he was going to get. She untied Durban's reins from around his chest.

She raised her face to the heavens and prayed, choking on the rain.

She climbed over him, keeping him steady, until she was kneeling on the carriage floor. Now, she thought, now. She drew a deep breath. She pulled with all her might.

She couldn't get him off the ground. She nearly yelled her frustration. Saying one "damn" and instantly tasting turnips, she jumped down from the carriage, got beneath him, sucked in another deep breath, and tried to stand and shove inward at the same time.

She couldn't lift his weight. Durban neighed, poked his nose beneath Gray's lower back and lifted his head. Gray slowly slid into the carriage. She and Durban had done it.

She quickly pulled the burlap sack over him and straightened him as best she could. She closed the carriage door, tied Durban to the back of the carriage, and climbed back onto the box. This time, she only lightly flicked the reins and spoke just above a whisper. "Let's go, boys. There has to be a village back this way. Find it for me, please."

The small market town of Court Hammering was battened down, everyone off the streets, including all the animals, as the rain drenched land and buildings. The road was already muddy. Jack was careful to keep the horses at a very slow walk. Finally, she saw an inn at the far end of the small town, set back from the main street—King Edward's Lamp.

There was no one in the yard. No wonder. She jumped down from the carriage box and ran inside. A very tall woman suddenly appeared from the small taproom to the left. The woman looked as if she would quite enjoy eating a board or two for her luncheon, perhaps nails for her dessert. She wasn't at all fat, just very tall and very well filled out. She was also, actually, very lovely, Jack saw finally, with surely much more beautiful pale blond hair than a single woman deserved to have, woven in fat plaits over her ears. Jack looked down at the light gold flagstones beneath her feet. "I'm sorry," she said. "I'm getting your lovely floor wet."

The woman crossed her arms over her magnificent bosom. "I see that you are," she said. "What do you want?"

Jack pointed back to the carriage. "Please, help me. Gray is in the carriage. He's unconscious."

"You look like a little drowned sparrow. You stay here, and I'll see to Gray. Who are you? Who is he?"

"I'm Jack, and he's nearly my husband," she said, immediately on the woman's heels. "By that I mean that I'm going to marry him tomorrow."

"I completely understand. I'm Helen. Now, don't move. Yes, stay."

Jack watched Helen stride into the rainstorm, her head up, paying no attention to the mud puddles that were slopping over the tops of her boots and dirtying the hem of her gown or the rain that was drenching her.

She watched Helen open the carriage door and look inside. Then Jack thought she heard a deep laugh. She saw Helen lean into the carriage. When she straightened a moment later, backing away from the carriage, she had Gray over her shoulder. She wasn't even breathing hard when she returned to the inn.

"The water is so deep right here in my inn yard," Helen said, "that I could most certainly launch a thousand ships from my very front door. Come with me, Jack, and let's get your nearly husband to bed." As she climbed the narrow inn stairs, Gray hanging down her back, she called down to the three men who were staring at them from the doorway of the taproom.

"Go on, you codbrains. See to the horses and the lady's carriage. Rub down the horses, they're all prime horseflesh, particularly the gelding tied to the back. Have a care or I'll discipline all of you, and I'll do it in such a way that you won't like it a bit."

If Jack hadn't been so scared for Gray,

she would have laughed. Just how would Helen discipline three codbrains? She watched the men run outside into the rain.

Helen said over her shoulder as she gently let Gray down onto the oak-planked floor, "No reason to get the bed all wet. You, Jack, go downstairs and ask Gwendolyn to give you some dry clothes. Just tell her that Helen requests it."

"But—"

"I'm starting to speak to you like I do to my pug, Nellie. No matter. Just do as I say. Go, Jack. I'll see to your Gray," and Jack went.

When Jack returned carrying a dry petticoat, a thin muslin chemise, and a voluminous gray cotton dress over her arm, Gray was in bed, covers to his nose, and Helen was looking down at him.

"Please, is he all right, Helen?"

"He's a finely knit man," Helen said. "Fine indeed. Now, we must keep him alive so the two of you can marry. Help me spread his clothes over the back of the chair so they'll dry. Yes, that's it."

"We're to be married tomorrow morning," Jack said, as she smoothed out Gray's breeches, "but Arthur grabbed me at Portman Square this morning and stuffed me into his carriage. That's the one outside that the three codbrains are taking care of. The prime horse is Durban. I stole him once, but he belongs to Gray."

Helen held up a large, very lovely white hand. "I wish to hear all about this, but first let me call for Dr. Brainard. The only reason I've allowed him to remain in Court Hammering is because he doesn't go out of his way to kill off his patients and he occasionally amuses me. You change into dry clothes and sit beside this fine young man and hold his hand."

Gray opened his eyes to see Jack not an inch from his face. He blinked and pressed his head down into the pillow. "Good God, Jack, back away or my eyes will cross."

"You're alive. Thank God, Gray, you're alive. How do you feel?" She'd taken his face between her hands and was stroking his chin, his ears, his nose. Then she kissed him, over and over, light, sweet kisses all over his face that would have made him smile if—

"Jack, quickly! Mathilda—chamber pot."

It was under his chin just in time. When he fell back against the pillow, white-faced, his head pounding, utterly exhausted, she said, "Here's some water."

He washed out his mouth.

"Ah, puked up your guts, huh, boy?"

Gray closed his eyes against the sight of the very small, completely bald man, thin as a windowpane, who stood in the doorway, water dripping off his thick black eyebrows.

His eyes flew open again, disbelieving what he was seeing. A mountain of a woman towered behind the little man, and she was really quite beautiful. She looked to have huge blond wheels over her ears.

He slowly turned his head on the pillow. "It really is you, Jack? Wearing a gown I've never seen before? How are you here? Where are we? Why am I in bed and you're not?"

"There is quite a bit to tell you, Gray, but first, this is Dr. Brainard. Helen said he won't kill you."

"Why do I need a doctor, Jack? What happened?"

"I was driving the carriage around the bend and you were riding Durban toward me and I couldn't stop the horses and Durban was terrified and you got thrown and hit your head against an oak tree."

"Thank you," Gray said and closed his eyes again. "Yes, it's starting to come back to me now."

"Here, eat a bite of this."

He didn't want to open his eyes again, it required too much effort. He just opened his mouth. He tasted a scone that rivaled the best of Jenny's. He chewed, then opened his mouth again. After three bites he managed to have both his eyes and his mouth open.

It was that beautiful behemoth of a woman and she was leaning over him. "I'm Miss Helen Mayberry. I own King Edward's Lamp."

"I didn't realize King Edward even had a lamp, particularly one that anyone would want."

"Sir, mind your irony. Miss Helen is the owner of this inn, and the inn is named King Edward's Lamp."

"I fancy, Ossie, that our young sir here is really a my lord. Am I right?"

Gray said, "Could I have some more scone?"

"Of course. Just rest and open your

mouth. When you're full, Ossie can tap your chest, peer into your ears, scratch your scalp, all to determine what sort of dreadful potion he wants to pour down your throat."

"I fancy that you're not just in the common way yourself, Miss Mayberry," Gray said.

"Here's your scone, my lord."

Jack just shook her head as she watched Helen feed Gray. Her day had begun very strangely, what with Arthur pulling a burlap sack over her head, and now here she was in King Edward's Lamp watching Gray eat a scone from the white hands of a beautiful, very large woman.

Suddenly a boy not older than ten years banged open the door. "Helen! Hurry, there's this man who's shouting and waving a gun about. He wants somebody named Winifrede."

Jack jumped a good foot in the air and whirled about. "Oh, dear. It's Arthur. I'll just wager he got that burlap sack out of the carriage and he's vengeful."

Gray threw back the covers, saw that he was naked, and pulled them back to his chin. "Jack, hand me my clothes and be quick."

"I can't, Gray, they're all wet. You'll become ill and—"

"Damn you, Jack, do as I tell you. I'm going to be your husband in less than twenty-four hours. You can begin your duties by obeying me now."

"My lord," Helen said, rising even as she shoved the last bite of scone into Gray's mouth. "Allow me to see to this Arthur. Now, quickly—this Arthur is the man who kidnapped you, Jack?"

"Yes, he wanted me to marry him. He was going to force me all the way to Scotland."

"Helen, he's coming up here!"

"It's all right, Theo, let him come." She turned to Jack. "What do you want me to do with Arthur?"

"Break his right arm," Jack said. "Maybe his left as well if you think he deserves it."

"Hmmm, a woman who knows her own mind. His right arm? We'll see," Helen said and walked to the bedchamber door.

"No," Gray shouted after her, "don't break any of that little swine's body parts. Bring him here, to me. I'll do all the breaking. Oh, yes, if you would please give me a gun. I must protect Jack."

"Arthur and Jack," Helen said to herself.

They heard Arthur yelling, his boots heavy on the oak stairs. Then he was coming down the corridor toward them.

"Don't worry," Helen said over her shoulder, calm as a sail in a windless sea. She planted herself squarely in the open doorway.

"My lord," Dr. Ossie Brainard said, "breathe deeply. I need to listen to your breathing. No, don't jump when I tap your chest. Miss Helen will see to this fellow."

"Jack, for God's sake, go behind that screen. I don't want Arthur to see you. He might start frothing at the mouth. He just might use that gun on Helen."

Jack wasn't about to leave his side. She compromised and moved one foot closer to the very old dressing screen.

"My lord, your breathing gallops. It is far too erratic. Please breathe deeply and don't excite yourself—something men never seem to learn not to do."

"If you were marrying her less than a day from now, I daresay you would be exciting yourself as well, particularly with her kidnapper not a dozen feet from her."

"My lord, you shouldn't speak of such marital sorts of things in Miss Helen's hearing. And don't forget, the fellow has to get past Miss Helen, which even her sire can never manage to do, and Lord Prith is a gentleman of great courage and charm."

"Miss Helen isn't listening to my outpourings or to yours, so close your mouth. Jack, dammit, get behind that bloody screen."

"All right," Jack said and moved another foot toward it.

They heard Arthur yelling just outside the bedchamber door, "Move aside, you big woman. I am here for Winifrede. Is she in here?

"No, don't even think to lie to me, I know she's in there. I saw my carriage. She tried to murder me. She actually kicked me out the open door of my moving carriage, then she stole my carriage and my horses and left me for dead. I've come to remove her. Give her to me now."

Helen turned back into the bedchamber at Gray's call. One very fair eyebrow was climbing upward. "What do you say, my lord?"

"I've never met Arthur, just heard of him. Do show him in, Miss Mayberry. This should prove a treat."

Arthur Kelburn, eldest son and heir of Lord Rye, ran into the room, then pulled up short at the sight of the young man in the bed and the small, older man hovering over him. It was Gray St. Cyre, Baron Cliffe, the bastard who planned to marry Winifrede and her groats. His chest was naked. What was going on here?

Yes, Arthur had seen the baron once outside of White's on St. James. How was it possible that he was here, and obviously the center of everyone's attention?

"Lord Cliffe," Arthur said, trying his best to stride manfully toward the bed, for the large blond woman was watching him, eyebrows raised. Then the large blond woman was directly in front of him. He shouted around her, "What the devil are you doing here? How could you possibly be here when my carriage is also here? Why the devil are you in bed, with this pathetic little bald man leaning over you?"

"Jack," Gray said, "you may come out now."

Jack peered around the end of the screen to see Arthur, red-faced and wet, standing toe to toe with Helen. Jack was quite sure that Arthur wouldn't go anywhere. Sure enough, he was carrying the burlap sack under his left arm, the bounder.

"There you are," Arthur yelled, waving his fist toward Jack. "Come out this minute. I will punish you with the sack. You deserve it."

"I've never before disciplined anyone with a sack," Helen said, stroking her chin thoughtfully. "I will observe to see what you have in mind."

Jack came out. Arthur nearly leapt at her. Helen said to Arthur with absolutely no inflection at all in her voice, "Move back right this instant or I will throw you out of that window."

"You're a female, you're—" Then Arthur, his survival instincts finally engaging, shut his mouth and took three quick steps back. He cleared his throat. He shoved the sack behind his back. He said, in a winsome voice, "Ah, there you are, Winifrede. Come, where's your cloak? We must leave now."

Jack could only stare at him. "Are you mad?"

"No, but if you don't obey me quickly, I just might become very angry indeed."

"I wouldn't go with you if you promised me my favorite sweetmeats."

He pulled out a gun and aimed it in her general direction. "You're stubborn. So be it. Come, Winifrede. Now. Oh, I understand what you meant. I believed you were calling me insane when you said 'mad,' but you weren't. I'm not as yet mad or angry with you. You are the mad one, what with kicking me out of my own carriage and then stealing the carriage and my horses."

Jack sat down on the floor, the old too-long gray gown spread out about her. "If you will just look toward the bed, Arthur, you will see Lord Cliffe, my betrothed, lying there. Unfortunately, I ran him down. If I hadn't escaped you, then he would have caught up with us quickly enough, and he would probably have wrung your miserable neck. All in all, you've been very lucky, more lucky than you deserve.

"Now, you will please leave. Go home. Tell my stepfather and your father that neither of them will get their hands on my dowry. All my groats will be in Gray's hands. Go away, Arthur."

"Yes," said Helen, "do go away. I would also recommend that you change out of those drenched clothes. I wouldn't want you to become ill."

"Change out of your wet clothes elsewhere, Arthur," Gray said. "Leave—now."

16

"No," Arthur howled. "It isn't fair. I need a new waistcoat, this one is nearly a year old. I loved it last year, but it's served its time and I need a new one."

"Ah, so your papa promised you clothes if you carted me off to Scotland?"

"Yes, and a handsome allowance. Come along, Winifrede. Get up. Just look at you. Your hair is straggling down around your face, you're wearing a wretched gown that makes you look bilious, and there's this woman here who's larger than I am and could probably snap my neck like a chicken's. She probably *could* toss me out of that window. Still, she's very pretty, and I fancy she would be very pleasant to have wrapped around a man on a cold night."

Dr. Brainard drew himself up and puffed out his meager chest. He waved a bottle of his own homemade dandelion restorative tonic at the young interloper. "You mind your manners, you coarse little puppy. Actually Helen could lie on you and suffocate you. She wouldn't need to exert herself at all."

Helen said, "Now, Ossie, the boy is merely upset and not thinking straight. Look to your patient and I'll look to the coarse little puppy."

Ossie dutifully looked at Gray, then said quickly, "Oh, goodness, my lord. Miss Helen is quite right. You're looking flushed. I beg you to lie still. Don't jump out of this bed, entirely unclothed, and strike this young man who's going to receive his just desserts any minute now from Miss Helen."

Gray's head felt as though it should be split open. The fact that it wasn't, the fact that he could actually see and hear everything that was going on, was heartening. He managed to stand, pulling the covers around him like a toga.

"You stole Jack from me?"

"Yes, of course," Arthur said. "She and I are going to marry. She sent me a note begging me to come take her away from your house on Portman Square. We were on our way to Scotland."

"Jack? Do you wish to marry this paltry fellow?"

"Goodness, no, Gray. He's a worthless sod, a wastrel, of no good to anyone I can think of. I think Helen should snap his neck or perhaps pound him into a pork kniver."

"Actually," Helen said, advancing on Arthur, "perhaps that might be a fine idea. You're boring me, sir. You are unduly exciting Dr. Brainard's patient. You insulted one of my maid's gowns that she very nicely loaned to Jack here."

"Stay back," Arthur said, waving the gun about. Then he looked crafty. "If you were dead, my lord, then there would be no one but me to marry Winifrede. That's her name, not Jack. That's the valet's name my father was yelling about."

"You'd hang for murder, you bonehead," Jack said. "Well, that's not true. I'd kill you myself before you were hauled to the gibbet. Give it up, Arthur. Go home."

Gray realized that if he didn't sit down he would collapse on the floor. The room was moving, and he knew he wasn't. Jack was on her feet then, running to him. How could she realize so quickly how he felt when he'd just realized it himself the instant before? "Please, Gray, you must lie down. You could be seriously hurt. Please."

Arthur grabbed her arm and jerked her back. Gray felt rage pour through him. He stepped around Jack, girded his toga, grabbed Arthur's other arm and yanked it up behind his back. Arthur screamed with the pain. The burlap sack fell to the floor. Jack kicked it away. Gray said in the most menacing voice Jack had ever heard from him, "Let her go, you idiot."

"No, she needs to obey me, she needs discipline—"

"Discipline, you say?" Dr. Brainard said, taking a step toward Arthur. "Now, Miss Helen here, she knows all about discipline. She's known to be exquisitely inventive."

"Let her go," Gray said again and tugged Arthur's arm up just a bit higher.

Arthur yelled again and let Jack go. This time she kicked Arthur's shin. He yelled again.

"Now, drop that nasty little gun," Gray said, not an inch from Arthur's nose, "before you shoot yourself in the foot or I stuff it down your throat."

"The gun or his foot?" Jack said.

"Be quiet, Jack."

"No, I—" Arthur screamed when Gray pulled his arm up higher behind him. "You're breaking my arm."

"It's all right. There's a doctor right here to bind you up. Drop the bloody gun."

Arthur dropped the gun. Jack quickly picked it up. Gray leaned close to Arthur's ear and whispered, "You've lost. Take your carriage and go home. If I see you again, I won't be pleased. Go away—now." Gray dropped his arm.

Arthur moaned and rubbed his arm. Helen said, "Why don't you come to the taproom with me, Arthur? I'll give you a nice mug of ale before you leave my inn, which shouldn't be more than ten minutes from now." She led Arthur Kelburn away, still moaning, still rubbing his arm, and said over her shoulder, "Ossie, see to it that his lordship is resting comfortably. Jack, you've got the gun. You can remain here and guard his lordship, just in case our Arthur here has cohorts."

"You mean like Lancelot?" Jack said.

They heard Arthur moaning his way down the hall, saying at every other step, "It just isn't fair. She would have begged me to marry her. All I needed was just a couple of days with her. I would have disciplined her and she would have loved it. My father taught me all about that, you know," and then he groaned again.

Ossie said, "I'll wager the puppy's father doesn't know any of the marvelous disciplines Miss Helen employs."

Gray, tucked back into bed, moaned and closed his eyes again. "Jack, your Lancelot comment was on the witty side. I can already see questions in your eyes—don't listen to any of this discipline talk, all right? Now, I really hadn't intended to spend the day before my marriage in this manner."

"Breathe deeply, my lord."

"Here's a scone for his lordship, from Miss Helen," said the maid Gwendolyn, who'd lent Jack the gown.

"Thank you," Gray said. "Give it to Jack and she will feed me."

"Your breathing is irregular, my lord. Perhaps if you chew on a bit of scone it will ease your choler."

* * *

Helen Mayberry sat in the chair that Ossie Brainard had pulled close to Gray's bed. Ossie sat at her feet on an old leather hassock. Jack was seated on the end of Gray's bed, her legs tucked beneath her.

As for Gray, he was propped up against three pillows, like a king, eating another scone, this one crammed with raisins.

"I see nothing for it, my lord," Helen said. "I believe if Ossie says you're fit enough, we should return you to London tomorrow morning. It is your wedding day."

Gray started to say that his head ached so badly a wedding day was the furthest thing from his mind, but he looked at Jack, who had the gun in her lap and looked pale and frightened. He said, "I don't have a carriage."

"I do," Helen said. "That's why I said that we should return you to London. I will accompany you. It's only an hour and a half away."

"Miss Helen's father is Viscount Prith," said Ossie. "We will borrow his carriage."

"We could," Helen said on a sigh, "but you know, Ossie, my father would demand to come with us." She said to Gray, "He loves to travel, even short distances. A trip to London would send him into raptures. He would also demand to come to the wedding. He attends every wedding not only here in Court Hammering but in all the surrounding counties. He married my dear mother three different times, when he was in a particularly romantic frame of mind. Thankfully, our vicar is a man of flexible bent."

Gray said to Jack, who was still looking blank-brained, "Jack and I should very much appreciate having you as our guests. It is to be a small wedding. It's possible that it will be even smaller if Douglas and Ryder Sherbrooke are still out chasing after you, Jack. Perhaps we'd best postpone the wedding until everything settles down, my head included."

"No," Jack said, so distressed that she nearly bounced herself off the bed. "Something else bad will happen if we don't get married. It's already started—my foot's asleep. Something else would happen, too. I just know it. My stepfather could kidnap Aunt Mathilda, not realizing that if she wished to she could orate him into the ground, then slit his throat. No, as long as you can stand upright, Gray, I should like to get it over with. Then you can go to bed for as long as you like."

"An offer a man can't refuse," Gray said to the bedchamber in general.

"Really, my lord," Ossie said, giving Helen an interested look, "there are ladies present."

"Not really," said Jack. "Until last week I was a valet and proud of it."

Douglas Sherbrooke stood beside Gray late the following Friday morning in the St. Cyre drawing room, having returned to London three hours before, just in time for an early breakfast. He'd had time to shave and change his clothes and rejoice that Jack was back where she belonged.

Bishop Langston, loose-limbed as a willow wand and endowed with a beautifully dark speaking voice, conducted the brief ceremony—so brief in fact, that Jack was married before she even realized her fate was sealed. "Jack, look up at me so I can give you a very modest kiss."

She knew his head still ached, but he was smiling down at her, and she thought he looked wonderful in his stark black formal garb and his white linen.

She closed her eyes and raised her face. She felt his fingertips touch her cheek, then cup her chin. He gave her a light, fleeting kiss, over before it began. But she found it very interesting, nonetheless. His fingers didn't immediately drop. She opened her eyes and looked up at the man she hadn't even known existed just three weeks before. Now he was her husband.

"How does your head feel?"

"Let's just not speak of that, Jack."

"Then I will tell you how very handsome you look."

"That's better."

"There's something different about you. About the way you're looking at me."

He could have told her that he was now seeing her through a husband's eyes, and that was a very different experience for him indeed. He was seeing her as a woman who would, this very evening, climb into his bed with him and Eleanor.

"You're very brave, Gray. Thank you."

His knuckles grazed her cheek. He said nothing. Bishop Langston cleared his throat, which brought some chuckles from behind them.

"Perhaps I'll become as romantic as Lord

Prith, and we'll get married several more times in the coming years."

"Perhaps at our next wedding I will have time to order a wedding gown."

If anyone believed that the pale yellow satin gown with its long, fitted sleeves and high-cut bodice wasn't suitable for a bride, no one remarked upon it. "Yes," Gray said, patted her cheek, then turned back to Bishop Langston. The bishop gave them a benign smile and nodded. "Now, my lord, my lady, I believe Quincy wishes to announce that an outstanding wedding breakfast awaits us in the dining room."

"With champagne," called out Lord Prith, Helen Mayberry's father. "Best thing about weddings—the champagne. Even when I don't know the bride and groom—as in this particular case—I always bring a bottle of excellent champagne to the festivities."

"I say," Aunt Mathilda, gowned in stark black, "that is an excellent course to adopt. Did you already give your bottle to Quincy?"

"You said an awful lot there, Aunt Mathilda," Jack said, watching Lord Prith eye Aunt Mathilda as he would a succulent pigeon. "I haven't ever drunk champagne."

"You won't drink too much," Gray said.

Before she could question this peremptory order, Mr. Harpole Genner was bowing deeply over her hand. "A lovely ring. Wasn't it your mother's, Gray?"

"No," Gray said. "It was my grand-mother's."

Mr. Genner said, "This is a very happy occasion, my lady. It is such a pity that Lord Burleigh is still too ill to attend. Ah, perhaps he will awaken soon. Yes, he will be de-lighted to hear of his ward and his godson becoming man and wife."

"There is no word yet if his lordship will survive his illness?" Gray asked.

Mr. Genner shook his head. "I visited just yesterday and his butler, Snell, told me his lordship still lies on his back, eyes closed, occasionally snoring—which is odd, his phy-sician says—with Lady Burleigh holding his hand and speaking to him as if he were there and listening, even interested. Snell also said that his lordship's color was better and that his whiskers were growing at a fine clip, which, Snell told me, gave the physi-cian reason for guarded optimism.

"At least they've gotten rid of the noxious sunlight from Charles's bedchamber. You recall how he much prefers the shadows."

"I do, indeed," Gray said.

"Charles will pull through, my boy. Now, I wish to speak to Lord Prith. Haven't seen Harry since Trafalgar. A sad day that was when we got the news of Nelson's death. I remember Harry fancied himself in love with Emma Hamilton once, a very long time ago. Odd how everything works out, isn't it?

"That daughter of his, Helen, what a splendid specimen of womanhood. She stands so many inches from the floor, yet it inspires a man to worship, not to fear. I must meet her. Is it true that she owns an inn?"

"Yes, indeed," Jack said. "It's called King Edward's Lamp."

"You wonder where that name springs from, Mr. Genner?" Helen said, resplendent in pale green silk, her magnificent hair piled atop her head.

"Yes, Miss Mayberry, I was wondering exactly that."

Lord Prith, taller by a half a head than his lofty daughter, boomed out from behind her, "The story goes that King Edward brought a very special lamp with him back from his crusade in the Holy Land. It's said to be encrusted with precious stones—diamonds, sapphires, rubies, and such. It has mysteries surrounding it; it supposedly has magical sorts of powers. Tales hint at supernatural sorts of things, like making men disappear, striking down enemies with a single thought, changing light into darkness, things like that.

"My girl here fancies finding it. She'd rather have the lamp than a husband. The good Lord knows, I've presented her with dozens of suitors over the years, but she just looks them up and down—usually down since it's the short gentlemen who normally swarm about her—and turns them out."

Douglas Sherbrooke, who had met Lord Prith when he was twenty years old and newly unleashed on London society, shook the older man's hand. "And Helen," he said, turning to the woman who stood exactly at eye level with him. "I read somewhere about King Edward's lamp. I'm sorry to say that the author believed the lamp to be a fabrication, a fanciful myth that just happened to survive into our time."

"Douglas," Helen said. "It's a relief to see that you've not grown shorter in your advancing years." Then she punched him lightly in the arm saying to Jack as she did it, "I was once desperately in love with Douglas. He was just turned twenty, and I was all of fourteen or fifteen. He would have patted me on the head like a bothersome little sister if I hadn't been the same height as he."

Douglas laughed. "You're right, Helen. I was hard-pressed to know what to do with this beautiful young girl who stared me square in the eye. Now, we must spend our time with Gray and Jack, then let's adjourn to the dining room and stuff food down our gullets. When Gray and Jack won't wish to be bothered by any of us later, we can have a long talk."

"Where's the champagne?" Lord Prith bellowed.

"Of course we'll want you to bother us," Jack said. "You're our guests."

"No, Jack," Aunt Mathilda said.

"What Mathilda would say if she'd wanted to enlarge upon her words is—"

"It's all right, Aunt Maude," Gray said. "I fancy most everyone understands the underlying wit at work here."

Actually, every gentleman in the circle was simply staring at Jack as if she were an idiot.

Helen just laughed and patted her hand. "We will see, Jack. We will see."

*   *   *

Just ten minutes before the newly married Lord and Lady Cliffe left the St. Cyre town house, Ryder Sherbrooke, clothes askew, hair windblown, strode into the entrance hall, saw that he'd missed the wedding, howled one mournful note, then kissed Jack and said, "Gray, you will give me just a moment."

Gray didn't have a chance to thank Ryder for all his trouble. Ryder immediately said, "Remember I told you I would have just one piece of advice for you?"

Gray blinked, then said, "Yes, I remember. You rode like a demon to get here in time to give me this advice?"

"It's important, Gray. Now, listen."

17

The St. Cyre carriage was well sprung, the carriage rugs soft and warm. A light gray rain tapped gently on the roof. The sway of the carriage was mesmerizing.

"I feel quite stupid," Jack said, leaning her head back against Gray's shoulder and closing her eyes. "I wish you would tell me what I didn't understand."

Gray, whose headache had finally subsided to a dull throb, was thinking about what Ryder had told him. "You married me. That wasn't stupid."

"No, what I said to Helen, telling her we wished to stay with our guests."

"Oh, yes, surrounded by our friends well into our wedding night. Everyone was amused. Even Douglas gave me this pat on the shoulder, grinning like a dog."

"But I still don't understand why—"

"I have a favor to beg of you, Jack."

He felt her cheek against his shoulder, felt her turn her face into his shoulder and kiss him.

"Um, the favor is that I don't wish to speak of this until tomorrow morning."

She gave him one more kiss, then leaned back. "Why?"

"Because between now and tomorrow morning, you are going to become a very well-educated woman. You will come to fully understand concepts that before were mere cloudy ideas swirling about in the ether. You will see with unusual clarity why no one would have expected the two of us to remain with them for more than one single champagne toast."

"Now," Jack said, very firmly. "I want you to educate me now."

Even the dull throbbing in his head was miraculously gone. He felt strong, powerful, so manly that his chest expanded. As for his body, he was quite ready to consummate his marriage in the next ten seconds.

"We're in a carriage. A man doesn't do educating in a moving carriage, at least not the very first day he's married. It wouldn't be well done of him."

She straightened up and kissed his neck. "I like the way the carriage is rocking back and forth." She lightly touched her fingertips to his chin, slowly bringing his face around to hers. "Why not? I think anything you do would be well done. My father always believed that education was an important endeavor."

He grabbed her hand and brought it down to his lap. No, that was far too close to the center of his attention. No sense in terrifying her. He quickly set her hand on his leg, near his knee.

"Jack," he said, looking at those tender little ears of hers, wondering what it would be like to nibble on them, just a bit, "you're a virgin. You don't know about things yet. When I'm ready to teach you, we will do it right. In a nice soft bed. In the very best bed-chamber at the Swan's Neck."

"Why?" She turned her hand palm down onto his thigh. He looked at her gloved hand, surely too far up his leg, inching upward more, her fingers now curving inward, not six inches from his groin. He pictured the glove off that hand of hers and the hand, all white and soft, lightly touching his flesh, since his clothes were miraculously gone, caressing him, and he nearly flung her onto her back on the carriage seat.

"No," he said chanting a litany. "No. I'm a man, not a randy boy so filled with lust that I'll stutter myself off a cliff if I can't gently lift you onto that other seat, gently pull up your gown, and gently come over you, all with a froth of petticoats. Yes, naturally I want to do it right now, right this minute, but as I said earlier, I'm a man, a controlled man who knows what he's about." He fell into brooding silence. He desperately wanted to make love to her right now. He couldn't think of a single thing more important than making love to her right now. Who cared about a soft bed? What did it matter in the scheme of things?

Odd how a man's brain worked, he thought, trying to get something in his head except lust. He lifted her onto his lap. "I've decided halfway measures won't be all that bad. Lie back against my arm. I want to look at you."

She stretched back against his arm, all boneless, trusting, innocent—his wife. He felt immense guilt for perhaps a single second.

He unfastened the bow beneath her chin and lifted off her bonnet. He saw the innocence and wickedness in her eyes and laughed. "You've got me in a bad way here, Jack. What am I to do?"

"You're to get out of that bad way, Gray."

"You have no idea what you're talking about. Be still. Ah, damnation." He leaned down and kissed her mouth, warm and soft, that mouth of hers. He felt her hand stroke his cheek. He reached up and unbuttoned the glove and pulled it off. He sighed deeply at the touch of her naked fingers against his flesh.

"Open your mouth, Jack. Yes, that's it. Not quite so wide or I'll fall in. Yes, just tease me." It was too good. He wanted more. Actually he wanted everything and he wanted it all at once. He raised his head and chanted again, "I'm a man. I'm a man who isn't a clod. My heart's pounding louder than a drum in the middle of a battle." He was amazed at how she was making him feel. He pressed his forehead against hers. "How can you, just a little slip of a girl, make me feel like I'm going to explode if I don't dive my hands under your petticoats right this minute?"

"Your hands can dive," she said. "Aunt Maude told me I was to be obedient to your wishes as soon as we were married."

His laugh was on the painful side, but he didn't really heed it because he was kissing her again.

"Gray," she said into his mouth when his hand lightly caressed her breast. "Gray?"

Just the sound of her saying his name was more than enough to make a sane man dive over the waterfall. He didn't want to rip her gown, but the buttons fought him, making his fingers trip over them, and finally, he simply jerked the fabric apart. Then he saw her chemise, another barrier that was all lacy and soft, and he couldn't bear it. He cursed, then ripped.

When her breasts were bare, he saw that she was staring up at him, her face a bit on the pale side, set in petrified lines. "No," he said. "Don't be embarrassed or afraid of me, Jack. I've seen your breasts, don't you remember? I saw them at great length, four days of great length. I saw them so much that I grew jaded. I remember turning away once to look at my dinner plate, at the mess of potatoes in the center of the plate.

"It's true that I looked at your breasts again as I was eating my potatoes, but I remember thinking food thoughts, like wondering if your breasts would taste as good as the potatoes. No, I don't suppose it was necessary to tell you that at this point in time. Don't panic on me, Jack."

"I won't panic. I was sick then. You had no choice but to look at me."

"And now you're my wife. I still have to look at you."

Then he touched her. Even as he closed his hand around her, he leaned down and began kissing her again. He said into her mouth, "Do you have any notion of how you feel to me?"

She squirmed on his lap, and he knew it was all over for him. "No, don't move. I'm very serious about this, Jack. That's right, don't even breathe. Now, let me look at you and touch you and you don't do a single thing, particularly move." She didn't move, just lay there looking up at him. He managed to find a smile for her, but it hurt, really hurt just to make his mouth move like that. He wanted his mouth on her breast. But not yet. He couldn't. If he did, he wouldn't be able to stop himself. Why was she making him feel so utterly out of control?

"A puzzle," he said. "This is all a puzzle. Tell me, Jack, when I touch you, like this"— he lightly laid his hand over her right breast—"when I just stroke my fingers over you, what does it make you feel?"

How to tell him that she wanted to rub herself against his palm? That she felt like someone had lit a fire in her belly and the warmth of that fire was spreading outward, making her tingle and ache and feel terribly urgent. She said, "I read a book. I saw several drawings. I want you to do those things to me right now. I don't want a nice soft bed. I don't understand how this will work, but you do. You've had nearly eight more years than I to practice and learn. Just do it, Gray. Please."

He shuddered like a palsied man. He cursed even as he lifted her up, facing him. He untangled her braids with his fingers, loosing her hair over her shoulders. He pulled the gown and chemise to her waist.

Then he stopped. He took a very deep breath. "What book did you see? Don't tell me you found this book in my library?"

"No. Aunt Mathilda gave it to me. She said she'd found it at Hookham's, back in a dark corner, where a clerk whispered prurient material was hidden. She said she wasn't up to explaining marital concepts to me, so I was to acquaint myself with the basic sorts of things. It all sounded impossible. And those pictures, surely they simply couldn't be right."

"Tell me about the pictures."

She was sitting on his lap, naked to the waist, his hands on her hips, and he was looking at her, just looking, nothing else, and waiting to hear about those pictures. "A man was leaning over a woman and he was licking her stomach, Gray—at least that's what it looked like. Isn't that silly?"

God in heaven, he was going to expire. "Close to unimaginable."

"Then there was a naked man and a naked woman, really close together. Actually, she had her legs wrapped around his waist. His hands were holding her against him and he was dancing around the room."

"We'll do that next Tuesday," he said. "Jack, don't you have the basic idea yet?"

"Yes," she said. "I have an excellent idea." She pulled away from him to sit on the other seat. She leaned toward him, those breasts of hers right there for his mouth, his hands, and pulled off her other glove. Then, smiling at him, she lightly laid her hands on him.

He jumped, then moaned. She pulled her hands back. "I'm sorry, Gray. Did that hurt you? I can't imagine why it would. I didn't pull or jerk you or anything."

It was then that he realized he simply couldn't wait for that very soft feather mattress at the Swan's Neck that Douglas had told him about, that particular bed in the third-floor corner bedchamber that Douglas had said Alexandra had adored to the soles of her arched feet.

"Dammit, it's still our wedding day. It's not even our wedding night yet. The sun's still out. I'm going to die. I'm going to educate you right now, Jack, all right?"

She nodded slowly, her eyes on his groin.

He was on her immediately, jerking her gown up, tangling his hands in her petticoats, trying to ease her garters and stockings down, all at the same time. He stopped, pulling himself back. "No," he said. "I can do this. I can even manage to do this with a modicum of self-control and finesse. I am not a pathetic excuse of a man who is so selfish he doesn't care if the woman is awake or asleep or simply a piece of fruit."

"In all the pictures both the man and the woman were naked," Jack said. Without another word, she began pulling up her gown.

He looked until he couldn't bear it. It was the stretch of stocking-covered leg that finally got to him. "No," he said, pulling her hands away from her garter, "this isn't the way it should be done. Jack, I want you to come back onto my lap and kiss me. Then we'll see."

She sat on his legs, her own legs apart, facing him. "One of the drawings was like this," she said. "Except the man and woman didn't have any clothes on. I think I could come to like this." She grabbed his face between her hands and leaned forward to kiss him.

Laughter helped, but not much.

He brought her tightly against him, kissing her ear, her jaw, his hands wild on her back, then beneath her gown, and he felt her hips. He froze.

She moved and he simply couldn't take it. He grabbed her leg and said against her neck, "Open your legs wider, Jack. Then push yourself against me as hard as you can."

He hadn't imagined how that would feel if she did it. His hands came from her hips around to her belly. He felt her suck in her breath. "No, no," he whispered. "It's all right. I've seen all of you, your belly included. It's a nice white belly. Just like your bottom is nice and white, and I've seen it too. Remember when you were leaning out the window at the inn? Well, I was behind you, enjoying the back of you. We'll talk about your legs later, and your feet, remind me not to forget your feet. Nice feet as well, but that's not what's important right this moment. That's right, Jack, just lay your face against my shoulder and let me feel you. No, ease back down and let me hold you on my hands. Ah, try to relax, but don't go to sleep, all right?" His breath hitched. His fingers eased inward to touch her.

She jumped, pulling back. "Gray? I'm feeling rather strange." He was but a layer of wool away from her.

"You don't know the half of it," he said. He unfastened his breeches, eased her open with his fingers, and came into her.

She was staring down but couldn't see him for the froth of her petticoats. But she felt him, oh, dear, did she feel him. "Oh, my goodness, can you really do that? I don't know, Gray. No, stop."

He stopped and she froze. Still he came deeper because she was damp and her body wanted him deeper. He said against her mouth, "It's all right, Jack. No, don't move. Let's just stay like this for a moment. My sex is inside you, just a little way inside you. Can you feel me? It isn't so bad, is it?"

She shook her head against his shoulder. "I don't know. It's the strangest thing I've ever felt in my life." He pushed her just a bit further onto him. She moved. "No, don't, Jack. When you do that it makes me explode. Trust me on this. I don't want to explode just yet."

"We can't dance," she said against his chin.

He laughed and pushed her forward just

a bit more. "That's for next Tuesday. Lie back against my hands."

She slowly leaned back, supported by his hands. Her hands fluttered around his arms. "You're inside me," she said. "I never imagined another person hooking up to me like this."

He stared at the mouth that had said those words and wondered how he could possibly survive much more of this. He eased her forward, bringing himself deeper, and felt her maidenhead.

He closed his eyes. Naturally she had to have a maidenhead, all girls did. "Don't move. Don't do anything. I'm praying for fortitude. I'm a good man. I deserve fortitude so I will remain a good man. I don't want to degenerate into a clod. A man who's a clod doesn't deserve much of anything. We're going to go slowly here. Tell me I'm going slowly enough for you, Jack."

"Since you're not moving, I suppose it's slow, but it hurts, Gray, sort of burns and pulls and feels raw. Does it burn you as well?"

"Oh, yes," he said. "Oh, yes." He brought her up again until she was tight against his chest. He was holding her up with his hands,

controlling his depth. When she was positioned just right, he let himself push upward
with all his strength.

Jack yelled, then her voice broke into
sobs. She hit him with her fists, and even
damned him once, twice.

As for Gray, he was beyond thought, beyond anything but finishing this business.
And he did. He was deep inside her,
breathing so hard he thought his heart
would burst. When finally he was through
jerking about and heaving like a palsied
man, he managed to say in a voice so dark
and harsh that he hardly recognized himself,
"It's over, Jack, all over. Are you all right? It
doesn't hurt so much now, does it?"

She didn't say a word.

He stroked her back, closing his eyes at
the feel of that soft white flesh, all his. He
was deep inside her, and he knew the pain
he'd dealt her had to lessen soon. He wasn't
about to leave her, not just yet. He would let
her get used to him. Yes, that was a noble
approach, and practical as well.

Within minutes, though, all nobility had
fled the carriage. He was hard inside her
again and she pulled back to look at him.
"Gray, what are you doing? I can feel the

change in you. At least we're all wet so it doesn't hurt so bad anymore, but—"

There was a shot. Then another. Leonard, the St. Cyre coachman, shouted and cursed, then pulled up the horses, making the carriage lurch wildly.

He was deep inside her. There was simply no time. Nor was there a gun inside the carriage. Robbers? During the day? On his damned wedding day?

He pulled the bodice of her gown back up. She held the front together with both hands.

When Arthur and an older man jockeyed with each other to peer into the carriage, Jack was seated on him and he was still deep inside her, her skirts and petticoats frothing all over them.

Arthur didn't understand.

The older man understood very well, and he yowled. "No, I don't believe this. You're a bloody gentleman, yet look what you've done to her. Here, in your carriage. Are you witless? I don't believe this. Hell and damnation. Arthur, get on your horse. There's nothing for it now. Even if we shoot him, it wouldn't matter. He's had her. She could have his child in her womb even now." He cursed some more, turned and slapped Arthur, then strode away to the horses.

Arthur shouted after him, "But she probably isn't with child. Let's take her. She'll have to marry me."

"You bloody fool, her virginity was your only leverage. You have no leverage now."

They sat very still, listening to the older man yell at Arthur.

"That," Jack said, "is Lord Rye." She squirmed on him.

"Yes," Gray said, grinding his teeth at the feel of her. Unbelievingly, he was still hard, still very deep inside her, and getting harder. But he managed not to move until he heard Leonard yell, "My lord, shall we proceed?"

"Onward, Leo, onward."

"Yes, my lord."

Gray took Jack's face between his hands, pulled her forward, and kissed her hard. Between kisses, he said, "For a wedding day, dearest, I believe we would capture all prizes for achieving the outrageous and the unexpected."

"You're still inside me, Gray. It doesn't hurt so much now. How did Lord Rye know that you were inside me? My clothes are covering both of us."

He laughed—what else was a man tottering on the edge of sanity to do? He wanted to tell her that Lord Rye might be a very bad man, but he wasn't an idiot. He felt her tight around him, felt the weight of her. He closed his eyes. He went deeper, not able to make sense of her words when she told him to stop this instant, when she yelled in his face that she didn't want him to do this anymore, that she liked the drawings in the book, but this wasn't at all fun.

"Stop!"

But he didn't stop, he simply couldn't. His fingers found her but he realized that it was much too late, for either of them. He heaved and shouted in ecstasy. Jack yelled in his face and bit his neck.

18

Jack stared down at herself, utterly appalled, once she got over the urge to yell that she was bleeding to death. Thank God she wasn't still bleeding; she would be all right, wouldn't she? She wasn't going to die. But what about the next time?

No, that was ridiculous. This sex business wouldn't have continued very long if it ended with the woman bleeding to death. Surely that would get out and other women would find out and run. They would also quickly learn how to use swords and guns to keep the men away.

Still, it was dreadful all the same. Now that

she knew she'd live, she shuddered, embarrassment seeping to her bones. He'd done this to her. He'd even looked at her while he was shoving inside her, making her bleed. He must have known what he was doing, what would happen when he'd finished. When Gray came around the screen a few moments later, she yelped like a wounded cat and grabbed up her wrinkled gown in front of her.

He saw the blood on her legs before she managed to hide behind that gown. Surely she knew about a virgin bleeding? He looked at her face and realized she was as ignorant as she was mortified.

"Well, hell," he said, instantly raising his hand. "I know, turnips. But believe me, a mild curse is appropriate in this instance." She'd bled. He'd been a clod—more than a clod, a careless bastard who should be shot. At least now maybe he could ease her through this. He saw the shine in her eyes and knew she was close to tears.

"You could have killed me."

As matter-of-fact as would a parent to a three-year-old child, he said, "No, Jack, sex isn't a killing business. Virgins bleed the first time. It's natural. It looks as if you're more virginal than most virgins. No, don't feel like you should cover yourself. We're married. I'm your husband. You're a mess. Let me help you get cleaned up." He held out his hand. "I'm really sorry, Jack. I will make it up to you, I promise. Next time—"

"Next time? Do you believe me a perfect dolt?" She stared at his hand as if it were a snake to bite her. "Go away. You did this to me. Go away."

His bride of less than half a day was clearly perturbed. Perhaps she was even beyond perturbed, perhaps close to violence. She did rather look like she would enjoy bashing him with a log, or worse. He was relieved she didn't have a knife close by.

Taking his life in his hands, he said, "I didn't know you could make your breasts blush."

She looked down at herself, blanched, grabbed her slipper off the rug, and hurled it at him.

He just laughed, grabbed her arms, and hauled her over to that big bed, the one Douglas had raved about, and shoved her down. He let her keep her gown as cover.

"Don't move," he said over his shoulder. "I'm going to clean you up. No, Jack, don't go all maidenly on me and squeak. I cleaned you up for four days. I cleaned you up until I could have done it blindfolded." As he spoke, he turned away to pour some warm water into a basin, float a bar of jasmine soap, and grab a soft cloth. When he was finished, he turned back to the bed.

Jack was gone.

His first insane thought was that Lord Rye had changed his mind and somehow slipped into the bedchamber and snagged her. But no, that was surely impossible. He'd locked the door when they'd finally got to the bedchamber. He was losing his wits.

"Jack?"

Not a hint of a sound.

He found her one minute later, under the bed.

Fifteen minutes later she still wouldn't look at him. She was, he believed, currently studying the intricate embroidery on the soft green counterpane.

"Enough is enough, Jack. As I told you, the bleeding is natural. It's nothing either to alarm you or embarrass you. It won't ever happen again. I told you I was sorry. You're being a twit. Stop it."

At least she was finally clean—thanks to

him; wearing her nightgown—thanks to him; and draped over with a lovely pale peach peignoir—yet again thanks to him. He sighed. He didn't think she was on the verge of thanking him for his kind attention.

"We will dine here, if it pleases you."

"It's still daylight, and I'm in my nightgown like an invalid. It's not right."

"If you would like to dress, we could stroll about the town."

"On the other hand, it will be dark very soon now."

"Yes, and there's only to be a quarter moon tonight. We wouldn't see much of the town and its surrounding scenery with such a small moon."

"A well-made point. After all, this is a lovely room."

"Yes, Douglas told me Alexandra particularly admired that bed."

At last that got her attention. She looked away from the embroidery and up at him. "You embarrassed me, Gray. You made me lie here on my back and you made me open my legs. Then you looked at me and wiped me down, like a horse."

He raked his hand through his hair. "I had to clean you up, Jack. I didn't mean to embarrass you. I'm sorry. It's just that I wanted to make sure I hadn't hurt you, ripped you or something. I've heard that sometimes happens."

"If you did rip me, then it's really bad, Gray. I hurt all the way to my stomach."

She was utterly serious. She was actually rubbing her belly. He laughed. He thought of Ryder Sherbrooke's secret to a successful marriage and laughed—until he felt her hairbrush strike his chest. He picked it up off the soft woven carpet at his feet and placed it on the dressing table.

He walked to the bed, gathered her stiff body up against him, and said against her pursed lips, "I promise our next time together you won't be seated on my lap in a lurching carriage. I'm sorry, Jack, it wasn't well done of me. As a matter of fact, it was exceedingly badly done of me. I lost my wits." He leaned back and studied her face. "You know, if you weren't so beautiful, so utterly delicious, I would have been able to exercise nobility."

"I'm not beautiful. I'm about as delicious as a green strawberry. You're just saying that because you feel guilty. And how like a man—you're trying to make it my fault, though I was but an innocent bystander."

"You're right. But you weren't exactly by-standing at the time. It makes me feel even guiltier that I feel so marvelous myself, all sated and manly and satisfied with life. Men are very straightforward creatures. It be-hooves us to remember that women are del-icate and easily shocked, and ever so tight inside."

She pulled back in his arms and stared at him as if mesmerized. "Goodness, you re-ally did say that, didn't you?"

"Yes," he said and kissed her, "I did. Ah, here comes our dinner. I ordered it and for-got. If you like, you can test me. Shall we bare your breasts and see if I can pay more attention to my meal than to you?"

"No, not yet. Listen, Gray, it isn't fair that you feel guilty, even though your reasons for feeling guilty are remarkably self-serving. No, I wanted you to do what you did to me in the carriage, I really did. I wanted to know what it was all about. Those drawings were so exciting, but I just didn't know it would be the way it turned out to be."

"You mean hurtful, messy, and not any fun at all?"

"I fear so, yes."

"Lovemaking is always messy. It should also be a lot of fun. Next time it will be, I promise you. And since you're no longer a virgin, it won't hurt anymore."

He started laughing again. He pressed his face against her hair and nearly swallowed his tongue, he was laughing so hard. "Oh, God, it's something to tell our grandchildren. Grandmama was hiding from Grandpa under the bed, all wrapped up like a mummy. Will they believe it?"

He still had a silly smile on his face when the innkeeper, Mrs. Hardley, came into the bedchamber, beaming at the newlyweds and carrying their dinner of roast duck, ivory peas, carrot puffs, and Monmouth pudding layered with raspberry jam, all on a huge silver tray crowned by a silver dome.

"Now, my dears," she said, "we must keep up your strength."

"Jack?"

"I'm asleep."

"Your stomach doesn't still hurt, does it?"

"No, I'm just very sore in places I didn't know could become sore."

"That's a good thing. No, don't breathe

fire on me. I'm chastened. I'm not going to leap on you. I want to talk to you about something else. I've been thinking about your little sister. I'm wondering how we can get her away from your stepfather."

He felt the bed give as she turned to face him. "You really want to have Georgie with us? Truly, Gray?"

"Yes," he said, turning on his side. "I want her with us."

"You're not just saying this because you still feel so guilty about hurting me even though I finally granted you absolution?"

"No. The fact is, I know you'll worry until we have her safe with us. You'll fret. You might worry so much that you'll never let me near you again. I'm not cut out to be celibate, Jack."

"I was celibate until this afternoon. All in all, it was preferable to all this."

"You were supposed to be celibate. You will look back on what you just said—not more than eight hours from now—and laugh at your foolishness. Now, back to your sister. What do you think?"

He could practically see her brain squirreling from one idea to another. Jack was smart—unless she lost all sense and crawled under the bed. He nearly laughed aloud again.

"My stepfather wouldn't ever let her go if he believed for a minute that we actually wanted her. He'll want revenge now, he's just that way. He'll use anything at all if he believes it will hurt us."

"Yes," he said, wrapping a handful of her hair slowly around his hand. "I think you're right. He mustn't know that we want her." He dropped her hair, turned onto his back again, and crossed his arms behind his head. "A puzzle to tease me, when you're tired of teasing me yourself."

"Will you teach me how to tease you?"

He stilled. His body reacted predictably. He breathed out slow and deep. "Naturally. You have but to tell me when to commence your lessons." He turned again to face her. He reached out his hand and stroked her hair. He could feel her warm breath, she was so close. He wanted her very much but had enough sense not to hurl himself on her.

"When will I stop hurting?"

He knew her flesh was chafed. "By morning," he said, cupping her face in his hand. "No later than by tomorrow morning. No more than eight hours from now. Go to sleep. We'll figure out what to do about Georgie."

When Jack awoke, pale dawn light was coming in the tall, narrow windows. She was warm, utterly relaxed. She was also lying on top of Gray, her face tucked against his neck.

Oh, dear, she thought. Would he think she was teasing him? Was this teasing him? Very carefully, she began pulling up her nightgown. He remained asleep, snoring lightly. She kept pulling up her nightgown. Her legs were bare against his. She couldn't believe the heat of him. When she finally had it up past her chest, every marvelous bit of him pressed against her, she whispered against his neck, between kisses, "Well, it's morning. At least eight hours, and a very bright morning it is."

"Good," he said with no hesitation at all, making her wonder if he'd really been asleep, and rolled over on top of her. "Now let me show you what this lovemaking business is all about, the right way."

Mrs. Hardley just smiled when she passed the earl of Northcliffe's favorite bedchamber and heard sweet, very excited female laughter coming from within. And a man's low voice, very deep and urgent. That bed was magic, her granny had told her some thirty years before. "Magic, that tester," Granny had said. It produced more babes than the entire village of Sudburn.

She was still smiling when she saw her son racing down the corridor toward her, yelling, "Ma, a messenger brought this for Lord Cliffe. He said it was real important."

Jack was kissing his neck when there was a loud knock on the bedchamber door. Mrs. Hardley called out, "Forgive me, my lord, but there's an urgent message just arrived for you."

Gray slowly raised himself onto his elbows. He was within three seconds of kissing her breasts. He felt every inch of her beneath him. He shook his head to clear it. He was not many seconds from doing other things even more far-reaching. He shuddered, pressing himself down against her, wanting to cry, when Mrs. Hardley shouted again, "My lord, please, the message."

"I'm sorry, Jack," he said as he lifted himself off her. "Believe me, I'm really sorry."

"Oh, dear, what message? What's going on?"

* * *

"She could be dead, Gray. Oh, God. The messenger went first to your town house in London, then came here. At least a day was lost."

Jack was hanging on by a thread. He knew it, but he didn't know what to do about it. He raised her hand and lightly rubbed her palm against his cheek. "It's possible, but it won't help to dwell on it. You're the most optimistic person I've ever met, Jack. Don't turn into a doomsayer now."

"She's so little, Gray, so very little. There's no one at Carlisle Manor for her, no one at all. She has Dolly, who's been her nanny since Georgie was born, and the other servants who care for her, but no one who really loves her. Thank God my stepfather even bothered to tell me. I wonder why he did."

"He did it to torment you." He gathered her against him, kissing her hair. "We'll be at Carlisle Manor by this afternoon. Then we'll see."

"He ignores her, Gray. I swear he doesn't even know she's there in his house."

The carriage was moving slowly along Church Street, past the grand clock tower, straight down West Street to Kings Road and the pier. It was a beautiful sunny day in Brighton. The smell of the sea was sharp and exhilarating, the breeze off the water billowing up a lady's skirts as she walked with her children along the pier.

"My father brought me to Brighton when I was ten," Jack said. "He said the Prince had just had the Pavilion interiors decorated in the Chinese style."

Gray rolled his eyes. "My father cursed every time anyone mentioned the Pavilion. He said the cost would eventually drive England into the sea."

"I should love to visit it."

He shaded his eyes to look out over the channel. There were at least a dozen ships coming toward land. "We will. It's enchanting. The Prince always serves such splendid banquets that you leave the table with your stomach bulging."

He stopped cold. She was crying, silently, the tears gathering and just rolling down her cheeks.

19

"It's all right," he said against her ear. "It will be all right." He thought of the message on that damnable piece of foolscap he'd so hurriedly unfolded: *Your sister is very ill. If you want to see her before she dies, you'd best come immediately. HWS.*

What was one to make of that? He closed his eyes and leaned his head back against the comfortable squabs. He held her until it began raining. She straightened, looking out the window. "Perhaps he lied."

"Yes," he said, "that's possible, given the few times I've met your stepfather. Remember you said that he'd do anything against us now, for revenge. Calm yourself. Relax against me, Jack. I like the feel of you."

They arrived at Carlisle Manor late that afternoon. Sir Henry was riding with Mrs. Finch, they were informed by Darnley, the hollow-checked butler who'd taught Jack how to polish the silver fourteen years before.

Jack grabbed his sleeve. "My sister, Darnley. How is Georgie? Please, she's still alive, isn't she?"

The old man looked surprised. "Of course your sister is all right," he said. "She's ill, that's true, but it isn't grave. At least Dr. Brace hasn't indicated that it's grave. He worried a bit that the cold could go to her lungs, but that hasn't happened." He paused a moment, then his face spasmed. "Oh, dear, is this why you've come in the middle of the day without warning? You believed Miss Georgie to be deathly ill?"

"That was the letter my stepfather sent us, Darnley. He said she was dying."

"No, no, Sir Henry mistook the matter. He must not have listened carefully to Dr. Brace. However, she is ill enough that Mrs. Smithers is with her now, as well as her nanny, Dolly. I'm dreadfully sorry you've been so worried, Miss Winifrede."

She looked ready to crumble. Then, just as quickly, she looked ready to kill. She said to Gray, "He did lie, for revenge. I'm going up to see her now."

Gray watched her gather herself together, stiffen her spine, and walk up the wide staircase. Halfway up, she turned to look at him. "Gray, I'll be back in a while."

"Do you want me with you?"

"No. If you would see Sir Henry when he returns. I really can't face him just yet."

"Don't worry, Jack. It would be my pleasure."

"Don't kill him, Gray, unless you're very certain you won't hang for it."

"I will consider all consequences before I act, Jack."

"My lord, I'm very sorry about this news Sir Henry sent you. I'm certain Sir Henry labored long over whether to interrupt your wedding trip with Miss Winifrede—or rather, her ladyship. Lady Cliffe. What a pleasant ring that has to it. None of us ever wanted her to be Lady Rye. It is not a pleasing thought. Ah, but Lady Cliffe, and you a pleasant young man who doubtless has a blameless reputation, despite the things Sir Henry was yelling about you. It is a pity Sir Henry interrupted your sweet time together for no reason."

Gray merely nodded and followed Darnley into the long, narrow drawing room, quite a charming room, with floor-to-ceiling windows at the southern end. It was a lovely prospect outside, an expanse of finely scythed lawn blending into a maple forest.

"Will you and Miss Winifrede be staying at Carlisle Manor, my lord?"

Gray hadn't even thought about that. What else should he be doing? "Yes, if Sir Henry doesn't object, which he might, I suppose."

"I will take your valises to the Oak Room," Darnley said. "I don't imagine that Miss Winifrede would like to stay in her former bedchamber."

"Why not?"

"Sir Henry tied her to a chair in the middle of that bedchamber and left her there for three days. She escaped by tying her bedding together. We were all quite pleased with her ingenuity. Now, my lord, I will see it done immediately. Then there will be no question. I will inform Mr. Potts that there will be two more to dinner." He added, more to himself than to Gray, "I must remember not to speak of Sir Henry in such a manner as to make one believe me unapproving of his actions."

"Thank you, Darnley."

When Darnley returned, Gray asked, "Oh, yes—who is Mrs. Finch?"

"She," Darnley said, drawing himself up, "is a widow who recently bought the Cit Palace over in the village of Brimerstock."

"Cit Palace?"

"I believe it is still called Curdlow Place by folk who are steeped in its local history and regard the past twenty years as the present and not at all history. However, since your lordship has your left eyebrow raised in further question, I would add that an ironmonger named Greeley from Newcastle bought it some twenty years ago and moved in his family, which consisted of thirteen children, all of them ill-bred boy louts and muffin-faced girl chits. Iron seemed to fall into decline and Mr. Greeley was forced to sell to Mrs. Finch. I would have to say that the lady is an improvement."

Although he didn't want to say it, Gray thought, wondering about Mrs. Finch. Darnley paused, hearing his master's voice from the entrance hall. "Excuse me, my lord. I believe Sir Henry and Mrs. Finch have returned. Please, wait here."

While Gray waited, he reviewed a possible course of action—a fist straight to Sir Henry's jaw, a knee to his kidney, an elbow to his neck. No, if he ended up selecting one of those satisfying options, it would only be fair to let Jack select her preference first.

Sir Henry had locked her in her bedchamber for three days? Amazing that in modern days such a thing could still happen. It was odd to remember that Gray had known her for fewer than three weeks. It was perhaps even stranger to realize that he had grown quite fond of her in a very short time, that she had a fighting spirit that pleased him.

He turned to look up at the portrait of a very lovely woman above the fireplace. She couldn't have been older than twenty-five when the portrait was painted. The angle of her head, yes, that reminded him a bit of Jack. Her mother, then. Whereas the woman looked exotic with her dark hair, golden complexion, and brown eyes, Jack was fair, blue-eyed, with white, white skin. There was no portrait of Thomas Bascombe,

Jack's father. Had he been as fair as Jack? Probably so.

Gray turned at the sound of heavy boots. The door opened and Sir Henry strode in. Behind him was an older lady who looked flamboyant and very sure of herself. She was nearly as tall as Sir Henry, showed a plentiful bosom, beautifully swathed in dark blue satin, and looked as if she knew just about everything that would make a man slobber in his brandy.

"My lord," Sir Henry said after a moment of staring at Gray. "This is Mrs. Finch. Maria, this is Lord Cliffe, my stepdaughter's husband."

Gray bowed over her hand. She gave him a smile that, had he been in a brothel looking for skill and utter complaisance, would have hardened him on the spot.

"We finally received your message, Sir Henry, in Brighton. Jack is upstairs with her sister."

"Oh, yes," Mrs. Finch said, stripping off her gloves as she walked toward the sideboard. "Poor little creature. Ah, well, it is probably for the best, Sir Henry. Who would like a brandy?"

Sir Henry nodded. Gray just shook his head.

"Who is Jack?" Mrs. Finch asked as she placed the brandy snifter in Sir Henry's large, smooth hand.

"Jack is my wife and Sir Henry's step-daughter."

"Oh? I thought her name was Winifrede."

"Things change," Gray said. "Now she's Jack."

"How perfectly hideous," said Mrs. Finch and laughed, which was meant to remove the sting but didn't.

"Who cares?" Sir Henry poured the brandy down his throat. He wiped the back of his hand over his mouth. "Whoever or whatever she is now is of no concern to me."

Mrs. Finch said, moving just a bit closer to Gray, "I understand you were just married."

"Yes," Gray said. He looked down at his fingernails, then over at Mrs. Finch. "As you said, Mrs. Finch, the poor little creature."

"I wish she'd taken ill when she was with my sister in York," Sir Henry said. "I don't like to see the servants as overworked as they are now. Everyone is unsettled. My meals are late. My valet nicked my neck shaving me this morning. I don't like it. It isn't comfortable."

Gray smiled. "I can see how that would disturb you, having your throat cut."

"I suppose you and Winifrede want to remain here until the little girl either dies or manages to survive?"

"Yes, if that won't disaccommodate you further."

"It will, but no one seems to care about me. That old fool Darnley was already smiling and nodding because Winifrede was back. Doubtless Mr. Potts will prepare a delicious dinner since Winifrede is here."

"I understand that Dr. Brace is more optimistic than you appear to be on the child's condition."

Sir Henry shrugged. "Brace is a fool. I heard the child coughing hard enough to bring up her guts. If she doesn't die of this, it will be a miracle."

Gray wanted so badly to smash his fist into Sir Henry's mouth that he was nearly shaking with it.

"My lord," said Mrs. Finch, "you and Winifrede were on your wedding trip? In Brighton?"

"A short wedding trip. Yes, we were in Brighton."

The drawing room door burst open. Jack ran in, yelling, "Gray! Hurry—oh, God, hurry!"

He was on her heels in an instant. He shortened his step when they reached the upstairs corridor.

"She can't breathe, Gray. She's been coughing, her lungs seem filled with liquid, but she can't spit it up. I don't know what to do. Neither does Mrs. Smithers or Dolly."

He was the last resort. He was terrified to his toes. He followed Jack into a large nursery at the end of the east corridor. There in the far corner of the room was a small bed. Standing by the bed was an older woman holding a small girl, shaking her, then pressing her against her bosom, crying, saying over and over, "You must spit it up, Georgie. Come, child, you must try."

The little girl was wheezing and struggling. She wasn't breathing well at all. Gray could hear the horrible liquid sounds with each breath she managed to suck out.

It was as if she were drowning. If she didn't get her lungs clear, she would suffocate. Gray grabbed the little girl, slammed her against his shoulder, and pounded her back. The wheezing was deep and raw. He didn't have much time.

He kept pounding that small back, saying over and over, "You can do it, Georgie, come on now, breathe. Breathe!"

He pounded her again, harder this time, then yet again, and a flood of dark gray liquid flew out of her mouth. He hit her back again, and more waste came out. Again and again, until finally the small body shuddered and collapsed. He felt her small chest expand, heard her suck in precious air, heard that her lungs were clear. Then she was still.

"Oh, God, Gray! No!"

"No, Jack, she's all right. She threw up all the waste that was clogging her lungs, choking her."

"We tried to get her to cough it all up, but she couldn't."

Mrs. Smithers was staring at the young man who'd just saved Georgina Wallace-Stanford. "Are you a doctor?"

Gray smiled. "No, ma'am. I'm just a very lucky man. She sounded just like a little boy I knew who almost drowned. I pulled him out of the pond and banged on his back until he vomited out all the water. Let's pray she got everything up. Perhaps now she can recover. She's sleeping. Come here, Jack, you can hear her breathing. Everything sounds clear, thank God."

But Jack, his pillar of strength, had fainted quietly at his feet.

When Jack opened her eyes a few minutes later, she looked up to see Gray seated on Georgie's bed, the little girl still in his arms.

"Hello. Georgie's fine for the moment. What happened?"

"I don't know. It's strange. I fainted, didn't I?"

"No wonder," said Mrs. Smithers. "We both believed she was dying, my lord," she added to Gray. "Here, lovey, drink some of this nice tea. Dolly just fetched it for you."

"Is Georgie truly breathing easily now, Gray?"

"Yes, she truly is. Mrs. Smithers sent one of the footmen for Dr. Brace again. We'll see what he has to say after he examines the mess that came out of her lungs. Now, drink the tea, Jack, then you can hold her and feel her lungs going in and out. That will convince you."

Quiet, sloe-eyed Dolly, Georgie's nanny,

said, "It was just like his lordship said. Miss Georgie was drowning from the inside out."

"Yes," Gray said. "We can hope she vomited out all the liquid in her lungs." He paused for a moment, his hand lightly stroking the little girl's back. "I couldn't think of anything else to do."

"I will give you anything you want, Gray," Jack said, swung her legs over the side of the bed and leaned into him. He pulled her against him with his free arm. He kissed the top of her head, then kissed Georgie's head. The little girl had black hair, just like her father. Her skin was as white as Jack's.

He looked up to see Sir Henry standing in the nursery doorway, his mouth twisted in distaste, watching Dolly clean the mess off the floor. "Is she dead yet?"

"No," Gray said. "She's not going to die."

Sir Henry grunted. "Waste of money, then, to bring Brace here again. If she's going to live, why do we need him?" He turned on his heel and was gone.

It was at that precise moment that Gray decided how he would deal with Sir Henry Wallace-Stanford.

Jack was standing, her hand, now fisted

tightly, on his shoulder. "I'm going to kill him."

"No," Gray said quietly. "There won't be any need. Trust me, Jack. Now, I think there's something else that might help Georgie."

Ten minutes later, the little girl was wrapped snugly in a very hot towel.

Dr. Brace, a solitary young man who'd wanted very much to buy the Cit Palace from old Greeley for his mother and his grandmother, arrived to see Georgie heaving up more liquid. "Hot towels? My God, it's working. How did you know to do that, my lord?"

"My grandmother wrapped me in hot towels when I was once very ill. I was all stuffed up and having a hard time breathing. Since I'm alive and in good health today, I didn't think the same treatment could hurt her."

Dr. Brace laid his palm lightly on Georgie's forehead, then her cheeks. He leaned down to listen to her heart and lungs. "She's nearly clear." He smiled over at Jack, who was seated on the floor, her legs crossed.

"She'll make it, Miss Winifrede. It's true that I feared it could become an inflammation of the lung, but it didn't progress that

far. You've got yourself an excellent husband here."

Jack looked at Gray with such naked gratitude in those very blue eyes of hers that he
winced. He wanted to tell her he didn't want
gratitude from her. Exactly what it was that
he did want from her, he didn't yet know. But
not gratitude, never gratitude.

After Gray threatened to haul her over his
shoulder and carry her down to dinner, Jack
finally agreed to leave Georgie to Mrs.
Smithers and a smiling Dolly.

She looked back once again, as if, Gray
thought, she was terrified to leave her little
sister. Georgie was sound asleep, wrapped
in another warm towel. For the past three
hours, when she woke up coughing, Jack
had been there to rub her back, to clean her
mouth, to whisper how much she loved her,
and to tell her to spit and keep spitting.
Every time, the little girl spit.

"Smile for me, Jack. You can do it. Just
think of the divine Mrs. Finch and smile."

Jack rolled her eyes.

20

On the way downstairs, Jack said very quietly, "I just realized that if you weren't my husband, my stepfather would have me in his control again. He would be able to starve me and beat me, whatever he wanted to do. That surely isn't right, Gray."

"No, but on the other hand, Jack, you could always knot your sheets again and climb out of your bedchamber window. Oh, yes, Darnley told me how all the servants thought you were brave, what with your daring escape."

"Mrs. Smithers tried to sneak me some food, but Sir Henry caught her. He threatened to dismiss her without a character if she tried that again."

He caught her against his side and kissed the end of her nose. "Georgie's sleeping, her lungs are clear, and it's time to fill up that skinny little belly of yours."

The antagonism between Jack and her stepfather was so thick in the air at dinner that one could have practically choked on it. The meal could have been a disaster. It wasn't, only because Gray engaged Mrs. Finch, a very willing accomplice, in a charming flirtation. When Jack rose, he said easily, "My dear, why don't you and Mrs. Finch go to the drawing room? Sir Henry and I have a few matters to discuss."

"No," Jack said, and he knew that there would be no private talk with Sir Henry tonight. He didn't blame her. She sat back down. Mrs. Finch stood beside her chair, and Darnley stood just a foot away from her, wondering what calamity would strike now.

"Very well," Gray said. Sir Henry raised a thick black eyebrow. "Maria, my stepdaughter is showing her ill-breeding. Forgive her. I will see you home." He flung down his napkin, nodded to Gray, and left the dining room with Mrs. Finch on his arm.

Gray looked across the lovely white table-cloth at Jack. He sighed. "I suppose you and I have a few matters to discuss as well."

"Forgive me for not obeying you, Gray, but I don't want you to deal with my step-father, not alone. I thought about it. He's a snake. I don't trust him. I wouldn't be sur-prised if he pulled his stiletto and tried to stab you. No, I won't leave you unprotected anywhere close to him. I can't, not after you saved Georgie." She crossed her arms over her chest and looked immovable.

He took another bite of Mr. Potts's Shrop-shire pudding. Mr. Potts had been generous with the brandy. His tongue was nearly numb. "I don't want your damned gratitude, Jack." He folded his hands over his stom-ach. "I guess you won't understand this, but I'll tell you anyway. Gratitude from a woman crushes a man, particularly if the man is her husband."

"That's unfortunate, because you've got it for life. I would be a very strange sort of per-son if I didn't feel gratitude. My intent is not to crush you, Gray. Now, what do you want to say to Sir Henry?"

He sat forward, shoved his plate aside. "Will you trust me on this, Jack?"

"Only if I can give you a gun."

He shook his head even as he laughed. "Yes, give me a gun and then leave me alone with your stepfather. I have a plan, but I doubt it would work with you in the room. It's my only plan, there is no alternative plan waiting in the wings that would include the both of us. Now, will you trust me?"

"All right, but I'll be worried until I know you're safe and sound with me again."

He rose, walked to her, and took her hand. "Come along. I'll go back up to Georgie with you, then I want you to get some sleep. I'll come to you when I'm through with your stepfather."

"I'm worried," she said. "You just don't know him as well as I do. He's capable of anything."

He kissed her ear. "Give me a chance to deal with him, Jack. Trust me."

Dolly was wrapping Georgie in another hot towel. The nursery smelled foul. Gray wanted to open windows but knew it wouldn't be wise. He also knew if he had to sleep in this room, he'd get ill just from the smells.

Thirty minutes later Georgie was tucked once more into another hot towel and lying on a pallet in front of the fireplace in the Oak Room, a corridor's length from the nursery.

"Yes," Jack said, "this was a splendid idea, Gray. Now if she wakes up I'll be right here to help her. I won't have to worry."

He left Jack sitting on the floor beside her sleeping sister, her arms wrapped around her knees. He'd kissed her left ear, lightly stroked his fingers over her neck, then turned to leave. "Don't forget your gun," she called out after him. He was thoughtful as he left the Oak Room. He'd never before in his life had someone be concerned specifically about him. No one. He realized it made him feel very good, made him feel as though he was very important in another person's life—and indeed he was.

He found Sir Henry in his library, drinking brandy, waiting.

"She's still alive?"

"Yes," Gray said. "She wasn't ever in any immediate danger. Apparently you panicked, Sir Henry, but no matter. I'm glad that Jack and I were able to get here so quickly. Dr. Brace is pleased and sees a complete recovery."

Sir Henry grunted at that, then steepled his fingertips and began tapping them together. "And you, my lord? Are you pleased as well?"

Gray shrugged and studied a fingernail. "The child has as much worth to me as she does to you."

"According to Dr. Brace, you sped her recovery immensely, perhaps even saved her life, since she hadn't managed to expel the liquid from her lungs on her own."

"Jack expected me to do something. The little girl will be fine now. When I take Jack from her in a couple of days, she won't be bowed by grief."

Sir Henry was staring into the fire, a sullen blaze. He said finally, "I realize now that Winifrede fooled me quite thoroughly, pretending she didn't care about Georgina. Ah, but that wasn't at all true, was it? I didn't realize until last night just how much she loves the child." Sir Henry paused, then picked up a quill from his desktop and said, "Don't you want to please your bride, my lord?"

Gray raised a sleek blond brow. "Please her? She's my wife. That should provide her with more than enough pleasure."

"No, you misunderstand me. She wants the child with her. I would imagine you would

have to drag Winifrede from her if you refused her the child. What do you think about
that?"

"I certainly don't mind if Jack wishes to
visit the child once or twice a year. Doubtless in six months or so I will be sated
enough to allow her to be away from me for
a week or so."

Sir Henry flushed. Gray knew he wasn't
mistaken, even though the candlelight
wasn't all that bright. "What do you mean,
'sated'?"

"I mean," Gray said, rubbing his finger
over his signet ring, "that Jack is a lovely
girl. I'm enjoying her youth and her innocence. In six months or so, she will have
nothing new to offer me. Thus she can come
here to visit."

The library was suddenly much darker,
and airless. It was difficult to breathe—the
air was so thick. Gray looked at his boots.
His valet Horace was a genius with boots.
He could still see his reflection quite clearly
even though it had been three days since
Horace had nurtured them with his secret
recipe. He waited, something he did well but
didn't like to do. Sir Henry seated himself
behind a mammoth mahogany desk, leaning

back so far that his head was nearly touching the bookcase behind him. He was still holding the quill, threading it through his fingers.

"Mrs. Finch doesn't like Georgina," Sir Henry said at last.

"Surely that isn't terribly important."

"I'm planning on marrying her. She doesn't want that pathetic little scrap as a stepdaughter."

"Ah."

"Ah, what? Damn you?"

"It isn't my concern, thank God. Now, I imagine that Jack won't wish to leave until she's certain her sister will indeed be all right. We will see you in the morning, Sir Henry."

Gray nodded and quickly let himself out of the library. He'd planted only a few seeds, watered them only a bit. But all in all, it appeared that Sir Henry wanted to be rid of the child more than he wanted revenge against Jack. He imagined that if Mrs. Finch weren't in the foreground of the picture, it would be quite a different scene. Now he'd wait a bit, give Sir Henry an opportunity to come to him. Yes, the gift of Mrs. Finch was unexpected, and quite a stroke of luck.

He was whistling as he stepped into the hallway. Jack was on him in an instant, silent as a shadow, slamming her fists into his chest, kicking his shins, her breath harsh and low, saying not a word.

He managed to grab her hands and force them to her sides. He kept his voice low and said right into her face, "Jack, what the devil is the matter with you? Jack, dammit, stop trying to kill me. What are you doing here?"

"You bastard," she said, breathing so hard she was wheezing. She went on her toes and bit his neck. He nearly yelled, but managed at the last minute to hold it in. The last thing he wanted was Sir Henry flying out here to gape at them.

"You miserable bastard. I should have known you were like all the other men in this benighted world. I hate you, Gray, I hate you."

He wrapped his arms around her and pulled her back to him. He leaned down and kissed her ear. She was trembling she was so angry. "How much did you hear?" he whispered into the same ear he'd kissed.

"Bastard."

"I suppose you came down because you

were afraid that Sir Henry would stab me in the gullet?"

"Yes—I wish he would have."

"Jack, I'm your husband. Didn't you tell me that you trusted me? Just thirty short minutes ago? Up in the Oak Room? Didn't you swear that you trusted me?"

"I was wrong."

He squeezed her more tightly. "Let's find some privacy. I don't want Sir Henry to come out and witness this. He's not stupid, Jack. Now, for the moment, I've got him right where I want him. Actually, he put himself right where we want him. Come along, Jack, let's go upstairs."

"Bastard."

He whistled all the way up the stairs.

She turned every few steps, shook her fist in his face, and continued with her refrain. "Bastard."

He pulled her into the Oak Room. She immediately jerked away from him and walked over to Georgie's pallet. She went down on her knees and lightly touched her palm to the child's forehead. She sat back on her heels. She said, not turning to face him, "I won't leave Georgie."

"No, naturally you won't."

She jumped to her feet and ran back at him. He managed to snag her wrists in mid-air. "What do you mean you won't want me after six months?"

He pulled her against him and kissed her closed mouth. She nearly bit him, but he was fast. He held her so tightly against him that he could feel the small tremors in her body. "Ah," he whispered in her ear, "your innocence and youth. An erotic and seductive combination."

"But not for longer than six months. Then I'll be old and used up and you'll be bored with me and not mind a bit if I leave you for weeks at a time."

"Jack, at the rate we're proceeding with the physical part of our marriage, I daresay you won't be used up and ready to leave for a good twenty years."

"Why are you laughing at me? I heard what you said to my stepfather. You don't want me and you certainly don't want Georgie. You said you'd be sated."

"You're wrong about that."

"Bastard."

He scooped her up in his arms and tossed her onto the bed, then followed her down. "No, don't yell at me, you'll disturb your sister. Just lie there and give me a magnificent frown." He kissed her, moving quickly when she tried to bite him again.

He pulled her arms over her head, holding her wrists against the pillow. "Tell me something, Jack. What do you want more than anything in the world?"

"Georgie."

He nodded. "Good." He waited. She said nothing. "No 'bastard' for me?"

Her eyes were narrowed and mean as she said slowly, "I'm considering this carefully. It will take me a while to go back over your conversation with my stepfather and filter out all my anger at you."

"Please do."

Suddenly her frown washed away. She actually smiled up at him, then stared at him in wonder. "Goodness, Gray, you're the shiftiest man I've ever met. You're trolling in very deep waters. You're playing as low a villain as Sir Henry."

"It took you long enough to recognize my great acting skills. However, I think what will really set everything right is your stepfather's desire to marry Mrs. Finch. She doesn't want Georgie, you see, and thus any revenge against us hasn't got a top ranking in Sir Henry's brain anymore."

"Do you think she's rich?"

"If she's not very, very rich, then Sir Henry's a fool, despite the level of his lust."

"He's wicked. He's not a fool. I just don't know about this lust business. Gray, you're lying on top of me. I can feel you."

He closed his eyes and shuddered, unconsciously pressing his belly against hers. "Yes, I can feel you as well, Jack." He released her and rolled to his side. She came up to face him.

"What will you do tomorrow?"

"I plan to have a nice talk with Darnley and Mrs. Smithers. I fancy they'll be excellent allies. I just want to cover all the possibilities. Now, it's late. I very much want to give you a teasing lesson, but I imagine you'll forget yourself and attack my poor manly self. We can't let that happen, Georgie's here. No, just sleep tonight, Jack."

Gray said nothing more to Sir Henry about his daughter for the next two days.

Jack spent most of her time with her stepsister. Georgie improved steadily. She was a tough little button. The first time Gray saw her awake, in the clear light of day, he blinked. Jack had just pulled her out of her bathing tub and wrapped her in a towel, and was drying her in front of the window. Gray paused a moment until she was finished. She was humming softly, kissing the child's nose every so often. He watched her run her fingers through Georgie's black hair, smoothing out the tangles. "There now, pumpkin, very nearly dry. But we don't want to take any chances with you. Let's go over to the fire and let your hair dry there."

Gray came closer and blinked again. Georgie had one bright blue eye and one gold eye.

No, surely he was mistaken. Different colored eyes—that made no sense. He took a step closer. The little girl stared back at him.

21

Jack looked up to see him. She grew very quiet. She squeezed her sister closer. "It doesn't make her bad," Jack said, all fierce and protective, but at the same time keeping her voice low and smooth so Georgie wouldn't be upset. He didn't know anyone else who could have managed to do that. "It doesn't make her evil, or a tool of the devil, or anything foolish like that. I don't care if a vicar once denounced her as an outcast from hell. He was a malicious idiot. I would have killed him if I'd had the chance. She's beautiful and very smart." She kissed her little sister's temple. "Ah, pumpkin, that bath tired you down to your little toes, didn't it? It doesn't matter, you did very well. You just nap now for a while, nice and warm in front of the fire."

Surprisingly, the child did just that, once Jack had wrapped her in blankets, smoothed her hair out around her head, and lightly patted her face.

Gray motioned her back toward the window. He said quietly, "Jack, when I was with your stepfather and Mrs. Finch that first meeting, she said something about Georgie's dying being for the best. Did she mean that just because she has eyes of different color?"

"Wicked, awful woman," Jack said. "Yes, she had to mean that. Sir Henry also believes Georgie is mentally deficient just because her eyes don't match."

Gray said slowly, smiling toward that small, very beautiful child, "I imagine that when she grows up she will have her pick of just about every eligible bachelor in London. She's beautiful, Jack, just beautiful. And unique, just like her stepsister."

Jack let out a very low, very undignified squeak and hurled herself at him. He was laughing quietly even as she knocked him backward onto the bed and landed flat on top of him. She kissed his face, stopping only when she heard Georgie say, "Freddie, w-w-ho is that m-m-an? W-w-why are y-y-you hurting h-him?"

Jack rolled off him and quickly came down onto the floor. She gathered her sister into her arms, blankets and all. "He's my husband, sweetie. I swear I'm not hurting him. We were just playing. He made me laugh, you see. Now, since I'm married to him, that makes him your brother. His name is Gray. He saved your life. He's nice."

Georgie peered at Gray over Jack's shoulder. "G-Gray? That's a c-color, not a n-n-n—"

"It's a name too. Now, let me comb my fingers through your hair and make you a bit more presentable. First impressions are very important. Yes, let's straighten that cute bow on your nightgown. There, you're the prettiest little girl in all of England, Georgina. Make your curtsy to Gray."

The little girl bent slightly in Jack's arms and gave him a very small smile.

"Hello, Georgie. Do you know something? I have a comb. Now, your sister did try to straighten your hair, but you're still not quite ready to see the queen. Would you come to me and let me comb your hair?"

Georgie sent an agonized look to Jack. "He's never offered to comb my hair, Georgie. I think we should let him try it first on you. What do you say?"

"I-I don't k-k-know, Freddie. L-lots of tangles."

After a good deal of laughter and coaxing, Georgie was seated on Gray's lap and he was combing the tangles out of her hair with both a small comb and his fingers, all the while delivering a monologue designed to entertain her.

"And after this tangle, I'll go west where there's a whole nest of them, trying to hide in the shadow of your little ear. If I were a very small little animal, I'd be afraid of falling into that nest, it's so well hidden. I'd be lost forever and starve because nobody could find me and feed me."

Georgie laughed. Her throat was still on the raw side, but it was nonetheless a sweet child's laugh and very nearly normal.

"How do you know what to do?" Jack asked him, sitting down on a small stool beside them.

He studied a knot of hair, then untangled

it with his fingers. "You met Ryder Sherbrooke very briefly the morning of our wedding."

"Yes, I remember. What about him?"

"Remember I told you he saves children. He's saved children since he was twenty years old. He and Jane—she's called Jane the Directress by Sophie, Ryder's wife—she takes care of all the children he brings to her. She told me about Jamie, the first child he brought to her. He was just a baby and someone had tossed him in a pile of garbage in an alley. Ryder saved him and brought him to Jane. That started it all. About six years ago Ryder built another house, close to his and Sophie's in the Cotswolds. I believe there are currently about fifteen children there, of all ages. When I was visiting some time years ago, Ryder introduced me to his own daughter. He was combing her hair and she very nicely allowed me to learn how to do it. She let me practice on her." He paused a moment, looking into a past that wasn't at all pleasant.

"Jenny's mother died, but Jenny lived. She isn't whole, mentally, but she's the sweetest girl you'll ever meet, Jack. Goodness, Jenny must be twelve or thirteen by now. And beautiful, just like her father.

"Since Jenny, I've combed lots of little girls' hair, even done some braiding. Now, would you like to know what Ryder told me was the most important ingredient for a marriage?"

Jack was blinking. He realized she was crying. "Oh, no, Jack. I didn't mean to make you weep. It's a good story, not a sad one."

He pulled her against him, holding Georgie on one side, Jack on the other. "No, don't cry. That's right, Georgie, pat her face—maybe even pull her ear. That will make her feel better."

She sniffed several more times, then raised her face to his. "I saw Ryder Sherbrooke, thought he was very handsome, and believed him a charming, probably heedless rich man. I'm horrible."

"N-n-not you, F-Freddie."

"You're right, Georgie. Our Jack—that's her name now, if you don't mind—she's the best of sisters, the best of wives. No, Jack, listen. It's just that we never really know anybody, do we? You meet someone for a short amount of time, then possibly you might learn a bit more about them. But with Ryder it was different. Not even his family knew what he was doing."

"How did you find out about what he did?"

"Well, actually, he helped me when I was in very deep trouble once, about five years ago. I found out everything as time went on. Ryder, naturally, never went into any detail."

"Goodness, Gray, what sort of trouble?"

He opened his mouth, frowned in a deep breath, then closed it. "It's better that you don't know. No one knows, actually. Yes, that's best."

"You mean like it was best that no one knew about Ryder's saving children?"

"No, nothing of the sort. No, forget it, Jack."

"I'm your wife."

"Barely."

"I-I-I'm your sister," Georgie said, beaming at Gray, her small fingers lightly touching his chin.

"You certainly are," Gray said and kissed those fingers.

Jack waited, but he said nothing more, probably because what he wanted to say wasn't proper for a little girl's ears. "All right. You don't want to tell me about that. Very well. Tell me what Ryder Sherbrooke said was the most vital ingredient to a marriage."

He looked up to see Dolly standing in the doorway, a small tray in her hands. "Ah, Georgie, here's Dolly with some milk and cookies for you. Would you like to go with her and eat your goodies? Then you can come and sleep in our room again."

"They're probably almond cookies, Georgie," Jack said, and that did it. Georgie went readily to Dolly.

"I'll bring her back shortly," Dolly said. She gave them a last look, then blushed, and quickly ducked her head.

Gray said nothing until Dolly had shut the door to the Oak Room, leaving them alone. He turned back to Jack, stared down at her mouth, parted slightly, and began kissing her. He whispered at last, his breath a warm sigh against her cheek, "Dolly knows what's on my mind. Yours too, probably. Now, I'll tell you when it's the right time. Not just yet, Jack. Not just yet. We will have a little girl joining us again all too soon. Patience."

"All right. I think I'll go eat a biscuit with Georgie. I'll bring her back with me, Gray."

Within the next hour both sisters were sleeping soundly. As for Gray, it was difficult for him to lie not six inches from his wife in a very soft bed, listening to the occasional little snorts and sighs. She was a restless sleeper. The third time she flung her elbow into his ribs, he gave it up. *Torture*, he thought, as he pulled her against him. He supposed that torture was better than pain, although where sex was concerned, it was many times one and the same. He fell asleep with his hand on Jack's bottom.

Jack said, "You're naked, Gray."

That woke him up faster than the smell of coffee under his nose. She was on top of him, her nose not an inch above his, and she was smiling. "I like the way you feel. It's just dawn. Georgie's still asleep. Her breathing is clear. I've been thinking hard about this. Gray, may I have a teasing lesson? I'll speak very quietly."

The day a woman needed lessons in matters of driving a man insane with lust, he thought, was the day pigs would take to the skies.

"All right," he said, agreeable and warm and already so hard he wondered how the devil he was going to keep himself together. "I can manage this if I really try hard. If I think about my ancestors staring down on me from their gilded frames, so ancient that I can't begin to imagine how they could have ever begat the next generation. It quite curdles the belly to think of it."

She was giggling, surely the nicest sound he'd ever heard at dawn. "First thing you do is hold very still." She did. It was an unspeakable relief, and at the same time terribly disappointing.

"Now, lightly stroke your thumb over my lower lip. Yes, that's it. No, don't press hard, just lightly rove around." Then he caught her thumb in his mouth. When he released her, she was staring down at her thumb, and said, "I didn't know a mouth could do that to a thumb. It should be silly, but it wasn't. It made me feel very warm all the way to my toes. I know, Gray—what if I stuck two fingers in your mouth?"

"You think to gain twice the pleasure? Make your toes twice as warm? No, it doesn't work that way. Let's do it again. Slowly this time, Jack. You decide when you want to slide your thumb into my mouth."

Jack was thorough, very slow and very thorough. He finally had to grab her wrist. "No, stop, Jack. That's quite enough of the thumb lesson." He drew a deep breath and said, "I'm strong. I have grit. I can do this. Kiss my throat, Jack, then go down to my chest."

She straddled him as she worked her way down, every so often raising her face to see if she'd gained his approval. Soon, he was beyond nodding. She was right over him. He was saved, or cursed, finally, when Georgie said in a soft whispery little voice, "Freddie, what are you doing on t-t-top of Gray?"

Jack twisted around on him and he thought he'd expire. Her flesh was naked and warm and very soft. "Georgie, good morning, little love. How are you feeling? Your voice sounds all clear and sweet as you are."

"I'm f-f-fine, F-Freddie."

"Let me climb off Gray and we'll get you the chamber pot." As she brought her bare leg over him, sliding slow across his groin, he nearly wept. "No more lessons, Jack, no more. I'm just a man. A pathetic creature who suffers more than you can imagine from your defection. No, go, there's no choice. I will gird my loins. I will survive this."

She laughed, leaned down, kissed his

belly, then sang out, "Now, where did I put that chamber pot?"

Gray heard Sir Henry yelling from the entrance hall. Darnley was nowhere in sight. Excellent.

He whistled as he quietly let himself out the front door of Carlisle Manor. It was a lovely morning, not a rain cloud in sight—an unusual occurrence in England on any morning. He breathed in the sweet smell of freshly scythed grass. He saw three gardeners tending bushes and plants on the east side of the house. Carlisle Manor was a beautiful property, a gem set amid green rolling hills and a thick oak forest.

Gray stayed away for a good hour. Upon returning, he saw Sir Henry standing on the stone front steps, hitting his riding crop against his boot. His face was red. Gray waved, dismounted, and gave the gelding over to a waiting stable lad.

Gray dusted off his charm and bonhomie and gave his host a big smile. "And just how are you this fine day, Sir Henry?"

"It's about time you deigned to come back here. Damnation, I won't allow this to continue." Sir Henry raised his voice to the heavens and yelled, "Get the child out of here or I'll send her to York forever."

"Child? York? Excuse me, Sir Henry, is there some sort of problem?"

"I told you my household wasn't running smoothly. I told you the meals weren't cooked well and were late. I told you my valet even nicked my neck. Well, now Darnley and Mrs. Smithers tell me it's either the child or them. They say they cannot tolerate further disarray. I've thought about it. Winifrede wants her little sister. Well, she can have her. Take her, my lord, today."

"I beg your pardon, Sir Henry. You're saying that you want to give away your only child?"

"If it were a boy child it would be different. The child is a girl, she is absurd-looking with her mismatched eyes, and now she's begun to stutter. Mrs. Finch doesn't like her, either."

Gray walked past Sir Henry into the manor.

"Well, my lord?"

Gray turned slowly and smiled. "May I inquire how you intend to make it worth my while to take the child?"

Jack pulled back beneath the stairs. *Oh,*

Gray, she thought, *please don't push him too hard*.

"What do you want?"

Gray struck a thoughtful pose. "Money," he said.

"You want money to take the child?"

"Yes," Gray said. "Let us say you'll give me one hundred pounds a year. This will take care of feeding and clothing the child."

"Clothing her like royalty! Ten pounds and not a sou more!"

"All right, fifty pounds, but that's the lowest I'll go. Don't forget I'll have to pay her nanny, Dolly. Also I'll require a signed paper from you that I will be Georgina's guardian. You will relinquish any and all authority you have over her, Sir Henry."

"Yes, yes, certainly." Sir Henry was nearly rubbing his hands together. He believed he'd won a mighty victory. So much the better.

"Let's see it done, then," Gray said. "Jack doesn't particularly like it here, as you can imagine. We will leave as soon as all the papers are signed. Is there a solicitor in the neighborhood?"

At three o'clock that same afternoon, Gray stepped up into the carriage and sat down on the seat opposite his wife and her little sister, wrapped up warmly in one of Jack's old cloaks. He tapped his knuckles on the carriage roof. He said nothing until they had turned out of the Carlisle drive and onto the country road.

"Do you think my stepfather will send you fifty pounds for Georgie's care?"

"Oh, no. It doesn't matter. I knew I had to appear to be as venal as Sir Henry, else he just might have seen through everything and offered Georgie to me only if I paid a vast sum for her."

"He's despicable."

"True, but if he marries Mrs. Finch, I have this feeling that he will receive just what he deserves."

"Why do you think that?"

"When I was thanking Darnley and Mrs. Smithers for their assistance in making Sir Henry miserable, they told me that one of the servants at Cit Palace found out—doubtless from eavesdropping—that Mrs. Finch was married to a very rich man who died shortly after their marriage."

"Was he very old?"

"Not above sixty. But that wasn't the point."

"What was the point?"

"Mrs. Finch has been widowed four times."

"Oh, dear." Jack pressed her knuckles to her mouth. "Oh, dear. But Gray, my stepfather isn't old or rich."

"Ah, so you believe Mrs. Finch loves him?"

"He is exceedingly handsome. He can be charming. My mother refused to believe ill of him until the day she died."

"Be that as it may," Gray said, leaning forward to straighten Georgie's collar. The child just stared at him, saying nothing. "It also appears that Lord Rye is interested in the lady. It also appears that she's seen in his company as well as in Sir Henry's."

Jack laughed. She couldn't help herself. She hugged Georgie close, kissing the top of her head. "Your hair, Mistress Georgie, is like silk, all slippery and shiny. What do you think of that?"

"I-I-I heard P-P—"

"Your papa?"

The little girl nodded. Gray wondered if she would ever be able to speak her father's name.

"He said to himself that he'd s-s-swallow

what he had to and marry the b-b-bitch. B-B-But not for l-l-long."

The two adults stared at the child. "Now this is a kicker," Gray said at last.

"You mean that the two of them just might try to do each other in?"

"May the best man or woman win," Gray said. He leaned over and lightly stroked his fingertips over Georgie's cheek. "You have an excellent memory, Georgie. Now, how will you like London?"

"W-W-What's Lunnon?"

22

I hadn't expected to fill my nursery quite this quickly," Gray said as he watched Jack tuck Georgie into a little girl's bed, quickly brought down from the attic, all draped with frills and gauzy material. Had it belonged to his grandmother? He didn't know. It was simply very old. He listened to Jack singing to her sister, rather a thin voice, but true.

"No, I hadn't either," Jack said quietly, her lullaby finished, looking up at him. She smiled toward Dolly as she said to Gray, "We're lucky that Dolly loves Georgie so very much and wanted to come with us. I was afraid of too much change for her.

When my stepfather's sister came to take her to York, I thought Georgie would just fold down. She became so quiet, as though if she were quiet enough everyone might overlook her and leave her be. The stuttering is new. All the change, the uncertainty, I suppose. But she'll be all right now, thanks to you, Gray."

Again, the dreaded gratitude he didn't want. Then she leapt on him, laughing, kissing his chin, the end of his nose, tugging his ear so that he bent down to kiss her. "Thank you," she said into his mouth. He didn't want to stop kissing her, but Dolly was standing there, looking down at her toes, blushing a bit, Georgie wasn't completely asleep, and Mrs. Piller had materialized not eight feet away from them. Gray pulled back and gently pressed his forehead against Jack's.

"My lord," she whispered, lightly touching her fingertips to his chin, "you're so smart I've decided to enroll in more of your teasing lessons. And I must practice what you've already taught me. I wouldn't want to forget anything or grow inept."

Where had this delightful flirt been hiding herself?

Gray said, as he pulled himself together,

"Dolly, this is Mrs. Piller. She's the best housekeeper in all of London. She's known me since I was three years old and has complained ever so long now that this house needed a child's laughter again. She told me you'll be in the bedchamber at the opposite end of the nursery. Thank you for coming with us."

And Dolly, all of eighteen years old, Jack's age, said with worship in her voice, "It's my dream, my lord. Being here in London. My dream."

Once Dolly had left with Mrs. Piller to see her own bedchamber, Jack once again looked down at her sister and saw that she was now asleep. Gray said, "I saw you looking at Dolly. I'm afraid I saw a bit of jealousy in those blue eyes of yours."

"Jealous of Dolly? It's true that she blushes quite a bit in your presence, but no, I swear I'm not jealous."

"No, no, Jack. You know that's absurd. She blushes because you're always kissing me in her presence. No, I meant that you're jealous because Dolly is so close to Georgie."

She thought about that a moment, and because she was a good foot away from him, he was able to observe her reactions with more dispassion than not.

"Oh, dear, I believe you're right. That brings me rather low on the worthy-person scale, doesn't it, Gray?"

"You'll slowly shed your less appealing traits the longer you're married to me. Trust me. I'll mold you into female perfection. You'll be towering over everyone female on that scale by the end of the year."

"My lord."

Gray turned, a smile on his mouth. "Yes, Quincy?"

"The earl of Northcliffe is here. He has brought his wife, the countess, to meet her new ladyship."

"News moves about London at an alarming rate. We've only been home an hour."

"Closer to an hour and a half, my lord."

"Thank you, Quincy. Come, Jack, and meet Alexandra Sherbrooke. She's a dandy lady."

Jack had no idea if the red-haired countess of Northcliffe was a dandy lady or not. She spoke, but only to Jack and Gray. Otherwise, she was silent. She didn't look at her husband, but took a chair as far away from him as possible. What was going on here? Was she sickening of something? Was she terribly shy? Did she hate Douglas Sherbrooke?

Alexandra was small, Jack saw, save for a magnificent bosom, which they'd all been treated to a view of when Quincy had gently removed her cloak. Douglas Sherbrooke, on the other hand, was a large man. He towered over his wife. Goodness, Jack thought, when they made love the earl would have to worry about crushing her. Or maybe, Jack's thoughts continued, as she wondered if something like it could work, the countess remained on top of her husband. Jack spent a few moments wondering what that would be like, wondering if such a thing would be possible. When Gray looked over at her, he saw that her face was flushed, her blue eyes gleaming.

He looked back at Douglas Sherbrooke. Evidently the earl and his countess weren't speaking to each other, of all things. If they indeed weren't speaking, then why the devil did they have to pick his drawing room not to speak to each other in? And what was Jack thinking? Her face was red. Was she sickening of something? And where were the aunts? He'd never before seen Alex stare down at her slippers and remain silent as a clam.

Jack, sitting on the edge of her chair, said brightly, "Your hair is lovely, my lady. The color is the exact shade of a woman's hair in a painting. Italian, I think. I like it all braided on top of your head."

"Thank you," Alex Sherbrooke said. "Call me Alexandra." She patted one fat braid. "All stacked up like this, I look taller. I'm surrounded by giants. Being short also seems," she added, tossing a killing look toward her husband, "to indicate a frail brain, at least to some people."

Douglas remained tight-lipped, looking not at his wife but at a globe that sat in the corner of the drawing room. The countess fell silent and studied her slippers again.

Douglas Sherbrooke cleared his throat and said to Gray, "Helen Mayberry is still in town with her father. You know, Gray, she is very enthusiastic about this King Edward's lamp, won't even consider that it's probably nonsense. She swears she rescued a very old and tattered parchment from one of the ancient abbeys near her home in Court

Hammering that spoke of the lamp and its powers—no outrageous specifics, however—and its supposed immense age. The parchment also questioned whether its powers represented good or evil at work in the lamp."

Gray said, "Miss Helen seems a very sensible lady. She carried me over her shoulder, Jack told me, after I knocked myself unconscious against an oak tree trunk. Didn't even wind her. When I came to myself I remember thinking she had blond wagon wheels over her ears."

Jack said, smiling and guileless, "Didn't she say at our wedding that she'd loved you, Douglas, since she was fifteen?"

Alexandra Sherbrooke stood abruptly, her hands on her hips. "You tried to deny that, Douglas. Now I know the truth. Thank you, Jack." Then she turned so quickly to face Gray that she nearly tripped on her skirt. "I could carry you as well, Gray. I'm fit and strong, even though I'm not such a huge grand specimen of womanhood as Miss Helen Mayberry. How dare she tell you that she loved you, Douglas? How dare you pretend that it didn't happen? How could you ever imagine that I don't know everything—everything, do you hear me?—everything that is said to you or said about you?"

"Alex, for God's sake, just stop this now." Her husband, at least a foot taller than his wife, was on his feet, ready to hover over her and thus intimidate her. "So all this is about Helen Mayberry? You're being a fool. Listen to me, Helen was simply reminiscing. She meant nothing by it. It was just conversation, nothing more."

"Ha! One does not reminisce in such a fashion to a married man, a very married man, and that's what you are, Douglas Sherbrooke, even though you don't have the same desire for me that you had before, and don't bother to deny it. You were behaving oddly even before I knew about Helen Mayberry, all silent and withdrawn from me, not even wanting to nibble on my earlobe when your mother would be coming into the room in only two seconds. So what am I to think now? Perhaps the mystery of your wretched indifferent behavior is explained. Just perhaps you'd already seen her. Yes, that's probably it, you sod. It's another woman you want, whose name is Helen Mayberry."

"Alex, stop it. If you insist upon getting your back up just because an old friend said something utterly meaningless, at least wait until we're alone. We're visiting Gray and Jack. We're in their drawing room. I'll wager they haven't even had a minor disagreement yet. They're still thinking only about making love, nothing else.

"Now, I won't have you acting like a fishwife. Sit down, Alex, fold your hands neatly in your lap, and smile. It would be preferable if you also kept your mouth closed. We are in company where you must act polite and well bred, not alone where you can shriek at me if it pleases you. As for the other, you're imagining all of it."

But the countess didn't sit down. She walked right up to her husband until they were standing toe to toe, in the center of a drawing room that wasn't in their home, unheeding of both Gray and Jack, their hosts. Alex poked her husband in the chest. "You don't have to keep talking about Helen Mayberry as if she's a saint and so intelligent and so lively and so attuned to those around her. Attuned? Ha! It just means that she wants you, you wretched clod. She saw you without me there to protect you from predatory harpies like her, and she knew she could pull the wool over your eyes. You're splendid, Douglas, but you're still a man, and that means your brain isn't always focused on what is proper and appropriate, particularly when there's a very big, very blond hussy around you."

Douglas stared down at his small, very angry wife. "I suppose this means that the dam has burst," he said slowly. "I'm sorry, Gray, Jack. I didn't realize she was so jealous of poor Helen that she would lose all her refinement and her exquisite manners in front of you."

His wife poked him in his waistcoat, hard.

He looked ready to pick her up and shake her, Jack thought, watching Douglas flex his hands. He took a step back from her. "Alex, for God's sake, get hold of yourself."

"You've been gone a lot lately, Douglas. All you tell me is that you had to take a trip to see to this, and then another trip over there to see to that. You've been gone at least three weeks in the past two months. Three weeks! You were with her at her ridiculous lamp inn, weren't you? My God, did you see her shortly before Gray's wedding? You did, didn't you? Just where is this ridiculous town, Court Hammering? You let her seduce you with talk of that lamp, didn't you?"

Douglas took two more steps back from his wife, whose face was now nearly as red as her hair. His back was nearly touching the mantelpiece. "Listen to me, Alexandra," he said, stern as a magistrate now faced with a roomful of ruffians, "This is beyond absurd. If you don't cease this ludicrous jealousy I will send you home. You will stay there, dealing alone with your mother-in-law—may God preserve you—until you learn how to comport yourself. I have never been to Court Hammering. Well, no—I visited Lord Prith once many years ago, but not since that time. Forget Helen.

"Very well, I remember now that I also visited Lord Prith at Grillon's Hotel after Gray's wedding. You weren't yet here. They invited me to dine with them. There's nothing more to it than that, Alex."

Then Douglas blundered. He smiled as he said to Gray, "One of the footmen tripped over a hassock. He would have fallen on his nose if Helen hadn't grabbed his collar and hauled him right up."

"Oh, yes, she's so fast and competent, isn't she? Oh, yes, I heard how she even faced down Arthur Kelburn, who'd kidnapped Jack. Well, Douglas, I could have faced him down as well. Just because I'm small doesn't mean that I'm stupid or a coward. I could have vanquished him. I could have saved that footman, too. A hassock would be nothing to me."

Douglas smote his forehead with his palm. "This is beyond ridiculous. Listen to me, Alex—you couldn't have faced down Arthur Kelburn. You're so small he probably wouldn't even have seen you. No, I revise that. If he'd seen you, he wouldn't have been able to look away from those breasts of yours. Yes, that's right. He would have just stood there, gaping and slavering over your breasts until someone thought to kosh him."

The countess of Northcliffe was shaking her fist at her husband in front of two very interested spectators. "Just listen to you. I will tell you, Douglas Sherbrooke, you haven't a notion of how one should comport. You're standing here talking about my bosom when a gentleman simply doesn't do such a thing."

"Oh, yes, gentlemen do it, just not in front of ladies. But you haven't acted like a lady for the last hour. All the way over here in the carriage, you just narrowed your eyes and stared at me. When I asked you what was wrong, you just kept shaking your head and saying 'Nothing, Douglas, nothing at all.' "

"You know, Douglas," Gray said mildly, "I was remarking to myself that if Jack were as well endowed as Alex, Arthur Kelburn wouldn't have cared about her money. He would have stolen her away because he was overcome with lust."

"I see," Jack said, rising slowly from her chair, turning to stare at her husband as if he were a roach in the corner. "But being that I'm just skinny and flat-chested, and utterly unappetizing, Arthur only wanted the money he'd get if he managed to drag me to the altar."

That's what I get, Gray thought, *for trying to distract Alex*. He looked up at his wife with a lopsided grin.

It was a pleasing, quite charming grin, disarming and wicked, but Jack wasn't going to be taken in. She was going to stand firm.

"Not exactly," Gray said, that grin now becoming white-toothed and even more wicked. "It's just that you require a bit of exploration, Jack, to truly appreciate all the lovely scenery you have to offer. Your terrain isn't obviously mountainous, you see, but—"

"Don't do it, Gray," Douglas said. "It won't work. Geographical metaphors filled with hillocks and valleys and forests and such, never work. Trust me."

"I'm strong, too," Jack said. She swooped down and jerked Gray's chair back, and he and the chair went toppling onto the pale blue and peach Aubusson carpet.

That gained everyone's attention.

"If I pull myself upright, what will you do, Jack?" He lay on his back, his legs still over the fallen chair.

"Jack," Alex said, "oh, dear, you mustn't argue with Gray. You've been married only a week. That isn't right. I was very wrong to leap at Douglas's throat in front of you. It wasn't well done of me. I apologize."

"Shouldn't you be apologizing to me?" Douglas said, taking a step toward his wife. "It's my throat you want to slit."

"Stop right there, Douglas. Now, tell me, my lord, why did you take the utterly charming and very strong Miss Helen Mayberry to Gunther's for an ice on Monday?"

The earl stared down at his wife as if

turned to stone. He cleared his throat, once, twice. "How do you know of that, Alex?"

Both Jack and Alex were looking at Douglas now. They were frowning. Gray, still lying on his back, was also frowning at Douglas, but his frown was not one of condemnation but one of *how could you be so stupid?*

Alex shook her fist in his face. "You believe, you faithless hound, that I wear blinders in my own house?"

Obviously, one of the servants had found out and told another servant, who probably told her maid, who naturally filled her little ears. He sighed. "It was a lovely day, Alex. Helen had never been to Gunther's. I escorted her there. I've known her for fifteen years. There was nothing more to it than that."

"Did she tell you anything more about King Edward's lamp?" Jack asked.

"Just that she's convinced it's somewhere in East Anglica, perhaps near Aldeburgh, close to the water. She told me that King Edward's queen, Eleanor, loved the coastline, the ruggedness of it, the savagery, especially at that particular spot. She believes that after Eleanor died, King Edward hid the lamp somewhere near there as a tribute to her, a shrine."

"I don't believe," Gray said, still on the floor, "that any man, even King Edward, would have hidden away a possibly magical lamp, particularly if it was covered with jewels."

Alex said, "You don't know your history, Gray. You're thinking the way most men think." She looked at her husband, then loudly cleared her throat. "Actually, King Edward—unlike most men—loved his wife, Eleanor, more than anyone on this earth. It's said that when she was dying, he was frantic, offering himself in her place, anything to spare her—unlike most men, I daresay. He, I might add, also adored his wife physically, sometimes even leaving his counsel chamber in the middle of the day to go to his wife. Unlike you, Douglas, who haven't come out of your estate room to hunt me down in more days that I can count, at least on those days that you've even been home and not out spending weeks away from me and refusing to tell me where you'd been or where you were going the next time. It is clear that you no longer love me. It is even clearer that you prefer to forget that I even exist."

"Bosh," said Douglas. "You're hugging conclusions to your ample bosom that have no more reality than a bad dream."

Alexandra Sherbrooke, small and delicate as a Dresden shepherdess, as sumptuously endowed as a Rubens model, topped with red hair more vibrant than an Irish sunset, yelled at the top of her lungs to her large, dark husband, who towered over her like a prize bull over a heifer, "You want a blond hussy who's as big as you are, Douglas? You want to feed Gunther's ices to a brawny trollop who can look you right in the eye? You're weary of someone half your size? Well, you don't have to be."

Alex pulled a chair up right in front of her husband, jumped on it, and stared down at him. "There, does this give you pleasure, Douglas? Am I tall enough for you now?"

"I can look straight ahead right into your damned cleavage," the earl of Northcliffe said, his wife's bosom at his eye level.

"Er, Jack, can I get up now?"

"If you keep your distance, perhaps it will be safe enough." Jack gave him her hand, her eyes never leaving the spectacle of the earl and countess, who were waging a very interesting war in her drawing room. Then

she drew her hand back. "No, Gray, I believe you'd best remain there a while longer.
It's probably the safest spot in the room. Do
you think I should order some tea or something?"

But Gray wasn't listening to her. He was
staring at Douglas. "No, Douglas," Gray
said under his breath, "no, don't do that,
Douglas. I strongly recommend you forget
that idea immediately." It was going to happen. Gray yelled, "No, Douglas, don't do
that."

But the earl paid him no heed.

He leaned forward and kissed the top of
his wife's breasts.

23

Alexandra Sherbrooke screeched, flew at her husband, wrapping her arms around his neck. She hung off him until he clasped his hands about her waist and gently set her on the floor.

Jack said, louder now, "Would you like some tea, Alex? Douglas?"

Douglas Sherbrooke looked over at his host and hostess and began to laugh. "Do forgive us. Normally we are quite comfortable guests."

Alex grabbed her husband's big hand and bit his thumb. "You may laugh, and jest about all of this, even try to shove me under the carpet, Douglas, but it won't work. I will not allow you to betray me with that dreadful Helen woman. I won't change my mind on this. You will not consider it, Douglas. I don't care how big and how beautifully strong she is."

"For God's sake, Alex, I didn't betray you. I wouldn't betray you." This time he did pick her up, bringing her nose to nose with him. "You will cease this jealous display."

"And after you took her to Gunther's and fed her two ices—yes, two!—you took her in your phaeton all around the park."

"Who the hell told you that?"

"Heatherington told me. He wanted to know who the blond goddess was who was laughing and sitting nearly on your lap and had you ready to lick her palm, blast you."

"Heatherington," Douglas said to Jack, "is a man so steeped in debauchery he isn't happy unless he can claim another man is just as low as he is. Alex, he was baiting you, nothing more." He finally set her down. "He enjoys baiting you because you won't ever let him seduce you. It's a game with him, nothing more."

Alex took a step back. "I have decided what to do," she said, flinging her arms out to include both Gray and Jack. "Yes, I have decided that I shall go riding in the park myself this afternoon. No, it's already afternoon. I shall ride tomorrow morning in the park. I won't be by myself. I shall be accompanied by a gentleman who will look ready to lick my palm. I will spend the remaining part of this afternoon searching out such a gentleman. I will discover where Heatherington lives. I wonder if he's as knowledgeable in matters of the flesh as you are, Douglas. Good-bye, Gray, Jack. Congratulations on your marriage. I'm sorry that marriage is the very devil."

Alexandra Sherbrooke grabbed her cloak and her small straw bonnet with a cluster of grapes cleverly perched on the edge of it and marched out of the drawing room.

They stood frozen, listening to Quincy, who was rushing to the front door, gasping, he was speaking so quickly, "No, my lady, surely you don't wish to leave just yet. Why, I haven't been asked yet to fetch tea or other interesting delicacies from Mrs. Post. She makes a marvelous almond pastry that would make you smile if you took but a single bite and—"

The front door slammed and Quincy trailed off into silence.

"Yes," Douglas said slowly, "congratulations on your marriage."

Gray, who was still sprawled on his fallen chair, said, "Thank you, Douglas."

"I believe I'll go home now and see my little girl. She looks exactly like me. She's nearly three years old now and adores me, unlike her twin brothers who look exactly like Melissande and adore me as well. That's Alex's sister," Douglas added to Jack. "She's so beautiful your teeth ache and your tongue falls from your mouth just looking at her. And now my two bright boys must share that same appalling beauty. They will be uncontrollable when they become men. No female will be safe from them."

Douglas sighed, looked thoughtfully toward the dark afternoon sky beyond the bow windows, and said over his shoulder as he was leaving, "I hope Alex doesn't find Heatherington today and bully him into taking her to the park. It will rain soon. Actually, he would go willingly with her. I hear that Heatherington prefers the weather to be dreary so it will match his dark soul."

"Goodness," Jack said some moments

later, after Douglas Sherbrooke had left. "That was an adventure. It was much more exciting than a play. And it was free, right in our drawing room. Do they perform such spectacular dramas often?"

"Actually, that's the first time I've ever seen any real discord at all between them. Certainly there's a lot of yelling and insults between them, but that's nothing unusual. Douglas is usually touching her or trying to bite her ear, or Alex is leaning up to kiss his neck, teasing him like I'm teaching you how to do." Gray stood up, then straightened the chair. He dusted himself off. "But this was different. I didn't like this at all."

"It's your fault, Gray, all because you insisted that Helen come here for our wedding. The poor countess, alone and cast out, all because of you bringing that temptress here. Did Douglas really kiss his wife's breasts? In front of us? And I missed it?"

"Yes," Gray said, grinning like a glutton over a plateful of pastries, "he most certainly did. Trust me, I would never have insisted that Helen come if I'd had a clue that this could happen. On the other hand, perhaps Alex and Douglas have gotten a bit too settled with each other, too predictable, each knowing what the other is thinking before he speaks, that sort of thing. This has certainly stirred things up, hasn't it?"

"But what if Douglas falls in love with Helen?"

"No, that won't happen. Ever. Now, it occurs to me that you haven't enjoyed my mouth on you in a very long time."

Jack swallowed, pleated her fingers through the soft muslin of her skirt, and said, "Did you mean that just exactly the way the words emerged from your mouth?"

"Oh, yes," he said, walking to her, "oh, yes."

It was Gray's immediate aim to remove Jack to his bedchamber in the next four minutes, strip her to her white skin, and wallow. He made it to the bottom stair, but no farther. Ryder Sherbrooke burst through the front door, flung his hat on the marble floor, and stomped on it.

"You'll not believe what those ignorant louts are saying!" Ryder shouted toward them. "I can scare believe it's happening myself. The lowness of some people.

"Hey, what is this? What the hell's wrong with you, Gray? You look ready to cry or yell. You have no reason to be irked. Now, listen to me. You must give me your opinion. I just saw Alex and Douglas in their carriage down the street. Were they visiting you?"

"They entertained us for a good half hour," Gray said. "They just left."

"I hope they didn't try to destroy your house," Ryder said. "I had to leave the Sherbrooke town house this morning because Douglas and Alex were yelling fit to drop the chandelier. It wasn't their usual sort of yelling either. I suppose they'll tell me what's wrong sooner or later."

Ryder turned on his heel and strode into the drawing room, leaving Quincy to pick up his hat and begin knocking the lumps out of it. "Come along," he called out over his shoulder.

"What now?" Gray said, an eyebrow lifted a good inch.

Jack sighed, looking longingly at her husband's mouth, and said, "I never knew there was such excellent entertainment in London. We don't even have to leave our drawing room."

"That's certainly true, curse it."

Ryder was pacing the drawing room. "To be brief," he said over his shoulder as Jack and Gray trailed into the room, "I've given this a lot of thought and I've decided to stand for Parliament. It's because of the children, of course. God knows that we need laws to protect children. It's disgraceful how our children can be treated here in England." He stopped pacing, turned red in the face, and yelled, "My damnable opponent, a Mr. Horace Redfield, who has a fat belly and sour breath, is telling everyone that Brandon House isn't a home for children I've saved. No, it's all my bastards that are housed there.

"My bastards! I was warned never to trust a damned Whig, curse their perfidious tongues. I should have known. He also has gout and a lot of cronies, blast him."

Gray whistled in admiration. "That would make you an excessively busy man for many years now, Ryder," Gray said. "It would also mean that you had a very understanding wife. How many children are there now?"

"Fourteen. But that number goes up and down. And that isn't all. Redfield even intimated that some of those children are also my brothers' bastards, that I'm the recipient of all the wayward lust in my family. I heard he was even whispering behind his hand that my brother Tysen, the vicar, has dropped a couple of his by-blows off at Brandon House. Good God, you know Tysen, Gray. He'd squeak and flee the neighborhood if any woman other than that priggish flat-chested wife of his even so much as winked at him. Damnation, I'm going to strangle that little Whig blighter."

"So Douglas doesn't know about this yet?"

"No, Jack, he doesn't." Ryder paused a moment, then took a longer look at her. "I think I remember you from your wedding day."

"Yes," Jack said. "Can't you simply tell the truth, Mr. Sherbrooke? Wouldn't that expose Mr. Redfield and all his lies?"

"Call me Ryder," he said, rubbing his chin thoughtfully. "I am fast learning that in politics there is no such thing as truth, there's only who's the best liar and how well he's able to twist things to his advantage, and how many cronies he has who lie as well as he does.

"Mr. Redfield is preaching about how he reveres the hearth and the family. And here I am, the debauched scourge of the neighborhood, a man with no concern for the spiritual value of marriage at all, living openly with all my congregated bastards and a downtrodden wife who goes along with the fiction."

Jack said, "But the fact that you have your bastards living near you should convince everyone that you're a fine, responsible man who cares about any child he brings into the world."

Gray rolled his eyes. "Jack, you're sweet and good and very naive. People's brains don't work that way. We'll talk about that later. What else, Ryder?"

"I hear too that Mr. Redfield is using bribery so that people will repeat this ridiculous tale to anyone still breathing. People are credulous, their lives are tedious. Give them a chance to wallow in wickedness and they'll leap into the mud as fast as a pullet escaping the hatchet. As you said, Gray, people's brains don't work in reasonable ways. It's true that they've all known about Brandon House for years. Good God, we order in huge amounts of food locally as well as bolt upon bolt of fabric for clothing. Do you know just how much leather for shoes alone we order? You know how fast the children grow, Gray. It's hard to keep up with them.

"Yes, they know the truth, but now because Mr. Redfield has intimated hidden lust and sex and scandal, they're eager to disregard what they've known for fact and leap upon this new wagon. It's just so more titillating than a simple haven for hurt children, and that's the truth of it, Jack.

"Right in Upper and Lower Slaughter, the very warm belly of England, I'm learning that anything to do with fleshly concerns brings people flocking to believe it."

"Have a cup of tea, Ryder," Jack said and pressed a cup into his hand. "It will be all right. We will come up with a strategy."

"Where did you get the tea?"

"Quincy came in," Gray said. "You were so engrossed in your tirade that you didn't heed him. Come sit down, Ryder. We understand the problem now. Let's solve it."

"I want to smash the blighter."

"The borough isn't controlled by a local family?" Gray asked.

Ryder shook his head. "No, not now. It was a rotten borough until the Locksley family died out some twenty years ago. Now it's free and clear, the elections, for the most part, aboveboard."

Jack said, "What's a rotten borough?"

"It's a borough that's controlled by a local aristocratic family. Some boroughs have fewer than fifty people living in them. It's disgraceful."

"Hmmmm," Jack said, "what a wonderfully easy solution."

Both men stared hard at her.

Jack gave them a beatific smile. "All right, Ryder. You'll simply make it rotten again. You're a Sherbrooke—control it. Your family must be more illustrious and have more influence than these Locksleys ever had."

"I hadn't thought about being as underhanded as Redfield," Ryder said slowly, looking at Jack with some respect. "What is involved, I wonder, in re-rottening a borough?"

"It can't be too difficult if those idiots in the House of Lords have managed to rotten them for the past hundreds of years," Gray said. "Come to think of it," he continued, smacking his palm on his thigh, "I'm one of those idiots."

"Let me consider this," Ryder said, gulping down his tea. "First, though, I must speak to Douglas. I hope that he and Alex have calmed their bile. Why were he and Alex shouting at each other, I wonder?"

"I believe," Jack said, "that it has something to do with a very big lady named Helen Mayberry. The woman who helped me save Gray."

"Oh, Helen. I took her to Gunther's on Tuesday. She told me Douglas had taken her there on Monday and she certainly did like those ices. Douglas and Alex were screaming at each other about Helen? Why, for heaven's sake? She's a good sort. Likes a jest and a mug of ale. And those Gunther ices. When we were driving in the park later, she knew at least half a dozen people. She said that Douglas had taken her driving the day before and introduced her to everyone. I'll have to tell Alex to get a grip on herself."

He rose and dusted his hands on his breeches. "Now I'm off to think. Re-rotten the borough, huh? That might be an appropriate solution, Jack. Thank you."

Jack just stared at Ryder's back as he accepted his newly reshaped hat from Quincy and left, talking to himself.

"Er, my lord, there are two letters here for you."

"I'll see to it later, Quincy."

"They appear to be important, my lord."

Gray grabbed both envelopes and stuffed them into his waistcoat pocket. He gave Jack a big smile, hauled her up in his arms, and took the stairs two at a time.

"Our boy is married," said Mrs. Piller fondly, standing beneath a large portrait of an eighteenth-century St. Cyre viscount. "Imagine, carrying a young lady in his arms in the middle of the afternoon, all the while kissing her and laughing. It would have quite scandalized my dear mother. In her day, she told me, things of that sort didn't happen in a gentleman's household."

"Your mother lied to you," said Quincy. "Everything has always happened in gentlemen's households since the beginning of gentlemen."

24

As for the gentleman in question, Gray was starting to breathe hard. Not because Jack was weighing him down but because he was randier now than he'd been just three steps before. "I swore that not another day would pass without me trying to show you that a woman's second time with her husband brings tears of joy to her eyes. The day is nearly over and I haven't yet done a blessed thing. Yes, it's late afternoon, nearly evening. We must work fast, Jack, while there's still daylight."

"What if it were raining?"

"I'd have to go by the clock in that case."

He set her down in the middle of his bed-chamber. "You've never been in here be-fore. It's my room. It's got a lot of light if you fling back those heavy draperies, but you might think it's a bit heavy with all the Span-ish furniture my father brought back from Cordoba. This second time, Jack, there's no blood and I won't hurt you."

"I imagine that chest at the foot of the bed is sturdy enough for you to give me teasing lessons on, Gray. What do you think?"

He groaned instead, and was on her. But-tons, he thought, usually his friends, were slipping everywhere but out of their holes. He cursed.

"No, don't say it. Your mother made you eat turnips. I promise you, Jack. No more bleeding and no pain."

"I believe you. You're being clumsy, Gray. Do you know how that makes me feel?"

He looked at her. "Like you want to run back to your own bedchamber and hide un-der the bed? Like you want to go find yourself another husband who could dem-onstrate a modicum of competence?"

"No, you're far off the mark. Every time your fingers slip and fumble, it makes me feel blessed. You want me so much you're losing control of yourself. I like that, Gray, very much." She laid her hands over his and together they unfastened the row of buttons that marched down the front of her gown.

Finally her slippers were tossed atop that Spanish chest, her stockings were off her feet, and Gray stepped back to look at her. "I'm exhausted from getting you out of all those bloody clothes, Jack. But now, at last, you're naked, standing here right in front of me, and I can touch you wherever I want to. I don't know where to start."

"Perhaps," Jack said, her voice a bit on the reedy side, "perhaps you could take off your clothes too? I feel very strange just standing here."

"All right, but you're so beautiful, Jack, I will have to get out of my clothes by touch. No, I can't look away from you, I won't. I love your breasts, did I ever tell you that?"

"Yes," she said and slapped his hands away from his waistcoat buttons. His buttons were larger than hers and easier to work out of their fastenings. "Do you know what I want?"

He gulped, reached out his hand to touch her, then dropped it to his breeches buttons. He began fumbling. "What?"

"I want to unbutton your breeches for you."

"Oh, God, I couldn't bear that. No, keep your distance. You have no idea what that would do to me. I'm already closer to the edge than I was our first time together and that first time I was barely hanging on by my fingernails, and then of course I lost my grip.

"No, it's better that you don't do anything except stand there naked and breathe very lightly, and let me stare and go all dry in the mouth. Very well, go ahead, unfasten my breeches buttons. Oh, yes, there are three buttons. Now you're on the last and your hand, Jack, my God, that hand of yours is—"

She touched him and he shuddered like a palsied man. It was going to be close. When he knew he simply couldn't have her touching him any longer, he pulled away. "No more," he said, panting, "no more."

It took another three minutes to get him naked. He kicked his left boot out of his way, grabbed her by the waist, and tossed her onto the bed. "It's a big bed, belonged to my grandfather. He died in this bed, but perhaps you don't want to think about that event at this precise moment."

He came down over her, closed his eyes,

tried to get hold of himself, then said, "Now, I'm coming up on my elbows so I can see your breasts."

"Gray?"

"Hmmm. I'm nearly ready to let myself touch you, Jack. No, I won't think about how my belly is against yours and I can feel every white inch of you. You're smooth and soft and—"

"Gray? I just wanted to say that I'd like to perhaps go over to the window and pull back the draperies."

His fingers were nearly touching her breast. He blinked down at her, his fingers still hovering. "I'm sorry, Jack. What did you say about the draperies? If you don't like them, then we can pull them down. Now—"

"No, please, Gray. You stopped teasing me. You mean business now. You're like a racehorse who sees the finish line and is going all out to get there first. I'm the jockey, Gray, and I don't even know where the reins are now. I'm not sure of any of this anymore."

It was the hardest thing he'd ever done, at least the hardest thing he'd ever done that he could remember at this moment. Jack was afraid. Curse it, she was right. He was galloping. She wasn't galloping. She'd come to a full stop. She'd lost the reins. He cursed, saw a plate of turnips, and rolled off her.

"I'm sorry," he said, coming onto his side. "This is a very odd thing, Jack. No, I'm not lying to you. If you hadn't stopped me, I don't know what I would have done. Probably you would have been left in the dust again, wondering what kind of a clod I was." He leaned down and kissed her breast.

She froze. He continued kissing her, light, nipping little kisses on her mouth, her chin, her eyes, nothing menacing or suspect. Slowly she began to ease. Gray kissed very well and he tasted sweet, and her interest grew. She placed her hand on his shoulder and brought him just a little closer to her. He raised his hand and lightly brought it down on her breast.

"Oh," she said. "Gray, this is all very nice. You're teasing me again."

"I'll tease you forever, Jack. I swear I won't forget anymore."

He kissed her breasts, then moved to her mouth while his hands caressed her. When she lifted herself toward him, he wanted to shout. "That's right," he said between kisses, "just enjoy yourself, Jack. I'm not going to roll over on you and crush you into the bed."

It was then that she arched up and kissed him herself. He started to say something more, and to his nearly hysterical pleasure, she slipped her tongue into his mouth. Not a moment later, she was pulling at him. She even tugged on his hair.

And he, an intelligent man of superb judgment, said easily, "No, Jack, not just yet." He smiled down at her as his palm flattened on her belly. Her muscles tightened beneath his hand. He didn't move his palm, just let it lie there, warming her. Finally, she said, "Oh, dear, Gray, perhaps you could consider remaining there for a while longer, even extending beyond the present reach of your fingers."

"I know," he said, "I know." When his fingers found her, she nearly trembled herself off the bed.

"Oh, goodness, this is just too much. It's—"

"Just wait, Jack." Without another word, he came over her. His mouth replaced his fingers, and Jack, embarrassed for perhaps a blink of an eye, forgot everything, even her own name, when she went over the edge into a blinding sort of pleasure that tossed her about like a leaf in a strong wind. She gasped for breath, arched her back, and tugged on his hair until he came into her. She simply couldn't grasp the joy of it, the utter belonging, the instant of being one with another person and that other person a man she'd met only a month before.

"I'm not going to live beyond the next minute," she whispered against his sweaty neck, enjoying his gulping breaths interspersed with kisses on her jaw. "Gray, if there is any enemy you wish me to rid you of, just tell me. I never imagined such a thing as this."

And Gray St. Cyre, Viscount Cliffe, closed his eyes, breathed in his wife's sweet scent, and the smell of sex and sweat, and settled himself atop her. His last cogent thought was that he was still inside her and it was more than a man deserved.

She must have dozed after Gray had showed her how she could sit astride him, and how she could treat him as her personal stallion and drive him as hard as she wished.

She smiled herself awake and welcomed his urgency as she felt his fingers probing each of her ribs three times. He was actually counting out loud. When he reached her lower ribs, he sighed deeply, kissed her slack mouth, and said, his nose nearly touching hers, "I'm adding rib counting to my repertoire. It seems to wake you quickly. What are you thinking about?"

"You kissing the back of my neck when you were inside me, your hands around me, pulling me back against you."

"Well, I did ask, didn't I? Ah, our third endeavor, you on your side with me curved around you. Was it just twenty minutes ago?" Already his heart was pounding, lust swirling through him. Since he was a man, he was eager. He supposed the combination was unavoidable. He also supposed that this was one area in his life where it was comforting to be predictable.

"And this, Gray? What does this do?"

She played no prelude, didn't digress to, say, his shoulder or just lightly touch his hip or skip to tickle his leg. No, she went to him immediately and touched him and held him.

He reeled with shock; he nearly yelled with the pleasure of it. "Jack, where this is going to lead—well, I know it will be to new heights, but that's not the point." He moaned. "Jack, it's going to happen very quickly if you continue touching and holding me like that."

There was a sharp knock on the bed-chamber door. "My lord?"

"Go away, Quincy." Was that his voice, sounding all blank and raw?

"It's nearly eight o'clock at night, my lord. Surely there must be some mention from one of you of sustenance by this time?"

He stared down at his wife, gritted his teeth, and sighed. "Quincy's right, blast him. I'm starving. I can wait for those new heights. What do you think?"

She leaned up and licked his neck. "Feed me," she said.

Georgie joined them for their late dinner, eating porridge sweetened with Mrs. Post's honey from her brother's farm in Sussex.

"How do you like the nursery?"

Georgie looked over her spoon at the man who was, like her sister, wearing a dressing gown and was feeding her sister bites of his bread pudding. "I-I-It's good, sir."

"I'm not a sir, Georgie," he said, looking at that one blue eye and one gold eye of hers. Unique, utterly unique. "I'm now your brother. Can you call me Gray?"

"You're old, like Freddie. But y-y-you're not as old as my p-p-papa."

"A name problem," Jack said. "What to do?"

"What do you think, Georgie? Do you think you could bring yourself to call her Jack instead of Freddie?"

Georgie gently laid her spoon beside her bowl of porridge and climbed up beside her sister on the arm of the wing chair. A thumb went into her mouth and she leaned against her sister. The thumb stilled for a moment. "Jack's not b-b-bad."

"I like Jack, too, sweetie. Why don't you think about it. You can call me whatever you wish. Ah, I'm so glad you're with me, pumpkin." She hugged Georgie against her, kissing her small ear. Gray saw tears swimming in her eyes. Jack pulled her onto her lap and began rocking her. "You and I are going to have such fun. I hear there's this place called Astley's. They have a horse ring with riders who do all sorts of tricks. Gray, have you ever been to Astley's?"

"Once when I was about ten years old Lord Burleigh took me. I'll take you and Georgie there next week."

Georgie took her fingers out of her mouth and said, "I like h-h-horses."

The next morning, Gray awoke early, feeling rested and remarkably energetic, feeling better, in fact, than he'd felt in a very long time. He stretched, hit a warm body with his hand and froze. For those few moment, he'd forgotten. His wife was sleeping next to him.

His wife. Jack.

He very carefully eased down again and pulled her against him. She fitted perfectly against his side, her face on his shoulder. He lay there, grinning like a happy fool, watching the morning brighten the bedchamber.

Finally he rose, careful not to awaken her, knowing she must be exhausted. He'd been the one to lead her to that marvelous exhaustion. He went to his dressing room and rang for Horace, his valet, a man recommended to him years before by Ryder Sherbrooke.

Ryder Sherbrooke had saved him from deportation to Botany Bay when he was ten and had been found guilty of stealing a gentleman's gold watch from his pocket. He'd been beaten thoroughly, and Ryder knew he would never make it to faraway Australia.

He bribed Horace's way out of Newgate the night before he was to be sent away.

Gray had been visiting Ryder and Sophie at Chadwyck House on Horace's eighteenth birthday. Speaking excellent English and being a gentleman's gentleman were Horace's dreams in life. He spoke English like an Etonian, thanks to Ryder. As for the rest of it, *Why not?* Gray had thought, and they'd struck a deal. They'd been together now four years.

They were also only four years apart in age. Horace told him everything, from Remie the footman's latest female conquest to the mood of Durban on any given morning.

When Horace, trim and fit and taller than Gray, his nose crooked from being broken years before, came into the dressing room, he was holding two wrinkled envelopes in his hand as well as a bucket of steaming water.

"What are those?"

"I found them in your waistcoat pocket," Horace said, handing them to Gray. "I, uh, understand from Mr. Quincy that you were rather in a hurry yesterday after Mr. Ryder left and didn't take the time to read them. Mr. Quincy was all aflutter—you know how he gets—because the boy who had delivered one of the letters said it was very urgent. Mr. Quincy wanted to know if you'd read it. Well, I told him I wouldn't know about that, would I?"

Gray stood there in his dressing room, naked, the early morning light spilling in the tops of the two wide windows, and unfolded one of the letters. He smoothed it out with his hand, then grunted. It was another threatening letter from that sniveling sod, Clyde Barrister. It was time, Gray thought, to follow through on his original promise to beat Clyde senseless. He remembered the other letter—it had arrived just before the great-aunts, and now, just a few weeks later, he was married.

"My lord?"

Horace cocked his head to one side, watching Gray.

"What? Oh, nothing, Horace, just another idiot letter from Clyde Barrister, the fool. I'll have to see to him once and for all. Give me the other one."

Gray read the second letter, then sighed. "Well, this is a relief. The note is from Lord Burleigh. He wants to see me, says it's urgent." Gray raised his head. "I wonder what it could be. At least he's got his wits back again."

He handed the note to Horace. "Look at the handwriting. He wrote it himself, but he's weak. You can barely make out some of the letters."

Horace read it once, then twice.

He looked up and said, "Lord Burleigh is your godfather."

"Yes," Gray said. "He is. He's also her ladyship's guardian."

"If Lord Burleigh is as weak as his handwriting appears, I believe, my lord, that you'd best bathe quickly and then we'll get you dressed."

"Yes," Gray said, climbing into the bathing tub. He began to lather himself, wondering what was so damnably urgent.

25

"My lord," Gray said as he grasped Lord Burleigh's hand between his own. It was difficult to keep his voice calm, his face relaxed. The powerful man he'd known all his life had been replaced by this slack-fleshed, frail old man who scarce had the look of Lord Burleigh at all. Gray wanted to weep at the inevitability of death and all its indignities.

"Grayson," Lord Burleigh said and smiled at the young man he'd loved since he held him in his hands when he had been but three days on this earth. "My boy, to see your face rather than that wretched physician's—the damned torturer. No, no, I didn't summon you to an old man's deathbed. I'm too fond of you to stick my spoon in the wall in front of you. Sit down, and Angela will give you a nice cup of tea."

Lady Burleigh, Lord Burleigh's wife of thirty-eight years, handed Gray a cup of tea, simply nodded at him, then sat on the other side of the bed, gently taking her husband's hand in hers.

Lord Burleigh's eyes were closed.

"He will rest a moment, then speak again," she said. "He is beginning to regain strength, but it will take time. He must go slowly. No, don't look so frightened. He will get well. Now, drink your tea, Grayson."

"I received an urgent note from him, my lady. I didn't read it until this morning."

"Yes," said Lord Burleigh, his eyes still closed. "You came. Now, my dear, would you please take Snell, who's always hovering over there by the door, tell him not to worry so much, and leave Grayson alone with me?"

"But, Charles—"

"No, Angela. Don't treat me like I've got one foot already over the edge. This is important. Please."

He fell silent again. Gray watched Lady

Burleigh and Snell the butler finally remove themselves from the sick chamber. He noticed that all the draperies were open, sunlight pouring into the room, making bright splashes of light across the counterpane. Didn't anyone care that Lord Burleigh hated the sunlight? He went to each of the three large panels of windows and pulled the draperies tightly closed. Gloom and shadows filled the room.

"Ah, bless you, my boy. I hate the blasted light. It hurts my brain. But my dear wife insists that it is from the sun that we gain life and well-being." Lord Burleigh laughed deep in his throat. "If she only knew," he whispered, and coughed.

"Mr. Harpole Genner reminded me that you preferred the darkness. Now, my lord, they're gone. This message you sent me. You said it was of the utmost urgency that I come here. What is wrong, sir? What can I do to assist you? You know I will do anything in my power."

"Your marriage," Lord Burleigh said, grasping Gray's hand between his. "My boy, I had no idea you were acquainted with Winifrede Levering Bascombe, no idea at all." He fell silent. His breathing was light as a moth's wing. His hands were now limp at his sides.

Gray saw the loose flesh on the backs of his hands. He looked at his own hands, strong, firm, the fingers sure and dexterous. He closed his eyes a moment, waiting. What was wrong? What was this about Jack?

When Lord Burleigh opened his eyes again, Gray said, "Yes, my lord. You were very ill when we needed to wed. Mr. Genner and Lord Bricker approved the match in your place. They believed, as did I, that since you are her guardian and I am your godson, you would be delighted at our marriage."

A muscle contracted in Lord Burleigh's cheek. Gray said, "I didn't know her until about three and a half weeks ago. Shall I tell you how it came about?"

"No, it doesn't matter now. As you will guess, Harpole Genner and Lord Bricker told me of your marriage when I was finally reunited with my wits again some three days ago. It was a shock, a dreadful shock."

"It was for me as well, my lord, but I'm very fond of her. Of course you know that I didn't marry her for her money. I married her to save her reputation. She's a marvelous girl, my lord, full of caring and spirit and loyal to her bones. She makes me laugh. I have her little sister, Georgie, with us as well. I don't despair that this marriage will succeed. I swear to you that I will do my best to make her happy."

"No, Gray."

His eyes were closed again. He was sweating. Gray picked up a soft, dry cloth from the bedside table and gently patted Lord Burleigh's forehead. "It's all right, sir. Just be easy."

"I can't be easy, Grayson. It's too late."

"I don't understand, sir."

"You can't be married to Winifrede Levering Bascombe. I can't begin to tell you how appalling it is."

Appalling? What the hell was this? "Good God, sir, why?"

Lord Burleigh grasped Gray's hand. His eyes were nearly black with intensity. "Listen to me, Grayson. I'm so very sorry, my boy, so very sorry indeed, but there's simply no choice for you. You must end it. An annulment. It's the only way."

"Sir, please. You must remain calm. I don't understand you. What is this about an annulment?"

Lord Burleigh's fingers strengthened

around Gray's wrist. "You can't have her as your wife, Grayson. Such a thing is cursed by God. She's your sister."

"No," Gray said very clearly in that still room. "No, that's utterly impossible. You're mistaken, my lord."

Gray didn't return to his home until late that afternoon. He didn't see Jack, thank God. He went directly to his dressing room.

Horace was there, waiting for him. He looked at his master's white face and said immediately, "Sit here, now. That's right. What did Lord Burleigh want?"

Gray sat on the dressing stool, leaned forward, and clasped his hands between his knees. He looked briefly toward the closed door that led into his bedchamber.

"No, her ladyship is out with the great-aunts. Aunt Mathilda expressed a wish to see Queen Elizabeth's tomb in Westminster Abbey. They took Georgie with them. The child was shrieking with pleasure. I believe Dolly wanted to shriek as well, but she couldn't, she's too old for it to be acceptable." Horace stopped. He couldn't think of anything else to say.

Gray finally looked up. "Lord Burleigh is my godfather."

"Yes, I know that."

"You also know that he is her ladyship's guardian."

"Yes."

"He told me that her ladyship is my half sister."

Horace just stood there, his hands limp at his sides, staring at the thick warm towels he'd heated in front of the fireplace for his lordship's next bath. Then he realized. "I forgot," Horace said, staring at those towels, anything but take those words into himself and give them meaning. "You bathed this morning. I heated the towels. You won't need them. You weren't at Gentleman Jackson's Boxing Saloon, were you?"

Gray shook his head.

"Then you've no need to bathe again. Do you?"

"No, I'm clean enough."

"Strange how I forgot something so ridiculous as that. Stay there, my lord. Just stay there. I'll be right back."

When Horace returned six minutes later, Gray was standing naked beside the bathing tub, holding a towel in his hand. Late-afternoon sunlight spilled over the tops of the draperies of the two wide windows.

"My lord? You wish to bathe?"

"What, Horace? Why, yes, I do."

"First drink this. Yes, sit down again and drink this. It will help."

Gray sat again on the stool. Horace put the snifter of brandy in his hand.

"Drink this."

Gray drank. Usually, brandy warmed a path directly to his belly. This time it didn't. It tasted cold, dreadfully cold. He sat there, balancing the glass on his leg.

Horace picked up the towel he'd dropped and put it over his shoulders. He said nothing, he merely stood there, his hand on Gray's shoulder, waiting.

"No," Gray said, looking up at him. "It can't be true, Horace, it just can't. Lord Burleigh must be wrong. He must."

He looked like a man who'd been dealt a killing blow. In the past years, Horace himself had dealt his master a few hard blows in the ring at Gentleman Jackson's Boxing Saloon, but not a blow like this. This was a blow to the soul.

His lordship was married to his half sister? He couldn't comprehend such a thing.

"No, Horace, he's wrong."

"You'll have a nice hot bath, then we'll see." Horace pulled the bell cord. It took a good long time for the footmen to bring the tubs of hot water to the dressing room. However, for the two men waiting inside, there was only endless time, and silence.

Gray knew he was being a coward. He simply couldn't deal with it now, he just couldn't. He slipped out of his home when he knew Jack was dressing for the evening. He remembered vaguely that he was supposed to escort her to some musicale, but the name of the host escaped him. He hid, in fact, until Horace assured him that even the great-aunts were employed in the drawing room, playing with Georgie, while Dolly, still flushed with excitement from their outing, looked on. Mr. Quincy was in the kitchen, fetching tea for the great-aunts.

Gray went to White's, sat alone, and ordered dinner. But he couldn't bring himself to eat. He knew he'd puke if he tried. He drank another glass of White's best smuggled French brandy. Odd, the brandy still tasted cold. Nearly frigid. He left White's and walked and walked, just as he had all afternoon. It was past midnight when he reached the river. He sat on the bank and stared out over the black water to the moored boats. He looked up at the quarter-moon, hovering clean and bright just above the far shoreline.

His half sister. No, no, it just couldn't be true.

He saw Lord Burleigh so clearly, his head a deep indentation on the soft pillow, heard his frail voice saying sadly, "I'm so very sorry, Grayson. You call her Jack. Do you know what her father wanted to name her?"

Gray shook his head. "No, I don't—" Then he remembered and he said slowly, "Graciella."

"Yes, it was as close to your name as he could imagine. Grace . . . Gray. But his wife refused the name. Did she suspect? I don't know. He never said. The girl baby was named Winifrede, according to his wife's wish."

Gray suddenly began to laugh. He slapped his hands on his thighs, he laughed so hard. He gasped for breath as he said, "Oh, God, do you know what this means as well, my lord? One hears there is always something good to be found, no matter how hideous a situation. And there is in this one as well. It means that that miserable bastard wasn't my real father. I don't carry any of that monster's blood. Well, that must be something."

"No, the man who raised you had no claim on you."

"He was an animal, you know," Gray said slowly. "He beat my mother."

"Yes, I know. There was nothing I could do about it. Actually, my boy, I know all of it. I just never saw the point in speaking to you of it or to anyone else, for that matter, not even your real father, Thomas Levering Bascombe, Baron Yorke. I remember right after your mother's husband died, Thomas came to me. He wanted to go to your mother, tell her that at last he would care for her, that if she wished it, he would look after you, his son. He wanted to assure her that he would be discreet, that no one would ever guess anything at all, that he would never allow a hint of scandal to touch you, now Baron Cliffe.

"Then the illness felled your poor mother and it was too late. Thomas was greatly affected. He also felt tremendous guilt, and tremendous sadness because you were his son and you would never know him as your father. I've never before or since seen a man so broken.

"It was some months later that Thomas came to me with the request that I become Winifrede's guardian in the case of his death. I asked him why, point-blank. He said he realized that life was a fragile thing. He said he didn't trust his wife because she was incapable of judging men. He said that if he died, the good Lord knew what sort of man she'd marry in his place.

"He laughed, I remember, and looked as if he would rather cry. He said, 'Just look at her judgment for her first husband. Yes, Charles, just look at me!'

"It was a shock when Thomas Bascombe, your father, died the following year. During that year he thought and planned how he could become part of your life. He wanted it so very much. He told me he just wanted you to know that he was a man to trust, that you could depend on him if ever the need arose. He knew everything about you. He would tell me of your exploits at Eton. But then he died and there was no more chance.

"I became Winifrede's guardian. Nothing changed when her mother remarried.

Thomas had been right—Sir Henry Wallace-Stanford is a paltry excuse for a man.

"I'm sorry, Gray. It saddens me greatly, always has. The man you believed was your father died. Your real father, a man you never knew, died not a year later." Lord Burleigh closed his eyes again. He swallowed. Gray held his head and gently dribbled water into his mouth. They both waited, silent.

"I'm so very sorry, Gray. It was a tragedy, the whole matter."

"You refuse to say it aloud, my lord," Gray said. "You really must face it, you know, for I have. I faced it years ago. I would do it again, with no hesitation. The man who called himself my father didn't just simply die."

"Thomas Bascombe never knew any of it. I refused to tell him. Your mother certainly didn't." Then, just as suddenly, Lord Burleigh was asleep, his hand limp in Gray's.

Gray's eyes were closed now. He listened to the soft splash of water against the stone water wall, not six feet away from him. The grass was becoming damp. He didn't care. He stared at the rippling waves beneath the moonlight.

He had wed his half sister. He'd made love with her four times the previous night.

What if she were pregnant?

Something that just the day before would have had him bursting with pride, with immense male satisfaction, now brought him to his knees. No, Jack couldn't be pregnant. She couldn't carry his child.

He lowered his face into his hands. He listened to the night sounds—the rustling of the leaves by the night wind on an ancient oak tree just to his left, the faraway shout of a drayman, the dip of a lone oar into the still water.

Hours passed. He rose to see the sunrise. Odd how his world had come to an end and yet everyone else's world had just risen on another day.

He walked home, weaving through the ubiquitous drays and wagons weighed down with the day's goods, dodging the early-morning carriages, not even hearing the children hawking mince pies or seeing the dozens of black-coated clerks, hurrying toward Fleet Street, their heads down. He had his foot on the first step when the door flew open and Quincy burst out.

"My lord! Oh, my god, my lord! What happened? Are you all right? Come in now, come in. Oh, my, just look at you, all soiled and wet, your beautiful boots all covered with mud and what—"

Quincy broke off. He stilled. He very gently took his master's arm and led him into the entrance hall. "Come now into your study. You will rest and I will bring you a brandy."

And Quincy led him, as he had when Gray was just a small boy, to his study. He sat him down and went to the sideboard to pour brandy.

"No, no brandy, Quincy," he said, raising his hand. "Do you know that brandy tastes cold to me? It's true. I had two glasses of the stuff yesterday, and it was cold and hard all the way to my belly."

"It's all right, my lord. I'm going to get you breakfast and a nice hot cup of tea."

"No, Quincy, thank you." He rose again. "I must go upstairs. I really must go." Then he stopped cold. Jack was upstairs, probably still sleeping in his bed. Had she worried at his absence?

Of course she had.

"What time is it, Quincy?"

"It is just seven o'clock in the morning, my lord."

He walked up the wide staircase, knowing that Quincy stood in the entrance hall, staring up at him, wondering, worried. But what could Gray have told him?

I'm going upstairs to make love with my wife who also just happens to be my sister?

He laughed. He was still grinning when he saw Horace striding toward him down the corridor.

26

"Come, my lord," Horace said, took his arm and led him to the dressing room.

"Am I to take another bath, Horace?"

"You're sorely in need of one."

This time, Horace said nothing more until Gray was in his bath, steam rising up around his face.

"There was hell to pay last night, my lord. Her ladyship flew around the house, searching every room, questioning everyone in the household. I'd hidden myself in the cellar with a good book so she couldn't find me and question me until I broke down. I heard she was like a dog with a bone in its mouth.

She just wouldn't stop. I remained out of sight until well after midnight. Quincy told me she'd taken three footmen and they were in the carriage driving around London, looking for you.

"She was afraid, naturally. There was no note from you, no message, nothing. Even the great-aunts were searching. The little girl started crying because her sister was obviously upset.

"Her ladyship returned in the middle of the night. Naturally they hadn't found you. She waited more, pacing the drawing room. Finally she went upstairs near dawn this morning."

Gray looked at his knee through the thick steam, then rubbed it with a bit of soap. "I suppose that was a grass stain." He rubbed the other knee, then looked up at Horace. "They wouldn't have found me. I was down by the river, looking at the water and thinking about how our lives have simply flown apart." He wiped a washcloth over his face. It came away grimy. "I'm sorry about my boots, Horace. Muddy water lapped over my feet last night."

"It doesn't matter. What does matter is what you do now."

Gray didn't say anything more until he was dressed, shaved, his hair brushed. He looked like a gentleman again; only his face, pale, the flesh too tight over the bones, bore the signs of wreckage.

He walked quietly into his bedchamber. The clock on the mantelpiece sat at only eight-thirty in the morning. Dear God, he felt as though a decade had passed. He looked toward the bed. He was beyond exhaustion. He was nearly numb, but not his head. No, his head pounded with the knowledge that had destroyed them both. He wished for just a veil of grayness, a sheen of blessed darkness to lessen the sharpness. But everything remained stark and real. He was appallingly clearheaded, his brain wide awake.

The bed was empty.

Jack was wrapped in a blanket in a window seat that looked out over Portman Square. He watched her white fingers trace an outline in the fog on the window. Her hair was tangled down her back.

"Jack."

Slowly she turned. If his face looked like wreckage, hers was worse because there was fear burning dark and hot in her eyes.

"Gray! Oh, God."

She was on her feet, stumbling over the blanket that had fallen. She went down to her knees. Before he could help her, she was on her feet again, the blanket left on the floor, and she was running to him. "Gray," she whispered, her face against his neck, her arms wrapped so tightly around his back that he was momentarily surprised at her strength.

Slowly, his arms came up to hold her against him. God, the feel of her. He closed his eyes. The thought of never holding her again, of never kissing her again, never again making love with her. It nearly broke him. A sister. She was his damned half sister. He didn't think he could bear it.

Then she drew back. "You're home, finally. God, are you all right?" Her hands were all over him, his shoulders, his chest, feeling his arms. Then she was on her knees in front of him, her nightgown billowing out around her, and she was running her hands up and down his legs. "Nothing's broken. Thank God. What happened?"

She stood again, pressing against him. He realized she was shivering violently. From the cold? He didn't think so. It was from fear. Fear for him. He closed his eyes a moment against the magnitude of it all.

God, he was a bastard, a selfish bastard.

"It's all right," he said, marveling that that calm, utterly emotionless voice belonged to him. "I'm all right, Jack, truly."

"But why didn't you come home?"

"Come, let's talk." He grabbed her dressing gown and gave it to her. She just held it loosely in her hands, staring at him, not looking at it. It was as if it were something she didn't recognize.

He took it from her and dressed her like a child. It was very pretty, all soft shades of peach, going wonderfully with her coloring. He tightened the sash around her waist. She didn't move the entire time, just stood there, staring up at him, saying nothing.

"Sit down," he said and pointed to a wing chair in front of the fireplace.

He knelt down and lit the fire. "It will be warm soon."

"I'm not cold," she said.

When the fire took, he rose again and came to her. He went down on his knees and closed his fingers over her bare toes. She was right, she wasn't cold. Even her toes were warm.

"I'm sorry," he said.

She waved away his words. "It depends on what you're sorry about." She looked at him closely. He knew he wasn't an inspiring sight. He knew what he felt like—a man who'd battled demons all night, and lost. She touched her fingers to his mouth, then shook her head slowly, putting off what he had to tell her, he knew. "Just a moment, Gray."

She rose and gave the bell cord a good pull. She kept looking back at him over her shoulder, as if she were afraid he would disappear. She walked to the bedchamber door, opened it, and went into the corridor. Every few minutes, she looked back into the room at him. She said nothing at all.

Some minutes later he heard her speaking to her maid, ordering breakfast to be served here, just coffee and toast, he heard her say, brought here, to their bedchamber.

Their bedchamber. He closed his eyes.

He leaned forward in his chair, his hands clasped between his knees, staring into the crackling fire. She stood beside him, her hand light on his shoulder. He wanted to fling off her hand, yell at her not to touch him. His sister wasn't to touch him like that, like she had every right to touch him, like she had the right to be his wife and lover. He knew he stiffened, but he remained silent. He didn't want to, but finally he looked up at her.

"Do I look as bad as you do?" she asked.

It brought a brief smile. "Yes," he said. "I believe that you do. Won't you sit down?" All night, he thought, while he'd battled his demons, she'd battled her fear for him. And he'd allowed her to do it. He'd left her alone. There was no excuse, none at all, but he knew, simply knew, that if it were to happen all over again, he would have done the same thing.

"No," she said. "I feel more in control of myself, more in control of this situation that I don't understand at all, if I'm standing." Then she was quiet, waiting.

"It's something bad, isn't it, Gray?" Fear crawled in her voice. "No, it's more than bad." Her voice was sad now, and distant, as if somehow she knew their world had ended. Just like that, it had ended. He heard her swallow.

Not for the first time since he'd visited Lord Burleigh the day before did Gray wish that the man had simply died, taking the secret with him to the grave. But he hadn't. And now Gray knew.

What if Lord Burleigh died now? Did anyone else know?

Gray didn't think so. If Lord Burleigh did die now, then Gray wouldn't have to do anything with the knowledge. He could continue his life as if nothing had ever intruded, nothing had ever broken him to his soul.

But he knew. God, he knew. And knowing made all the difference.

"Gray?"

She'd spoken. He looked up at her, an eyebrow raised. "Yes, Jack?"

He saw it in her eyes, those lovely blue eyes of hers. She didn't want to know now. She knew, deep down, she knew there was something bad out there and it was just a matter of time before it flattened her.

"Nothing. Here is our breakfast." She left his side quickly.

When they were seated across from each other, each holding a cup of Mrs. Post's specially blended coffee, Gray said, "It looks to be clear today. At dawn this morning it was cloudy, the fog deep and thick, but now the sun is out. Yes, it will be a lovely day."

"Yes," she said. "Sunny."

He wasn't hungry. Neither was she. They both fidgeted with their coffee cups for a moment, then Jack jumped up and said, "I will see to Georgie."

"Jack, no, please. Stay here, with me. I ran away and I suppose it would be only fair if I allowed you to do the same. But I can't. We must speak."

"I have nothing to say," she said, still not seating herself again, standing behind her chair, her fingers gripping the top of it tighter than death. "Well, yes, I do. The aunts are returning home today. They were very worried about you yesterday. So was Georgie."

"I will miss them," he said. He gripped the edge of the table until his own knuckles showed white. "Remember that note Quincy gave me yesterday when I was hauling you upstairs and couldn't be bothered?"

She nodded, leaned down, and picked up a piece of cold toast, tore off a piece, then dropped it back on her plate.

"I read the note this morning. It was from Lord Burleigh. He wrote that he had to see me on a matter of the gravest urgency. I went. I found out what he wanted to tell me."

She saw the pain in him, and something else as well. It was the memory of the utter shock, perhaps of disbelief. But of what? She realized that what she saw on his face now was acceptance of whatever he'd found out. No, no, surely she was imagining things. But the pain she felt coming from him, it was real, all too real. She didn't want to know anything more, she didn't. She was trembling. She sat down in her chair again.

"I'm very sorry that I didn't return home yesterday. I couldn't. I guess I'm a coward. Weak, pathetic really. It was just such a shock. I couldn't deal with it; rather, I had to try to deal with it by myself first."

The shock. Yes, she'd seen the shock, he saw that she had. She remained silent, stiff, as if awaiting a blow. But she couldn't begin to know.

He couldn't keep it back any longer. "He told me that you and I share the same father, Jack. Thomas Levering Bascombe was my father as well as yours."

She stared at him, her mouth open to say something that wouldn't be said now. No, she hadn't heard him correctly. Her mind was shifting in and out of the shadows, wanting to hide, and that's why she had heard something utterly ridiculous, utterly unbelievable. No, he was going to tell her that he didn't want her anymore, or that he was bringing a mistress to the house, or—yes, she knew now—he didn't want Georgie living with them. She could deal with any of those things.

"You're my half sister."

His what? A half sister? Surely that couldn't be true.

"That makes no sense."

"That's what I would have sworn as well. But now I believe him. What he said, it was convincing. It's what Thomas Levering Bascombe—your father—told him."

She rose from her chair slowly. She leaned forward, pressing her palms against the tablecloth.

"It is ludicrous. I don't believe it. I refuse to believe it."

"Your father wanted to name you Graciella. You told me that yourself. It was because my name was Grayson. He wanted our names to be close. Your mother preferred Winifrede. Did she know about me? Lord Burleigh didn't know."

"You want me to believe that my father made love with a lady of quality, impregnated her, and then didn't marry her? My father was an honorable man. He never would have done that, never."

"Evidently what happened was that your father and my mother fell in love. He was sent to the Colonies to negotiate the peace between the Colonies and England. He didn't know my mother was pregnant until he returned and discovered she'd had a child—me. She'd married the man whose title I now carry. As much as I loathed my father, it still isn't particularly fair that I, not of his blood, now control all that was his." He frowned over that. "No, I take that back. Given who and what he was, he deserves to be in hell. Any man could have his title and it would be a vast improvement."

Jack said, "Show me evidence that this is true."

"There is nothing in writing. There is only Lord Burleigh's word for it."

"And you believe what he told you?"

"Yes. I didn't want to. But by the middle of last night, I realized that the truth is that, simply the truth, and there is no hiding from it, no pretending that it doesn't really exist, or that if it does, it can be hidden."

Jack drew herself up and took two steps back. "I see," she said slowly. "Yes, I see everything now. Throughout the long night you kept yourself apart and alone and agonized about this. And this morning you have emerged from your pathos a philosopher. Well, I haven't had the time you took, Gray, the time to work your way through this— whatever it is. I'm leaving now. I'm going to see Georgie, then I'm going to take her to the Parthenon to shop. I will buy her a pink ribbon for her hair."

"There are decisions to be made, Jack."

"You ran, Gray. It's now my turn. We will speak of this again tomorrow. Perhaps, like you, I will return a philosopher."

27

It was eight o'clock that evening when Jack walked into his study. The draperies were pulled and a sluggish fire burned in the fireplace, sending an occasional streak of orange light into the dark shadows.

She finally saw Gray seated behind his desk, his head down on his arms.

She went to the large branch of candles on his desk and lit them. He slept on.

"Gray."

He thought he heard his name—a strident voice, fierce, a voice he didn't recognize.

"Gray."

Louder now, that voice. Hard and cold as

well. He slowly opened his eyes. He looked up to see Jack's face in the candlelight.

"Hello," he said. "I suppose I fell asleep."

"Evidently."

"I dreamed I heard a harsh voice. I wasn't wrong. I just didn't realize it could ever be you."

He thought her voice had sounded hard. Actually, she wasn't feeling at all hard. Rather, she felt as fragile as a mirror; one good crack and she would shatter into so many pieces that she'd never be whole again. But she knew more clearly than she'd ever known anything in her life that he had to believe her to be hard, determined. If he saw through her to her frightened soul, then she knew she would crumble. There'd be nothing more to do but crawl away, her life over. She drew a deep, gritty breath and said, "I've come to tell you what I've decided."

He was completely awake now, more alert than he'd ever been in his life. She looked unbending, as cold as a moonless winter night.

"First, Gray, I would like to ask you a question."

"Of course."

"Do you love me?"

She was going right for his guts. He had to keep his head about this, he had to keep his distance, to protect himself, to protect her. He said slowly, lightly tapping his fingertips together, "I don't believe in that French notion of lightning striking when you see a certain person and that person then becomes your mate for life. I've known you a short time, Jack. I'm fond of you. We laugh together. We seem to suit each other well enough." Then he knew he had to draw back, and so he said, placing her firmly in the past, "To me, that was a great start, but naturally, that's all it was."

She felt hard, focused determination, all on the surface to this point, there only as a fragile screen to protect her, begin to burrow deep inside her. She actually smiled at him. "I didn't know what you would say. Whether you'd lie one way or the other. This lie wasn't as awful as what I feared. No, I can work with this." Remarkably she smiled more widely at him. "Yes, I would even agree with you. What we have is a great start. You notice that my start for us is in the present, however, not the past."

He stilled; his hands dropped to his lap.

He had to make her understand, to accept what couldn't be changed, what would remain truth no matter what one wished with all of one's might. He said very gently, "But there's no longer a start for us, Jack. We've got to face up to it. It's all a matter now of how we'll deal with this situation. I'm very worried that you might be pregnant."

And she said, her determination still growing, "I wouldn't mind that at all."

He opened his mouth, but she stalled him, raising her hand. "No, Gray, listen to me. I told you, I've come to a decision."

Oddly enough, even though he'd come to accept that they would have to obtain an annulment, he still didn't want to hear her say the word. He hated the word. It meant the end. He didn't think he could bear it.

"Yes?"

"Lord Burleigh is wrong. My father wasn't your father as well. I refuse to believe it. Thus, there is only one thing to be done. You and I together must disprove the entire tale."

He could but stare at her. "You don't believe what Lord Burleigh told me? You call it a tale, as in a myth or a fiction to tell a child at bedtime?"

"That's right." She turned from him and began to pace some fifteen steps away from him, then back again, in her long-legged stride. She whirled about to face him at the far side of his study. "I don't understand why you would so completely accept what Lord Burleigh said. Listen to me: *he has no proof.* Nothing in writing. No sworn statement attested to by anyone. Yes, it's a tale, one he believes firmly, but nonetheless still a tale.

"I've gone over this many times in my mind, Gray, throughout today. Listen, Lord Burleigh has only my father's *belief* that he had impregnated your mother. Nothing more. You, Gray, bowed to his opinion, his consummate belief. No wonder—you've known him all your life. But I've never even met Lord Burleigh. Nor was I there with that sick old man, hearing the anguish in his voice, the sorrow for you, for both of us. No, you gave me only the facts—and the facts don't tear you apart with their sorrow and tears. They're cold and dry and don't clutter or numb your brain with the pain of it all.

"And so I tell you, it's not true. There are no real solid facts. Nothing to prove Lord Burleigh's allegations. Now, my question to you is how are we going to discover the real truth?"

He rose slowly to his feet, splayed his palms on the desk- top. "Jack, I'll admit it. When I left Lord Burleigh, I felt flattened, overwhelmed. I felt impotent. I was scared out of my mind that you could be pregnant because I did believe him. It's true that Lord Burleigh's pain and sorrow touched me deeply, scored his beliefs into my very soul, whereas you got a diluted version.

"But it doesn't matter. The truth remains the truth. I have no reason whatsoever to disbelieve Lord Burleigh. He was frantic. He didn't want it to be true, trust me on this, but he'd accepted the fact that he couldn't allow this marriage to continue.

"You're right, I was immensely floored by what he said, by how he said it. He believes this with every part of his being. Could I do less? No, I don't think so. I must believe him. Don't you think I wanted to fight against it?"

She didn't answer. She picked up her dark gray wool skirts and nearly ran back to his desk. She leaned over it, her face nearly in his. "You are not my damned brother. I cannot believe that you are so willing to simply give up, to simply toss me out of your life, to toss each of us out of each other's life.

"Now, since your mother and your father are dead, we must find another member of your family who was around your parents in those days."

Slowly Gray shook his head. "My mother isn't dead. Most everyone believes she died some ten years ago, but she didn't. She lives on my country estate near Malton, on the River Derwent, not many miles northeast of York."

"She's alive?" Jack nearly jumped up and down with joy and relief. "By all that's holy, that's wonderful. There's no problem now, Gray. I don't understand why you simply didn't tell me we would go immediately to see your mother. She would certainly tell you the truth, wouldn't she?"

"Yes, I suppose so," he said. "If she were able to." He dashed his hand through his hair. He looked away from her, toward the far wall covered with bookshelves.

"What, Gray? What is the matter?"

When he looked back at her, his eyes were shuttered, looking inward toward a vast wasteland of remembered pain. "I suppose you deserve the truth. My mother has been quite mad since the day I murdered my father. Or rather, since the day I shot the bastard who was beating my mother to death."

She said nothing more, simply walked around the desk and leaned against him, her arms around his back. He'd killed his father? She felt the wrenching pain in him and for a moment couldn't comprehend the magnitude of what he'd said. He'd carried this within him for so very long. She would wager that she was the first person he'd ever told of it. He'd been so alone. She didn't think she could bear it. She squeezed him more tightly, not caring that he'd stiffened, tried to steel himself from his half sister. "I'm so very sorry," she said against his shoulder. "So very sorry. I knew your father was a bad man, but this?"

"A bad man? My father? No, that doesn't begin to describe what he was. He was a monster. He beat her as long as I can remember. Then he started beating me. She screamed and cried, but did nothing.

"One day, when I was twelve years old, I heard my mother screaming. I ran into her bedchamber to see him hitting her with a belt. She was on her hands and knees, her head down, making these keening cries, and he was standing over her, his legs spread, wielding that thick belt. I couldn't stand it. I remember that I yelled at him to stop. He turned to face me and he was smiling. He said to me, his voice all jovial, nearly caressing, I remember, 'Well, boy, you want me to stop hitting the bitch? What will you do if I don't stop?' I stood there, frozen, just as I'd been since I was old enough to realize what he did to her. He laughed, turned, and struck her so hard she went down flat. I ran into his bedchamber and got his gun that he kept in a lower drawer of his armoire. I didn't even stop to see if it was loaded. I simply ran back into my mother's bedchamber, saw him raising that belt yet again, and yelled at him to stop it.

"Again, he turned to face me. He saw the gun in my hands. I'll never forget what he said to me for as long as I live. 'You dare raise my own gun to me? Do you know what I'm going to do to you for that?' and he started toward me. I shot him.

"I shot him dead center in his chest. He stopped, one foot still lifted to take his next step toward me. I remember the look of utter surprise on his face. 'You shot me, you puling little whelp?'

"I said nothing at all. He came toward me, blood dribbling out of his mouth, falling onto his white shirt that was already drenched with blood from the bullet in his chest. I raised the gun and shot him again. This time the bullet struck him in the throat. I don't think I realized until then that the gun held two bullets. He cursed me, took one more step toward me, blood now spewing out of his neck like a great red fountain. Then he just crumpled to the floor."

She held him more tightly. She could see that boy, see his mother. But she couldn't see that horrible man who'd terrorized both the mother and the son. What Gray had done had taken great courage.

"My mother got herself together and crawled over to where he was lying. She looked up at me, tears streaking down her face, and she said, 'You killed the only man I've ever loved.' Then she fell over him, crying and crying. I went to the butler, Jeffrey, and told him what I'd done. He took care of things.

"I remember that Lord Pritchert, the magistrate, came to speak with me. Jeffrey and all the other servants stood with me. But there was nothing to fear. Evidently everyone in the neighborhood knew what kind of man my father was. He was neither admired nor respected by the folk thereabouts. He was probably hated, although no one ever said that to me.

"Lord Pritchert just asked me to tell him what happened. I did. He didn't even ask to speak to my mother. He just patted my shoulder and left.

"It was over almost as soon as it had begun. I killed my father and he was buried the next day, and my mother was quite mad from that day onward.

"Lord Burleigh came to the funeral. I remember he sat with my mother. She was simply silent in those days before and following the funeral. I don't believe she said a single word to him. It was Lord Burleigh who saw me through Eton and then Oxford, who introduced me into London society, who put me up for membership in his clubs. And never once, until yesterday, did he ever let on that there was any sort of question at all about the man who'd sired me. I assume that he believed having a rotter for a father was preferable to being a bastard and knowing it. Naturally, had it ever come out, I would have lost my title and my estates."

Jack eased back from him. She looked up at him, touched her fingertips to his cheek. "You were a brave boy. You put an end to the violence, the endless cruelty to both you and your mother. You became an excellent man. You're my husband, not my brother.

"We will go to Malton and see your mother. We will do what we can to prove that none of this is true."

"What if you are pregnant, Jack?"

"By the time we discover if I am or not, we will know that we are in no way related and we will rejoice."

He marveled at her. He realized quite suddenly that she was right. He'd held Lord Burleigh's hand, listened to his tortured words, and taken everything he'd said as truth. He'd simply given up. He'd not questioned a thing, not really, not like Jack had.

He gave her an odd smile, one that held a great deal more than she saw. "How old did you say you were, Jack? Surely you can't be just a green young twit?"

She laughed. She didn't know where that laugh had come from, but it was there, and it had burst free and she enjoyed that brief jest from him.

"Women are born wiser than men, particularly brash young men who are more handsome than they deserve to be. You will simply have to accept it, Gray."

Horace and Dolly rode together in the second carriage, perhaps enjoying each other's company more than one would imagine. Georgie spent half her time in each carriage, even Jack admitting with an exhausted laugh that six hours in a closed space with a five-year-old little girl would give her gray hairs before she was twenty. As for Gray, he discovered that any possible gray hairs wouldn't be all that bad. Georgie now smiled at him. He'd earned that smile. He'd played Chase the Chicken with her for one hour and twelve minutes, without pause, never once succumbing to a headache, as Jack, the weakling, had done earlier. It was Georgie who said she wanted to bird-watch. He'd shown her a black bird in the first three seconds of looking out the carriage window. Georgie had then taken his hand, rubbed it against her cheek, and said, "I like p-p-porridge."

Gray had stared at his hand, cocked his head to one side, and asked, "My hand feels like porridge against your cheek?"

Georgie laughed. "I l-l-like p-p-porridge with honey." She never answered his question. After seeing three crows flying just over the trees, she fell asleep, sprawled boneless on his lap.

If it hadn't been for Georgie, he didn't know how he and Jack would have survived the journey. If Gray had been Catholic, he would have believed them in purgatory, with no real idea of what would happen to them. One moment he felt blinding hope; the next, he was thrown into shadows, crushed by those shadows, knowing he would never escape them.

The nights spent at inns, Jack slept with her little sister and Dolly in another bedchamber. She didn't say a word to him about it, just took Georgie's hand and led her away. Each night he'd been both immensely relieved and angrier than he'd ever believed a man could be. He wanted to strike out, viciously. Horace was there, always there, saying little, but Gray appreciated his presence, his stolid support, his silent companionship. During those nights at the inns,

Gray listened to Horace's steady breathing in sleep, and it became like the steady beat of a clock, predictable, soothing.

They arrived at Needle House, Gray's country estate, four days later. It was a small red-brick Georgian house, three stories tall, a long rectangle, only one hundred years old. Gray's great-grandfather, the third Baron Cliffe, had built it early in the last century.

At least Gray prayed that the third Baron Cliffe had been in truth his great-grandfather, that the third Baron Cliffe had indeed spawned the man who must be Gray's father's father. Monster or no, Gray wanted his father's blood in his veins more than he'd wanted anything in his life.

The grounds weren't extensive, but they were neatly bounded by hedgerows lining the long drive. Beech and pine trees surrounded the side of the house set along the riverbank.

It was a cloudy day, the air chill. Gray hadn't been here in eight months.

"You've grown very quiet in the last hour," Jack said as the carriage pulled to a stop before the house.

"Yes," he said, nothing more.

She took his hand, shaking it a bit. "Listen, Gray. It will be all right. We will get through this."

He nodded; he didn't look at her, didn't smile.

She wondered what he was thinking. She wondered if behind those doors of his home dwelt nightmares he didn't want to face. She said nothing, but just held his hand and didn't let it go.

The front doors opened and a very old man with thick, tousled white hair, taller than the birch sapling beside the front steps, took very careful, measured steps outside. Then he stopped, shaded his eyes with his hand, and yelled, "Is that you, my lord? Is it truly you? Or is Mrs. Clegge wrong and it's the vicar instead come to gather up old clothes for the orphans?"

"It's Baron Cliffe, Jeffrey," Gray shouted back, although he wasn't further than fifteen feet away from the old man.

He said to Jack, "Jeffrey has very weak eyes. They worsen by the year. As for his hearing, it's always been very nearly nonexistent. Speak very clearly and loudly. He's a grand old man, tells stories about the Hell Fire Club, and came with my mother when she married my—" His voice simply stopped.

"We'll see," Jack said. She wanted to hug him, but she didn't, not now. She said to Georgie, "Pumpkin, here comes Jeffrey. He looks nice, doesn't he?"

"N-n-no," said Georgie. "He looks like God."

"Yes, he does," Gray said, "what with all that white hair. Yes, I've always thought Jeffrey looked older than dirt."

Georgie laughed a stuttering laugh.

Jeffrey couldn't see the new baroness very well, but her voice sounded bright, and so he grinned at her fatuously and deigned to bow her into the Needle House drawing room himself, calling over his shoulder, "Mrs. Clegge? Where are you now? You must come out to meet her new ladyship. Ah, I think I can smell you. I do enjoy that lavender scent. Don't forget your special lemon crumpets. The little girl will like the crumpets. I'm sure I heard a little girl, at least some sort of child. His lordship hasn't spoken yet of a child, so I don't know. Hurry now, Mrs. Clegge."

"Actually," Gray said quietly to Jack, "it's Mrs. Clegge's daughter, Nella, who's now the housekeeper. But her voice sounds surprisingly like her mother's. Jeffrey has never accustomed himself. He fancied the mother once a long time ago, but I was told she fancied the gamekeeper.

"Every so often, even to this day, Jeffrey kisses Nella on the cheek and tells her that perhaps someday they will eventually wed. Nella, thank God, is a sensible woman with a very big heart. She laughs and tells him he has far too much hair for her. That and he's far too smart for any woman with only middling wits."

Gray paused, stared out a wide window that gave onto the side yard at a deer who was grazing quietly, then added, "She also takes excellent care of my mother."

Jack wondered at the pain it brought him to see his mother. Did he remember her tears, her screams, her escape to madness, when he looked her?

She looked back at Georgie, who was sitting very close to Nella Clegge, a stout woman with large hands and a kind face. It appeared that Georgie liked Nella's lemon crumpets. Jack fidgeted the entire time her little sister ate her treat. She wasn't hungry, nor was she at all thirsty. What she was, in fact, was terrified. She didn't believe for an instant that Gray was her half brother, but she was afraid they wouldn't be able to prove it. She knew, she knew it all the way to her bones, that without positive proof, Gray would insist upon an annulment. He would hate it; it would kill him, but he would do it. His honor would force him to do it.

When she couldn't stand it, she said, "I can't wait another minute, Gray."

28

"I can," he said, drawing a deep breath. "I could wait an eternity. But you're right. Let's go."

Georgie, a lemon crumpet in her small hand, was quite content to sit on Nella's lap, and look at Jeffrey, saying every few minutes, "H-H-He is God, isn't he?"

"Well, little love," Nella said, looking down into Georgie's face, "you certainly look like the perfect little angel, so perhaps you're right."

The dowager baroness was in the largest bedchamber at the eastern end of Needle House. Actually it was a suite of three rooms, decorated with pale yellows and greens and white. *Lovely rooms*, Gray thought, wondering how much his mother had ever even noticed them. He'd spoken to Nella a few minutes before coming up. Nella had leaned away from Georgie and said, "She's very quiet, my lord. She frets with the fringe on her various shawls, endlessly she frets. She's healthy, her color good. Dr. Pontefract believes she'll outlive us all. He spends quite a lot of time with her, just speaking of the weather, of places he visited when he was in the Navy, of the towns over in the Colonies. She's not unhappy, my lord, don't ever think that she's in a pathetic condition. I don't understand her world, but whatever is in it, she's not unhappy.

"Perhaps she'll venture out of her world and into this one if she understands that you're married and her daughter-in-law is here to visit her. Now, I'll keep my eye on the little girl. Those eyes of hers, they're incredible, aren't they? One blue and one gold; it's marvelous. Ah, I'm going on and on. My husband just shakes his head at me when I chat with him. Forgive me, my lord.

"You and her ladyship go up. I'll bring tea shortly. Your mother adores tea and my lemon crumpets. Mr. Jeffrey likes them too. They were my mother's recipe."

Gray found he was walking more slowly the closer he got to his mother's rooms. Finally, though, he and Jack were there, outside the thick oak doors to the baroness's chambers.

"You heard what Nella said. Over the years my mother occasionally speaks, occasionally knows who I am, sometimes even realizes who she is. I don't know, Jack. I don't know what we'll find out from her, if anything at all."

"I know," Jack said. "I know. It's all right."

He gave her a twisted smile, then lightly tapped on the door before turning the knob and walking in. He kept Jack behind him. "Wait a moment," he said, then walked over to the row of windows that faced the south, over a small garden, exquisitely planted, some of the flowers just beginning to bloom, and beyond to the home wood, a large area covered with oak and pine trees.

It was a beautiful prospect if one were mad and had nothing else to look at.

Gray came down beside his mother's chair. He gently lifted her hand, kissed her fingers, and said quietly, "Hello, Mother. It's me, Gray, your son. I've come here to visit you."

The beautiful creature with lustrous thick blond hair plaited atop her head turned slowly to look down at him, on his haunches beside her. He had his mother's light green eyes, the slant of her eyebrows, the darker color of both brows and eyelashes.

He hadn't thought to ask Lord Burleigh if he resembled Thomas Levering Bascombe. As for the man he'd believed was his father, he simply didn't remember if he bore any physical resemblance at all to him.

He squeezed his mother's hand. "Mother? It's your son, Gray. I've brought you a surprise."

There was a flicker of interest in her eyes. She said, "A surprise? I do love surprises. Dr. Pontefract brings me surprises occasionally. What a lovely man."

She was speaking. That was something. Her voice was low and soft. He said, "I've married, Mother. I've brought you a new daughter. She's my surprise to you." He motioned for Jack to come over, and she did, walking more and more slowly the closer she got to the woman who was Gray's mother.

Only Jack heard the pain in his deep voice. She came down beside him and looked up at his mother. "My lady? My name's Winifrede. Gray and I were married just a short while ago. We wanted to come and tell you about it."

Alice St. Cyre, dowager baroness Cliffe, sucked in her breath, and raised her hands to her face, covering her eyes. "No," she said, her voice nothing more than a die-away whisper. "Not you. Oh, God, go away. I don't want to see you."

"Mother? What's the matter?"

"No! Go away!"

She kept her face covered with her hands. She was crying now, deep, gulping sobs.

Gray slowly rose, then pulled Jack to her feet. "It's no use. I'll get Nella."

Jack trailed out of the lovely bedchamber after him. She looked back once over her shoulder. The dowager baroness was staring toward her, her face filled with—what? Fear? Hatred?

Jack didn't know what to make of it. She felt herself shudder. She followed Gray from the room.

* * *

He wasn't in their bedchamber. Jack felt a moment of panic, then realized he would be as far away from her as he could. This was the last place he would willingly be.

Jack sighed as she walked to the fireplace and lifted her hands to warm them over the flames. She'd just kissed Georgie good night. She was quite content to sleep with Dolly, particularly with Nella just down the hall and Jack only two rooms away.

Where was Gray?

He'd been so silent after they'd left his mother's room. It was now ten o'clock at night. Was he brooding? Was he planning how he would annul their marriage?

She simply didn't know. She began to pace the length of the beautiful bedchamber with its autumn colors. The big downstairs clock stroked twelve long times.

Midnight?

She wasn't at all sleepy. She wanted Gray. If she but knew where he was, she would have gone to him in an instant. She wanted to hold him, kiss him, even though she knew he would fight that with all his strength.

More time passed until at last she simply couldn't bear it. She picked up a candle and left her bedchamber. She walked down the dark corridor to the end of the east wing. She raised her hand to knock at her mother-in-law's door, then slowly lowered it.

What if she were sleeping? It was after midnight. Then she saw the light shining from beneath the door. She gently twisted the doorknob. If Alice was asleep, with candles lit against the gloom, she would simply leave.

Alice St. Cyre was sitting in the same chair, not moving. There was a branch of lighted candles at her elbow. There was a book in her lap. Her eyes were closed, her head resting against the soft cushions of the chair back.

Jack didn't know what to do. She just stood there, staring at the beautiful woman who wasn't moving. She read books? If she did, then surely she wasn't all that mad, all that unaware of the world.

"Why don't you just come here?"

Jack nearly jumped a foot off the floor at the sound of that soft, feathery voice.

"Yes, ma'am."

"Come sit in that chair so I may see you more easily."

Jack brought the chair closer, then sat down.

"I'm sorry to disturb you, ma'am."

"You're not at all sorry. You're bristling with energy. What do you want?"

Alice still hadn't looked directly at her, even though she'd said she wanted to. No, she was looking down at that slender volume of Voltaire.

A madwoman read Voltaire?

"You couldn't bear to look at me when you first saw me this afternoon. You covered your face with your hands. You said you didn't want to see me. You told me to go away." Jack paused a moment, then said something she didn't want to say, "You recognize me, ma'am? Do I look familiar to you?"

Alice said nothing. She was utterly still. The beautiful Norwich shawl, all varying shades of blue, fell off her shoulders.

Jack said, "Gray looks a great deal like you. Perhaps you believe I look like someone you know? Perhaps someone you used to know?"

"Thank God he left."

"Who left, ma'am?"

"Lev. He left. I will never forgive him. He

was a monster. Not like my dearest husband. Why did Gray have to kill him? Why?"

"He shot your husband because he was beating you, ma'am, viciously. Gray was afraid he would kill you. He had to do something. He had to protect his mother. To my way of thinking, he saved both of you."

"I didn't need to be saved. All I needed was Farley. He loved me."

Gray was right, Jack thought. This was a sort of madness that was beyond her ken. How to regain any sense in all this? She said, "Ma'am, who is this Lev? Did you love him?"

For the first time, Alice looked at her squarely in the face. "You're very young. I haven't been young for longer than you've lived. Has he struck you yet, my dear?"

"No, ma'am."

"Ah. You'll know he loves you truly when finally he feels free to punish you as well as reward you. I learned so much from my dearest Farley. Dr. Pontefract says that Farley wasn't sane—that no sane man would strike a woman—but what does he know? Yes, Farley tried and tried to teach me to please him, to please myself. But Gray murdered him. Is Gray trying to teach you?"

"Yes, he is. But he hasn't ever struck me. He agrees with Dr. Pontefract. Gray would never strike a woman." She wondered what Gray would be thinking were he to hear what his mother was saying. What memories would her words resurrect?

"Do you recognize me, ma'am?"

But Alice, dowager baroness Cliffe, turned away from Jack. She pulled the shawl back up onto her shoulders and knotted it between her breasts. She picked up the thin volume of Voltaire from her lap, looked at it dispassionately, and tossed it to the floor. "I'm tired," she said. "Finally, I believe I will sleep. Go away. I don't want to see you anymore."

Jack slowly rose, not knowing what to do.

"Take that boy with you, the one who murdered my dearest Farley. I wish he would stay gone from here. When he leaves I hope that he'll never come back, but he always does. I rarely even speak to him, but still he returns. He's stubborn. But it doesn't matter. He stole all that I loved from me."

"He's your son, that boy. He loves you. He loved you then and that's why he shot Farley. He was protecting you. He did the only thing he could think of to save you. He shot the man who was beating you to death. Why won't you remember it as it truly happened?"

"My dearest Farley beat me to death? What utter nonsense—lies, complete lies. I didn't need to be protected!" Alice jumped up from her chair and hurled herself at Jack. Her thin hands went around Jack's throat. God, the woman was strong. But Jack was much larger and much stronger. However, she wasn't as enraged as Alice obviously was.

Finally Jack managed to pull Alice's hands away. They remained curled inward, ready to strike again, ready to rip the flesh from her throat.

"Stop it," Jack said low, grabbed her shoulders and shook her hard. She struggled, but Jack held firm.

"Stop it," she whispered now right in her mother-in-law's face. She shook her again, snapping her head on her neck. "Just stop it. Damn you, do you recognize me? Who is this Lev?"

Alice sagged against her. Jack clasped the woman close. She whispered against her soft, beautiful hair, "Tell me if Gray is your son. Tell me if you ever loved Thomas

Levering Bas—oh, my God, that's Lev, isn't it? You called my father Lev? Oh, God, you said he was a monster. What did you mean? You said he left? Please, you must tell me!"

She stared helplessly down at Gray's mother, whose face was pale as a winter's day. And just as empty, no hint of feeling, or pain, of memory. Just a beautiful face with no person behind it.

Jack had nothing to lose. She drew a deep, steadying breath. She said, "If you will but tell me about Thomas Levering Bascombe, I will keep the boy away from you forever."

"He murdered my Farley."

"Yes, I will keep him away from you, if you will just tell me about Lev."

Alice fell utterly limp against Jack. As gently as she could, Jack eased her back down into her chair. She waved her hand in front of her face. Soft tendrils of blond hair lifted off her cheek. "Ma'am? Are you all right?"

"Lev wanted to marry me," Alice said in a low monotone, not looking at her or anything else for that matter, as far as Jack could tell. "He begged and begged me, but I had met Farley and he was the one I wanted. We were alone one evening, Lev and I, out in my family's garden. It was a warm evening, thin white clouds trailing over the moon. Lev pleaded with me again. Then he kissed me. I told him to stop, but he didn't stop. Lev took my virginity that evening. He raped me. Then he told me, even as he stood over me, his legs spread, his hands on his hips, that I would have to marry him, that I was ruined now, and there was no choice. I was his."

Alice began to sob, ugly soul-deep sobs. Jack leaned down and gathered her into her arms. "It's all right. It was a very long time ago." And even as she spoke, hope was withering inside her. Her father had raped this woman? Oh God, she couldn't imagine it. Not her father, not the man she'd adored. She remembered so clearly sitting in front of him astride his great stallion, his strong arms around her, humming. Yet now she felt the angry, helpless tears of her mother-in-law hot against her neck. She closed her eyes, but there was no hope for it. She simply had no doubt that it had happened just as Alice had said. "It's all right," she whispered again against Alice's hair. "What happened then? Can you tell me?"

"Lev told me he would call on my father the next day. They would arrange a marriage contract. Everything would be all right."

"Didn't you tell your father what he'd done to you?"

Alice shook her head. "It wouldn't have mattered. He would have blustered about, then he would have done exactly what Lev knew he'd do. He would force me to wed him. I can even see my father blaming me, accusing me of seducing Lev, forcing him to marry me, not the other way around."

"What happened?"

"I had met Farley. I loved him. I ran away, to him. He lived in London, in rooms on Jermym Street. He took me in. I knew my father was looking for me, but he'd never imagine that I would come to Farley. I stayed with Farley, and then we married. Gray was born just over nine months later."

Jack stumbled back. She folded in on herself. Everything was over now. No more hope. Nothing that was good, that was joyful, remained. She knew she was crying, but there was no noise. Everything had burst inside her, and she was left with nothing at all, except this emptiness that would be with her forever, until she died, and she would die alone. She would never know Gray as her husband, as the man she would share her life with. It was over before it even began. She simply couldn't stand it. She rose slowly, raised her face to the sky, and shouted, "No!"

"What's wrong?"

It was Alice. Suddenly she sounded perfectly normal, as if they'd been speaking of the spring daffodils.

"I am married to Gray and I love him and he is my half brother and that is what is wrong."

She wanted to kill the woman, simply take her white neck between her hands and squeeze until this damnable pain that was eating her lessened.

But it wouldn't lessen, ever.

"You are Lev's daughter," Alice said. "My son told me this afternoon that he had married you."

"Yes, I am Lev's daughter."

"You have the look of him. It frightened me how much you look like him."

"Yes, I know. I also have something of the look of your son, Gray, who also has the look of you and of his father, Lev. Haven't you noticed? We are both fair. My eyes are blue and his are green, not much difference there."

"What are you talking about? You make no sense, girl."

"Lev is my father. Lev is also Gray's father. That's what you just said."

"You believe Lev is Gray's father?"

Jack just stared at her stupidly, wondering how much madness was within herself and how much in her mother-in-law.

Alice waved her white hand in Jack's face. "Oh, no, you silly girl, you don't understand. When Farley took care of me, I meant that he saved me. I miscarried Lev's child four weeks later, just before we married, and I nearly died because the bleeding wouldn't stop. He nursed me, saved me. Oh, I remember he was so desperately pleased that I wouldn't bear another man's child. I remember that he got drunk, he was so relieved. But to my beloved Farley, it didn't matter that I wasn't a virgin, that Lev had taken me first. It didn't matter until later, because I was so very slow to learn, to admit my guilt in the matter. Farley was always trying to get me to understand my guilt, to admit what I had done, to pray to God every night that I owed Farley more than I would ever owe another human being. And it was true."

Jack said slowly, "Evidently Lev always believed that Gray was his son. He told Lord Burleigh that Gray was his son, made him believe it."

For the first time, Alice smiled, a beautiful wide smile. "Yes, I know. It pleased Farley to let him believe it. Then he would punish me. All of it pleased him."

"Lev named me Graciella, wanting me to be close in name at least to Gray."

"Lev was a fool. I wish he had died when he went to the Colonies. He haunted me, the bastard. He came here to Needle House after Gray murdered Farley. He wanted me yet again, I know it. I know he wanted me to admit that Gray was his son. I refused to see him. Jeffrey told him of my dreadful illness. He had no choice but to leave. He finally died, did he not?"

"Yes, Lev finally died. Will you tell Gray that Farley is indeed his father?"

"You promised I would never have to see him again."

"That's right."

Alice rubbed her chin with her white hand.

"I would never have to see that murdering boy again. I could forget that he even existed. But I would have to see him to tell him that Lev isn't his father."

"No, you wouldn't. You could write it all on paper for him to read. Will you write down that Lev isn't his father, that I am not his half sister?"

Alice squared her shoulders and jumped to her feet with all the grace of a young girl. She looked into Jack's face and said, "I have thought about it. My answer is no. He killed his father. He killed my Farley. If there is suffering, then he will suffer. He deserves to suffer. There's no reason he should be happy after what he did. It is ridiculous that he should be happy with a wife. No, let him believe that his wife is in reality his sister. That will bring him more misery than he can stomach, and he deserves it. He is the monster, not his poor father. He murdered my only love."

The dowager baroness Cliffe turned away and walked to the far windows. She pulled back the thick green satin draperies and stared out into the black night. She said nothing more.

Jack stood there, mute, unable to think of a single word that might change the woman's mind.

What was she to do now?

29

Jack hurried back to their bedchamber, flung open the door, and ran into the darkness. There was a fire in the fireplace, no other light. Gray hadn't been here. She pulled up short. She realized it wouldn't matter if he were here or not. He wouldn't believe her. He would have to have proof.

Where was he? Probably hidden away somewhere in this house, pondering how he would gain an annulment, wondering what he would do with her, a wife he cared about who soon wouldn't be his wife if he could help it.

Slowly, she sank to the floor in front of the

fireplace. She looked at the one stump of wood that was just beginning to burn. She lowered her face into her hands.

She didn't move when she felt his hand on her shoulder, gripping her tightly.

"Jack, don't cry, damn you, not now, not just yet. We're not beaten. Come along. I just remembered that there's a large portrait of my father painted when he was not too much older than I am now. Just after I killed him, I pulled that portrait down and dragged it to the closet beneath the stairs on the first floor. Come, let's go see it."

He wasn't making annulment plans. He sounded excited. He sounded hopeful. She looked up at him and swallowed the damnable tears.

"Gray," she said, "a portrait of your father?"

"Yes, I never wanted to see the miserable bastard again as long as I lived. I wanted to erase him. Come along, Jack. It's nearly one o'clock in the morning. I was down in the library searching for anything my father wrote that could concern me, Thomas Bascombe, or my paternity. I didn't find anything as of yet, but that doesn't mean there isn't something, somewhere, I will contact his steward tomorrow. Don't worry, Jack. Don't give up. What's wrong with you? Come, let's go find that portrait."

He hadn't given up. She jumped to her feet, smoothed her skirts, then took his face between her hands. "I'm sorry I collapsed on you. It wasn't well done of me. Let's go."

Ten minutes later, Gray and Jack together dragged out a four-foot-tall, two-and-a-half-foot-wide portrait that had to weigh more than the boy who'd dragged it in here all those years ago. It was wrapped in a thick white Holland cover. Jack was spitting out spiderwebs from her mouth as they emerged from the deep under-stairs closet.

"Let's bring it into the study," Gray said. Once they had it clear of the closet, he hefted it up onto his back, saying over his shoulder, "Bring the candle branch, Jack. Yes, close the door first. That place was black as night and dirty as well. I'll tell Nella about it."

She followed him silently, her eyes on that huge covered portrait. She was praying as hard as she could. There had to be something in that portrait, she thought, just a simple something, some sign, a small proof.

She watched Gray prop the painting up

against his desk. Slowly he pulled off the cover. He wiped the cloth over the painting. She knew he wasn't yet looking at it. He rubbed for a few more minutes, tossed the cloth away, then looked at her. "Come here, Jack. We'll face this together. Why are you hanging back? No, don't be frightened." He walked to her and gently took the branch of candles out of her hand and set it on a side table near a settee. "What's wrong?" He gently pulled her against him. "You were so certain that everything would be all right. You made me ashamed that I'd believed it all without a single question. Then I remembered the painting. Come, let's face it together." Gray lightly touched his fingers to her white cheek. There was a small veil of spiderweb. He wiped it away.

She pulled away from him, grabbed up the candle branch, and set it atop the desk. It cast bright light over the painting. She took several steps back to stand beside Gray. Together they looked at the painting.

She stared at a tall, very lean man who was standing outside a stable. He held a bridle in a black-gloved hand. His other hand—not gloved—lay negligently on his hip. One leg was bent slightly, but still, he stood tall and proud. He was handsome, beautifully dressed in riding clothes, his head thrown back as if he'd just laughed at something someone had said just beyond him.

Gray breathed out slowly. "I'd forgotten what he looked like. I suppose I didn't ever want to remember."

He was as dark as Lucifer. One simply knew that beneath his white-powered wig his own hair was black and thick, opaque, without a single swatch of lighter color in it. His skin was swarthy, his eyes as dark as a bottomless pit, probably as black as his hair. His eyebrows were thick and arched, black slashes scoring his brow. Those eyes stared back at them, soulless, without light, filled with nothing that meant anything to Gray.

"I hated him," he said quietly. "I hated him more than anything or anyone in my entire life. He looks like Satan, doesn't he? No humanity in him, just endless cruelty, endless delight in dominating, endless belief in his own power—and he wallowed in his power, Jack, I do remember that. No one went against him. I remember now that he enjoyed simply looking at my mother, touching her beautiful hair, lightly stroking his fingers over her face, her shoulders. An angel and the devil. That's how they looked together. Her fairness fascinated him."

His voice sounded faded, as if he were seeing himself in the past, seeing everything through a child's eyes.

"Yes, he must have been something," she said in a very adult, very matter-of-fact voice. "A splendid fellow, don't you think? He beat his wife, beat his son, showed no mercy until his son, only a boy, was brave enough to stop him. Now, on the surface of things, he doesn't seem to have a single feature that he passed on to you. Let's study it more closely."

She took his hand and pulled him forward.

"Look at the black hairs on the back of his hand," Gray said, pointing to the ungloved hand that posed on his father's hip. He held up his own hand, letting the candlelight flow over it. "His hand is square, mine isn't."

"He has long legs. So do you."

"Many men have long legs," Gray said, staring now at the boots he was wearing. "His feet are long and narrow. So are mine. Many men have long, narrow feet. There's nothing to any of it, Jack."

"He has a very heavy beard. You can see

it, and given the angle of the sun the artist has painted in, it can't be later than noon."

"Yes, he was quite dark. I'm not. I fear I'm most like my mother, Jack."

But Jack wasn't listening. She was staring at Farley St. Cyre's wig, powdered stark white, tied in a black ribbon at the nape of his neck. Very slowly, she touched her fingertips to his forehead. "Look closely, Gray."

"What is it? He's wearing a wig. It was the style then."

"No, see how the wig doesn't completely conform to the line of his hair? Don't you see it? He has a widow's peak, Gray. You can see the arrow of black hair that the wig doesn't cover." She turned to smile up at him and touch his forehead. "Just as you have a widow's peak, a small one, but it's there."

He stared down at her, mesmerized. "I never knew there was even a name for it. Widow's peak? Isn't it common?"

"Oh, no, not at all common. Yours isn't all that visible because your hair falls over it, to the side, but look at his, straight and right in the center, a sharp arrow. Yours isn't nearly so dramatic, but it's still there."

"A thing called a widow's peak," he said slowly, stepping away from both her and the large portrait. "To accept this monster as my father because we share this same uncommon hair growth?"

"Well, there is something else as well," Jack said, and she told him how she had gone to his mother's room, and what his mother had told her.

"Do you remember Thomas Levering Bascombe coming here after your father's funeral?"

"No, I have no memory of him at all, ever."

"She said she refused to see him. She knew he wanted her again, wanted to marry her."

"She's quite mad, Jack."

"Perhaps, but there was no madness in the story she told me, Gray. My father raped her in order to force her to wed him. But it wasn't his child that grew in her, it was your father's, her new husband's. There was no reason for her to lie about the miscarriage, about how your father nursed her, ultimately blamed her for not coming to him a virgin, and beat her, but evidently cared for her nonetheless."

"A very strange sort of caring. I daresay she could have been a saint and he still would have beaten her."

She shuddered at the truth of what he said. "Strange indeed. She wasn't making it up, Gray."

"You said she refused to tell me of this? You said she refused to write it down? That makes no sense to me. Why wouldn't she want to tell me?"

It was hard. She didn't want to say it, but now there was no choice. "She won't write it down because she wants you to suffer."

He said nothing for a very long time. He simply seemed to stare into his father's black eyes. "He never hit her face, I remember that now. He worshiped her face, touched her face whenever he passed her. But her back, my God, Jack, she must have been scarred endlessly from the beatings of his belt on her back."

"Yes, more than likely. But it was a long time ago, Gray. Unfortunately, your mother still lives in that time, still sees him as the man who, when he wasn't pounding her, worshiped her. She can't seem to bring herself to forgive you."

"You mean she's always spoken so little

to me when I visited because she hates me?"

"Probably. I think now that seeing me so unexpectedly, seeing my father in my face, she let down her guard. She had to speak. I suppose I was the catalyst." Jack knew what she'd just said was true. She also realized that whatever madness gripped his mother, her feelings of hatred for her son were deep and abiding. She thought of Gray as that twelve-year-old boy, saving his mother the only way he knew, and she'd hated him for it. She wanted to weep for the pain he'd endured from these two people who were his parents and should have loved him and nurtured him, but hadn't.

Gray said, "All these years and I simply didn't realize it. Jesus, that bespeaks a fine sensitivity on my part, doesn't it?"

He was wallowing in guilt, and she was appalled. She said matter-of-factly, no hint of emotion or pity in her voice, "What it bespeaks is the demented spirit of a woman who could never accept the truth of things, who didn't have the strength to stand up to a man who hurt her, who turned herself into a victim and sought his cruelty as a drunkard would seek drink.

"I plan to speak to her again tomorrow. You will listen, hidden, perhaps, and she will tell it all to me again.

"Now, my question to you is, Gray, will you believe the proof of your father's widow's peak combined with the words from your mother's own mouth?"

"But why was Lord Burleigh so convinced?"

"Because my father believed it so deeply. My father was a very serious man, a proud man, a very intelligent man. I also believed him honorable and loyal and infinitely honest. I was wrong. He committed a grave crime against your mother. He is dead, so there is no retribution for him.

"I must also believe that my father wanted to recognize you as his son because he failed to sire a son by my mother. He had me and that was it. Gray and Graciella." Jack shook her head. "Such tragedy, Gray. But it's not our tragedy. Let it remain in the past where it belongs. We're free of it. You are not my bloody brother. You're my bloody husband, thank God."

Still he held back. "I want to hear my mother speak of it. I must."

"Yes," she said, and she even managed to smile up at him, "I know you must."

Jack held Georgie's small hand, saying even as they walked into the dowager baroness's sitting room, "She is a very lovely lady, Georgie. She rarely leaves her room, but that's all right. That just means that we always know where she is." And, Jack prayed, *I hope she will not scare you witless.*

Georgie just hummed, staring around her. "P-P-Pretty room," she said, broke away from Jack, and dashed to the brilliantly colored silk shawl that lay in shimmering folds over the back of a chair near to the windows.

"Who are you?"

Jack walked quickly to Alice's chair. "That is my little sister, ma'am. Her name is Georgina. She loves bright colors and soft materials." Jack called out, "Georgie, love, do come here and meet her ladyship."

The dowager baroness sucked in her breath. "Her eyes, goodness, how very strange she looks. One gold eye and one blue eye. How very odd. And delightful."

Georgie stood her ground, staring at the lovely woman who was staring back at her.

"She's as delightful as her eyes," Jack said. "May we stay with you for a while? I promised Georgie she could see your beautiful room. Is that all right?"

Jack said nothing more for a good ten minutes, simply waited, watching Georgie eye the woman, then slowly walk to her and stand beside her chair, looking up at her. No one could resist that face, Jack thought. She was right. The dowager baroness wrapped the shawl around Georgie's head, telling her that she was a sweet young miss protecting her hair from a stiff wind, and wasn't this lovely? Then she draped it over her shoulders. She was behaving quite normally, just as someone who liked children would behave. Jack never once turned to look back toward the bedchamber door.

Finally she said, "Georgie, if her ladyship doesn't mind, why don't you carry that lovely shawl over to the window and hold it up so that the sun can shimmer through it and make colorful patterns on your arm. You can make it magic with the sunlight."

"That was well done," Alice said, after some moments of watching Georgie waving the shawl through the bright sunlight pouring through the windows. "You brought the child in here to pave your way. She is not Lev's daughter?"

"No, she is my half sister. After Lev died, my mother remarried. You're right, of course. That's exactly why I brought Georgie with me. I worried that you would refuse to see me again."

"What makes you think that I still won't refuse to speak of anything to you? I am merely polite, you know. The child is adorable."

"Yes, she's mine now. Her father didn't beat her, but he didn't care if she lived or died. She's safe now with me."

"What does Gray think of her?"

"She quite has him dancing to her tune. Your son is a very good man, ma'am. I truly don't believe it's right for you to want to make him suffer. It isn't fair to him. Nor is it at all fair to me or to Georgie."

"Fairness has nothing to do with life," Alice said staring up at Jack, her voice sharp and cold. "Look what happened to me and then speak of fairness again. You'll find it impossible."

"I see a woman who has known tragedy, as many women have. I see a woman who can have anything she wishes to have simply by asking. I see a woman who likely hasn't done a bit of work in all the years she's been sitting dependent and lazy in this lovely room. I see a woman who can't face the present because she prefers to nurture a long-dead past, a pathetic past, truth be told. I see a woman who holds the past close, lovingly remembers everything that happened to her so that she can better feel her own pain, remember her own misery, wallow in her own sense of ill-use.

"I see a beautiful woman who is as sane as I am, and the good Lord knows I'm dreadfully sane, more sane than is probably good for me and all those around me." She stepped close, leaned down, and clasped the arms of Alice's chair. "Why don't you think about walking out of this damned bed-chamber? Why don't you think of running down those elegant stairs and flinging open the front doors? Why don't you go riding with Dr. Pontefract, ma'am? There is a lovely mare in the stable named Poet. Your coloring and hers would fit together quite nicely. Ah, I see you turn all sorts of pale and lean back away from me, like I'm a witch.

"Well, perhaps I am. Perhaps it's wise of you to be afraid of me." Slowly Jack straightened, folding her arms over her breasts. "Don't you look just lovely sitting there all useless, worth nothing to anyone, waiting for someone to lightly caress your forehead and tell you how lovely you are, how very fragile?

"But you're not at all fragile, are you? Oh, no, you're unforgiving, you're cold. You wish to hate a man who probably saved your life many years ago. That hatred is the only thing you nurture inside you because there is naught else but emptiness. What a wondrous thing: your present and your future—both faded before they can even come to pass because you've done nothing to fill yourself with anything good and worthwhile.

"You hated a twelve-year-old boy—your own son—because you simply couldn't face life by yourself, making your own decisions, never again having anyone tell you what to do."

"Damn you. Shut up, you miserable little bitch!"

Jack rose tall. She tapped her foot. She looked mildly bored. She raised an eyebrow and said in some surprise, "Me? A bitch? At least I'm an honest bitch, ma'am. I don't practice my die-away airs to gain my way, to garner sympathy. I don't cut off my own flesh and blood because I'm incapable of seeing the past as it really happened."

"No, you're wrong. You are cruel, unfair. You don't know what I've suffered."

Jack smiled down at the woman whose cheeks were becomingly flushed with healthy, furious color, whose chest was heaving with more passion that she'd probably felt in the past dozen years. Her smile widened. "You are very lucky, ma'am. Madness becomes you. May you enjoy your madness for many years to come. May you hold it close and find it warm as a lover and nurturing as a mother because it is all you will ever know, all you will allow yourself ever to know."

She turned on her heel, calling over her shoulder, "Georgie, love? Are you ready to take your leave of her ladyship?"

The little girl, who was blessed with sound hearing, turned slowly to her sister and the beautiful woman whose hands were fisted on the arms of her chairs. "T-Thank you, ma'am, for letting me p-p-play with your sh-shawl."

Alice looked at the flowing shawl that had filled and overflowed the little girl's fingers.

The sight had warmed her. Speaking to the child, the first child she'd seen in so very long, had made her wonder why she'd shut herself away from such a very simple joy. She looked at Jack, then beyond to where her son stood, arms folded over his chest, leaning against the wall beside the door, his face pale, the skin stretched tightly over his bones. The cast in his eye, that slight looking both outward and inward at the same time, it was from her.

She rose, standing tall beside her chair, and said very calmly, "You're quite legitimate, Gray. The man you've despised for so very long now—you carry his blood. Yes, my face, but his blood. Perhaps someday soon you'll want to give this girl here lessons on how to be a proper woman. Then, perhaps, your father's blood will show itself. Go away, both of you. Take the child with you. She's frightened by all the loud voices."

"Thank you, Mother."

Alice simply waved her hand at them, saying nothing more.

"G-Gray," Georgie said, tugging on his breeches, "that lady is s-s-strange, but she's ever so b-b-beautiful."

"Yes," he said, leaning down to pick her

up, "but perhaps she isn't quite as strange now as she was just thirty minutes ago. Do you know something, Georgie? You're a very special little girl. Now, how would you like to have lunch with me and my wife?"

"J-J-Jack told me I was s-s-special, but I didn't b-b-believe her," Georgie said. She smiled up at both of them then placed a small hand in each of theirs.

30

Gray said quietly to Lord Burleigh, the man who'd watched over him since he was a boy of twelve, "All these years, sir, you've held this secret close. I thank you for that. But now it's over. I am my father's son. Believe me, it's less distressing to accept that I carry that monster's blood than to believe I was a bastard, the result of a rape of my mother. Actually, I suppose that blood-wise it doesn't matter. They were both dishonorable men."

Lord Burleigh was sitting in a large chair, a plaid woolen blanket covering his legs. His skin had lost its grayish pallor, and his eyes were bright again with awareness and intelligence, thank God. He was still too weak to leave his bedchamber, but he was improving daily, Lady Burleigh had assured Gray when he and Jack had arrived. His voice was strong and deep again, and that relieved Gray enormously.

He sat back and closed his eyes. "I still have difficulty believing that Thomas Levering Bascombe did such a thing. Ah, what a man will do when he loses his heart. He must have loved your mother very much."

A man could be excused anything, Gray thought, his jaw clenching. He could rape a woman and have it seen as love. But he managed to keep his voice calm and low. "I would never call rape a possible consequence of love, my lord. As I said, given that particular show of brutality, I don't believe him so dissimilar from my own father."

Lord Burleigh sighed, closing his eyes for a moment. Finally he said, "I suppose there's some truth to that. I knew him for so very long, and yes, I admired him. You're positive, Gray? There is no doubt at all in your mind?"

Gray smiled. "No, sir, not a single doubt. I'm a very relieved and lucky man. My wife is waiting downstairs, enjoying tea with Lady

Burleigh. Would you like to meet her, sir? She's lovely, you know, and I imagine that just being with her will keep me alert, keep my mind sharp for a good many years to come."

"Yes, I should like to meet her. Bring in this young lady called Jack."

And so Jack finally met the man who'd believed in his very soul that she and Gray were brother and sister.

"I'm very pleased that you have found each other," Lord Burleigh said, tiring now, his wife saw as she moved closer to him. "I'm more pleased that I can say that there is nothing more to disturb your future."

Jack knelt beside Lord Burleigh's chair. "You forced us to confront ourselves, my lord. If things had turned out differently, then perhaps I would have been tempted to shoot you, but now I suppose you can hear my relief and my happiness shouting from my very bones.

"It's over—and do you know what?"

Lord Burleigh smiled down at the bright, glowing girl beside him. "Tell me what."

She leaned up and whispered in his ear.

"Ah," he said, "that's excellent."

Gray stepped forward at a sign from Lady

Burleigh. "Jack, my dear, his lordship is ready for a bite of lunch and a rest. We've worn him down, I fear." He helped her to her feet. She gave Lord and Lady Burleigh a lovely curtsy, took her husband's arm, and nearly danced out of Lord Burleigh's bed-chamber.

He was laughing. "You told him you would have wanted to shoot him. That's good, Jack."

"Nothing but the truth."

"What did you whisper to Lord Burleigh that pleased him so much?"

"Oh, just a pleasant little something, nothing all that remarkable, something that you, for example, could probably guess without a moment's hesitation."

He stopped just before they reached the upper landing and lightly closed his hands around her neck. "Tell me or I'll strangle you and toss you down the stairs."

She touched her fingertips to his mouth. "To have your mouth on mine again—as a lover's, as a husband's—you can't know how wonderful that is."

"You don't believe I understand all about wonder?" He leaned down and kissed her. When he raised his head he was smiling.

"Since we're in another person's house, I can't very well take this any further. You won't distract me, Jack. Tell me now what you whispered to Lord Burleigh. If you do, I'll let you kiss me again."

"I just told Lord Burleigh that I love you with all my heart and I will do my very best to make you the happiest of men."

She'd dropped into his placid, well-ordered life not much longer than a single month ago. She loved him? Her words surrounded him, slowly seeped into him. He felt something warm begin to fill him, something he'd never felt before in his life. He realized in that instant that what he'd come to feel for her was buried deep in the midst of that warmth and it was vibrant with pleasure and endless promise. But the words to express what he felt weren't yet part of what he'd become, and so he said, his voice as deep as the feelings that were swirling inside him, all the way to his soul, "All your heart? As in every small fiber in your heart is dedicated only to me and my happiness?"

"Every single fiber is yours."

His thumbs caressed the pulse in her throat. "In that case, then, I suppose I'd best keep you around. I like being happy." He kissed her again, more deeply this time, what he was feeling for her building and expanding, and he supposed then that it would continue to fill him. He couldn't imagine anything better than that. Snell the butler, the only witness to their display of affection, harummphed only very slightly to remind the young couple that this wasn't, after all, their own house, then turned away. Only two footmen were still staring when Snell closed the front door behind Baron and Baroness Cliffe.

When they returned to the St. Cyre town house, both of them nearly incoherent because they wanted each other so badly, they were stopped cold by Colin Kinross, the earl of Ashburnham, who nearly leapt upon them the moment they stepped into the entrance hall.

"She'll be fine!" he shouted, grabbed Gray's arms and shook him. "Did you hear me? Sinjun won't die birthing our babe. Dr. Branyon is an excellent fellow, Gray. He told me that she has wide hips, that she was created to make as many babes as she wants to. Or that I want to. He wasn't quite certain whose wants would take precedence, but that doesn't matter at all. All that does matter is that Sinjun will be here to torment me until the hands fall off my clock and I stop chiming.

"When Sinjun's time is nearing Dr. Branyon and his wife, Ann, will travel to Scotland and stay with us at Vere Castle.

"Ah, yes, it's about time you've returned home. From your wedding trip, wasn't it? Fresh love, there is nothing like it. Well, there is, but I needn't go too deeply into that. But neither kind of love is as important as Sinjun being healthy and all ready to birth babes."

He grabbed Jack, hugged her tightly and lifted her off the floor. "Your incredible new husband sent me the man to save my wife's life." He swung her around and around. Jack was laughing so hard that when she tried to punch Colin lightly in his belly, he laughed, twisted to the side, and nearly dropped her. It was Gray who plucked her out of Colin's arms and righted her again.

He pressed his forehead to hers. "I'm sorry, love, but I don't think Colin would understand if I pulled up your skirts right in front of him."

"He might," Jack said, then quickly stepped back at the look in Gray's eyes.

He'd called her Love. She wished Colin Kinross to the devil in that moment.

Colin said to Gray, "I couldn't very well dance around with you. You're a man and you're too heavy. You're still laughing. Does that mean you're pleased with yourself or that you wish me to Hades so you can have your way with Jack right here, right now? No matter—forget your lust for the moment. Just imagine it—Sinjun will be around to plague me for the rest of my days."

"I've just arrived to begin the plaguing," Sinjun announced from the open doorway. Quincy was standing beside her, grinning so widely that Jack could see the gaps left by missing teeth in the back of his mouth. "My husband no longer yanks at his hair when he looks at my stomach. He is pleased, Gray, as am I. We thank you very much."

"Congratulations, Sinjun," Jack said and hugged her. Sinjun looked over at her large husband, gave him so provocative a smile that it threatened to melt the brass fittings on his boots, then said to Gray and Jack, "Thank you both, very much. Whilst Colin has been suffering and making me suffer with him, I suppose you two have had nothing more on your minds than kissing and doing delightfully silly things to each other, and other things as well. I suppose you're wishing us as far south as Italy right now."

Gray brushed an invisible speck of lint from his jacket sleeve. "Italy is to the south, true enough, but you know, Greece is even farther south. A grand place, I hear. No, Sinjun, what I was actually thinking was that my Jack adores silly things. She likes to sing me ditties while I'm shaving in the mornings, just one small example. Our 'other things' were proceeding apace when Colin sprang himself on us. We, like you two old married fossils, are very happy, and we also plan to plague each other until the next century." He turned to his wife, lightly touched his fingers to her cheek, and whispered, "What do you think, Jack? Will we still be able to plague each other in another eighty years or so?"

"I'll do my best, my lord, to dodder along after you."

He patted her cheek, then dipped down to kiss her lightly on the mouth.

Sinjun rolled her eyes. "I remember when Colin and I were newly married, he was always finding the slightest excuse to kiss me, to haul me away to a handy bedchamber, or kitchen, or up in his tower room—"

Colin interrupted her without a by-your-leave, laughing as he said, "Finding the slightest excuse to kiss *her*? Finding the slightest excuse to haul *her* away to wherever? Now that's an observation that can't bear examination. The truth of it is that Sinjun managed to be just everywhere I was, Gray. She would hide herself behind the stairs, behind a door, behind the dressing screen, all so she could leap out at me, catch me by surprise so I wouldn't have time to protect myself or to escape or to find excuses to put her off. No, she would always have her way with me. Actually, now that I think on that a bit, she jumped out of her armoire just yesterday morning to waylay me for a good hour."

"Well," Douglas Sherbrooke said from the open doorway, beaming at everyone, "this reminds me of a party I attended before my marriage. The only difference is that there were six ladies present and I"—he sighed—"was the only poor male present. They didn't let me leave until nearly noon the following day."

"You keep speaking like that, my lord, and

your wife will surely take a knife to your gullet."

The four people in the entrance hall stared at Douglas Sherbrooke, his wife, Alex, and Helen Mayberry, who stood behind Alex, towering over her, her beautiful blond hair fashioned in thick coils atop her head.

"Er," Quincy said, "may I relieve anyone of his hat? His cane? Ah, I know, cloaks abound. In addition, there are all those other outer items the ladies wear. Shall I take anything you wish to give me?"

No one paid Quincy the slightest heed.

Colin Kinross said to his wife, "I believe it is time that you and I returned home and made plans for our offspring." He bowed to his wife and formally offered her his arm. The countess very properly touched her fingers to his sleeve, then turned and winked at Jack. "We will see you soon, my dears. Good-bye and thank you. Douglas, Alex, don't hold poor Jack and Gray for long. They're newlyweds, you know."

Alex Sherbrooke waved to Sinjun and Colin and paid no attention to Jack or Gray as she marched up to her husband, stuck her chin up, clutched his shoulders, and said, "Where did this happen with the six ladies? I demand to know the address. I demand to know their names. You will list them all out for me, and I will patiently explain to them that you are no longer available for such orgies."

"But Alex, this happened before we met. Over eight years ago. Look at me. I'm a staid old married man."

"With too many fond memories of your wild days, my lord. However, I just realized that I'm probably still blessed with enough vigor to enjoy myself in such a situation. Eight gentlemen, that's what I need." She struck a pose, a very clever one, pacing, looking more serious than a philosopher, her fingers stroking her chin.

"Your jest doesn't amuse me," Douglas Sherbrooke said, his voice as austere as a judge's. "You will cease speaking of such things. It displeases me. It would most certainly displease my mother, your mother-in-law, whom you've yet to win over."

"I know," Alex said, brightening, and ignoring her husband, "I will see Heatherington. He knows everything there is to know that is wicked. I remember the first time I met him—I was alone and he wanted to be my shepherd. I was so furious with Douglas at the moment that I didn't give him the proper consideration. Perhaps he would participate. Now that would be amusing—"

Douglas picked his wife up, held her above his head, and shook her, making her auburn hair come unmoored from its fastenings and stream down her back and over her shoulders. "You will not see Heatherington. You know he will only try to seduce you. He wouldn't even allow you to find other men for your orgy. He would insist that he could give you the pleasure of a dozen men. This is not true. It's a gross exaggeration. You won't speak to him, Alexandra."

"I believe," said Helen Mayberry, "that I really should like to meet this debaucher. Is he tall, Douglas?"

"He is your height, Helen, no taller. I, on the other hand, am at least two inches taller than you are. You wouldn't care for him at all. His is an exhausting life, filled with licentious entertainments that would surely make you blush."

"Me, blush?" Helen laughed and lightly poked Douglas's arm. Since he was still holding his wife over his head, he couldn't react. Slowly he lowered Alex to the floor, brought her up against him, and kissed her hard on her mouth. "You won't speak of these sorts of entertainments again, Alex. I will be your only shepherd. You will forget Heatherington. Helen, are you mocking me? Your eyes are rolling in your head, and your lips are pursed."

"I'm making certain I won't forget his name, Douglas. Heatherington. I wish to meet him. Perhaps I can convince Ryder to take me to a party where he will be present. Sophie still hasn't come to London. Ryder's still a free man."

Alex stepped away from Douglas and walked up to Helen. She gently shook Helen's arm. "Listen to me, you mustn't think that you can just do as you please with Ryder. You don't know Sophie. She becomes a termagant, an ill-tempered shrew, utterly loses her sweet nature, whenever another woman approaches Ryder. She isn't kind and understanding like I am, Helen—although," she added, a frown about her mouth, "I was ready to throw you into the Thames, and Douglas after you, because I didn't see things clearly. Yes, I'll admit it. I was jealous and it wasn't well done of me, but when you're married to a man as splendid as Douglas, it's difficult not to believe that every other woman in the world isn't just as much in love with him as you are. And of course they are, all except you, who managed to survive your infatuation with him.

"But I finally realized that Douglas hadn't withdrawn from me because he was inflamed by your beauty. No, he finally admitted that he's been to France twice in the past two months, on some sort of mission for the war ministry. That is why he was distracted. That is why he ignored me, despite my varied and wondrous attempts at seducing him.

"He felt guilty because he didn't tell me that his precious life was in danger. He knew I would have locked him in a closet. When I finally accused him of infidelity, then he had to tell me the truth. I forgave him. He is to go on another mission in two weeks, and I am still deciding how I will react to this.

"I believe I will travel with him. My French is so excellent now—after eight years—that I, like Douglas, will be accepted as a native. Yes, Douglas, I will go with you and protect you." And small, slight Alexandra Sherbrooke stood there, her hands clasped, beaming.

Douglas said to Gray, "Actually, she did break me. I had to tell her, although I knew it wasn't a good idea. You see, I'm used to speaking to her of all things that occupy my mind, and thus when I didn't, I changed toward her and she took it to heart in a woman's way, which is never accurate in the least. Believing I was unfaithful to her. Ha!

"As to her French, the good Lord preserve us. It isn't a whit better than when she shouted at Georges Cadoudal *'Merde!'* And then something like, 'I'm going to Paris tomorrow with my husband—*Je vais à Paris demain avec mon mari'*—in Hookham's eight years ago and hit him in the nose with a book. Heatherington overheard it and was mightily amused, the damned bounder."

"Heatherington again?" Helen said, stroking her chin with long, slender fingers. "I must meet this debauched gentleman who appears to be everywhere of interest. I don't believe I mind that he isn't taller than I am, Douglas."

"Forget Heatherington, Helen," Douglas said "You might be big for your age and have a modicum of sense, but he is wily and cunning and knows how to make a woman—

any woman—want to toss up her skirts for him.

"Now, Alex," he continued, his voice suddenly soft and cajoling, "this is to be my last mission. The first two trips to France were preparatory to this final one. I am to bring out an old gentleman who has provided Wellington with excellent, perhaps even vital, strategic information over the years. It won't be dangerous, Alex, I swear it to you. I'll leave on Thursday and be back with you again by next Wednesday. All right?"

Alex was silent for a long moment, studying his face. Finally, she nodded slowly. "I will allow it, but only if I can accompany you to Eastbourne and wait for you there. You will also tell me all your plans so that I won't feel utterly helpless. All right?"

Douglas cupped her face in his two large hands. "You are my torment and all that I hold dear. I will expect to see you waving to me from the beach when the boat returns from France." He kissed her.

"Well," said Gray, "it appears that we now all understand why Douglas wasn't making love to Alexandra three times a day as was his wont before two months ago."

Douglas raised his head. "I've a lot to make up for, don't I?"

31

Gray realized in that moment that his entire staff was very likely enjoying this titillating performance by an earl and countess of the realm. He looked up to see Maude and Mathilda standing at the bottom of the stairs, staring benignly at everyone.

Jack said, "Oh, dear."

Mathilda said, "What orgy?"

Maude said, "What Mathilda would say if she wished to tread further down that particular path is that—"

Mathilda said, "Eight men? A good number. Don't bring Mortimer."

Gray simply grabbed Douglas's arm and

said, "We're going into the drawing room. Jack, bring Helen. Aunt Mathilda, Aunt Maude, won't you please join us? Quincy, bring refreshments, but knock first. Don't just come in with the tea tray, all right?"

Quincy said, "I could slither in, my lord, or I could creep in on mice feet. No one would even notice that I was in the drawing room with the tea tray. I could—"

"Be quiet, Quincy," Mathilda said and walked quickly toward the drawing room. She called over her shoulder, "Tea, if you please, not manly brandy."

Once everyone was gathered in the drawing room, Helen said to Douglas, who was still holding his wife close to him, "It's a pity Alex didn't realize that I have never fancied married gentlemen. They've been broken by another woman's hand, you see. They carry her mark, her imprint, if you will. Yes, you are well taken, Douglas."

"Helen, you are jabbering like a nitwit," Douglas said. "What is this nonsense about breaking and imprints?"

"What I could have said instead," Helen said, her lovely eyes twinkling with amusement, "is that you, Douglas, are obviously very much in love with your wife. I'm relieved that you finally told her the truth, regardless that it will worry her. A man should never keep things from his wife. It isn't healthy for his innards. Imagine the discipline Alex would have to mete out if you were to do it again. Now you will once more be reasonable and trust her."

"What sorts of discipline?" Alex said, all her focus now on Helen.

"You are very nearly *en pointe,* Alex," Douglas said, looking vaguely alarmed and also, truth be told, a bit intrigued. "Forget this discipline business."

"You may feel free to write me, Alex," Helen said. "Now, I've intruded far too long—actually, all of us have. Aunt Mathilda, Aunt Maude, it is a pleasure to see you both again.

"Now, here are poor Jack and Gray, still in the throes of bliss, their first week of marriage barely completed. Good-bye. I'm off to find this Heatherington."

Helen slipped out of the drawing room, leaving Alexandra staring thoughtfully after her. "I will write to her about this discipline business. Do you really think Helen will search out Heatherington?"

"I hear Quincy prowling outside the door,"

Gray said. "Is everyone finished saying their lines in this extraordinary play? Is everyone thirsty from talking so much?"

"I don't believe I'm thirsty," Douglas said. "I believe I have a lot of making up to do with my wife. Do you have anything more to say, Alex?"

"I don't have anything to say, my lord. Do you think that if we left Gray and Jack they would feel slighted?"

"Doubtful," Gray said and laughed.

Mathilda said to Douglas, "Beautiful man. Come back soon."

"I will, madam," Douglas said and kissed Mathilda's veiny hand. He gave Maude a winsome smile and lifted his teacup to his mouth.

Douglas and Alex drank half a cup of tea, if that, before they left, laughing, nearly dancing to their waiting carriage.

Mathilda said to her sister, "Everything goes well. We can leave now."

"I have heard," Gray said, "that Featherstone is fully restored to its former beauty, all traces of the wretched fire and flood long gone. But that is no reason for you to leave. You are quite my favorite great-aunts. I should like for you to remain."

Maude briskly shook out the skirts of her puce gown, smiling at both of them impartially. "No, we're through here. I meant to tell you, my boy. I hear that Jack's stepfather is going to marry that Mrs. Finch, a lady who isn't at all a lady, but at least she's wealthy." Maude patted Jack's hand. "She will keep Sir Henry in good form, Jack. She is a very strong woman. Actually I feel a bit sorry for him. I daresay his life will become less pleasant."

Jack said, "On the other hand, she seemed to be quite a passionate lady."

Mathilda said, "Animal pleasure—that's all any of them want."

"I agree," Maude said. "No need to give him more. Come along, Mathilda, the two young people wish to quote sonnets to each other. I recognize the signs. We are going to a walk in the park." And off they went, with Quincy fluttering after them, offering shawls, bonnets, gloves, even raspberry tarts.

Jack laughed and said to her husband, "We have had a very unusual homecoming, Gray."

"Actually," he said, taking her hand and

gently placing it on his arm, "I would like to regularize it a bit now."

"Perhaps all afternoon, just the two of us?"

"Yes," he said, kissed the tip of her nose, shouted a laugh to the ceiling, and galloped up the stairs, Jack running at his side.

Quincy stood very still in the doorway of the drawing room. He slowly ate one of Mrs. Post's orange tarts. When Horace reached around to snag a lemon cake, Quincy said, "There have been so many changes since her ladyship arrived on the scene."

Horace, closing his eyes in bliss as he chewed on the lemon cake, said, "Everything is finally right and proper, thank the good Lord. My liver nearly scared itself out of my body there for a while, but not any longer. I believe I'll go upstairs and see what Dolly's about." He grinned down at Quincy, wiped his hands on his breeches, grabbed an apricot tart, and walked away, whistling.

What was right and proper now that wasn't right and proper before? Quincy wondered.

Two Weeks Later

It happened so quickly, Gray saw only the slash of movement hurtling out of the deep shadows before the knife came down. He managed to jerk away, but the knife tore through his jacket and shirt, sliding into his shoulder, not deeply, thank the Lord. He felt a punch of freezing cold, then numbness.

He whirled on his heels, crouched down, and brought his fist up into the man's jaw. The man grunted in pain and anger and staggered backward several steps. It gave Gray room and precious seconds. He said to Jack, never looking away from the man, who was shaking his head, the knife still held ready in his right hand, "Stay back, Jack."

Jack looked frantically around for a weapon, anything she could wield to help. They were only fifty feet from home, it wasn't even fully dark, yet this man had attacked them.

The man was coming at him again, and Gray shifted to the right, light on his feet, as Gentleman Jackson himself had taught him, and looked at his opponent's eyes. "Always in their eyes, milord," the Gentleman always said.

The man's eyes flicked with pain, then purpose, then direction. Gray was ready for him. He kicked upward, striking the man's wrist, spinning as his leg came down, to the right, out of harm's way. The knife went flying toward the street. He heard Jack running to get that knife. What should he have expected, anyway? For her to stand there cowering? Perhaps whimpering? Not Jack. Not his wife. He smiled even as he sent his fist beneath the man's chin. It lifted him off the ground. The man howled, cursed, then fell hard onto his knees, his palms out flat in front of him on the ground to keep himself up. "Ye bastid," he said, wheezing, choking, shaking his head, trying to get himself together. "Ye bastid. He told me, he did, that ye'd be a treat to butcher, the bloody lying bugger, making me think ye'd be easy, so I wouldn't back out. Ye ain't no treat attal."

"No, I'm not a treat," Gray said, standing now over the man. He came down beside him, jerking his right arm up behind him, high and higher still. "Tell me who this bloody lying bugger is. Who hired you to kill me?"

The man moaned softly, then keeled over.

"Gray!" She was at his side in a moment, the knife in her hand. "He hurt you. Oh, God, he stabbed your shoulder."

"It's all right, Jack. Don't fret. The damned bastard passed out before he told me who'd hired him. I hope he's carrying some papers." He leaned down and searched through the man's pockets. In his breeches pocket he found a folded piece of paper.

He couldn't make it out in the darkness. "Well, there's no hope for it." Between them, Gray and Jack dragged the man across the square to his own town house.

Quincy had the door open but a moment after Jack's yell. "My lord! Oh, my goodness, what has befallen the poor gentleman?"

"This is no gentleman, Quincy," Gray said. He and Jack heaved the man onto the marble entrance hall. He grabbed his shoulder, swayed a moment, then straightened.

"Quincy," Jack said, trying to keep her fear from bubbling out, "send one of the footmen for his lordship's doctor. This man stabbed him." Her voice shook, she couldn't help it. "Quickly now!"

Gray was gone. She saw him walking into the library. "Gray!" She ran after him. He was standing by his desk, unfolding the bit of paper. She watched him read it in the glow of the candles.

He swore softly beneath his breath, but it wouldn't have mattered if he'd only thought the curses, Jack heard him. "No, it's all right. Curse if you want to. Gray, what does it say? Who is this man?"

"This fellow is simply a hired assassin, Jack, sent to me by a villain whose wife I saved three months ago. Before the aunts and you arrived, I got a letter from him, telling me that he would make me suffer as I had made him suffer. He sent me another letter some two weeks ago, the bastard."

Jack was fair to bursting with questions, but she saw his hand pressed against his shoulder, the blood seeping through his fingers, and said very calmly, "Come to the kitchen, Gray, and let me see how bad the wound is."

He called over his shoulder as he followed Jack to the nether regions of the house,

"Quincy, get Remie in here to sit on this fellow if he awakens."

"Aye, my lord, Remie is on his way. We'll not let the bastard breathe too loudly."

Jack seated Gray at the kitchen table and helped him off with his coat. Her hands were trembling. When she got his shirt off, she looked at the two-inch wound that slashed along the top of his shoulder. "I don't think you'll need stitching, Gray. Let me wash you. It's not bleeding very much anymore."

"No, my lady, I'll do it." Mrs. Post took very purposeful steps toward the baron, her eyes glittering. "How did this happen to ye, milord? Some little thief, I'll wager. Bring him here to me. I'll put a fish 'ook in the little bugger's mouth and throw him in the sea. It's nasty, it is, but not all that bad. Now, if yer ladyship will jest step out of me way, I'll fix up my poor master all right 'n tight."

Gray never made a sound. When the wound was clean, Mrs. Post had Tildy, her scullery maid, tear a clean muslin towel into strips. "Be careful, Tildy. No, ye brainless twit, don't tear it with yer teeth."

Gray was walking back to the entrance hall when Dr. Cranford arrived. "See to the fellow there, sir. I'm just fine."

Dr. Cranford insisted on examining Gray's shoulder before he left. "Nasty, but clean now and not deep," he said. "Excellent, my lady. Do I see your fine hand at work here?"

"I tried, sir, but Mrs. Post, our cook, shoved me out of the way. His lordship is hers to see to, she said. You swear he'll be all right?"

Dr. Cranford, tall and lanky, blessed with thick black curly hair, grinned at her. "I've known Lord Cliffe since he was a wild young lad up to London from Oxford. I do believe this is the worst shape I've seen him in. Well, there was that one time when you were so foxed you fell off your horse and your friends didn't realize you'd fallen because they were all in their cups as well. No, no, don't be alarmed, my lady. That's a tale best forgotten. Now, his lordship will mend just fine.

"As to the ruffian in the entrance hall, he's just a bit dizzy from the beating you gave him, my lord. You didn't break his jaw, and that surprises me. He's tough. He'll survive, but maybe that's a pity. The magistrates will be delighted to toss him into gaol."

"I have a feeling he won't be unknown to

the magistrates," Gray said. "I do know who sent him and that's far more important."

There was deep, calm rage in the baron's voice, and Dr. Cranford tilted his head in question. "I know it's probably none of my affair, but I strongly advise you not to take on this man tonight. You've lost a goodly amount of blood. I don't want you to hurt this shoulder perhaps more. Can it wait until to-morrow?"

"Oh, yes," Gray said, looking into the rus-tling coals in the fireplace. "I fancy he'll be-lieve his henchman has succeeded. Even if he finds out that I'm still breathing, I doubt he'll be worried. How was he to know that the stupid sod he sent to kill me kept his instruction?"

Dr. Cranford, not wanting to know any more, took his leave.

32

"Tell me," Jack said, pressing as close as she could to Gray's side. "Tell me about this woman you saved. I don't understand this."

Gray sighed. His shoulder throbbed, the laudanum was beginning to drag at his voice and his mind, slowing both. He turned his head slightly and kissed the tip of her nose. "I finally have you as my wife again, but here you are, lying against me all neutral, not a lustful bone in your body, not a lustful thought in your female brain."

She lightly stroked her palm over his belly. He sucked in his breath. "No, don't prove me wrong. Well, go ahead if you truly wish to. Despite my manly wound I will eventually feel lust begin to fill my bones and my brain."

She laughed, kissed his mouth, and let her hand move lower to touch him. He trembled and jerked and sucked in air. Then she kissed him one last time and quickly moved away. "No, you need to build your strength, not deplete it. I won't tease you any more, it's not fair. Now, tell me about this woman you saved, or let's sleep. One or the other."

"A hard woman you are, Jack, very hard."

She laughed at that, wanting to touch him again, to feel the heat of him. She didn't even have time to sigh with regret. He rolled over on top of her, jerked up her nightgown with his left hand, and nearly lost his wits at the feel of her naked against him. He forgot his manly shoulder wound, forgot everything but how he wanted her now, no more waiting, no more talking, just her body and his, together. "I think it's time I made you pregnant," he said and came into her. Her body was ready for him and accepted him, but he realized quickly that Jack's mind was still on his wounded shoulder, the man who'd tried to kill him. He hadn't given her enough time.

Well, hell.

He came up, balancing himself on one hand, and said, "I want you to forget everything but me inside you. Do you hear me, Jack? Think of me pushing in you, deep. Ah, yes. I love the feel of you, how you squeeze me, how you shift and tighten around me. How do I feel to you?"

"Inside me?" Her voice sounded thin and scratchy. "Hot, Gray, you feel hot and—" She gasped, arching up, pulling him down on top of her and kissed him wildly. He was laughing and moaning when he felt her tense beneath him, felt her legs tremble and lock. Then he threw back his head and cried out to the ceiling beams, knowing that this woman had been fashioned only for him and he'd been as lucky as a man could get that he'd caught her stealing Durban.

"Jack, I'm done in."

"No wonder," she managed to whisper as she helped him ease over onto his back again. "That was a very nice experience for me, Gray. Thank you."

"Anytime," he said. "Well, if you're still interested, give me another five minutes." In the next moment he was asleep, the laudanum and his utter relaxation drawing him quickly under.

Jack lay beside him on her back, her head pillowed on her arms. Her nightgown was bunched up around her waist, her thighs were sprawled apart, and she too was relaxed, too relaxed even to bring her legs together.

She stared up at the dark ceiling. "Thank you, God," she whispered. "He is my husband. Thank you." She began whistling softly into the still room.

"And he loves me," she said as she turned her head to see the distant stars through the windowpane just beyond Gray's side of the bed. "I know he does."

"Yes," Gray said beside her. "Of course I love you. Do you think me an utter idiot?"

"You're never an utter idiot, Gray. You truly love me? You swear it?"

"I swear it. How could I not? You come dressed to my house as the valet Mad Jack, you steal my horse, you have the gall to get deathly ill on me, you have the nerve to make me want to protect you. Oh, yes, I love you."

After that utterly wonderful monologue, Jack had no time to tell him she'd kill for him, she'd do anything he ever wanted her to do. He began snoring, soft fluttering little sniffs that made her smile even as she grasped his hand in hers and fell asleep.

"That's how I met Ryder," Gray said the following morning at the breakfast table. He kissed her fingers, then released her hand just a moment to take a bite of his eggs. "He saved children who were abused, as I already told you, and I tried to help women whose husbands abused them."

Jack heard his calm voice, looked at his beloved face, and thought, *That doesn't surprise me after what you saw your father do to your mother.*

"I was twenty years old, wild because there was no reason not to be, and thoughtless, enjoying myself far more than a healthy young man should. One night I had just left two of my friends and wasn't more than a mile from home. I remember the sky was beautifully clear, with a smattering of bright stars and a half-moon. I felt good. I was whistling, kicking pebbles out of my path lightheartedly, when I heard a woman cry out.

"I saw a woman in a drawing room through partially open draperies. A man was hitting her. I didn't stop to think, didn't stop to wonder what was going on, to question, to do anything. No, I ran up to that house and tried to burst through the door. It was locked. I ran to the window of that room where the man was hitting the woman and managed to shove it up high enough to climb inside.

"I remember the look of utter astonishment on the man's face when he saw me crash into his drawing room. He looked at me, looked at the woman, hit her again, really hard in her ribs, and it was then that I knew he was the sort of man who made hitting women a habit.

"I told you that my father never hit my mother's face. Neither did this man. Her ribs and her belly were his targets. He was just like my father.

"He shouted at me, demanding to know what I wanted, but I just ran to him, jerked the woman free, and beat him into the floor.

"It was the woman who stopped me. I remember she was pulling at my hands, saying over and over, 'No, he's not worth it, please don't kill him. He's not worth it.' And so I stopped hitting him. He was unconscious, not dead. Nor was he going to die, more's the pity.

"The woman was his wife, and she'd angered him by visiting her sister without getting his permission. It took her a while to trust me, for, after all, I was a young man and she was a married woman of at least thirty. But when she finally told me the entire truth, I realized that it would simply continue if I didn't intervene. She was in exactly the same situation as my mother had been.

"The only difference was that this woman hated her husband. She wanted to leave him despite the resulting scandal; she didn't care. But she couldn't leave because she was afraid of him. He'd told her that he would kill her if she did. There was one little girl, Joan, and a little boy, William.

"I didn't know what to do, not really, but I just knew that I wouldn't let this continue. I couldn't leave her to face the bastard. I tied him up and gagged him and pulled him behind a settee.

"Then I waited while she packed and got her young daughter and son ready to leave. I took them both to my house.

"They remained there for three days. That third day I met Ryder Sherbrooke. He was arguing with an older man in White's. The old codger was saying that all the irritating trash in the streets should be eliminated once and for all, all of them sent to the Colonies or to Botany Bay. He was referring to children who were forced to beg or steal to keep from starving. Ryder never raised his voice, just said that it was adults who brought these poor children into the world and then abandoned them. What were the children supposed to do? Leave all good people alone, the old codger was saying over and over. I managed to introduce myself to Ryder when he stepped away, leaving the old man muttering into his brandy snifter. Oddly enough, within ten minutes of meeting him, I was telling him of the lady at my house and what had happened.

"Within two days he knew all about my past. It was Ryder who helped me figure out how to protect her—"

"Who was she, Gray?"

"Lady Cecily Granthsom."

Jack just shook her head.

He said only, "You will doubtless meet her soon, Jack. I believe she and her children are currently in Scotland visiting her husband's family. She will be charmed with you."

"What did you do with the husband?"

"Ryder and I went to see him. He was enraged that his wife had escaped with her lover, so he screamed at us. He would kill the bitch, he yelled, and that damned lover of hers. He didn't recognize me as the young man who'd beaten him into the floor.

"That was when Ryder and I explained the situation to him." Gray smiled, seeing the past, Jack realized, seeing a triumph that had remained with him.

"Lord Granthsom was beyond fury when I told him that I'd been the one to hit him, that I was hiding his wife and children, until I had some believable assurance that he would never strike her again, or the children. He kept screaming that it was none of my affair, that she was a slut and an adulteress and she deserved whatever he did to her.

"That was when he attacked me." Gray rubbed his hands together. "I thrashed him again. I remember the butler came to the door, saw what I was doing, just nodded, and left. Everyone always knows when there is violence in a household. There is no hiding it. No keeping it secret. After he was bleeding and on the floor, I asked him what he thought I should do with him.

"Granthsom wasn't stupid. He claimed he

wouldn't hurt his wife again. I didn't believe him. He signed a paper swearing he'd never touch her again, or her children. He swore he wouldn't retaliate in any way. Ryder and I left. Two days later, Cecily returned to her home. I accompanied her. Lord Granthsom seemed calm, accepting. Cecily seemed convinced. I left.

"Three days later the man I'd hired to keep watch over them came to my house to tell me that he was beating her, and it was bad. I took my gun and went there. The servants were all white as death, listening to her screams, yet unwilling to do anything. What could they do? They were nothing compared to him.

"I shot him in the leg. He kept hitting her. I shot him in the other leg."

"What happened?" Jack looked at the piece of toast she'd been holding an inch from her mouth for the entire time Gray had been speaking. She dropped it onto her plate and leaned forward. "What, Gray? What happened?"

"Lord Granthsom is in a wheelchair. It's been nearly six years now. He is dependent upon the servants and his wife for his very existence. One of the bullets caused enough damage so that he'll never walk again."

"My God, what an exquisite punishment," she said, jumping to her feet and throwing herself into his arms. He moaned from the wound in his shoulder, then clasped her close, bringing her onto his lap. "Yes, it worked out well. Cecily is her own woman now, in complete control of all his estates because she controls him. He is not a happy man and that pleases me inordinately and Cecily as well. You will meet her daughter, Joan, and her son, William, when they return from Scotland in the middle of the summer. Cecily is beloved by his family for her kindness, her selflessness, her caring for the fallen earl. They believe that he fell from a horse. Because of his pride, he hasn't ever contradicted her."

"The husband is an earl? *A peer of the realm?* An earl was beating his wife?"

"Yes. There are no class boundaries, Jack. It's true that poverty tends to drain the spirit, and thus many men lose all hope and take their hopelessness out on their wives and children. Also, some men are simply animals, no rhyme or reason for it."

"And you save the women?"

"I try. Since Cecily, there have been ten women. It's Cecily who has helped me over the years assist them in dealing with their various situations. Every one is different. I have spent hours scratching my head, trying to figure out the best way to save a woman. Two women I've saved were exactly like my mother. They cursed me for interfering. I've simply not involved myself with them after I discovered that."

"This man who wanted to kill you? Who is he?"

"He is the Honorable Clyde Barrister, a little weasel who would doubtless be in excellent company with your stepfather, Sir Henry.

"I've gotten several threatening letters from him. I wrote him after the first letter and told him that if he didn't swallow his threats and leave me alone, I would beat him and throw him in a ditch. I guess he didn't believe me because another letter from him arrived at the same time as the urgent request from Lord Burleigh to see me. After seeing Lord Burleigh, you can understand how simple it was for me to forget about it.

"Clyde must have panicked after sending me the letter and decided the only thing to do to save his hide was to hire an assassin to kill me."

"What will you do?"

Gray gave her a kiss in the tip of her nose, nuzzled her neck, then kissed her mouth. "What I'm going to do is pay the gentleman a long-overdue visit."

"Do you believe he is beating his wife again?"

"Oh, no. His wife, Margaret, is living with his older brother and his family. He is the head of the family, and incidentally, the very deep well from which our gentleman here draws enough groats to keep himself in luxury. He can do nothing against his brother, thus he would like at least to remove me, the bane of his existence."

"Let's get him, Gray. Let's show him what's what."

"Ah, Jack, you do please me so."

But Jack wouldn't let him go until she'd looked at his shoulder. "I wouldn't want you to hurt yourself," she said, as she gently re-bandaged the wound. "It looks fine, but I don't want you to hit him very hard. It could reopen the wound, and Dr. Cranford wouldn't like that."

They were donning cloaks when Quincy

answered the knock at the front door. It was Ryder Sherbrooke, windblown, tanned, healthy and smiling, his Sherbrooke blue eyes light and full of life. It felt as though he brought the sunlight into the house with him.

"You'll not believe what I—no, wait, what happened here? What did you do to your shoulder, Gray? Jack, what's going on? I leave for a very short time, and you get yourself hurt? Damnation, Gray, I must move in with you so that I can keep you whole-hided?"

"No, no, Ryder. Come in for a moment. I'm fine. Quincy, bring us some tea and whatever Mrs. Post has available in the kitchen. Now, Ryder, what's happened?"

"No, I will not tell you my news until you tell me what's happened."

Gray did, quickly and cleanly, leaving out more than Jack would have left out, but she managed to keep herself quiet.

"So, the two of you were going to see our little weasel to speak to him about his lack of manners?"

"Actually," Gray said, "I haven't decided just yet what to do with the Honorable Clyde, the mangy little sot."

Jack said with relish, "I vote we break his

neck, but in a very subtle way so that everyone believes it's an accident."

Gray laughed and hugged her against his side. "Don't ever try to hurt me, Ryder, else you'll have my wife to deal with. Now, tell us your news."

"Yes," Jack said. "Have you decided how to re-rotten the borough?"

"No, there wasn't even time to act. You see, my children took a hand."

"Your children?" Jack said.

"Yes, all fourteen of them."

33

I went home to see just how easily I would be able to re-rotten the borough, and if I couldn't manage to do that, then just what else I could do about that little fop, Horace Redfield. I soon learned that he'd spread his groats and his venom throughout Upper and Lower Slaughter.

"My Sophie was fit to shoot his ears off. Ah, she's so very lovely when her eyes are sizzling with rage. I nearly forgot my own ire when I remarked upon her eyes and her lovely heaving chest. So then I—no, never mind that.

"Where was I? Oh, yes, it turns out that

Oliver and Jeremy were home from Eton—"
He looked over at Jack, adding, "Jeremy is
Sophie's younger brother, and Oliver is all
of sixteen now, and a glorious young man.
Douglas is very fond of Oliver as well and
plans to train him to be the future steward
of Northcliffe, but that's neither here nor
there.

"In any case, the boys soon discovered
what was going on. They got all the children
together and told them that they were going
to 'squish the bad man.' " Ryder rubbed his
hands together and grinned into the distance. "Ah, my sweet boys."

"What happened?" Jack asked.

'Jeremy and Oliver rightly decided that Mr.
Redfield was doubtless a scoundrel and
they took turns following him. They quickly
discovered that he was seeing a woman in
a small cottage just east of Upper Slaughter
in the village of Primpton. Then they sent the
children, in pairs, to see this woman. Her
name is Fanny James, a former actress who
was down on her luck, and because, she
told Jeremy and Oliver, she couldn't sew or
cook, and scrubbing things would ruin her
beautiful hands, and she didn't want to
starve, she became Redfield's mistress.

They told her that since she knew all about treading the boards, they wanted her to teach them how to act and perform a play.

"Fanny James was charmed, needless to say, particularly after all fourteen children trooped to her cottage door, sat at her feet, and listened reverently to every word that slid off her tongue.

"She visited Jane at Brandon House, met all the other staff, and Sophie as well."

Ryder stopped, stared down at his boots, then threw back his head, and howled with laughter.

Gray waited until Ryder had quieted a bit, then said, "This Fanny James didn't know what Redfield had done to blacken your good name, did she?"

"No," Ryder finally said, shaking his head. "No, she didn't know anything. In short, she fell in love with the children, with Jane and all the other women at Brandon House, and naturally with my Sophie. Ah, yes, and I don't want to forget Sally, a jewel, Gray, who has the children eating out of her hand. She's one of the cooks," Ryder added to Jack. At her still obvious confusion, he said, "Gray saved her from a brute of a drunken husband and brought her to me. She's very happy, Gray.

"Now, all the children decided that what Brandon House needed was a resident theater artistic director to live at Brandon House to instruct the children in the art of playgiving, which is, actually, a splendid idea. It will keep the little heathens occupied and entertained, particularly during the long winter months."

"Was there a play, Ryder?" Jack asked. At his impudent grin, she smiled herself, unable not to because that Sherbrooke grin of his was so warm and so filled with laughter. "Come, tell us, what did you do? What happened to Horace Redfield?"

"Oliver and Jeremy told Fanny what Redfield was doing. She turned as red as the sunset before a storm, Jeremy said, she was so infuriated. So she wrote a short play about this absurd fat little man who could only get elected mayor of the town if he blackened the name of his opponent, who was an honest man. He did this by claiming every child in the town was a bastard and he himself was in search of the father to bring him to justice. It was staged in the middle of the afternoon on the green in Lower

Slaughter. Thank God the afternoon was warm and sunny.

"There was no warning about what was in the play, just that 'Ryder Sherbrooke's bastards were going to perform for the townspeople.' Horace Redfield came, all resplendent in a yellow waistcoat, happy as a clam, ready to hammer in the final nails to my coffin by pointing his pudgy finger at all the children and wagging that finger, and remarking that they all resembled me and no one would feel sorry for them and thus vote for me no matter how many free plays they performed.

"All the nails hammered were on Horace Redfield's coffin. Ah, the children were magnificent. Fanny was superb. One of the children's teachers, Mr. Forbes, played Mr. Redfield. He was splendidly oily. He'd tied a fat pillow around his waist and wore a bright green waistcoat. Every time he saw a child, any child, even those in the audience, he yelled 'Bastard!'

"In the end, Fanny James stood up in front of the good two hundred people present and said she was casting her vote for me, the man who took in abused children and fed them and clothed them and made certain they grew up straight and not crooked, like some men she could name. She stared at Redfield, who was by this time standing utterly alone. Even his wife had left his side.

"The election is next week. I do believe I shall win, thanks to my children and a very nice woman who is now in my employ and won't have to worry about becoming a mistress to any more scoundrels."

"What an ending, Ryder," Gray said. "I wish we could have been there."

Jack turned to Gray, took his hands in hers, and said, "I was thinking that Georgie would very much enjoy meeting all Ryder's children. Perhaps, too, acting would help her with her stutter. May we go to visit?"

Gray arched an eyebrow in Ryder's direction. "Come," Ryder said. "I'm going back home tomorrow. I returned to London only to speak with members of the Tory Party about final strategy, to tell them what happened, which will make them chortle and crow until next week, and to sign some papers. And, naturally, to tell the two of you what had happened. So, Jack, I didn't have to re-rotten the borough. Now, as to coming to me, why, you're both welcome anytime. Who is Georgie?"

"Our little sister," Gray said. "You'll like her, Ryder. Speaking of little sister—" They all turned to see Dolly standing in the doorway, holding Georgie's hand.

"I-I-I heard you," Georgie said. 'I heard a g-g-gentleman sh-shouting."

"Not shouting exactly," Ryder said, striding to the little girl. He dropped to one knee and looked her straight in her one golden eye and her one blue eye. "I must have a big full voice so that all fourteen of my children can hear me."

"F-F-Fourteen, sir?"

"Yes. When you come with your sister and Gray, you can increase my number of children to fifteen. Would you like that, Georgie?"

Even as Ryder was speaking, Georgie, her shy Georgie, had released Dolly's hand and begun to move closer to him. By the time he paused, she was right in front of him, smiling. Jack had never seen anything like it. Georgie continued to move toward Ryder until she couldn't be more than a single inch from his face. "Oh, yes, sir, I would I-I-love to see your children."

"And you, my little sweetheart, will soon be a favorite with everyone. I think you will make a splendid actress. Now, would you like to select a tart that you think I would like?"

Both Gray and Jack held silent, simply marveling, as Georgie was soon seated on Ryder's leg, laughing and feeding him an apricot tart. She was speaking quickly between her spurts of very natural and joyous laughter, not stopping when she faltered or stuttered, just tumbling her words one over the other, smiling, so very happy, near to bursting with it.

"He is amazing," Jack said, swallowing around the sudden lump in her throat. "I never would have believed it."

"I wonder how Parliament will react to him," Gray said and laughed.

"I just hope the prince regent isn't so charmed that he wants to sit on him. He'd break Ryder's legs."

Because Ryder was Ryder, he didn't leave the St. Cyre town house, even though members of Parliament were awaiting him, until Georgie, still pleased and excited, had finally fallen asleep with her head on Ryder's shoulder. He hugged Jack and shook

Gray's hand. "Go take care of Clyde Barrister now."

"Yes," Jack said, her eyes lighting up with viciousness, "let's go."

But the Honorable Clyde Barrister had left his town house, obviously in a hurry. They were met by his butler, who looked a bit dazed, able to say only that his master had mumbled something about leaving for Greece, that there were bad people after him.

"He'd best stay far from England," Jack said, a great disappointment in her voice.

"I imagine he will. He's not stupid. I wonder if he left his brother with a mountain of debts. At least Margaret is safe now."

Late that evening, after they had both decided that life was possible after lovemaking, Gray kissed her temple and said, "I am very pleased with you and with this marriage, Jack, very pleased indeed."

"I as well. Actually, there can be no more pleasing me, Gray. You've pushed me to beyond pleased."

He kissed her left ear, pulling the tangle of hair back from her forehead, and kissed her eyebrows. "And what do you say to that?"

She didn't say anything for a very long time. She was thinking that no woman could be more blessed than she, more blessed or more pleased. But what were mere thoughts when a man like Gray was her husband? She kissed his neck and whispered, "I say thank you, Gray. Thank you with all my heart for catching me when I stole Durban."